The Liquid City

The Liquid City

Curtis J. Hopfenbeck

To order additional copies of this book, contact:
Xlibris Corporation
1-888-795-4274
www.Xlibris.com
Orders@Xlibris.com
79548

"I mourn the morn that is won as one."

Curtis J. Hopfenbeck

In Memory of Robert B. Parker
1932 - 2010

My surrogate father and silent mentor.
Sleep well Mr. Parker . . . perchance to dream.

In Dedication:

To my God, my Family, my Police, and my United States Military . . . Thank you for providing me with my Life, my Love, my Safety, and my Freedom!

In Acknowledgement:

I would like to thank my mother, Jinny Hopfenbeck; my sisters, Kary Burin, Jan Zimmer and Lynn Demerse; and my brothers, Paul Hopfenbeck and Mark Hopfenbeck; for their patience, time, encouragement and critical review. And most importantly, for a lifetime of love and laughter, for which I will be enternally grateful. That in me which is of value, I owe in great part to them; that which is not, I must take credit and responsibility!

I would also like to thank Sir Jeffrey Driggs, my editor extraordinaire. A man of regal air and impeccable character. A thespian and philosopher of amazing wit and infinite wisdom. It is an honor to call of man of his caliber my friend and counselor; and I thank him for his countless hours of camaraderie and corrections. From one man who married well to another, I thank you, Sir!

And my thanks as well to those of you who chose to read this book, may it leave you at some point with a tear in your eye or a smile on your face. If so, my work is done!

CHAPTER 1

The Seattle Rain Festival lasts from approximately January first through December thirty-first of every year. And this day differed little as I sauntered down Fifth Avenue, entering and emerging from beneath the occasional historic overhang as the Puget Sound's tangible atmosphere fell from the skies, seemingly without respite. At least, I was trying to saunter. I'd seen Cary Grant saunter suavely through a Monte Carlo casino once in *To Catch a Thief* and I'd always wanted to emulate his elegant gait. By the look on the faces of the occasional passersby, I still needed work. I bet Cary hadn't got it right on the first try either!

One must make peace with Seattle's liquid ambience upon first introduction or infinitely suffer the daily consequences. I, for one, partnered early. To me the rain, and the ensuing mist and darkness, were at once both cloak and confidant—providers of darkness and distance from people and problems. It was an embraceable escape from reality that sheltered me from asking too many questions of myself and judging my life too critically. Sunlight always seemed too harsh and penetrating to me. It exposed and illuminated the detritus of my life that was better left nocturnal. Not that I'm a bad person, I argue for the opposite, but to be absolutely just, one must be justly absolute. But at this point, I was just absolutely drenched and happy to have reached my destination.

I'd never been to the Heritage Club at the top of the Legacy Tower in downtown Seattle before, but then again, most of the members had probably never been to some of my clubs before either, so I guess we were even. The Heritage was where the Washington rich and powerful went to prove their prowess and prosperity, although mainly to each other. Some might find the decorum pretentious, but I was quite fond of the fact that my surroundings were as ostentatious as they were exclusive. It befitted the breeding and boasting for whom it was intended. From the time you stepped off the heated, seated elevators you were immediately hit by the grandeur of unlimited wealth and infinite finery.

The daily polished Italian marble floors led you along twenty-foot-high, smoke-mirrored walls until you hit the expansive main lounge and the huge floor-to-ceiling windows that looked imperially out over the Sound. The rare imported furniture was of the finest fabrics and the rarest wood grains. The colors were the darkest shades of forest green and ocean blue, with the Midas touch of gold, luminously interwoven throughout each theme. Huge, imported, black oak pillars shouldered fifty-foot ceilings and sprouted ambient, grand crystal chandeliers that shone with the quiet light of iniquity.

The epicurean five-star restaurant and lounge veered off to the left in fitting elevated status, and the tantalizing odors of garlic-laced sauces, imported cigars, and old money traversed the corridors in search of aromatic appreciation from the resident sybarites. To the far right were the labyrinth of private conference rooms where heads of state and corporate magnates practiced political pandering and questionable jurisprudence. It was also said that there were several luxuriously adorned private suites available for those gentlemen to whom monogamy was thought to be only for the poor and the underprivileged.

It was one of the conference rooms with the Russian Ruble monetary symbol on the door, in which I now stood. I had been led past the

English Pound Room, the Japanese Yen Room, the Mexican Peso Room, the French Franc Room, and the German Marc Room. I had asked my tuxedoed guide to seat me in the Sri Lankan Rupee Room, but my humor was either lost on my octogenarian escort or he was much too much the gentleman's gentleman to laugh uproariously at a great one-liner. I envied his ability to keep a straight face in the company of a master comedian.

As I stood at the hundredth story window of the Russian Ruble Room and the magnificent vista it offered, I tried to think back upon what I had heard and read of Seattle's resident presidential hopeful. Republican Senator Richard Marcum was not necessarily an icon of virtue, but a man born and bred for politics—a good-looking man in his early sixties, tanned, reasonably fit, a winning smile with matching handshake, and the proper political pedigrees to continue kissing babies and bottoms ad infinitum. He was a good inch over my six-three but nearly twenty pounds short of my two-hundred and thirty, and I imagined it was proportioned a little differently since the life of leisure seemed to be manifesting itself mainly around his waistline.

I've never met him personally, but have watched him wax philosophic on enough national Republican Party talk shows to wonder if he lacked a certain honorability. 'On her ability' he'd been accused of, 'honorability' he seemed able to circumvent at will. It was rumored that he was involved in a few nefarious scandals during his tenure, but always remained distant and dormant enough to avoid the long arm of the Judiciary Committee.

I was beginning to ponder the auspicious occasion that would require my presence here when a panel that I hadn't noticed before opened from the dark walnut wall. A group of rather serious-looking, suited individuals entered the room and patted me down for anti-tank guns and small nuclear devices. And upon seeing that I posed no immediate threat, gave the go-ahead to the rest of the entourage to enter.

"He's clean. No weapons, no wires," shouted one of the agents to those yet unseen. I was about to warn him of my rapier-like wit, but figured why alienate myself before the proper introductions had been made.

"Twisted steel and sex appeal," I replied, and smiled winningly—which was met by an unimpressed, "Whatever!" from the lead leviathan.

Senator Marcum strolled into the room with a spring in his step and a broad, white smile on his too tanned face; the consummate politician. He walked over to me quickly with his hand out, took my hand in his and put his other hand on my shoulder. *Grandfatherly!*

"Well, you must be Shad Kilbourne," the senator said matter-of-factly. "I appreciate you meeting with us like this, I really do."

The senator was resplendent in his taupe, double-breasted Armani suit, white wool-cotton blend Brooks Brothers' shirt and a navy blue iridescent silk tie. I thought the European class wing tip shoes were a bit much, but a three thousand dollar ensemble doesn't come without its eccentricities and extravagances.

"It's a pleasure, Senator Marcum, but I'm at a slight disadvantage in that I don't know why you requested this meeting. Mr. White was a little vague over the phone."

"Ah, right to the point, eh? I like that. Okay, we'll play it your way," the senator said with the practiced grin as he unbuttoned his coat and seated himself heavily into the chairman's seat at the head of the football-field length conference table. "Shane, you wanna handle the intros?"

Shane was Shane Lowe, an acquaintance of mine and probably the top legal mind in the largest law firm in the West. And, I felt, the nation's leading special prosecutor. I'd known Shane casually from the club for years and had found him to be an excellent individual. But it was not until he'd had an article written about him six years ago in the *Law Review* that I had actually sought him out. The article was based on a draft that he'd written in law school twenty years earlier, regarding the fact that the judicial system didn't go far enough to convict felonious career criminals and keep them in jail, regardless of evidence or proper arrest procedures. His essay went on to say that life sentences were a waste of time and that the death penalty was not only a deterrent, but a fitting end to those who obviously disvalued life in the pursuit of their own criminality as well. The piece in the review written by a young, liberal idealist charged Shane with circumventing the law to prosecute individuals without a preponderance of evidence. Seeing the possibility of a valuable ally and alliance, I'd met with him for a private lunch and we'd been good friends and confidants ever since.

"Shad here already knows me, but this is Nicholas White, the senator's lead counsel; Malcomb Arbreau, his Campaign Manager; and Rik Ryles, Chief of Security, and the rest of his security staff."

The staff consisted of four other ill-fitted suits who, along with their wireless radio earpieces and probable secret decoder rings, took themselves far too seriously. As did Rik Ryles himself, whom I'd met before when he was handling security for other sport and movie celebrities that had patronized a few of my clubs. We weren't friends. But he was big and tough and did a pretty good job, from what I'd heard, so I gave him an ambivalent nod and let it go at that.

"And now, gentlemen, if you'll leave us," Shane said to the four overly engineered agents still standing against the wall with their hands folded in front of them, just like in the movies, sunglasses still on and all, "we can get started."

All four looked at Ryles as if on queue. Ryles jerked his head toward the door and they each vanished without a word. Good head jerk! I'd have to remember to work on mine. Two points for ol' Rikky.

When we were all seated, Shane looked at the senator, the senator looked at his manager, and the manager looked at the lead council. I, on the other hand, crossed my legs and looked at the shine on my shoes and admired the fact that the rain hadn't spotted them. Always the sign of a good shine, I thought, the rain rolls right off. No spotting. I was trying to think of the dishwashing detergent that made the same claim, but my thoughts were interrupted before I could place it. Now it would bother me all day.

"Mr. Kilbourne, it has come to our attention via our external legal counsel here," Nicholas White gestured to Shane as he formulated his thoughts and postured for effect, "that you have quite some influence here in the greater Seattle area and are . . . oh, how should I put this . . . somewhat resourceful and industrious when need be?"

I smiled and tried to look modest. "I am but a humble barkeep, pure and simple."

White grinned a dubious grin. "I have heard that you are neither humble, pure, nor simple Mr. Kilbourne, which is why we are all here."

White started to go on, caught himself, and asked, "Mr. Kilbourne, can I assume that everything we talk about here today, without exception, will be kept in the strictest confidence?"

"No," I said.

"No?"

"No!" I repeated.

White started to get a sickly look on his face and looked to Shane for help.

"Go ahead, Nicholas," Shane offered, looking at me and shaking his head, "he just means that if what we talk about puts him or anyone he cares about at risk, he will make up his mind at that point in time as to whether or not he remains quiet. You can trust him. I do, and have, with my life."

That seemed to be sufficient enough because some of the color returned to White's face and he decided to go on without a confidentiality agreement signed in blood. He had been the senator's legal counsel for over twenty years, so he deserved to be a little frazzled. His work had left him almost completely bald and beset with a nervous twitch in his right hand that flared and flailed when he spoke. His waistline spoke of too much fine dining and his varicose nose spoke of too much fine wine.

"I'm sorry, Mr. Kilbourne, it's just that what we are about to discuss is of a very private and personal nature, and could be devastating to the senator's presidential campaign if the press were to get wind of it."

"Mr. White," I sympathized, "I did not get to where I am by speaking recklessly about the clandestine conversations I have had with those who are in need of my assistance. I can guarantee you that I won't purposely try to jeopardize the senator's presidential run based upon the information proffered here today. That will have to be sufficient."

White was about to continue when Ryles broke in. "Where exactly are you, Kilbourne?" he said with obvious distaste.

"Excuse me?" I said, a little bemused by Ryles' outburst.

"You said, 'I didn't get where I am . . .' where is it that you think you're at exactly?"

"Shut up, Ryles," White said sharply as he turned and glared at the Chief of Security.

"Well, who the heck does he think he is? He's a freekin' club owner, big deal! He's not the damned chief of police for crissake."

I stared hard at Ryles and was tempted to get out of my rather comfortable Italian leather chair with the built-in lumbar support and kick his teeth in, but figured it would ruin my spotless shoeshine and the ruckus might disturb the delicate decor. Though I did envision a rather brief encounter and a spectacular and much heralded victory. I wondered if they still did ticker-tape parades!

"Ryles, you wouldn't rush a Girl Scout camp without a gun and backup," I said as I simultaneously checked that morning's manicure.

"So unless you're fully insured and looking forward to a long hospital stay, I'd suggest you do what you're used to doing . . . what you're told!"

Ryles was just stupid and angry enough to come out of his chair, but before he could, the senator burst into laughter.

"I'll be damned, Kilbourne," the senator said, laughing so hard I thought he'd choke, "wouldn't rush a Girl Scout camp without a gun and backup. That's funny stuff. I'll have to remember that."

Shane stepped forward as Ryles and I just glared at each other. "May I remind you Mr. Ryles, that you are the chief of security, not the chief of insecurity?" Ryles switched his glare from me to Shane and then back to me. "I charge by the hour and I can think of more prudent things to do with the senator's campaign funds than to spend them on expensive, albeit deserved, attorney's fees."

"Me too, gentlemen," Malcomb Arbreau, the campaign manager, finally chirped in. "We have a press conference in two hours, senator, and you haven't even been briefed yet."

The senator wiped his eyes with his monogrammed handkerchief, stuffed it triangularly back into its breast pocket and nodded at White to continue, yet still with a smile on his face and a glint in his eye. He seemed truly sorry to have the fracas come to an end. But White looked relieved to have everything back in some semblance of order. And with his confidence renewed, he got back to preamble.

"Mr. Kilbourne, do you have children?"

This time *I* looked at Shane for help.

"Nicholas," Shane implored, "if you could please just get to the subject at hand. I think we're all past the drawing of parallels at this point."

"Right, Yes. You're perfectly correct." White arose with great effort and then leaned on the conference table without much alacrity. "Let me get to the point then. Ten years ago, when she was sixteen, the senator's daughter ran away. The whole family was living in DC at the time, as they normally do during session. She was a troublesome youth to say the least, and we feel she eventually turned to prostitution to support her obvious growing drug habit. As you might expect, the senator being as great a father as he is a leader, did everything in his power to bring her back into the fold, so to speak. But she was just too far down that lonesome and loathsome road and he had to disown her for the sake of the rest of the family, as you could imagine."

I, personally, could not imagine disowning my own daughter, much less for the sake of the rest of the family, but I again felt it better not to comment—an area I've been urged to work on with great frequency.

"Well," White continued, "when people asked about her we naturally told them she was off to the finest European schools and to see the world with friends. People wouldn't know just how hard the senator had tried to reunite his loving family, and frankly, we were afraid it might reflect poorly to the voters and his constituents."

I was watching the senator admire his own manicure, which I might add is the true sign of great intellect and breeding, but if this story of the loss of his daughter brought back painful memories for a loving father, then he was sure hiding it well. You'd think they were talking about a fictional character for all the emotion he seemed to be exuding.

"We've had some people trace her whereabouts," White went on, "and they have it on good authority that she came back to Seattle some five years ago and has continued down the same tragic path. But the trail has gone cold from there. We've had Mr. Ryles here look into it, but after an exhaustive investigation he has also come up empty and believes she is either dead or has left the state again."

I nodded at White and turned to look at the senator. "Have you had anyone competent look into it?"

Ryles did come out of his chair this time, his face as red as his close-cropped military haircut. "I don't have to take that garbage. I had my men comb the city, there's no sign of her anywhere. We checked every street corner from Vancouver, Washington to Vancouver, Canada. She's gone."

I looked at Ryles's face and couldn't help but laugh. "No offense here to the great finder of lost children, but he's in charge of a security firm. By 'competent,' I meant have you contacted local social services, prostitution alternative programs, hooker halfway houses, drug rehabs, soup kitchens, Jane Doe death certificates, hospices, homeless shelters? Have you hired private detectives, or bounty hunters, or runaway experts?"

Everyone turned and looked at Ryles and rather than return their inquisitive gaze he sat slowly back down. "If she were around, we'd have found her," he said quietly and mainly to himself.

No one said anything for maybe thirty seconds. Outside our slightly tinted windows, seagulls floated bouyantly on the rising currents, and I felt the soft, cool caress of the pneumatic air-conditioning as it kicked quietly back to life, the almost silent white-noise an unconscious welcome to the heated emotions that lay just beneath the surface.

Since no once ventured an answer, I decided to continue, "So what is it exactly that you request, gentlemen? Do you want Ryles's accounting of her non-existence in Seattle verified? Or do you wish her logistical whereabouts established? And if she can be located, should contact be made? And if so, by whom?"

I looked around the room at each of the players, who were busy looking at each other. There was finally another utterance out of the normally mute, Malcomb Arbreau. He was probably at least five years younger than Nicholas White, whom I'd read was about sixty, but looked ten years older. He lacked the follicly challenged status of White, but his face and eyes bore the stress of multiple campaigns and pulling the senator's proverbial bottom out of innumerable fixes and fires.

"Mr. Kilbourne," Arbreau pontificated, "I believe the answer to your question is that we would like to ascertain her whereabouts as soon as possible. Because of her lifestyle, I do not think she could be found if she is not in the Greater Seattle area. She would hardly be high profile." He stopped and lowered his head to push his small rimless glasses higher up on his rather bulbous proboscis. As he did so, I noticed that he glanced quickly at the senator who did an almost imperceptible singular nod with his head. "Once she is found and confirmed you can contact Mr. Ryles here and he can make the initial contact and take it from there. Any other questions?"

"Just one," I said. "Is the impetus and immediacy behind the search for the prodigal daughter based upon love or liability?"

Shane initiated a cough and gave me the "shut up" look that I seemed to get a lot from people, and the question seemed to relegate Malcomb back to mute status. White, though, was up to the task and quick to refute any improprieties.

"Mr. Kilbourne, the question in and of itself is insulting enough," White said, while trying to look aghast and feign seven levels of sincerity at the same time. "The senator's intentions are beyond reproach. Just as any loving father would . . ."

"Don't waste your breath, boys, Kilbourne's not an idiot," the senator said as he rose slowly from his chair and walked to the window looking out over the Sound. He rested his chin on his chest and pushed his hands deep into his pockets and stayed that way for maybe ten long seconds. I remembered a photo of Nixon profiled like that during the Watergate investigation . . . I was hoping this would turn out better. Finally, he seemed to come to some sort of internal conclusion, took a deep breath and said, "No bull?"

I smiled and said, "If you don't mind stepping out of character for a minute."

Both White and Malcomb reached coronary status that time, but the senator just laughed and raised his hand for them to be quiet. "All right, Kilbourne, you shape up like pretty much of a man, and Mr. Lowe over there says you can be trusted." He turned back to the window then and crossed his arms. "The Democrats would love to get something on me. Most of the cracks I've managed to get my tail into, Malcomb here has been able to spin my way out of. But the liberals would deal with the devil to find out I had a daughter who turned trix for fix, or whatever terminology they're using these days."

He turned from the window then and walked over to where I was sitting and looked me straight in the eye. "I could'a been a better father, but I loved the body politic, and the senate was my mistress. I've got a damn good shot at winning this giant BS contest and Chrissy could sink me. If she's alive, I'll try to get her some help and if she's dead, I'll make sure she's memorialized somehow. But what I can't have is this wandering liability walking around. Chrissy's a political time bomb and I'm fresh outa foxholes." He stopped abruptly then, a little surprised I think, at both his forthrightness and conviction.

I, on the other hand, liked the fact that he attempted honesty, seemed sincere, and that he finally gave his daughter a name and personalized her. I imagine he probably cared more for her than even he realized, but had been trying to distance himself from her for so long he probably still couldn't allow himself an honest emotion.

I held the senator's gaze for a few more seconds and looked past Arbreau and White to Shane, who tilted his head and raised his shoulders as if to say "your move." I turned the other way and looked at Ryles. "What do you think?"

Ryles, surprised at first that I'd seek his opinion, deliberated for a second and then said, "I think you're an egotistical arse, but we're in a hurry and short on reliable resources. And," Ryles smiled devilishly, "I'd love to see you fail and fall flat on your face."

I turned back to the senator. "Well, I'd be a fool to turn my back on all this love and admiration, so . . . ," I paused for only a second, "I'll have it looked into!"

I excused myself after extending the obligatory good-byes and stepped outside the partially opened door and had the pleasure of watching as Shane worked his usual magic. He took out some contractual paperwork and placed it on the conference table. "Gentlemen, I am confident that Shad will be able to come to some conclusions and possible closure within thirty days, regardless of Chrissy's current state of being. But there is still the question of compensation." Shane paused here to make sure there were no misunderstandings. "One million dollars and future markers will need to be credited to certain accounts prior to any effort on his part."

White visibly blanched as the figure was iterated. "I still think it's an outrageous sum of money, Senator." The senator looked at his lead counsel and shook his head. "We're too far into this little dance contest to change partners now, Nicholas. And besides, never question a closer's contract in the ninth inning."

White turned from the senator still seeking approval and retrained his focus on Arbreau. "What's your take, Malcolm? I'd like to make sure we have consensus on this thing before moving forward." "Let me put it this way," Malcomb started as he swiveled his chair around to face his peers, "if this were two weeks before the election and she surfaced . . . we'd pay ten million dollars to make the situation go away." White then turned his attention to Shane. "What is this about future markers, Mr. Lowe?"

Shane looked at all three men individually to make sure that each was paying attention. "It is simply guaranteeing Kilbourne the right to ask favors and have them granted, going forward." White started to object for the umpteenth time, but the senator cut him off short. "Then let's light this fuse, fellas," said the senator, "before we're the ones blown out of contention."

I spoke privately with Shane in the hallowed halls and left him to tie up the details. I'd have to meet with the senator or his staff tomorrow to fill in the holes and get some pictures and background, but if Chrissy was still in the Puget Sound area, I was sure we could locate her. But before I bid my fond farewells to the Heritage Club, the same elderly tuxedoed gentleman who had escorted me in was now painfully slow escorting me out.

"What's your name?" I asked, being the great conversationalist that I was and intrigued by the hunched over old man. Even though he was old, slow, and slightly bent with time, you could tell he still tried to carry himself with a great amount of dignity and pride.

He stopped and turned slowly toward me, looking up with raised eyes from his permanently stooped position. "Are you inquiring as to how I am addressed by the Heritage members, sir?" he asked in return, without much inflection or interest. When I said that I was, he owned up to the fact that the members called him Smythe.

"First or last?" I asked since he didn't elaborate. But before he could answer, a December-gentleman walked by with a well-displayed May-lady who seemed to be slightly inebriated and more than a little giggly. Smythe bowed his head slightly as they passed, as if in respect and repose. May looked at me like I was dessert and December looked at me like I was demented for talking to the help.

"Just Smythe, sir, no one is interested in the rest," he said after the couple had turned the corridor's corner. And with a seasoned smile added, "And you're the first to ever ask."

I followed him the rest of the way to the grand entrance in silence and took one last look at my rather surreal surroundings. Smythe pushed the elevator button for me and stood to see that I boarded safely, or at least that I didn't steal the silverware, I wasn't sure which.

"What is it they call you at home, Smythe?" I pried as the hum of the private elevator's electromagnetic rollers grew increasingly louder with its ascent.

"They don't, sir." And this time he paused and looked at the floor before going on. "For six weeks and five days there's been no one at home to call me much of anything."

I watched as his shoulders started to shake ever so slightly. His loss was obvious, but I knew somehow that he was a proud man in his own way and would not want me to question his private pain. So I just stood with him in the high-priced silence and said, "I'm sorry for your loss, Smythe."

As the elevator doors finally opened, I took a business card out of my suit pocket and handed it to him. He took it in both hands out of reverent habit and turned it over.

"It is elegant, sir, but it is only a telephone number."

I smiled at the bent and broken old man, his seen-everything eyes still bright with moisture. "My name is Shadoe Kilbourne, Smythe, and the number is for you if you should ever find yourself in need."

He looked up from the card a little confused. "What is it that you do, sir?"

I stepped into the elevator and to the cool, smooth tones of Sinatra. "Whatever it takes, Smythe," I said. "I guess, I just do whatever it takes."

And then the highly polished elevator doors shut without sound, and there we were again, just Frank and me.

CHAPTER 2

By the time I got back to the Liquid City it was almost four o'clock and the traffic on Fifth Street was starting to congeal, the weather coming off the Sound feeling gelatinous after the quiet, climate-controlled conditions of the Heritage Club.

The Liquid City was Seattle's hottest and most exclusive nightclub, taking up the bottom three open floors of the city's tallest high-rise. I took over the Liquid City six years ago when the previous owner died of cancer. I'd done some heavy work for Red McCrady about a decade ago and I guess giving me the City at his death was Red's way of paying me back and, in his own way and on his own terms, saying thank you for my help and friendship. When I took over the City, it was a relatively small but popular bar that captured the overpaid suits and their undercompensated secretaries as they headed home from work. It was placed strategically on the third floor as the corporate inhabitants came down from their ivory towers and had to abandon the elevators and continue down to the bottom two floors on the escalators. It was the perfect place to see and be seen and proved to be an excellent repository for singles in search of sociosexual gratification.

Since taking over, I had completely overhauled and expanded the place. The Liquid City now took up the first three floors of the Paragon Tower in open-air, delta'd fashion. Upon entry into the City you walked

"Das right, Bawse," he said. "I used to weigh a fat and frustratin' 302."

I stole a piece of chicken from Slice's bowl. "Really? What do you weigh now?"

Bama smiled brightly, "Now, I a lean and mean 298!"

I laughed and almost choked on my chicken. "Wow! That's some transformation," I said as I headed across the ocean floor. "Just remember our insurance plan doesn't cover anorexia." I could hear them start to laugh as I ascended the stairs, so I yelled back over my shoulder, "And nobody likes a skinny bouncer."

Halfway up the crystal staircase, I stopped at the hostess podium and checked the reservations for the Falling Waters restaurant. It looked like another frenzied Friday night. I noticed a few illustrious names on the list, so I made a mental note to drop by those tables later on with a bottle of Dom Perignon and acknowledge their much appreciated patronage. And any opportunity to sip on ice-cold Dom was worth any effort and expense on my part. And since I was going to quit drinking tomorrow, a couple of glasses of champagne couldn't hurt tonight.

"Hello, Handsome!" said the loving and familiar voice behind me.

"Hello, Lady Di!" I replied as I turned to receive my daily hug and kiss from one of nature's most dazzling creations. Diana Fontaine was my general manager, and handled all aspects of the City: hiring, firing, ordering, scheduling, etc. She was also a no-nonsense knockout and Bryn Mawr MBA-dynamo whom I loved dearly and respected greatly . . . and invited over regularly for business sleepovers.

"Do you really think I'm handsome?" I said as I returned the hug and kiss. "Or did you just say that because you have perfect vision and impeccable taste?"

"Actually, I take pity on all God's creatures," she said, "especially the ones that prove He had a sense of humor during the design phase."

I looked through a litany of messages as I tried to dodge the verbal onslaught. "Am I to assume that your disparaging remarks are directed solely at me or are all men subject to your rhetorical diatribe?"

She walked over and took my face in her baby-soft hands and squeezed my cheeks together so that my lips did that fish-pucker thing.

"Just you, Schmoopie, and of course, the two womanizing widgets with whom you dilly-dally daily; who, by the way, are in your office waiting for you in a heated debate."

"Heated debate about what?" I asked as she smacked me affectionately on the bottom and headed back to check on the kitchen.

"I think it was something about superheroes, but when I told them I liked the *Hulk* because my favorite color is green, they kicked me out of your office."

"What about *AquaMan* and *the Green Hornet?*"

She stopped at the swinging kitchen doors and turned around and gave me her most mirthful and mischievous grin. "The *Hulk's* got bigger hands!"

Ah, the truth at last! I made a mental note to start buying larger gloves.

I ascended the rest of the stairs gingerly as the lingering effects of the previous day's squat workout continued to wreak havoc with my quads, calves, and glutes. The high price of vanity paid in full, once again!

The third level, Atlantis, or L3, was my personal favorite. The "Quiet Light" semi-opaque floors were done in the colors that mirrored water ripples when reflected by the sun—a nautical mosaic of transcendent blues on gray-white acrylic. Since the city would not give me a permit to have actual aquatic floors at this level, and since my insurance company laughed at the liability request, this was the next best thing. The sub-surface lighting rolled subtly underneath the entire length of the floor every ten seconds to mimic the roll and undulation of waves, and a

Gio finally put the *Seattle Times* away and chimed in. "So we basically have a Jane Doe, who . . . if she is still alive, could be anywhere in the world."

"Technically yes, but all we've been hired to do is to determine if she's vertical and in the vicinity. Figuring she's horizontal and hell-bound doesn't get us anywhere. And, to further muddy the waters, she is definitely of background status: drugs, theft, prostitution. Very lo-pro."

"So we gonna deal with the General and Gat-Gun upfront or wait?" Deity asked.

"We're going to wait on the twin terrors," I said. "I imagine that if she were in the General's current employ, Ryles would have turned her up somewhere. We'll go around them for now, and stay away as long as we can."

The General was Damien "General" Lee, who ran the Greater Seattle's prostitution ring and was pretty much the corridor Skin Czar from Portland, Oregon to Vancouver, Canada. His "black iron fist" was another rather roided out brutha by the name of Derek "Gat-Gun" Gatlin, who was the General's first lieutenant and main enforcer. The nickname Gat-Gun came from the size of his arms, not to mention the rest of his notable musculature. Like a lot of bodybuilders, he was short on stature and long on attitude, all of it bad. Considered the meanest man in the metro, he took great pride in his moniker and seemed to be cruel just for the sake of being cruel.

Gio got up and walked over to the aquarium wall and flipped the electronic control switch that turned the glass from frost to clear so that he could look down on all three levels. I'd had 3M install the privacy glass after I'd been alerted to the fact that some of the latest hi-tech audio and optical technologies could penetrate mirrored glass. The polymer dispersed liquid crystals are sandwiched between two layers of transparent conductive film. The film is then laminated between two pieces of glass. When electricity is applied to the film, the liquid crystals line up and the window is clear. When the power is turned off, the liquid crystals return to their normal positions and turn the glass from clear to frost. It is a great state-of-the-art effect and ensures privacy both optically and audibly.

Gio watched as a small leopard shark cruised by. "I'll see what Seattle's Finest have on her and see if maybe the FBI has a file tucked away somewhere, since they undoubtedly have something on her presidential papa."

Deity poured himself a double mandarin orange vodka and Red Bull at the rotational bar that also spun around and doubled as a bookcase when not in use. Affectionately known as the "twirly bar," it was an important crime-fighting tool and used in all emergency situations . . . like thirst, stress, celebration, boredom, and depression. "I'll make some stops and talk to the local Lolas and see if anybody knows of her," Deity said. "You got some glossies I can flash to the flesh?"

I walked around the desk and down the steps to where Gio was standing in front of the massive aquarium glass wall and looked down on the City coming to life. "I have a meeting with Marcum in the morning to get her photos and bio, so I'll have something for you then. D, if you got the streets and G has the beats, I'll call in some favors and see what I can come up with as well."

Deity brought me over a Barbancourt and Diet Coke and handed Gio a Glenlevitt and soda. We all watched as the majority of the bouncers came ambling up the stairs from L1 to L2 to grab some steak and taters before their shift; twenty massive bodies in Armani tuxes: Trey-Deuce, Rock, Play-Maker, Dante, Semi, Gaud-Almighty, Romance, Nines, Poolside, Tree-Top, Yard-Bird, Baby-Cakes, Kon, Trinity, Rhino, Breeze, etc. All the frontline employees went by nicknames here at the City, allowing them to maintain a modicum of privacy and assume secondary personalities if they so desired. It wasn't a big deal for the bouncers or bartenders other than mere fun, but since the restaurant's waitresses and cocktailers were also some of Seattle's aesthetically elite, I didn't want customers knowing their names or other personal information unless it came specifically from them.

"Damn, Bawse, datta whole lotta humanity," Deity said as he sipped his drink and nodded in appreciation. "Maybe we oughtta start invading small countries on our days off!"

I looked at Deity. "It would take a small country just to feed 'em." We maintained our vigil until they all filed into the kitchen and then took our usual positions. When I got behind my desk, I turned on the array of video screens to the left and checked to see the line already stacking up outside the glass doors to the City, even though it wasn't even four-thirty yet.

"It looks to be another busy Friday night. Why don't you guys go down and brief the staff and security, and we can plan on updating on the other matters at hand on Sunday after brunch," I said and looked away from the screens and gave them an inquisitive look, "unless there's anything I need to know about now?"

Gio drained his drink and set the empty glass down on a marble coaster. "Nah, we're good until Sunday. Need to wire some funds and refine-n-define the details on two new targets, but other than that we're pretty squared away."

"Excellent! Let's not worry about it until then. Are you both doing pickups and drop-offs tonight?"

Gio smiled the Mona Lisa smile. "I have a date."

I looked at Deity and he just smiled and shrugged. "Well, this is an auspicious occasion indeed," I said. "Who is she?"

"Let's just say it's an ember from an old fire," Gio said.

"Not an ash?" I said.

"Nope," he said.

"But not a flame either?"

"Nope."

"Could die out."

"Yup."

"Could flare up."

"Yup."

"Hard to know."

"Hard to care," he said.

"Good point!" I said, and joined my boys at the twirly bar for another medicinal beverage.

CHAPTER 3

I stepped off the elevator and into my penthouse high above the sights and sounds of the city streets, glad to be home from another frenetic Friday night at the City. I didn't bother to turn on the lights. Dark was my friend and I didn't want to disrespect him with a luminous insult. And as everyone knows, Dark loves the Rat Pack, so I grabbed the universal remote and sang along with the boys of eternity. I threw the keys to the Range Rover on the entry side table and navigated my way through the plethora of furniture to fix myself a Barbancourt and Diet Coke at the bar. As I picked up the universal remote to turn on the gas fireplaces, my cell phone rang.

"Hi!" was the soft and sleepy mew at the end of the line. I always loved the way Jessie's voice sounded when she was really sleepy—an almost breathless and buoyant purr—as if she was speaking from an ethereal dream.

"Hey, you!" I said softly into the phone, unconsciously whispering like people tend to do when it's late and the other person is in bed. "I take it you've already made it home to San Fran and crawled in."

"Um-hmmm, and it feels heavenly to be in silk sheets again, except for my everlasting lack of you," she said with an inflected pout and giggled ever so softly, her voice trailing off in the rustle of sheets and pillows as she tried to make herself more comfortable.

"Ah, the perils of solo slumber," I replied and laughed into my drink as I walked to the moisture streaked floor-to-ceiling theatre windows. I looked out over the rain covered radiance of downtown Seattle. I loved the city at sleep. I loved the way the skyscrapers and corporate towers held their nightly vigil and stood stoically over the city and its unconscious occupants. And I loved the architectural rebirth that seemed to take place with every downpour; each street and structure gleaming brightly from the shimmering sheets of iridescent rain.

"I hate sleeping without you," she said. "And it's even more painful waking up without you. What's the quote that I love so much by that poet?"

I thought about how many times that quote had entered the transoms of my mind and how much those nine words meant to me. And for a split second I let it take me to a place . . . and a person, but I felt the always instantaneous tug at my heart and blow to my solar plexus and immediately tried to suppress it—to put it back where it couldn't hurt me anymore.

"I mourn the morn that is won as one," I said, while fixing myself another rum and Diet Coke. "And his name was Curtis St. John."

"Was? Is he dead?" she said with genuine concern.

"Suicide. I've seen his picture before in magazines and on the Internet and he looked like pretty much of a stud. It's weird too because in every picture I've ever seen of him he's either smiling or laughing—surrounded by lots of friends at an infinite number of social gatherings, but I read his stuff and you can tell he's the saddest and loneliest guy on the planet—outwardly heaven, inwardly hell! The guy must have had some serious pain issues."

"Hmmm, that sounds a little like someone I know and infinitely adore," she said, ever so carefully. "Maybe kindred spirits are at play here."

I plopped acrobatically on one of the couches in front of the large main fireplace and silently congratulated myself on not spilling even a drop of my drink. "What? Are you kiddin' me? I'm the happiest guy you know. When have you ever even seen me down?"

I could tell she had just sat up in bed and I could sense the change in her mood. "I hate that about you, Shad. I hate that you won't let me in there. I hate that you won't let us go to that place inside you together. I hate that there's something terrible and painful somewhere dormant in your past and you won't even admit it or share it with me." I could hear her start to lose it and at the same time fight to maintain control, but tears always came easy to Jess and there was no stopping them now. "I hate that you won't let me move there, and I hate that you won't marry me, and I hate that you do things that put your life in jeopardy."

And then there was nothing but the painful sound of her crying, and the fragile remnants of a conversation we'd reenacted a thousand times before. I took a long sip from my cocktail and waited until the sobbing subsided. And then I heard her start to laugh through her tears. "And I hate it when you don't say anything when I get hysterical." And then we both laughed, and talked into the wee hours of the morning.

I put down the phone after our reluctant good-byes, and closed my eyes and tried to imagine her as she slept. She'd be in her suite at the Mark Hopkins Hotel in her ridiculously expansive bed, lying luxuriously on her stomach under silk sandstone sheets. She'd have on my cobalt blue silk pajamas, switching to her matching teddy and tap pants if I was there. Her face would be to the side facing away from the door and her long honey-colored hair would be placed carefully over her pillow or down along her smooth, flawless back. And if I knew Jess, there'd be the slightest hint of Bordeaux on her breath.

Seeing her in my pajamas always made me laugh until my stomach hurt. One of her tan, voluptuous shoulders would always be hanging out of the too-big neck, and the six-inches-too-long sleeves she'd roll up and pin back with a pair of yellow sapphire cufflinks she'd bought me at Tiffany's for our first year anniversary. The waist she'd roll up high along her narrow hips so that the pant legs didn't drag on the floor. It was always comical to see her that way, especially if she'd just awoke and an added aura of dishevelment was making an unexpected appearance. On those mornings, I knew exactly what she must have looked like as a child . . . precious, precocious, and perfect!

I'd met Jessie two years ago when she was still singing back-up for Sarah Brightman. But now that she had her own bourgeoning career she was traveling nationally and internationally a lot and our time together was less frequent, but no less intense. Both of which probably added to her current state of mind and heart. But this was all I had to give, and I didn't foresee that changing in the near future. She has the voice and beauty of an angel, the body and soul of a romantic, and the patience and understanding of a fruit fly.

I poured myself another cocktail and clicked on *Headline News* with the mute on. It had been a fun night at the City. Rob Reinner, Meg Ryan, Tom Hanks, and his wife Rita were in town for a *Sleepless in Seattle* reunion and they surprised me with a little dinner party in the private dining room in The Reef. It was a nice evening for everybody, including the other patrons who got to have their photos taken with the infamous group. Meg had to head out early for another project she was filming, but it was good to see her again. We'd had a few fun months together several years ago, so I was happy that she wasn't still harboring any ill will over our parting of ways. It's tough when your sweetheart is also America's sweetheart. Anonymity, autonomy, and alone time seem to be the first casualties of dating the infinitely famous, and 'twas not the life for me.

I'd have to stop in and see Senator Marcum tomorrow afternoon and find out what information I could gather on his daughter Chrissy, hopefully along with some photos and a little more pertinent background. I'm sure we could find her if she was around, but how quickly and in what condition I couldn't be sure.

We also had other matters at hand and I didn't want to get too distracted with a runaway and lose focus on the important issues. But fortunately, my most important issue at the moment was that of going to bed, especially since it was 5:00 a.m., so I made another cocktail for the long walk up to the master bedroom. And in fitting tribute, I clicked a button on the "do it all" remote and the Carpenter's Greatest Hits accompanied me on my way . . . maybe *Solitaire* was the only game in town!

CHAPTER 4

I woke up that same morning, eleven fifty-nine to be exact, with a spring in my step, a hitch in my giddyup, and a charley-horse in my left hammy. I always hated squats, especially the second day afterward when you could really feel it. I'd have to remember to do a little more stretching or a little less weight, both of which held their virtues. But a quick cup of coffee and a frosted blueberry Pop-Tart before I showered, and a PowerBar and Diet Coke for the road and I was good to go. Pop-Tarts are truly the breakfast of champions and critical sustenance for the genetically perfected; and since I couldn't quite justify rice crispy treats first thing in the morning, I felt I was going with the healthier alternative.

I took my private elevator downstairs and Roiko was waiting at the car with the door open and the heater on at full blast. Roiko was in my employ as a favor to an old friend of my father and his cryptic cronies when they were in the CIA together. I had never met my father's secretive counterparts, but since his death umpteen years ago, they called occasionally to check on me as promised to my father. It was like having an invisible moral minority lurking in the shadows.

The big old Russian, who was now in his early sixties, was in the witness relocation program for several years before he was exposed and dropped off at my doorstep. He turned out to be a top-notch driver, body-guard, cook and bartender, and a good and loyal friend. His time with the Russian mafia had left him a little mentally and physically scarred, but I always felt a little safer and less exposed when Roiko was around.

"Good morning, Roiks," I said energetically as I hopped in the back.

Roiko looked at me with a skeptical grin. "Morning has come and gone, comrade. But that is what happens when you arise at the crack of noon."

"How nice to have you here, Roiks, for those times when I miss my mother's criticism! Oh, how I miss a good lecture every now and then!"

Roiko laughed his deep rolling laugh. "We Soviets are all maternal at heart, comrade, why do you think they call it Mother Russia? Besides, cognitively challenged young men of dubious means and questionable hours need all the advice they can get."

"Remind me again how much I pay you?" I said, shaking my head.

"Your government pays me, you pay me nothing."

"Well, I just want you to know you're worth every penny."

With that said, Roiks shut the door on my coat and our conversation, and we were on our merry way. I had decided to go with my blue-gray Armani suit, a black, cashmere mock, a blued 9 mm glock, with matching Andy Arratoonian block and hand-bone back holster and my navy light-weight overcoat, the outfit of the modern day D'Artagnan. I figured the senator would be decked out in a suit and tie and I had to compete with the type of attire that could only be purchased at taxpayers' expense.

We crossed the five-twenty enroute to Bellevue, and Roiko pulled up to the curb in front of the senator's campaign office and dropped me off. I entered the nearly empty building and noticed what the Good Gentleman from Seattle lacked in substance, he most certainly made up for in taste. Should the senator's political career dry up, his success in the field of interior design was most assuredly guaranteed. And his receptionist was no exception.

"Can I help you?" she asked plainly, already in denial of her obvious attraction to me, no doubt.

"Yes, you May, me Tarzan!" I charmingly replied, taking note of her nametag and cleavage in one furtive glance.

"Huh?" was her ingenious retort.

Ah, I was obviously in the presence of a true verbal master. "I'm sorry," I said. "It was a play on words, your name being May and the obvious connection with the 'You Jane, me Tarzan' dialogue of yore."

Again, the vacant stare and just a hint of annoyance! Maybe I wasn't as funny as I thought I was. Naaaah!

"How can I help you, sir?"

"Sir? Ah good, then the senator was kind enough to alert you as to my knighthood, how kind of him," I flirted. "I personally don't like to brag about it, but it gets me into all the nicest places."

"What?" Again the clever repartee, her mental acuities were staggering.

"My apologies, I was trying once again to be funny. 'Sir' is a titular prefix to the forename of a knight. Henceforth, the jest, though not the joust!"

Have you ever noticed that initially attractive receptionists are not nearly as attractive when their mouths gape open and their eyes glaze over?

"Do you have an appointment?" she finally uttered when the cognitive fog had cleared.

I started to say "with destiny," but thought better of it. She was dangerously close to slipping into a coma and I didn't want to be held responsible. Though the opportunity for mouth-to-mouth resuscitation and repeated chest compressions gave me a moment's pause!

"Yes, I do. Could you please tell the senator that Shad Kilbourne is here to see him?" I could see the fog begin to clear in her eyes as we finally entered a realm she was familiar with. Not necessarily competent in, but familiar with nonetheless.

I was told that I could sit in the waiting room until the senator was off the phone; but at least the chairs were comfortable and the magazines were recent. I checked *People Magazine* to see if I had made the annual "50 Most Beautiful People" list, but was once again let down by my international obscurity and their blatant bias of the genetically gifted. Periodical stardom had once again slipped through my grasp!

When the senator finally appeared, he was once again the jovial political juggernaut. But surprisingly enough was in black jeans, ebony, ostrich-skin cowboy boots, and a white, suede, button up shirt.

"Nobody told me it was Casual Day on the campaign trail," I said, as I rose to meet his handshake.

The senator laughed and reciprocated the handshake. "For better or worse I'm afraid I'm a ranch-hand at heart. I'll take a saddle and a sunset over a Senate Subcommittee any day of the week."

"Good decision," I said.

"I'll take it," he said as we headed into his office. "Could be the only one I make all month."

"What? A self-deprecating senator? You'll be kicked out of the Congressional Conceit Club."

"You're right, forget I mentioned it," he said. "Pretend we're off the record."

His office was done in early Loius L'Amour and had a great rustic texture and western warmth to it. A magnificent twelve-foot spread of Texas Longhorns adorned the wall above his desk and fireplace, and a huge sun-bleached buffalo skull was showcased under glass on a black marble column in the far corner. Genuine leather chairs and cowhide rugs completed the theme. There were pictures on the woven reed walls of the senator with former presidents, movie stars, music stars, and those of revolving infamy. I saw no pictures of family, other than his wife, but maybe that was to discourage familial questioning about the kids . . . and their whereabouts.

After we were seated I said, "I reckon I ain't dressed proper for this here meetin', Sheriff."

"Don't worry, Deputy," he joked. "I'll rustle us up some grub and we can sit a spell and tell a few yarns over vittles!"

"Giddyup!" I said.

The senator pushed some buttons, and within a few minutes we had an assortment of pastries and some freshly brewed coffee—black as Deity and nearly as strong.

I took a chocolate-on-chocolate, nut-encrusted donut and tried not to think lesser of the senator by not having Pop-Tarts or rice crispy treats on the tray. "By the way, I think I'm in love with your Mensa candidate at the front desk."

Marcum started to laugh and almost spilled his coffee. "Yeah, she's a package, isn't she? How'd you know she wasn't very bright?"

I took a welcomed bite of my donut. "She didn't proposition me the minute I entered the room."

"Silly girl," he said.

"I know, physically fortified but mentally marginalized," I said. "But maybe on the way out I can offer to show her my home in Paris and see if that changes her mind."

"You have a house in Paris?" he asked.

"No."

The senator got a confused look on his face for a minute and then finally understood and nodded his head in bemusement. "Ah, I get it now. Sorry, I confused the promise with the premise. You'd be a good politician, Kilbourne. How would you like to be my vice president?"

"If Vice President is anything like Vice Squad, I think I'll pass."

This time the senator did spill his coffee, but luckily on his black pants and not on his white shirt, which I'm sure, is why he was eating a powdered-sugar donut. "They actually have multiple parallels, but you're either going to have to quit making me laugh, Kilbourne, or I'm going to have to get more graceful."

I threw the senator a napkin. "Well, when you're president, you can make me the U.S. Ambassador to France so that I'll have a home there to impress beautiful but befuddled receptionists with."

"I'll make it the top priority of my administration, Shad. You have my solemn promise as a Congressman."

"You're a senator," I said.

He smiled the political smile. "See how easy that was!"

The senator's intercom chimed in and his Girl Friday told him he had an important call, which ended up being a lobbyist offering a Cabo San Lucas fishing trip in the interest of fun, food, and pharmaceuticals. When he got off the phone he wrote something down on his calendar and gave me a wink. *Co-conspirators!*

"I'd heard you were a threesome," he said when he mentally returned from Cabo.

"I felt I could risk a sardonic senator and a rabid receptionist on my own," I joked as I reached for another donut. "Gio and Deity are both good men and good friends, and manage security at all my restaurants and clubs. If it's a situation where I feel they'll be needed, then they're typically close at hand."

"Gio? Deity?" he asked?

"Gio is short for Giovano Gianinni. Deity is Deity Jones, who was left at an orphanage when he was only a few months old with nothing but a pacifier and an old, worn blanket with the initials DET embroidered along the tattered trim, and he's gone by "Deity" ever since."

"I've seen them with you a couple of times at some different functions," he said. "They look . . . oh, how should I say it . . . formidable!"

I chuckled as I thought they would both appreciate and enjoy the adjective and the inevitable epitaph. "Formidable they are, senator. Gio is ex-police and FBI, and Deity is ex-military and mercenary, and both of them are about as lethal on all levels as it gets. And both are very adaptable. They seem almost indigenous to each event."

"Who's tougher?" the senator asked, like we were school kids talking about cowboys and Indians. I thought about it for half a second, "I'm not sure, typically when individuals are that evenly matched it ends up being situational rather than physical. But if I had to choose, I'd say Deity, just based upon the fact that he's less methodical and less remorseful. But these days it's irrelevant since bullets replaced bravado a long time ago. Seems like in these dark days of despair every eight-year-old is armed and dangerous. It ain't the way it used to be, Senator."

The senator looked contemplative for a minute while slowly nodding his head in agreement. "There was a passage I read once in college about the after-effects of war, and then I thought about it again after 9/11, and your statement reminded me of it . . . 'Nothing is as it used to be: no men as they were, no day as before, no hope nor want of dawn.'"

"Ah yes, the evolutionary echo of change," I said, " . . . especially catastrophic change!"

Our cerebral stream was interrupted at that point when his secretary knocked and entered with a couple of files and a large manila envelope. I smiled smugly at her as she set her gatherings down, to which she playfully stuck her tongue out at me unbeknownst to the senator. Maybe there was life on that planet after all!

The senator spent the next hour showing me a few old photos of his daughter, Chrissy, and going over as much history as he knew, remembered, or cared to speculate on. The only item of real relevance and permanence that he had heard was that she now had "Crystal" tattooed on her left wrist and "Marcum" on her right, which if we did find her, would make identifying her that much easier.

When we were about done, the senator pushed his chair away from his desk and propped his ostrich-encased feet up. "Well, what do you think, can you find her?"

I thought about all the young girls who had met their fate on the back streets and in the back alleys of cities and towns all across America—rich girls, poor girls, pretty girls, plain girls, smart girls, dumb girls—the girls that were loved and the girls that were left behind. The chances of us finding her were slim, and the chances of us finding her alive were even slimmer, but it didn't hurt to take a peek around the crimson curtain occasionally and see what lurked behind.

"Let me put it this way," I said. "I think we can find out 'about' her. I think maybe we can find out what happened to her or where she ended up. But I'm sure you already know that there is a significant chance that she may not be around . . . or even alive."

As I completed that last sentence I looked the senator straight in the eye to catch some glimpse of a reaction: good or bad. And maybe, just maybe, there was the slightest spark of a dormant emotion that lay beneath the rough western and political exterior. Deep down, dark, cold, unknown and unexplored, but there!

CHAPTER 5

Roiks dropped me off in front of the City after a quick stop at Taco Time, thankfully without reminding me to take my vitamins or to play well with others. When I climbed up to the Falling Waters Restaurant on L2, Diana walked up quickly with a very serious and official look on her face. Instead of the usual exchange of pleasantries and much awaited peck on the lips, she looked over at one of the booths nearby and said, "Excuse me, Mr. Kilbourne, but a Mr. Ramirez is here to see you." Just loud enough so that he could hear.

I looked over to see a Hispanic youth about ten years old in an ill-fitting, navy-blue suit a few sizes too small, scuffed black tennis shoes with white socks, and a wrinkled white shirt and battered red tie under his smallish jacket. He was looking around the restaurant like a kid in a candy shop, and pretending he couldn't hear our conversation.

With her back to the young boy, she gave me a wink and said, "He said he has no appointment, but only requests a few minutes of your time . . ." and she smiled, "man to man."

I looked past Di and saw the young man look up sheepishly from under his too-long hair, and look away nervously as I met his gaze. "Please tell Mr. Ramirez that I need to make a phone call and then I will be pleased to meet with him." As I walked away I got to see a bright, wide smile light up his bronzed face as Di told him that I would see him shortly. If only everyone were that happy to see me!

On the way up the crystalline stairs to my office, I smiled with admiration at the courage it must have taken for the boy to come here presumably alone and ask to meet with an adult he'd never met. I was eager to find out the reason behind his visit so I made my calls quickly to those who might assist me in finding Chrissy and waltzed like a muscle-bound, matza-ball down to my meeting.

As I walked up to the young man, he stood, but before I could get there Di waltzed over equally as balletically and reminded me that I still needed to return a few calls and taste-test some of the new appetizers. I wasn't great at returning phone calls, but I was quite possibly the greatest appetizer taste-tester the world had ever known. Always good to know your strengths and weaknesses!

I turned around and greeted the young man, "Good morning, Mr. Ramirez. Shad Kilbourne."

The wee lad smiled a little nervously, but shook my hand firmly, "I know of you senor, you have been a good friend to us . . . my people, I mean. I am Pablo Aurelio Ramirez."

"It is a pleasure to meet you, sir," I said, and motioned him to sit.

As we both sat, Di appeared at our booth and asked us if we would like anything to eat or drink. I asked our friend if he would like anything and he asked for water while I went with a Diet Coke. As she started to walk away, I saw Pablo reach into his pocket for change and said, "How much would a Diet Coke be, senora?" She smiled her loving smile and said, "There is no charge for handsome and charming young men." And was off.

He watched her go and was obviously very proud of the complement he had just received. "Would you care for anything to eat, Pablo?"

"No, gracias, Senor Kilbourne." But the thought of food must have reminded his stomach of its emptiness, and a soft growl was heard above Mozart's background music.

"Well, then, Pablo, what is it that I can do for you this day?"

He hesitated for a few seconds and looked down at his hands in his lap, and when he looked up, his eyes were shiny with moisture. "I need a job, Senor Kilbourne, my father has lost his job and my mother is sick. And I have three little sisters. And I have heard my mother speak of you and how you are a great man, and how you helped fix the playgrounds and build the community center for the Mexicans. And I am strong like a bull, Senor Kilbourne, and I work hard. Harder than any other boy my age, I promise you."

He was so earnest and forthright that I almost started to laugh but caught myself as I realized it was important for him to be taken seriously . . . man to man. But before I could answer, Di returned with our beverages. "Here you go gentlemen, is there anything else?"

I looked at Pablo. "What is your current consulting rate, Pablo?"

"S'cuse me, Senor Kilbourne? My what?"

I looked at him seriously. "Your consulting rate. If someone were to ask you to paint their fence, or mow their lawn, or give them financial advice, what would you charge them per hour?"

Pablo looked down at his lap again and thought about it for a long ten seconds. "I think, senor, that I would charge them ten dollars for that hour."

"Okay, then, I need your help. I have to pick out some appetizers for the children's menu for the lounge downstairs. I will meet your fee if you have an hour to spare. Do we have a deal?"

Pablo was so excited he could hardly contain himself. "Si, Senor Kilbourne. You and I, we have a deal. I am on spring break so I don't have to be home until dinner."

And so we shook on it and Di brought out the sixteen appetizer samplers that we had narrowed it down to. Over the next hour, Pablo, Di, and I, along with Fraank my executive chef and his experienced kitchen crew picked out our four new menu offerings. It was done with much discussion and much laughter as we watched Pablo make faces according to his appreciation or dissatisfaction at the moment. It was an hour well spent.

Before he left, Fraank walked over to where Pablo was sitting and looked at him evaluatively. "You have a good palate young man. You and I agreed on all the same blind tastings and sauces." Fraank looked at Pablo again for a few seconds before sticking out his hand. "It has been a great honor to meet you, Mr. Ramirez. Come see us again soon."

I watched my typically itinerate and egotistical executive chef walk back to the kitchen whistling along with Beethoven, and saw the look of pride envelope Pablo's entire body.

He looked back at me with a huge grin on his face. "That was the best food I have ever had, Senor Kilbourne, other than mi madre's, of course."

I studied the eager, young face for a minute and came up with a plan. "Mr. Ramirez, I have no cash on me in which to pay you your consulting fee," I lied. "But I also have some errands to run, one of which is to the bank, and I can use some more of your consultation if you have the time."

"Si, Senor Kilbourne," he said with a large and excited smile, "I think I will do this work for you."

I called Roiko and had him bring the limo around. Where I was headed was only a few blocks away, but I wanted to give Pablo the full treatment. Once we were comfortably seated inside and Pablo was through trying every button in the limousine, I opened the mini refrigerator and grabbed us each a Gatorade.

"Okay, Mr. Ramirez, I need to stop at Maurice's first and get a haircut and a manicure, so I'll need your advice on the best cut."

Pablo looked a little sad and said, "Senor Kilbourne, I know nothing about haircuts and manicures."

I smiled at my young protégé. "You know far more than you think, Pablo. Trust your experience when you have it and your intuition when you don't. Even if your decision is wrong, it will add to your experience and ability, and hone your judgment. Bad decisions are the best teachers, and good decisions are the best guides."

When we walked into the salon, the clinicians greeted us warmly and the owner practically ran over to us. "Messieur Kilbourne, how great to see you! How can we assist you today?"

"Good afternoon, Maurice," I said. And then pointing to Pablo I said, "My associate and I are in desperate need of a haircut and a manicure, but we will be discussing matters of utmost concern while we are being attended to, so we may need some refreshments."

"Oui! Anything for you, Messieur Kilbourne." Maurice snapped his fingers and we were whisked off to the executive suite in Seattle's most posh salon.

"Am I to get a haircut too, senor?" Pablo asked with obvious excitement and trepidation as we walked down the mirrored and marbled halls.

"Hey, if I gotta get a haircut, you gotta get a haircut."

Pablo giggled for the first time that day and then jumped up into the chair with an ease and alacrity I lacked. The very attractive and attentive clinicians arrived shortly thereafter and showed him several different cuts and styles. He chose the "Freddy Couples" for me and the "Tony Gonzales" for himself. They also made much ado about Pablo and flirted with him shamelessly.

Afterward, we checked our reflections in the full-length mirrors. "Ya know, Pablo, I think you made the right calls on the haircuts. We are two handsome men."

Pablo stepped up closer to the mirror and looked with obvious pride at his haircut, and then looked down at his hands at the manicure. "I have never had a manicure before, Senor Kilbourne."

"Did you like it?"

"I think so. The senoritas, they were very beautiful, weren't they?"

"Yes, Pablo, they were, and to be honest with you, they're the best part of the whole deal."

Pablo looked up at me in the mirror and smiled. "I think so too, Senor Kilbourne, I think so too." As he turned to look at himself in the mirror again, his face was flushed with excitement, but when he looked at his suit, and then at mine, I could see his face lose some of its luster.

"All right, my young consultant, we're off," I said as we departed the salon quickly to avoid more of Maurice's hugs and kisses.

"Where to now, senor? The bank?"

"Not yet, we have one more stop to make and more business yet to discuss."

On our way to our next stop, Pablo told me a little more about his father and his situation.

"Mi padre, he worked construction and got laid off two months ago and can't find work. And I am afraid he will go back to the Diablos if we don't have any money. He promised me and mi madre that he would not, but I know they pressure him to come back and it is hard to break away."

"El Diablo, the gang?"

"Si, senor. I'm not sure what he did for them, but I know he was one of the leaders, and it was dangerous, and my mother cried all the time. But people from the bank are trying to take our home, and even though he won't say it, it hurts the pride of my father and the heart of my mother to worry about such things."

"I thought members in Diablos were bangers for life and weren't allowed to leave the gang?"

"They can't, but my father, he is very strong, senor, and very brave, and I know he is a great caballero, um, how you say . . . soldier?"

I looked at the likable young man as he peered out the window. I could tell he was awaiting an answer from me and was nervous to find out if I could do anything for him.

"All right, Mr. Ramirez, here's the situation. I am always in need of a world-class dishwasher, kitchen assistant, and personal consultant, so let me know when you can start work, and Diane, the nice lady you met today, will get you all set up. But," I said very emphatically, "honesty, honor, and loyalty are the hallmarks of a man's character, and I demand all three from all my employees. Can you promise me you will always maintain all three?"

Pablo nodded his head frantically with nervous excitement. "Si, Senor Kilbourne, I am all of these things you speak of. I will work hard and be on time, I promise you this."

"Well, then, it looks like we have deal. Welcome aboard, Mr. Ramirez, and welcome to the Liquid City family."

With that, Pablo leaped into my arms and gave me a hug that I hadn't expected. I hugged him back and he began to cry, softly at first, and then with a rush of tears that must have been held back for those two long months.

After a while the tears abated and he sat back down and wiped his face with the back of his tattered jacket. "I am sorry to cry, Senor Kilbourne, but this is great news for our family."

I smiled as I looked back at him. "No harm in crying, Pablo," I said. "I do it every time I get out of the shower and look in the mirror."

Pablo and I both laughed this time, all the way to our next stop. This time Roiko got to stay in the car as the tuxedoed and top-hatted greeter stepped forward from the curb, let Pablo and I out, and ushered us in to Jean-Paul's haberdashery.

"What are we doing here, Senor Kilbourne?"

"Well, Pablo, I noticed at the salon that we were both in the need of a new suit and shoes. What do you think? Should we pick it up a notch?"

At that point, Pablo started jumping up and down and spinning around with his hands up in the air. "I have never had a new suit, Senor Kilbourne. Not even one. Never in my life, senor! I cannot believe it! Think what my mother will say, senor, and how handsome my sisters will say I look!"

Pablo kept talking so fast, and sometimes in Spanish, that I only caught a little of what else he said. But I caught all of the surprise and all of the joy; and for the first time in my life I felt like I knew what it would be like to have a son; and it was a good thing.

Once again Pablo's consulting expertise paid off as I was fitted for a cobalt-blue, double-breasted Armani, with a thin bright-white pinstripe. Pablo picked out a solid black double-breasted suit and shoes, and I picked out a navy blazer for him as well with three sets of shirts and slacks, and another pair of shoes and socks.

Pablo looked wide-eyed at the clothes piled on the counter, then up at the aging Jean-Paul, and then turned to look at me. "All of these things are for me, Senor Kilbourne? To keep? For good?"

I smiled and said, "These things are for you to keep, for good, as long as you keep your word, and your word is good. Do you understand this?"

"Si, senor, I promise!"

I had to leave my "Pablo Original" with the tailor for some "tweaking." Unfortunately, a size fifty-four jacket comes standard with a size forty-six waist. For some reason an eight-inch drop was about as close as they could accommodate, so all my suits had to be custom-made for a thirty-two-inch waist. But I didn't want to disappoint Pablo, so I told him that some minor adjustments would need to be made. He asked if he could wear the double-breasted home to show his parents, and I told him they were his suits and he could do as he pleased.

Back in the limo, he asked why I preferred double-breasted suits. "Well, Pablo, for one reason they are more formal, which I tend to be. For another reason, they don't gape at the waist like a standard and show the shirt underneath, which I think sometimes looks sloppy. For another reason . . ." and I thought about this for a second. "Do you know how it feels when your mother or your sisters come up from behind you and wrap their arms around you and give you a big hug from behind?"

"Si, Senor Kilbourne, I love it when they do that."

"Well, that's kinda the way double-breasted suits feel to me, Pablo. Like a great big, long hug from behind, just like my mother used to give me when I was a boy your size and age."

Pablo looked down at his suit and wrapped both sides around him and then fastened the top two of the three buttons like I had shown him. When he looked up at me, his face was bright with understanding. "Senor, it does feel like a hug from behind. I will think of my mother and my sisters every time I put it on."

Pablo and I rode in silence for a few minutes, both alone with our own thoughts—Pablo, smiling because of the excitement of the day, and I, smiling because of Pablo's excitement!

Pablo turned to look at me all of a sudden. "Can I ask you a question, Senor Kilbourne?"

"Of course, Pablo, go ahead."

"How come when we go into those places, you never pay for anything? Do you have a charge there?"

I laughed. "No Pablo, no charges. I have all the tuxes for my security and bouncers at my clubs custom-made there, so all my things are free as Jean-Paul's way of thanking me for my business. And at Maurice's, I did him a favor once when he was in trouble and needed my help, so his services are free for me there as well."

Pablo nodded to himself as he thought about that for a minute. But before he could ask what kind of trouble I had assisted Maurice with, I interrupted him. "Speaking of favors, I might need some help from your father. Do you think you could have him come by and see me?"

"Can you get him a job, senor?" Pablo asked as he almost came to his feet inside the limo. "Can you please, senor?"

I smiled at his eagerness. "I just may know somebody, Pablo . . . I just may know somebody who can."

With that, I got another billion-dollar hug from Pablo and another when we got back to the City after the bank. I gave Pablo five twenty-dollar bills as I left him at the curb.

"But, senor, I was only with you for three hours. That should only be thirty dollars, not one hundred."

"I know, Pablo, but your mother and sisters might be sad if you come home with nice things and nothing for them. So go buy them a treat so they can share your joy and not be jealous of it."

"Really? Oh, thank you, Senor Kilbourne. Muchos gracias!"

"My pleasure, Pablo, and no need to thank me. Remember, you are family now. And speaking of family, your uncle Roiko will take you to get some things for your family and drive you home."

Roiko glared at me, but grinned when he caught Pablo's disbelieving gaze.

"You mean it, senor! He will drive me to my house?"

"Absolutely! Just let him know where, and he'll take you there. And don't forget to call Diane and get set up for your new job."

"Si, senor. I mean, no, senor, I will not forget, not in a million years I would not forget." He looked up at Roiko again, "Gracias tio Roiko!"

Tio Roiko. Uncle Roiko! I laughed for the hundredth time that day and waved good-bye as the limo pulled away with the City's newest top executive tucked safely away inside. But as I turned to walk into the City, I caught a glimpse of brake lights reflecting off the mirrored windows and looked back around to see Pablo's window rolling down. He stuck his head and half his small body out of the window and yelled, "Senor Kilbourne, this has been my best day ever!" And with that, they were gone with a wave. As I walked through the turnstile doors, I watched the limo pull off in the distance and said out loud to myself . . . "Me too, Pablo, me too."

CHAPTER 6

Once I was back in my lair, I made a phone call to Rich Jordan, an old friend who owned Puget Sound Construction and informed him of a new employee he was going to hire.

"Things are slow, Kil, I don't have enough work to keep the crews that I already have busy."

"Okay," I said, "I'll take care of that too. Expect a call."

I hung up with Rich and called a County Commissioner that owed me a few favors. I gave him my highly valued opinion that he should move up the construction date on an upcoming project and award it to Rich.

"But Rich is always more expensive than the other bids," he said.

"I know, but he does better work," I responded back.

There was a short exasperated pause on the other line and then a long exhalation of breath. "Hey, remember this is the government you're talking to, we take low cost and low quality over expense and expertise. It's part of the bid process."

"So raise property taxes already," I said. "What are you waiting for?"

"I can't. I'm a Republican, remember!" he said, "And it goes against principle."

I started to laugh. "Politics prohibits principles."

"Oh yeah, I forgot," he said. "Anyway, it doesn't matter. I'll just place the cost under the minimum bid requirements, scale down the scope, award it to Rich, and then extend it in phases."

"Then do we have a deal?" I asked.

"Do I have a choice?" he asked in return.

"No," I said matter-of-factly.

"Then, I guess, we have a deal," he said, but not without some humor. "I take it for granted that Rich is expecting my call."

"As a matter of fact, he is."

"Well, isn't that a coincidence?" he said.

"Ain't it, though!"

With another job well done, I buzzed Diane and asked if she'd get a hold of Mr. Ramirez and ask him to come by the restaurant on Sunday at noon with Pablo and meet with me. The City was closed on Sundays and the employees all gathered for a free Sunday brunch and the opportunity to socialize with each other. I could introduce Pablo to everyone and let him get to know his new adopted family.

I always brought in a guest speaker for a half hour every Sunday as well, to speak on various subjects that the staff had requested . . . investing, parenting, economics, benefits, religion, politics, logic, self defense, etc. We were a family and it was fun to just relax and enjoy each other for a couple of hours every Sunday and have someone wait on us for a change. And just so the kitchen crew could partake as well, we had guest cooks brought in from other restaurants to showcase their wares.

The next call I placed was to Jenner DeBrille, quite possibly the gayest and most flamboyant man in Seattle, and my usual contact for dealings within that lifestyle. But he also was a partial sponsor for a reform and assistance program for prostitutes called "Vertical Alternatives," and would probably have an idea of where my search for the senator's daughter should begin. Jenner came to the United States from Britain as a boy and was forced into prostitution by his sponsor family—a fate that awaited many a child when shipped across the pond and landed ashore without family or resources! But he was a famous interior and fashion designer now, with a global clientele and an impeccable reputation.

"Greetings and salutations, Noble Knight," Jenner said in his most extravagant British accent as he came to the phone. "How may I assist the stoically straight today?"

"How do you know I didn't call just to say I was joining the 'great gay way' and needed to borrow a lavender ascot for a fraternity tickle fight?"

"Don't tease dear boy, you'll make an old man's heart swoon with hope!"

"Well, try not to get too discouraged. I promise to keep watching the fashion channel and buying Streisand albums and we'll see what happens. I do have a favor in your area of expertise though."

"Fashion, cuisine, or travel, young Othello?"

"Actually, more along the lines of prostitution, Jen. I'm looking for a young girl who disappeared into the oldest profession about six years ago here in Seattle. Her father is on somewhat of a quest to find her dead or alive and put the past to rest or the present in progress. Any idea where to begin?"

"Well, you know I do love a good Victorian quest every now and then, but I'm afraid with my hectic and harried schedule these days, my finger is not as close to the pulse as it was in earlier years."

Jenner paused at that point to think about what to do, so I put the phone on speaker and walked down to watch the aquanauts at play.

"Well?" I called back to the speaker phone after an abnormally long pause, even for Jenner.

"Where have you gone, Joe DiMaggio?" Jen asked as he giggled into the phone for being clever. "You have a faraway sound to your voice all of a sudden."

"Don't worry, Queen DeBrille. It's geographical not emotional. You're on speaker and I'm fixing a cocktail and making faces at the fish."

"I thought you were going to quit drinking?" he said.

"I am," I said. And then he finished the sentence with me . . . "Tomorrow."

"All right, my bonified-befriender-of-fish, I'll tell you what I'll do. If you'll make me a reservation for four for nine o'clock tonight, and spoil me with your food, looks, and wit . . . and buy me some ridiculously expensive champagne, I'll dazzle you with my presence and insight later tonight."

"Four people for tonight? I'm booked solid for months, you know that."

"Yes, my lovely Lothario, but think of the review I'll give you in Sunday's *Seattle Times*."

"Good point," I said. "See you at nine o'clock."

I checked the Rolex and realized it was almost five o'clock and that the doors were about to open. I called Diana and it looked like everything was in order and good to go. I turned on the array of camera monitors; the ones outside showing a large contingent of the thirsty, already waiting to imbibe. I looked at the aquarium, and the fish seemed in especially good spirits too; even the itinerate eels seemed anxious to receive the masses.

I noticed on camera three at the Island Bar on L1 that PlayMaker and BigTop were already at their posts at the front of the doors to check IDs and screen for the code, the rest of the bouncers all heading to their designated areas.

I walked down to L3 looking down on L1 and L2 when Makes checked his watch and looked up at me. I nodded the go-ahead, and he got up to punch the code to unlock the electronic doors—Toppy trying to trip him as he went by, and both of them laughing into their fists as Makes almost fell. Just two So-Cal boys who grew up in the projects together with only each other to make sure they made it. No real education—just the streets and the sheets, and an unshakeable friendship.

I remembered three years ago when they both walked into my private office with Deity, two huge guys, both over six foot six and 280 pounds; Toppy maybe an inch or two taller and at least twenty pounds heavier. But Makes was older and smarter and treated Tops like a little brother he'd been left in charge of, which in a way he had from what Deity had said. They'd known Deity from the "old days," though no one ever bothered to explain to me exactly what, when, and where the old days had been.

Makes was the first to speak. "D said we should come talk to you, said we could trust you, said your word was good."

I looked at the two solid and stolid giants in front of me and then looked at Deity. He nodded. I looked back at the twin towers. Toppy looked a little nervous, and avoided eye contact by looking around my office and rubbing the arm of the Corinthian leather chairs, and nodding in appreciation.

I looked back at Makes and said, "You can and it is. What is it you gentlemen have in mind?" You could see a hint of a smile cross Toppy's lips, as if he liked being called a gentleman.

"I get right to da point," Makes offered. "We be needin' us a legit J.O.B. for life—salary, bennies, an 'tirement." Toppy finally looked straight at me and bobbed his head in firm agreement.

I looked at Deity and started to smile. "Looks like maybe somebody's had some coaching."

"We go back a ways," said Deity, his big smile as mischievous as it got.

I looked from one to the other and asked, "And what do I get out of the deal?"

"You take care a us, we take care a you," Makes said.

"What kind of yearly are you expecting?" I asked, trying to keep a straight face.

Makes looked a little nervous, like maybe he was hesitant to ask and risk being turned down because it was too much. "We be thinkin' fifty K a piece."

"Of course, you were." I was going to look over at Deity again, but I could tell he was already enjoying himself way too much. I thought about that for a second, but they obviously mistook my pondering as hesitation, so Toppy finally spoke up, "We could make do with less, we got nuthin' else an nowhere to go." As soon as he said it, Makes gave him a hard look and quickly looked back at me.

I thought about it for a few more seconds and said, "Can you gentlemen excuse us for a minute, please?"

Both Makes and Toppy looked at each other and then at Deity, and then got up from their chairs to turn to walk down the stairs, so I said, "If you want, have a seat at the bar and order some lunch from the bartender on me."

Toppy turned around and asked, "Can I order me a steak, Mr. Kilbourne?"

Makes stood there shaking his head, but I just smiled and looked at Toppy. "Yes, you can order a steak, but a guy your size should probably order two." Toppy smiled big for the first time and his whole face lit up. "Reckon I will then!" On the way out, Makes got him in a headlock and rubbed the top of his head affectionately as they both laughed all the way out the door.

Seems like a long time ago now, and both of those young men were still eating their weight in steak every year . . . and I was still taking care a them and they were still taking care a me!

The next couple of hours went very smooth. A few minor incidents outside when a couple of bodybuilders tried to cut in line. But, fortunately, DJ and Trey-Deuce had a few extra minutes in their schedule to teach them that there's a difference between strong and tough. It looked like a painful lesson for the roid boys, but one probably well deserved.

The only other minor altercation was when *The RawkDawgs*, the nation's hottest heavy metal band tried to "famous" their way into getting in. Diane had pinged me on the headset saying that they wanted to make an "appearance" at the City, but they had shown up in questionable clothing and dubious demeanor. Diana had explained the code to their manager over the phone prior to their arrival, but they probably figured they had enough international notoriety to garner special entry. But since Deity, Gio, and I weren't avid fans of heavy metal, we took special pride in turning them away.

Their manager and promoter called a half-hour later from their limousine saying they'd acquiesce to the rules, but since they had gotten a little belligerent with the staff, I told them I would think about it the next time they were in town. But being the softy that I am, I gave them free entry and VIP Room passes to H2O, one of the dance clubs I owned downtown. And they had to promise to do a set when the house band was on break.

By the time Jenner arrived, the City was packed to the rafters, if we'd had rafters; the Island Bar on L1 was at capacity, and the Falling Water's restaurant on L2 had only one empty table, appropriately reserved for Seattle's resident Liberace. Jenner was ushered in through the VIP door downstairs and he and his entire entourage made a grand entrance as they climbed the crystal waterfall to the restaurant, kissing both T-Bone and Blade on the cheek, much to their dismay, as they unhooked the royal purple velvet ropes to allow his ostentatious ascent. Most of his party of men, women, and those somewhere in between decided to stay at the Island Bar, while he and what looked like three supermodels, complete with matching boas and giggles, challenged the remaining steps and waved gratuitously to those below.

I came down from Atlantis on L3 after checking on a few of the illustrious that were dining exquisitely at the Reef and Breakers, or L4 and L5, the private dining rooms that sat royally and reclusively behind the aquariums and peeked out secretly on those at Atlantis. The governor and mayor were dining with some foreign dignitaries concerning some Sister-City trade negotiations, and a private Corporate CEO Society was hard at work one-upping each other in relation to earnings and ownership, which I admired greatly.

Jenner got up from the table as I approached and made much ado about my timely arrival, kissing me on both cheeks and giving me a friendly hug. Jenner was immaculate in a lavender Gucci blazer, pale pink shirt and bright yellow bow tie with matching lavender and pink polka dots. After introducing me to the three beauty queens in their very low-cut diaphanous gowns, who happened to all be sisters from Brazil, we cracked the champagne, ordered the hors d'oeuvres and toasted the night's festivities. After an hour of merriment and mirth, Jenner asked if I could have Gio and Deity give the three Latinas a tour of the facilities while we talked.

"Well, Casanova, here's the scoop," Jenner began, turning to face me in full animation. "I will have my minions scour the files and the databases at Vertical Alternatives and see what they can come up with, and I will put out an APB (All Prostitutes Bulletin) to be on the lookout for your girl, but I also have another idea that might bring a better return on investment if your girl has fallen off the beaten path." Jenner looked around conspiratorially as if we were trading national secrets.

"There's a woman you might want to talk to, an amazing artist who lives up on Queen Ann Hill. She does a lot of volunteer work with women in need. In fact, that's the name of her group: WIN—Women

In Need. But she works with a variety of groups and diverse lifestyles, especially those that may have been subject to abuse of any kind or are in fear of abuse. If she can't find the information you seek, she may know of someone who can. She's incredibly well connected in a street or cause sense, and adored and respected by all."

At that, Jenner stopped with a smug look on his face and held out his champagne glass for more Dom Perignon. "So, did I perform up to expectations?" he asked like a precocious child.

"Jen, you always surpass all expectations, in dress and in lifestyle," I said. "Why would she have access to information that others wouldn't?"

"Mainly because of the trust that she imbues in some of the more leery organizations, but also because she is always willing to donate her time, money, and energies, and because she has a special penchant for those women that may have fallen through the cracks with nowhere to turn," Jen said and started to smile. "She can come off cold, but has a heart of gold. So try not to act like a petulant adolescent upon first introduction."

I let that pass since I couldn't mount a substantial counterclaim of adulthood. "Where's she getting her funding from?"

"Self funded. She's an incredible artist! Her works sell for gazillions, and the majority of her profits go back into the program. Her work is all painstakingly custom, and extremely emotional. I cry every time I attend one of her viewings."

"Yeah, but you cry at Lassie reruns too."

"Only the one where Timmy falls in the well, you emotionless drone! Besides, haven't you ever cried?"

"Nope, tends to rust the armor. But if it makes you feel any better, I think my eyes moistened once when I saw Old Yeller as a kid."

"Oh, dear D'artagnan, there may be hope for you after all!"

"Dare to dream," I said. "So I take it you're talking about Kathryn Rae?"

"The very one."

I bit off a piece of roasted garlic prawn and washed it down with more bubbly, anticipating the tangible and inevitable effect of good food, friends, and French champagne. I watched as staff and guests milled about in various stages of merriment. I was by nature a voyeur; people and their interactions interested me greatly. I loved to sit and watch as the young and the old, the sober and the inebriated, the confident and the cautious intermingled in ignorance and ambiguity, aware of only their individual and transitory interests. If there was a public square in Seattle, I would sit there in my old age and sip a warm beverage and watch the world unfold at my feet. Until then, Pike's Market would have to suffice for my observational outpost.

"I'd heard she shuns the limelight," I said as I got back to task. "Is she elusive, reclusive, or repulsive?"

"A little elusive and reclusive," Jenner said, "but she is very committed to her art and causes, and does shun most fanfare."

"She sounds like a great gal," I said sincerely.

"Oh yeah, you'll really like her," Jen said and then smiled brightly, "but she'll hate you instantly."

"Why's that?" I said as I finished surveying the room and looked back at him. "And why does that seem to give you great joy?"

Jenner started giggling again mid-drink and almost choked. "Because you're big, you're built, you're bright, you're beautiful, and you're blatantly heterosexual."

"So I take it I'm the evil oppressor and the sole source of feminine fatality?" I said.

"Yup!" Jenner said, a little too happily.

"She gay?"

"Yup!"

"Openly?"

"Yup!"

"Overtly?"

"Yup!"

"Cuz she likes women or because she hates men?" I asked as if it mattered.

"I'm assuming the perfect marriage of both," he said with a sly wink.

"She good looking?"

"Extremely."

"Is she well built?"

"Exceptionally."

I thought about that for a second. "Maybe I can convert her?"

Jenner shook his head with feigned pity. "Doubtful, dear Dante, doubtful!"

"Well," I said as I rose, "though I am grateful for your information and your obvious glee at my shortcomings, could you at least set up an appointment for me to meet with her?"

Again the arrogant look of overachievement as he pulled out a piece of paper from his breast pocket. "Way ahead of you, my woeful Wyatt Earp, she is expecting you at seven o'clock tomorrow evening at her studio-slash-home."

"And," he added with a mischievous grin as I started to walk away, "she said she's heard of you, too!"

"Yikes!"

Many hours later, I locked the electronic doors to the City from my office sanctuary, and lowered the ambient lighting as I watched the last vestiges of my employees exit the building. BigTop and PlayMaker usually were the last to stay, to walk the few remaining cocktail waitresses to their cars and make sure they got off safely.

It had been another good night at the City. Jenner and his accompaniment had added another level of levity and theatrics to the evening, as they always did. And Deity and Gio had decided to abandon me at the pleading and beckoning of Jenner and the three Brazilian beauties, and go for more cocktails and club hopping. I had politely denied the invitation, making up a number of excuses. Gio had pointed out that that would leave one extra diva, so I called a good buddy of ours, Jake Jorgensen, to help pick up the slack. Being the true friend and compassionate humanist that he was, he said he would be more than happy to escort an incredibly beautiful, highly inebriated, barely dressed, surgically augmented, international supermodel for the evening. True friendship ne'er waivers!

I looked at the clock and saw that it was nearing 3:00 a.m., so I turned off my computer, strolled down the stairs, and entered the emptiness that was the City after dark. It was my favorite time at the City; a quiet and a void beyond description, but not without great anticipation and appreciation—just me and my free-floating friends.

I went behind the Atlantis bar and turned on *Solitaire* by Karen Carpenter, and then flipped the switch on the audio panel that would put it into a continual loop, playing again and again without respite. Then I poured myself ten rum and diet cokes, since I was going to quit drinking tomorrow, and set them up in a line and walked back across the bar and sat down on the stool in front of them. Ten good friends! That's all a guy really needed, was ten good friends; friends that he would always be happy to see; friends that would always be there for him; friends that would help him feel better; friends that would help him forget; friends whose passing he would mourn.

I looked at my friends and felt the same sense of comfort and relief that I always felt. That in a few minutes, I would be transported out of my current state of being and ushered into that great state of grace where life would be less complicated, less stressful, less painful. I put a straw in the first one and sucked it down in one long draw. I wanted to make sure I didn't get drunk too fast, so I ate a peanut. Then I put the straw into my second friend and repeated the previous process. I did the same thing with friend three and marveled at how well we were all getting along. I looked at my other seven friends still sitting on the bar and thanked them for their presence and support. It was a comforting feeling knowing that they were there for me. Victory was close at hand; the emotional void would soon be vanquished.

I sat for a few minutes and closed my eyes, and just listened as Ms. Carpenter narrated my life . . .

> *And Solitaire's the only game in town*
> *And every road that takes him takes him down*
> *And by himself, it's easy to pretend*
> *He'll never love again*
> *And keeping to himself, he plays the game*
> *Without her love, it always ends the same*
> *While life goes on around him everywhere,*
> *He's playing solitaire*

After a few precious and painful minutes, I opened my eyes and felt the nuance of alcohol's first hug. That was another nice thing about friends, there's the warm, familiar embrace that only old friends can proffer. I decided that one peanut was nowhere near enough to ward off the ill effects of alcohol, so I decided to eat a pretzel as well, which made me thirsty, so I invited friends four and five over to discuss how to proceed. They suggested I continue to drink to combat the ill effects of thirst, so I was pleased we had reached a healthy consensus and that dissension hadn't impeded our progress.

My cell phone rang and I glanced at the number, which seemed to be a little fuzzy for some reason, it was Jess. I looked at my friends and knew that I had promised to spend the night with them, so I just let it ring. Jess would understand. She hated talking to me when I'd been out with my ten friends, anyway. I gathered friend six over and decided the ice cubes were drowning and that I'd better save them from certain death. To celebrate my life preserving heroics, I decided to have another pretzel and a peanut. But it was rude to double up on food and not double up on the drinks so in the spirit of duality and parallel universes, I enlisted the help of seven and eight to even things up. Parity and fair play are very important among good friends, so I felt it was the least I could do.

I walked behind the bar again and unlocked my special drawer, the one that contained my Cubans and my cards. As I sat back down at the bar, I caught a glimpse of myself in the mirror and said hello. It was good to see me, as it always was. I enjoyed my own company very much, and was never lonely when alone. Though I experienced loneliness often, it was typically in crowded rooms, but for far greater and much more agonizing reasons.

As I looked closer into the mirror, I saw what God and life had carved out of the clouds. I reached up and felt the scars on my chin and cheekbones from numerous fights, and the mark left from the grazing of a bullet on my forehead, over my right eye, by a highly agitato Mafioso. Fortunately for me, I was not always the super athlete I claimed to be. When I saw Johnny Shotz pull the gun in the old, abandoned warehouse, I tried to stop too abruptly from a full sprint toward him and my feet came out from underneath me as I slid on the ubiquitous sawdust. Had I remained athletic and upright, I would be dead now. Gio and Deity had seen it as me hitting the deck just in time, but it had really just been a serendipitous slip and a lifesaving one at that.

So I toasted my great blessings and occasional clumsiness by summoning the celebratory sanctuary of friend nine for further festivities. After ardent discussion and much camaradic consultation it was decided that continued cocktail consumption was the requisite of the night and not to be mitigated prematurely.

As I bid adieu to nine and sipped on friend number ten, I got up once again and went behind the bar to grab a bottle of Crystal and a bottle of Krug Grand Cuvee, both chilled to perfection, and a bag of stick pretzels. I walked over to the Oasis couches, lit my cigar, poured my champagne, and dealt a hand of solitaire. When all was in readiness, I looked up at the glass-domed ceiling and the smiling stars that shone down undaunted through the Puget mist, and I made a heavenly toast to her, to all that she once was, and to all that we once had.

CHAPTER 7

Sunday morning came early as the sun broke through dawn's grasp and woke me with its penetrating prisms of brilliance. I looked around groggily and noticed that I had fallen asleep on the couches, for the millionth time, with the only witnesses being two empty bottles of champagne turned over in a now-melted bucket of ice, a half-smoked cigar, and a half-eaten bag of pretzels. It was 8:15 a.m., and I knew that the cleaners would arrive at nine followed by the caterers at ten o'clock. So I rose stiffly from my soporia, not unlike the phoenix from the ashes, and once more entered the sanctuary of my office and the small private bed and bath that sat covertly behind the other false bookcase next to the twirly bar.

An hour later, showered, shaved, and seductively dressed in my Sunday best, I released the electronic locks, and the cleaners sauntered in to begin the urban renewal. At noon all was in place and my Liquid City family trickled in with their wives, husbands, girlfriends, boyfriends, and significant others.

As I entered the main foyer, I saw Diane's five-year-old daughter Taylor, at her Shirley Temple best, entertaining the troops and loving the affection and adoration that she seemed to conjure up wherever she went. When she saw me, her whole face lit up and she jumped off Diane's lap and into my waiting arms.

"King Kilbourne!" she yelled as she ran across the floor. I caught her in my arms and gave her a long hug and a couple of dizzying twirls.

"Princess Taylor, it is so good to see you, Madam," I said. "How is My Lady this fine April morn?"

I set her down and she stepped back and curtsied in her frilly ivory-silk dress with much flare and fanfare and said, "Just marvelous, Your Majesty." And then broke into girlish giggles and my heart melted as it always did.

I picked her up once more and carried her over to the table where Diane, Gio, Deity, and various others were already sampling the omelets and pastries. I set Taylor down in the chair between Diane and myself but she immediately climbed back on my lap and snuggled up. After a few minutes of catching up with the crew as they came by to wish us good morning, Taylor looked at Diane and said, "Can I ask him, Mommy, can I?"

"Ask me what?" I said as I asked the server to bring me some steak and eggs. "What is it that I can do for you, Pookie?"

She took a deep breath, "Well, Mommy and I want you to take us to the zoo next Saturday and if you do, then we'll fix you a picnic in the park afterward if it's not raining." And then, she looked me right in the eye and said with much excitement and volume, "And I'll make the sammiches!" To which, at that point, the entire table and those around us broke into laughter. Goldilocks had struck again!

At around two o'clock, Pablo's father, Rama, came to pick him up, and Gio and Deity reluctantly threw in the towel after Pablo had already beaten them in checkers ten times in a row. We all shook hands and Gio and Deity took Pablo to get his belongings while Rama and I went up into my office to discuss things of greater relevance, but less enjoyment, than checkers.

Once we were both seated in the lower couch section of my office, I grabbed us each a Diet Coke and sat down across the coffee table from him. Rama was probably about my age or a little older, with thick, black hair worn longish and a Fu Manchu mustache. He was probably only around five-eight, but weighed around two hundred pounds if I wasn't mistaken. He was thick and muscular with plenty of visible scars and gang tattoos, dressed in faded black jeans, worn tan work boots, and a denim shirt under a khaki construction jacket.

After staring at me hard for a few seconds to size me up, he said, "I need to thank you for all that stuff you did for my Pablo. He hasn't stopped talking about it since he come home the other day. It is a good thing you done."

I pulled out a couple of coasters from the side drawer next to the couches and set the Diet Coke down on it and slid one over to Rama. "He's a great kid," I said. "It was the first time I ever wished for one of my own. And by the way, he thinks you're ten feet tall and bullet proof."

Rama almost smiled. "Well, more like five feet tall and bullet ridden. But he's got a good madre and hermanas that think he is a gift from God, and I try to keep him and his sisters away from the bad things, you know? But I been a bad guy for so long, sometimes I don't know how to be nothing else. But I love that kid so damn much it makes me want to be a better padre, you know? I ain't never been much, but I love the heck out of them and they deserve better than a banger and a bandito for a father."

"So you're trying to get out?" I said.

Rama's demeanor changed visibly and his whole body seemed to stiffen. "I am out. If I say I'm out, I'm out. Nobody tells Rama what to do or when to do it. They know that, and they don't mess with me much. I stay in touch and I . . . what did Pablo call it . . . 'consult,' when they need me to. But I'm out, I just need to find some honest work again to take care of mi familia, you know?"

I grabbed two bags of peanut M&M's out of the other drawer and threw a bag to Rama. "Well, I think maybe we can help each other there. I know a foreman who needs a good man, and I may need a favor someday from a guy with connections into the Mexican mafia."

Again the hard stare of Rama as he thought about what I just said. "I won't sell nobody out, not for no amount of money," he said.

"I'd never ask you to, and I know you never would, anyway. You wouldn't be the man I think you are and the man Pablo knows you to be if you would sell somebody out. What I need is to purchase future favors from you, but only those favors you're willing to provide, nothing else."

Rama nodded his head in contemplation and took a sip from his Diet Coke, set it down gently on the circular coaster, and sat back in his chair. "What does the job and the favors pay?" he asked.

"The construction pay you'll have to work out with Rich, but I can assure you it will be sufficient, and for the favors . . . what do you owe on your mortgage?"

"I don't know, we been there forever, around thirty thousand maybe, why?"

"Okay, here's the whole deal," I said. "I'll pay off your mortgage and get you a job, but you gotta invite me to Pablo's college graduation, which I'll pay for along with your girls, if they all pull the grades."

I wasn't sure what his reaction was at first as his face got kind of contorted, but after a few long seconds I saw him fight harder to hold back unexpected emotion, and in the end his obsidian eyes merely got shiny as he got himself back under control.

"They must be cooking onions in the kitchen," he said with a slight smile.

"I thought maybe it was the carbonation in the Diet Coke."

"That too," he said, and we both laughed and shook on it. After we discussed the specifics of both situations in detail, we walked back downstairs and he turned and asked, "Will you need a resume or anything?"

"No, I've already met your resume," I said as I looked over his shoulder at Pablo who was arm wrestling Deity; Deity trying his best to look like he was straining mightily.

Rama looked back as well and laughed, and then turned back and shook my hand once again, but this time his face was more solemn. "A son should not have to pay for the sins of his father."

I looked from Pablo back to Rama and said, "And a father should not have to punish himself for the sins he committed for his family."

Rama just nodded his head and slapped me on the shoulder which was probably as affectionate as Rama got. I told him Rich would be giving him a call and then he headed over to gather Pablo and save Deity and Gio another embarrassing arm wrestling defeat.

As Rama and Pablo were walking out hand in hand, Pablo was asking his dad something that I couldn't hear. Rama stopped and got down on one knee and said something to Pablo, and with that Pablo jumped up and gave him a big hug and then ran across the room at warp speed and gave me a running hug that practically knocked me over.

"Thank you, Senor Kilbourne, thank you from mi mama and mi hermanas. It will be a great night at our casa tonight!"

After that, the little speedster ran back across the room and climbed on his father's shoulders and got carried royally out of the restaurant. When I turned around to go back up to the office, Gio and Deity were just standing there grinning at me.

"You big softy," Gio said, while Deity put his arm around my shoulders.

"I know," I said. "Do you think God grades on a curve?"

CHAPTER 8

Seated comfortably back in our happy headquarters, it was time to get back to business and to the world in which we were better equipped to dwell, and hopefully thrive. With Deity sprawled out on the couch, and Gio back in his usual chair with his feet up on the coffee table, the room seemed to grow more serious and intense as it always did, and probably always would. I went through the usual electrical ministrations to detect or counter any audio or video surveillance, and as all lights flashed green it looked like we were good to go.

"All right, gentlemen, where are we?"

Deity was the first to speak. "In regards to those projects already in play, we have confirmed kills on Maresca, the molester in Iowa, and Pearson, the cellar dweller, who had those three teen girls locked up in his basement in Louisiana. Both went down smooth, no tells and no trace, very clean, Bawse."

I gestured to Gio. "Who'd we use for Pearson? It always makes me a little nervous when the mark is getting that much attention from the press."

Gio leaned forward, "Same triple blind relay to the body broker we typically use for that type of termination and geography. The newspapers say he hung himself in his cell, so I'm sure the broker either had leverage with the guards or the inmates, and the rest is history. Nothing in the papers about it being suspicious, it came across as just another serial rapist taking the easy way out."

"Excellent! What about Maresca? That guy was a freak of nature?"

Deity spoke up this time. "He was out on bail, which was allowed temporarily because of some Search and Seizure violations that the local cops messed up on. This one was quick and easy."

"Jericho?" I asked.

"Just like Palladin . . . 'Have gun will travel'. Looked pretty basic from the police reports, Jericho probably just walked up behind him when Maresca was walking by himself at night and shot him with a twenty-two in the back of the head at the base of the spine, and let the ricochets inside his skull do the rest."

Jericho was a shooter out of New York, and that was about all we knew of him. But he was a favorite of one of our main east coast body brokers and seemed to like the work and the travel. I didn't like using any one hitter too often, but this guy was good and dependable, so for him the usual caution was discarded.

"Okay, let's talk new business." I got up from my desk and walked down to where they were both sitting and grabbed a handful of pretzels.

"You're obviously both aware of the guy who shot his four kids last week because of a lost custody battle. The old 'If I can't have them, nobody will' deal! Sounds like he beat up his wife pretty bad in the process too and supposedly made the kids watch. So let's make him the next object of our affections."

Deity saw me eating the pretzels and gestured to his wide-open mouth so I threw a pretzel his way and he caught it his mouth. Not to be outdone, Gio made the same gesture but he caught his in his teeth. He looked over at Deity and just smiled. "Showoff!" was Deity's only response.

"So G, if you can do your usual background on this guy and find out if anyone suffers if he goes away, and D, if you can work the kill-logistics on this, we can get this guy gone."

Gio and Deity both nodded in agreement and then looked at each other covertly. Finally, it was Gio who spoke up. "Boss, what about Phinney?"

Glancing at both of them, I could see the seriousness in their eyes. Johannes Phinney was a well-known wise guy who owned a large and lucrative real estate investment and development firm in San Diego. As of last week, he was also a "person of interest" in the death of his wife and two stepdaughters in a suspicious car wreck. His wife had filed for divorce a month earlier and accused him of molesting her two teenage daughters. He hadn't been named an official suspect yet, but all consensuses pointed to him as the architect of the so-called "accident."

I looked at both of them and blew out a lungful of air. "I know how you guys feel about trash like Phinney. But let's take this one slow. He's about as high profile as you get and has deep political and mob connections. Plus, we can be pretty certain it wasn't him that pulled the trigger, and nothing's been proven yet."

"Yeah, Bawse, but we all know Phinney and his goons. He's dirty as hell," Deity said. "Most of the smack that comes north over the Mex border has his fingerprints all over it."

"And," Gio said as he looked at Deity for concurrence and then back to me, "we want to do this one ourselves."

I saw the implacability on both of their faces and knew the hatred they both had for child molesters and child abusers in general. But, with the rapes thrown in on top of that, it just heightened their animosity. And since Phinney was a well known arrogant idiot and general sleazebag, it would make our day to deep-six him and his operation. It didn't mean that there wouldn't be another sleazebag in place before his body even got cold, but anybody looked better than someone as notoriously ruthless and cruel as Johannes Phinney.

The other delicate deliberation was letting Deity and Gio do it themselves. That was a major risk factor for all of us and not something I liked to tempt the fates with. They'd done a dozen or so personally over the last five years when they got restless or took personal interest, but this was a whole different paradigm.

Shaking my head, I said, "Phinney is heavily protected and connected on both sides of the law, guys. He's definitely sportin' the hi-pro glow. I don't mind you guys tagging targets that are more lo-pro, but he's practically got celebrity status down there. I'd prefer, if we do this, to do it quick, quiet, and cross-country."

Gio nodded toward Deity. "Hey, at least all I want to do is take 'm out, D wants to torch 'em."

I looked over at Deity with an incredulous smile. "You want to torch him? Like literally . . . fuel and flames, as in a Phinney flambé?"

Deity donned the big grin. "We owe it to his wife and daughters to burn'em once before the devil does it for 'em. Besides, you know I hate them mutha's, Bawse. Me and G will beat 'em half to death before we torch him anyhow, so maybe he won't even feel the flames till he's halfway to hell."

Gio shook his head in laughter and walked over to the bar to sharpen his mixology skills. "Ya know, Boss, I'm usually not as medieval as D, but if ever there was a goon who deserved a gasoline good-bye, this is the guy. He's contracted more killings than Capone, and he typically doesn't care if women and children get caught up in the collateral damage."

Leaning back in my chair, I thought about all the things that could go wrong and the connections back to us that could be made, and I thought about risking the lives of the two guys I loved and trusted most in the world.

"Okay, here's the deal," I said as I accepted a rum and Diet Coke from Gio, . . . since I was gonna quit drinking tomorrow. "If we move forward, and I do mean 'if' . . . we'll move forward with you two, but if there's any hint of threat or exposure, you pull out and we put one of the irregular regulars on it. I don't want this to get personal beyond the realm of reason. Deal?"

Gio clinked cocktail glasses and bumped fists with Deity, and said, "Road trip!"

Deity took a long pull from his cognac and coke, wiped his lips eloquently with the back of his massive, calloused hand, and replied, "Road kill, my brutha, road kill!"

CHAPTER 9

I arrived at Kathryn Rae's home-slash-studio on Queen Anne Hill Monday night as scheduled. It was a very large, old, and elevated two-story townhouse with a unique black and brown brick façade with lush foliage adorning every inch of the expansive tiered grounds. The lights emanating from the windows disclosed what looked like the living quarters on the bottom floor, and I guessed her studio to be on the upper, as the crests of easels peeked imperially out the windows of the upper floor. I parked the Range Rover at the bottom of the hill and had to walk up the winding, warped wooden steps with the gnarled timber and thick marine rope railings to get to her front door. It had a great adventurous "Swiss Family Robinson" look and feel to it and someone had obviously taken great care and expense to semi-authenticate the effect along with the rest of the abundant and meticulous landscaping.

I rang the doorbell and waited patiently, quietly singing a virtual duet of *That's Amore* with Dean Martin and pretending I wasn't out of breath from my recent ascent. After waiting for a couple of minutes with no response, I rang the doorbell again and followed it up with a gentle knock on the heavily glassed double doors a few minutes later. After another brief expanse of time with no answer, I peeked in the glass windows but saw no sign of life other than the bright light that illuminated a welcome warmth. Once again left alone at the altar!

I was certain that our appointment was for tonight at seven, but maybe Jenner had gotten it incorrectly or she had had a change of heart. I walked back down to the Rover and called Ms. Rae's number to leave a message on her machine, but someone actually answered the phone, which took me by momentary surprise.

"Hello?" spoke the non-indicative voice on the phone.

"Ms. Rae?" I asked.

"Yes, this is she."

"Hello, Ms. Rae, this is Shad Kilbourne. Sorry to interrupt your Monday evening, but I believe Jenner DeBrille had set up an appointment for us this evening at seven."

"Yes, he did," she said matter-of-factly.

I paused for a minute, a little confused. "I just rang your doorbell and no one answered."

"Yes, I heard the doorbell," was all she said.

I was still confused, but I was starting to get used to it. "And yet you didn't answer the door?"

There was a pause on her end of the line this time. "Mr. Kilbourne, what time was our appointment?"

"I believe it was supposed to be for seven o'clock this evening."

"And what time did you arrive?"

I looked at my Cartier and said, "Around twenty after seven . . ." And before I could finish my sentence it dawned on me where I had erred.

"Exactly, Mr. Kilbourne, when it means enough to you to be on time, it will mean enough to me to answer the door." And at that the line went dead, and I knew that I liked her immensely already. A no-nonsense gal who would neither be trivialized nor denigrated!

I thought about my immediate predicament for a moment and then hit redial. Again the same "Hello."

"Hi, Ms. Rae, this is IM Punctual from the American Society of Sorry, and I was wondering if I could stop by your home tonight at seven-thirty and discuss our program?"

I heard a quick laugh on the other end of the line, but I could tell she was trying to conceal it. After a moment's thought, I seemed to have gained my reprieve, "Come on up Mr. Kilbourne . . . and don't be late!"

Ah, a governor's pardon for the conspicuously guilty! I took the steps three at a time and was at the door at precisely seven-thirty.

After what seemed like a long time the door finally opened, but Jenner had not done her justice. Kathryn Rae was without question . . . stunning!

She answered the door with one hand on the door and the other on her hip, looking just a little irritated. "Mr. Punctual, I presume?"

"You're breathtaking!"

She laughed eloquently this time and opened the door wide enough for me to enter. "No, I'm Ms. Rae, and you're forgiven." She turned and walked away and said, "Please come in."

I entered her home and it was all that an artist's hideaway should be—lots of soft light, blonde hardwood floors, mosaic walls, dark walnut trim, and comfortable-looking eclectic furniture—all done in warm but vibrant tones and textures.

As I followed her to the kitchen, I caught the faint smell of fresh soap and soft perfume. She was dressed in form-fitting black tights, sockless black alligator flats, and a royal blue shirt much too big for her that she tied high on her waist with the sleeves rolled up above her wrists. Her hair was dark brown with some lighter highlights, shiny and in a soft ponytail, and her eyes were so startlingly green that they almost shone. The only jewelry she seemed to be wearing was a delicate gold chain around her tanned waist, and her makeup was almost non-existent or done so precisely that it was practically imperceptible to me. And as she was walking in front of me toward the kitchen, the rest of Jenner's description looked equally as anatomically correct.

"You have a beautiful home, Ms. Rae. It feels comfortable and well lived in."

She handed me a glass of red wine, which tasted like exquisite Cabernet, without asking me if I'd like some. "I rarely leave the house unless it is for a charity or one of my art openings. I prefer my home, my music, my art, my books, and my own company."

I noticed that she didn't offer for me to call her Kathryn, but before I could come to any conclusion on that, she gestured me to an expansive living room and to a large six-piece sectional that was just as comfortable as it looked, and the real wood-burning fire added an even greater degree of comfort and coziness. The artwork was all of fine origin, with most of it done in impressionistic oils and acrylics. A large Steinway stood majestically and opaque next to the full-length bay windows, with an old, well-worn guitar sitting juxtaposed in antiquity next to the gossamer sheen of the piano. There were framed photographs everywhere of what I assumed to be family and friends, the only repetition of significance being that of Kathryn as a little girl at various ages with a Cary Grant-esque gentlemen, and Kathryn with an equally stunning blonde woman in various global geographies, who I assumed to be her significant other.

As we sat across from each other, she tucked her legs underneath her and took a small sip of her wine, and then looked at me over the rim of her glass. "You realize of course, Mr. Kilbourne, that the acronym for the 'American Society of Sorry' is 'A.S.S.'!"

I smiled sheepishly, "If the shoe fits . . . !"

"Wow, self-effacement, Mr. Kilbourne. I wouldn't have thought you capable."

"I am often referred to as the great dichotomy," I said.

"I have heard you referred to as many things, Mr. Kilbourne. It is one of the reasons I acquiesced to meeting with you here tonight. To get a sense of who and what you really are."

I could feel the assessment already in play, but it seemed important to her to be able to categorize me, so I went with the flow.

"Who I am, is Shad. What I am, is merely a businessman."

"Mr. Kilbourne," she said, ignoring the subtle offer to call me Shad. "I have great doubt that you are 'merely' anything. For, I am most certain from what I've heard and read that you are quite capable of being 'largely' everything."

"You flatter me, Ms. Rae."

At that, she sat up on the couch, set her wine glass down on a blue mosaic tile coaster with a lime-green palm tree, and clasped her hands in front of her mouth. I could tell that she was enjoying my inquisition and was used to classifying and analyzing all those to whom she came in contact.

"Flattery was not my intent, Mr. Kilbourne. I only insinuated that you appear beyond mere trivialization in any aspect of your life. You seem to do things with great grandeur and flare. It seems to be your defining characteristic."

"And your theory is predicated on what presumptuous pretext?"

She looked at me with her eyes slightly squinted, like she was sizing up a side of beef. "Your stature is large. Your intellect is large. Your personality is large. Your income is large. Your restaurants, clubs, and businesses are large. Your charities and donations are large. Your reputation is large. And that's just to name a few. That which involves and is of essence of you, if not large, is overt." With that she sat back and smiled like the Cheshire Cat.

"All you forgot was my huge heart and grand humility," I said. "But I enjoy the finer things that the fruits of my labor have proffered, and most things are grander in relation to scale or expense. And that being the case, it seems that we lack similitude, for you seem to be the quintessential enigma wrapped in mystery. Was it not the New Yorker that called you 'The Veiled Voyeur' and 'The Absentee Artista'?"

She smiled a little coyly. "You forgot 'The Private Princess' and 'The Reticent Renoir,' Mr. Kilbourne. Congratulations on doing your homework."

She uncoiled gracefully from the couch and poured both of us more wine, again without request or acquiescence. "I am not a public persona, nor do I wish to be. I cherish my personal privacy and public obscurity. It means much more to me to be known for my art and my causes."

"Both of which are to be commended by the way! Jenner speaks incredibly highly of you. In fact, to hear him speak highly of anyone but himself is in and of itself a monumental anomaly."

At that she laughed with great mirth and the lingering effervescence of a warm smile as she thought about our mutual friend. "Jen is a dear friend and confidant," she said with obvious affection. "He is part genius, part child . . . and part Mad Hatter."

We both laughed at that and were quiet with our "Jenner memories" for a moment. When I glanced back at her, she was staring peacefully into the fire, quite alone with her thoughts. I looked past her out the window and saw the traces of a gathering storm, which I hoped was neither ominous nor foreboding. As I looked to the top of the windows, I noticed for the first time that the raised and recessed ceiling was painted in the soft, broad strokes of great artistry. And then it hit me that it looked incredibly similar to one of my favorite artists. When I looked back down, she met my gaze and looked to the ceiling as well.

"Is that Jergen Gorge by any chance?" I asked.

This time she looked at me, or on second thought maybe inside me, for a long thirty seconds without saying anything, and then set down her wine glass and sat back with her arms wrapped contemplatively around her.

"As a matter of fact it is. He's a good friend and mentor," she said barely above a whisper. After another fifteen seconds of visceral evaluation, she stood up abruptly, topped off both our wine glasses and said, "Would you like to see some of my work, Mr. Kilbourne?"

I took this as a better omen than the weather. "As a matter of fact, Ms. Rae," I said as I stood, "I would love to see your artwork and your studio."

With that, she smiled a genuine smile, grabbed another bottle of already opened wine, and led me upstairs to her private studio, which seemed expansive, brittle, and barren compared to the controlled warmth and innate comfort of her downstairs dwelling. It was all windows along the fifty-foot, east-facing wall, with crimson-colored antique brick encrusting the other three walls, absorbing the fading brightness of the floor-to-ceiling theatre windows, every odd one enshrined in striking stained glass.

The vaulted, ebony ceiling was latticed in ivory-iron beamery and nuanced with bright fiber optic pin-lighting that hung down in choreographed coordination, with the in-progress paintings that stood stoically within themselves at about ten-foot wide circumferences. I counted about eight in entirety, all in various stages of completion. As I walked forward, I noticed I was alone and that she had stopped a number of feet back. When I turned to her to wait, she outstretched her arm in indication that I was to proceed on my own.

I took about twenty minutes to look at all of the brilliantly articulated pencil and charcoal works and then she joined me at the last large easel with an inquisitive look on her face. "Okay, Einstein, you're on," she said with a mischievous look on her face. "You have five individual words to describe my work. Tread lightly."

I looked at her for a few moments, which I'm sure she thought was to grasp a sense of her inner aura, but it was in fact an incredibly selfish opportunity to just stare at someone who was painfully beautiful. Something I'm sure she would have found to be sexist and repulsive, but I was enjoying my secret moment immensely.

I turned from her and looked at the drawings in great thought and intensity. "Five words, Ms. Rae?"

"Five words, Mr. Kilbourne!"

"Okay, here goes," I said in great synthesis, and then expelled my adjectives in plodding and pondering order. "It is without question both intelligent and intimate. There is a cognitive craft that obviously pervades thematically throughout your abstract detail. But if I had to add three adjectives to intelligent and intimate, it would be melodic, emotive, and elegant."

Again the evaluative, piercing stare from her for a long ten seconds. "You continue to surprise me, Mr. Kilbourne. From a man of your reputation, I expected maybe 'sex' or 'erotica' to be uttered in your grouping."

I looked back at the drawing. "Your paintings are all suggestive of those labels, but you can tell they surface and immerge merely as suggestion and innuendo, not as intrinsic intent. The adjectives already opined are more inherently . . . and, therefore, artistically, honest."

"Well, Mr. Kilbourne, I am impressed. You are as described. In fact, when I asked Jenner about you, he categorized you as a 'cerebral rogue'."

I laughed at Jenner's classification. "I prefer the term . . . The thinking man's thug!"

"I'll bet you do," she said with a mischievous grin.

We stood there for a few seconds in silence and just looked at each other. And in those few seconds, something genuine passed between us—nothing sexual or romantic, but maybe just her realization that I was no longer the enemy. It wasn't much on the grand scale of things, but it was something!

"May I ask you a question, Ms. Rae?"

"Yes, you may, Mr. Kilbourne," she said as she poured us more wine.

"Why, in all your drawings does the fiber cloth paper have tear marks only on the left side?"

Again the sidewise glance from her, like maybe I'd said something smart. Oh, how I cherished those rare occasions.

"It's a trademark of sorts—pages torn from the story of my life. And very few people notice that detail since it is typically so close to the mounting and framing. I am once again impressed, Mr. Kilbourne."

"But can't pages also be torn out from the right?" I said.

"Yes, good point. But we're a left-to-right society," she said.

"The Republican Party will be happy to hear of your endorsement."

"No, you Neanderthal," she said with a laugh. "A page with the tear on the right has theoretically already been turned. So in essence, it implies duality. It is not only the page, it is the page yet unturned."

"Ahh," I said. "So your drawings only portend to those things already lived and/or experienced."

"Yes, I guess. It keeps me grounded in reality, keeps me from being too publicly wistful and wishful, I think. I try not to dwell on, or intellectually invest in, those things beyond my immediate physical, financial, or emotional control."

I pushed the envelope a little. "What could you possibly wish for that is beyond your physical control or financial means? Your work is very public, yet you are personally very private. It seems incongruent and disingenuous, if you don't mind me saying so. And if we had known each other longer and better, I would say that there's a missing piece to your persona."

She turned and walked from me at that point and stood diagonally about twenty feet away, looking mournfully out the expansive windows—a profile in repose. From my vantage point, I could see the bobbing of multicolored masts as they rocked and rolled from the occasional lumbering wake on Lake Union. Various sea birds danced on the rolling winds and a lone boat whistled noisily, voicing its solo journey to those within earshot. It reminded me of Cary Grant and Debra Kerr in *An Affair to Remember* . . . 'I don't like boat whistles!'

Lightning lit up the sky in the distance and the inevitable thunder came calamitously within seconds, the thick blankets of rain following in entwined unison. Only moments later, more lightning struck and the lights flickered sporadically and then went out completely, and Ms. Rae didn't even seem to notice! Lightning lit up the sky once more encorishly, and this time the flashes of static ions reflected and exposed the trails of tears down her face.

She hugged herself tightly and continued to stare obliquely out of the windows. "There are writings on the back of each drawing that are too personal and painful for me to publish."

"Yet you feel the need to do it?"

"Yes," she said softly . . . carefully.

"Aren't you afraid that they'll be discovered and read?"

She looked at me briefly and turned back slowly to the window. "No, I write it in a special medium called Egyptian eggshell ink, which is incredibly fragile and fractious if disturbed or disinterred. And the glues I use are singular bonds which would make the writings indiscernible if removed or peeled back."

"Doesn't that pose a certain amount of artistic risk, regardless?" I said, trying to be inquisitive without sounding argumentative.

"Or a certain amount of literary restraint based upon that risk," she said flatly.

I considered what she had just said. "Or a certain amount of personal pleasure or pretense based upon the risk of that discovery?"

She turned away once again from the dull light of the windows and looked at me serenely. "It is my therapy, I suppose. So you see, Mr. Kilbourne, in actuality I am a silent writer, with my art as my vehicle and veil."

I stood in the emptiness as she became only a silhouette against the glass, the gathering darkness robbing the room of light. Only the warmth and the emotion remained. "So the writings are destroyed almost upon creation?"

"No, the writings are intact. They are only destroyed if someone attempts to access them."

"So it is important to you that they are in existence, but not accessible."

"Yes."

I walked toward her and topped off our wine glasses on the way. After handing her hers, I said, "Are you sure we're not talking about you?"

"Excuse me?" she turned and said a little defiantly.

"You. Extant but inaccessible."

She turned quickly and slapped me, not hard, but emphatically, as if the gesture was enough, regardless of the force exuded. I had trespassed on an emotional geography and crossed an imaginary line of demarcation that she was clearly not yet ready to concede. But after a few seconds, the softness and sorrow returned to her eyes, and then the crystalline stillness was finally broken. "I'm so sorry. I've never slapped anyone before. I don't think anyone's gotten so deep inside me so quickly before. I apologize. I am a terribly private person and it scares me to be read or revealed so easily, especially by a man . . . and I've never told anyone that before either, . . . about the writings I mean."

"Why me?"

"Because you're the first to seek beyond the art, I guess. Because you're the first to ask about the why instead of the what. Because you seem to be genuinely concerned, genuinely compassionate, genuinely interested, and annoyingly astute and interspective. It's funny, you are both the reasons I am a lesbian and may someday choose not to be."

I rubbed my cheek and pretended it didn't hurt. "Don't forget, I am 'The Great Dichotomy'!"

"I know you are just being funny," she said. "But I have a feeling you are probably as overtly and as ostensibly dichotomous as anyone I have ever met."

"I am many things."

"Yet one," she said.

"One under the many," I said.

"No, one encompassing the many."

"Nothing," I said.

"*Everything*," she whispered as almost a confirmation to herself.

I took that as an opportunity to change the subject. "You mentioned lesbianism as a choice, why a choice?"

"Is this your non sequitur since we were closing in on *your* psyche for a change?" she said with a knowing smile.

"It is as close as I let anyone get," I said. I leaned up against the windows as the rain streaked and scoured the panes. "Why lesbianism? Why a choice?"

She looked up and stared piercingly at me for a few seconds; I could almost feel her getting into my head to see if it was permissible to continue. I knew that she was much further out of her comfort zone than she was used to going and that she was risking a lot to proceed. But whatever conclusion she was seeking must have been resolved because she turned from me at that point and walked a few feet away—the supposed safety of distance. She wrapped her arms around herself again, more of a personal hug and haven than merely a crossing of arms.

Again, in the distance, the fading forlornness of a boat whistle, and then another which answered in obeisance. The approaching night had darkened and dispersed the reluctant light, leaving us without shadow or separation, just an encroaching blackness that granted visual reprieve in which to speak freely and without consequence.

"My mother died in a car wreck when I was five so I have no real memory of her. Just a trunk full of pictures and letters that she had sent to my father, and those he had sent to her. Those are my treasures. Those and a bottle of her perfume, 'Eternity' ironically enough, which I spray and wear once a year on her birthday. It scares me that someday it may be gone."

She took a sip of wine. "My father was a Colonel in the Navy, a fighter pilot. He was tall, smart, handsome, funny, charming, and strong . . ." She stopped then and turned to look at me quickly, and then once again turned away, "he was *everything*."

She paused for a minute and then continued, "He was always off on some exotic adventure in some remote and romantic part of the world, and I missed him dreadfully. But when he was home, he was all mine. We spent every second together . . . shopping, trips, movies, Broadway plays, the ballet, the symphony, the circus, the zoo, long walks, long talks . . . and every night we'd fall asleep together on the couch reading a book that we had chosen together or an old movie that held special meaning to just us. Nothing ever came between us when he was home. It was a little girl's silent wish . . . just a princess and a king and a dream."

I could see her shoulders start to shake before I heard her start to weep, and then, just as the rain had done earlier, the tears came in buckets and her whole body shook with the memories of events and evenings passed. After a few moments, she gained enough composure to proceed and I looked around for a tissue and handed her one.

"I always had the best of everything, Daddy made sure of that. But all I ever wanted was him, for him to come home for good. When I was still very small, a few years after my mother died, we counted up how many days until he had put in his twenty years and could retire and we could be together forever . . . 5475, 5474, 5473 . . . It was the first thing I did every morning when I woke up. I would jump out of bed and go cross a day off the calendar that he had had made especially for me in Beijing that was dated up until his retirement."

She stopped for a moment and stared out of the window, lost in the infinite fog and intricate webbing of remembrance. "When I was fifteen I was at my private school in my geometry class, in my crisp uniform just like a good soldier, when the headmistress came to get me from class with my favorite teacher and our school counselor. I thought maybe I'd won another award or some kind of scholarly commendation. We went to her office and there were five men there in uniform, two of daddy's friends in the Navy whom I knew, a Navy Chaplain, and two fellow officers. I remember my first reaction was excitement because I thought he was playing a trick on me or had a special surprise that everyone was in on. But when I looked at each face . . ." and again the flood of tears came . . . "and they all had tears in their eyes . . . I knew . . . I knew he was dead, I knew Daddy was gone . . . I knew that we had died that day."

More tears, more pain, more body racked and reticulate in anguish. She leaned languidly against the large bay window and slid slowly down it until she was on the hardwood floors, slumped over in an emotional agony that I was unfortunately only too familiar with. I wanted to go to her, but somehow knew it would be an invasion of sorts, an intrusion on a very personal and emotional repast. So I moved closer, wishing I were more.

After what seemed like an eternity of tears, she turned and looked at me, still sitting on the ground, leaning up against the cold and uncompassionate pane. "I could feel and almost hear my heart ripping apart, my head exploding, and then I must have passed out. Because when I awoke, I was on the couch and they were all encircling me, and all crying, and I wanted to die. I wanted to be with him in heaven. I couldn't believe that God would take him, especially without taking me too."

She turned back to the outlying night. "I must have screamed for hours at the horror of my loss, almost as if I screamed loud enough, it would purge me of the excruciating experience and all would be as before. As if God would realize it was too painful for me and He would turn back time and return Daddy with His apologies. Finally, a doctor arrived and sedated me and when I woke up again, I was at my grandparents' estate. So alone and inside myself I thought I would implode."

I thought about the abyss of betrayal, physical betrayal; to have a part of you unceremoniously ripped from your essence and existence by forces unknown and not understood. To know that the only friend and cure you had now would be death or time. But how much time, and how imminent death?

"When my mother died, my father had hired a nanny from a very poor family that he had known in Spain. She was quiet, beautiful, and simple about most things, and was my whole world outside of my father. We never went anywhere. I was either at school, or lying in bed, or on the couch with Maria at my grandparents' manor. She was a little girl at heart too, so we just played mostly, and spent quiet time together. She was my refuge, my rock, and my retreat for many years, and I loved her dearly, almost physically. When I went off to college and my grandparents died, she went back to Spain to take care of her ailing mother, and I immersed myself in my schooling, in my art, and eventually in my causes."

She stopped and looked up with wet and swollen eyes. "Could you pour a sobbing wreck some more wine, please?" she said with a weak smile.

I got a new bottle from the wine rack next to her brushes and pencils and did the honors for us both. She took a deep staccato'd breath and wiped her eyes once more. And then she continued.

"So to answer your question, I don't know why I chose lesbianism or am a lesbian. It may be because no man could ever live up to my father, or the memory of my father, or the dream of how my father would be. I wasn't old enough and we weren't together enough for me to discover his faults, or for us to argue, or for him to have to discipline me. Or maybe I would feel too guilty replacing him somehow, that it would dishonor him, or my love for him, or my memory of him, somehow. Or maybe I transferred my emotional love for my mother to physical love of other females since I never got to love my mother in a physical, demonstrative sort of way. Or maybe I think of women how I thought of Maria, as safety and security, and quiet and uncomplicated intimacy. Or maybe I'm not a true lesbian, maybe it's my way of making sure that no man can ever hurt me or leave me like my father did, and maybe the fear of devastation outweighs the physical attraction of a man. I don't know. I quit trying to figure it out a long time and several hundred therapy sessions ago." She smiled again and I grabbed her hand and helped her to her feet. "Sorry you asked?" she questioned.

I smiled at her with genuine affection. "No, not sorry at all, except that I have an overwhelming urge to apologize for not being there for you in some way."

She looked at me intensely and said, "You're sweet. You're a sweet, kind, generous man, Mr. Kilbourne. And you must think I'm nuts!"

I laughed out loud and put my hand gently on her face, and looked into her eyes. "No, Ms. Rae, you're not nuts. You're a wreck. Probably not often, and definitely not long, but you're a wreck."

We both laughed at that and then she took my hand and pressed my palm harder against her cheek and closed her eyes. When she opened them and looked up, she said, "May I kiss you?"

I didn't know what to say, but rule number two in my book of wisdom said never to say no when a beautiful woman requested a kiss, so I just said, "I wish you would."

"Will you allow me to do it without touching me?" she asked sweetly.

"Yes," I said, "of course."

And then she put her hands on my face and kissed me, softly, tentatively at first, and then more strongly and passionately for a few long memorable seconds. When we were through, she pulled away but we continued to look at each other, and she continued to stroke my cheek with one hand as she touched her own lips lightly with the other.

"Someday, will you tell me about you?" she said after a while. "Jenner says there's been loss in your life as well."

"That is just supposition on his part, and he talks too much," I said with a smile.

"Yes, he does. But he loves you and cares about you also."

"And you as well, Ms. Rae."

"Yes, me as well," she said knowingly. "But how do you get by, how do you deal with it?"

I puffed out my chest and made my voice deep and said, "I am a rock, I am an island," and then she quoted Simon and Garfunkle with me while rolling her eyes, "a rock feels no pain, and an island never cries."

"You are a liar, Mr. Kilbourne."

"And you are quite lovely, Ms. Rae."

She smiled brilliantly and I brushed the softness of her cheek with the back of my fingers. "It's getting late," I said. "And I'm sure you're tired. I'd better go."

She kissed my hand and gave it back to me and I told her that I would see myself out. As I was walking across the muted timber flooring, I turned to look at her once more before heading down the stairs and to my car.

"Thank you, Shad," she said softly, "for caring."

"Thank you, Kathryn," I said, "for sharing."

As I walked down the stairs, I remembered that I had not even accomplished what I had come there to do, to find out about Chrissy and where she might be or where I might look. But it had been a nice night all in all, and I had met an incredible woman.

When I started to get in my car, I looked up at Kathryn's second-story studio and the lights flickered and then came on at full strength, lighting up the neighborhood once more. And then there she was, looking down at me, a silhouette in the descending brightness. I waved once more and she blew me a kiss. It was, without question, as pleasant and painful an evening as I could remember. I got in the car, opened the moonroof, and looked up at the now clearing night sky. "Good night, Mr. Rae. Rest well. You raised one heck of a daughter!"

CHAPTER 10

Tuesday morning brought me to my office, but not necessarily to my senses, and the inquisitive looks of the two grinning idiots I called my best friends.

"Morning, Bawse," they said in suggestive unison as I walked up the stairs to find them kickin' it once again on the couches. "How was your night? You were supposed to meet us for cocktails after your clandestine rendezvous with Kathryn Rae."

I shook my head and told them that I was unavoidably detained, which they didn't buy.

"Ahh, c'mon Bawse, who you trying to kid," said Deity. "Ya'll are holding out on the posse, we need details. Raw, unrefined, graphic details, and if you ain't got any, you needs to be making some up."

"Tell you what, I'll read a Harlequin romance novel and come up with a good story for you later."

"No night of rapture?" Gio asked.

"Unfortunately for me, but fortunately for women everywhere . . . she's gay," I said. "Pals, not paramours."

"She 'cide she gay 'fore or after she saw yo ugly mug," Deity said and both of them started laughing and knuckle-bumpin'.

I had to laugh at that one too, but hated to give in. "All right, you two adolescents. Quit living up to my low expectations. So what's up in our world?"

"Well," Gio said sitting up. "A letter was hand-delivered by a messenger this morning that is now adorning your desk, and Diane called up just a second ago and said that an elderly and elegant gentleman of great etiquette was downstairs and would like a minute of your time."

I looked down at my desk and there was indeed a red envelope. A 'Scarlett Letter' perhaps!?! I didn't recognize the quite beautiful calligraphy, but the perfume that seemed to accompany the penmanship was subtly familiar. I opened it, and the letter read . . .

Dearest Shad,

My apologies and my thanks for last night. You are as irritatingly exceptional as Jen had conveyed! It was a night not without embarrassment and painful emotion on my part, so my heartfelt thanks for your discretion, kindness, and caring. Irrelevant of future events, you will forever hold a special place in my heart for our short time together.

After you left, I remembered that I let you leave without fulfilling your magnanimous mission. In speaking with Jen and some of those I am in contact with, may I suggest assignation with a dear friend and confidant of mine who goes by the name of Casper. He is probably in possession of the information you seek in relation to Ms. Marcum, and if not, can direct you in circles of which I remain blissfully unaware. I have asked him to contact you upon his earliest availability as I know time is of the essence.

Shad, there is still much left unsaid and much cause for clarification. If I haven't scared you off already, I would love to see you again under more sane and less emotive conditions. And I would also enjoy the honor and opportunity to call you "friend." Come see me again soon (don't be late!),

Always,
Kathryn

That was sweet of her to take the time to pen the letter and to steer me in the right direction; hopefully her lead would prove to be of value and viability. I was also excited for the opportunity to sit with her again and talk without past or pretense.

I put the letter in my top drawer and looked down again at the gruesome twosome. "Okay, what's this about someone downstairs?"

Gio looked at the note he had written on the side of the sports page and said, "Diane buzzed us to tell us you were on your way up so to put away our toys and comic books, and also to tell you that an elderly gentleman had just walked in and was wishing for a moment of your time."

"Did she say who it was or what it's regarding?"

"Nope," said Gio grinning. "Just that you'd want to see him because he looked like a nice old man."

"That sounds like Diane. Okay, tell her to tell him I'll be down." I pushed some buttons on the City's electronic surveillance system and looked at camera eight to see who was waiting on L1. I couldn't tell at first because he was kind of stooped over, but when I panned in with the toggle switch, I could finally recognize the face. Smythe!

"On second thought, never mind," I told the boys. I punched in Diane's wireless headset code and she pinged back. "Yes, your majesty?"

"Finally, some love and respect!" I said.

"Well, some respect anyway," she retorted, and laughed into the receiver.

"Insubordination. I'm surrounded by insubordination," I complained to the guiltless. "If you wouldn't mind defusing the verbal onslaught for a while, could you please escort the distinguished gentlemen up to my office?"

"You want to see him in your office?" she said a little incredulously.

"Yes, his name is Smythe, and he is an acquaintance of mine."

"We'll be right up," she said.

I put down the headset control and walked down to my boys and the couches. "What's up, Bawse?" asked Deity.

"Smythe is a gentleman's gentleman that I met at the Heritage Club last week," I said. "Definitely a grand old man, but we'll have to wait until he gets up here to find out exactly what he needs."

A few seconds later my Star Trek slidey door opened and Smythe ambled up the stairs via cane as dignified as he could with Diane helping him sweetly by holding his hand and arm. He had on a grey tweed suit and bow tie, both of which bagged with the cruelty of time. But his shirt was bright white and his shoes were shined to an incandescent glow. His white hair was recently barbered and combed perfectly back, and his black cane had a white ivory penguin handle that looked of quality craftsmanship and expense. He looked to be about seventy, but I was a lousy judge of age, so he may have been ten years to either side of that. He looked like the grandpa in the old Disney flick *Parent Trap*.

I walked over and met him at the top of the main level and shook his hand. "It is good to see you again, Smythe."

Smythe smiled and looked around my office, first probably at all the electronics and the relational accoutrements, and then at the continuous aquarium that looked down upon the other floors. It was only after a thorough survey that he noticed Deity and Gio as they rose to greet him as well.

"Good morning, Mr. Kilbourne," he said softly, but not without strength. "And to you as well gentlemen," he said to Deity and Gio.

Diane smiled and winked at me as she helped Smythe down to the sitting area. When we were all seated, Diane was at her hostess-best and asked us all if we'd like anything. Smythe said he'd have a cup of coffee and the rest of us concurred as well.

"Would anyone be in need of artificial augmentation?" Diane asked with a smile that could light a city block.

Smythe looked at me questioningly so I was first to speak up.

"I'll take a shot of Bailey's in mine, Diane," I said as Gio and Deity acquiesced as well. "Smythe, would you like a little 'comfort' in yours?"

He looked at the three of us and said quite matter-of-factly, "'Tis a weak and immoral man that drinks before ten in the morning, gentlemen."

I checked the Rolex. "It's ten-o-three, sir."

Smythe looked at me and winked and looked back up at the lovely Diane and said, "In that case, you'd better make mine a double, Ms. Fontaine!"

With that, we all laughed and bid Diane a fond farewell as she departed to go get us our refreshments.

Smythe looked at us frankly. "Do you think she's in love with me?" he said.

I smiled at the genuinely funny and distinguished old man, and thought he must be the mold from which God made grandfathers. "I am almost sure of it, sir. But may I also ask a favor of you? If your intentions are not honorable and you have no plans to ultimately marry her, then please let her down easy."

"My word as a gentleman, young Kilbourne," he said with a twinkle in his eye. He looked over at Gio and Deity. "What is it that you gentlemen do?"

"We are our brother's keeper," Deity said in his best diction. "We ensure his health and prosperity."

Smythe looked at all of us and said, "And what of the prosperity of his posterity?"

I smiled. "You are quite eloquent and articulate, sir. But we are men of a singular existence. Are you familiar with the Faerie Queen?"

He smiled and said, "Yes, Sir Edmund Spenser. Many eons ago, I was a professor of Early English Literature at the University of Washington. Up until a few years ago, I still held Status Emeritus there."

Somehow I knew he would know. "Then it would suffice to say that Gio and Deity are twin Talus' to my Sir Artegall."

Gio looked at Deity and asked, "Do you know what the heck they're talking about?"

Deity smiled. "Rarely, but I'm thinking it be a compliment."

Smythe studied me for a minute then and gave equal gaze to Deity and Gio. "That is a compliment. And it is also a rather ominous and telling response, Mr. Kilbourne. But, if true, it gives me partial hope for what I've come to talk with you about today."

"What is it that we can do for you, Mr. Smythe?" I said, enjoying his company immensely already.

"Well, first of all, you can call me Reginald. And secondly, I hope you can help me . . ." Smythe's eyes immediately began to fill with tears, which ran unabated down his cheeks as he dropped his head and took a moment to himself.

"I'm sorry, gentlemen," Smythe said when he had regained some semblance of composure. "I had hoped for a better showing than this. Please accept my heartfelt apologies."

"No need to apologize, Reginald," I said. "Most people tend to cry when they're stuck in the same room with the three of us."

"I thank you for your graciousness," Smythe said with a weak smile. "But my loss is still recent, as I assume it will always be. To make a long story short . . . fifty-one days ago, when my sweet Mildred was walking home from bingo around dusk, the doctors said she must have slipped or tripped or had some type of medical issue, because she fell and hit her head on the sidewalk and passed away before they could get her to the hospital."

Smythe finished his accounting of the incident with great difficulty, stopping intermittently to fight back tears and probably much more. I was saddened by the fact that he knew exactly how many days it had been, and I was sure that he knew the hours and minutes if asked as well.

"We're sorry, Reginald," we all said in unison or some variation thereof. Our mood was interrupted briefly by Diane as she set down our coffee setups and ponies of Baileys Irish Cream. Sensing the emotion in the room, she departed quickly with thanks from us all following her down the steps and out the door.

Smythe took a deep, cleansing breath and continued, "We'd been married fifty-eight years, and her death was nearly the death of me, for loneliness is an ugly and unmerciful companion, gentlemen, and I would wish it upon few. But three days ago, a shopkeeper whom Mildred and I patronized almost daily, finally told me that some individuals whom he referred to as skinheads were hassling her because of her surmised Jewish heritage and pushed her down when she tried to maintain her dignity and her purse. I guess they had seen our friend, the shopkeeper, through the window and told him that if he said anything to the police or anyone else, they would kill him, and his family, and burn his beautiful little store."

Smythe pulled a monogrammed handkerchief out of his breast pocket, wiped his nose with gentle elegance, and placed it neatly back inside his tweed blazer. I think I knew where this was going, but it would have to be stated and asked of him without inference or interference from us.

"The little area we live in has changed greatly over the last twenty years, but it has been the only home we've ever known so we've been reluctant to leave. Unfortunately, a criminal element has started to take root and most of us of antiquated status have come to know fear. Demetri, my shopkeeper friend, said that he and most of the other small shopkeepers of minimal means have to pay these so-called skinheads a thousand dollars a month or they threaten great bodily and structural harm. We are a poor and simple neighborhood, Mr. Kilbourne. We have no way to protect ourselves from these ruffians."

Gio broke the tension by pouring us each coffee and assisting Smythe as much as he could without insulting this proud gentleman.

"I have no right, nor means, for that which I ask, gentlemen," he said. "But we are presented with a minimum of resources and I am boldly asking in great humility for your assistance, in whatever form that may be. Maybe you have some pull with the authorities that you could leverage or maybe you know someone with expertise in this area. I have talked with many of my neighbors, and most of the shopkeepers who aren't too afraid to take action, and I can present whomever with close to ten thousand dollars in cash."

I think he meant to continue but he seemed exhausted from the emotion and the telling of his communal predicament. He sank back into the couches and rested his eyes. I looked at Gio and Deity and they both nodded their head in acquiescence, a look of great concern and anger on Gio's face, a look of benign curiosity on Deity's. I assumed Gio's facial depiction was because he had parents and grandparents that were still living and I'm sure he took Smythe's plight personally. I assumed Deity's look was that of eager anticipation for another opportunity to test himself against others, or that another operation was to be put in place where he could utilize his talents.

"Mr. Smythe, though I appreciate the offer of money and the opportunity to have Deity's and Gio's weekly bar bill paid off, I will respectfully turn down your kind offer of financial assistance," I said. "I will also assume that you've already gone to the police and that they can offer no specific relief without cooperative witnesses or evidence. But what I can offer you, Mr. Smythe, is that we will have it looked into and the situation corrected to the advantage of the neighborhood. All I ask of you in return is that I have your honorable word that this stays strictly between the four of us and that no mention of us is ever uttered again, regardless of future events."

After several more cups of coffee, greater detail, and as pleasant a morning as I could remember, Smythe rose slowly to his feet, which I assisted in as we stood as well. A grateful and tearful smile encompassed his face. "I don't know what to say, gentlemen. I had no grand aspirations of such generosity and involvement. You have my word as an Alzheimer's patient that I will forget this conversation ever took place, but I will never forget that on this fine and glorious morning I met three great and valiant men."

We all laughed at the promise of our new patriarch, and walked with him to the doors downstairs, all the while being entertained by Smythe's stories of youthful exuberance. When we found out he had taken a taxi, I suggested that Gio and Deity give him a ride home as well so that they could do a little reconnaissance and familiarize themselves with the area near the outskirts of Tacoma. As Gio and Smythe exited the building arm in arm, Deity turned to me and asked, "How do you want to handle this?"

"Same as always, D. Find out who the players are, who they're connected to, if anyone, and who gets hurt if they go away."

Deity grinned with pleasure. "You gonna be in on this, Bawse?"

I peered out of the window and saw Smythe showing Gio a wallet-sized photo of a woman, who I assumed to be his recently deceased Mildred.

I looked back at Deity. "Yeh, I'm gonna be in on this." And then I turned and headed back to my office. "I'm gonna be all over this."

CHAPTER 11

Within the next seven days, I had gotten in two rather painful gym workouts with the boys, got a call from Kathryn's friend, Casper, who said we could meet with him the next day, and also received an update from Deity and Gio regarding Smythe's little slice of life, south of Tacoma.

It was the latter matter that we now tackled. Gio and Deity had spent part of the last week and nights doing "reconnaissance, research, and ramification" on the skinheads, which as we had assumed, turned out to be a Hitlerian sect of Neo-Nazis amounting to about forty individuals of ill repute. It looked like they had taken over the drug distribution business in that sector of the city from some of the smaller and weaker gangs and were trying to make a name for themselves. They had allegedly accounted for two murders and a couple of rapes within the last month alone, adding to their repertoire of grand theft, armed robbery, and extortion; and seemed to be emboldened by their recent successes. From the research we'd done, it looked like there were about eight individuals who formed the nucleus and strength of the operation, and from past experience we knew that if you took out the legs, the body would fall. We'd also spoken to Pablo's father, Rama, and he confirmed most of the information we'd received.

"Just be careful, gringos," he told us. "Those boys are a hornet's nest. They gotta lotta meat, a lotta heat, and a lotta hate. If it moves they'll rob it, rape it, or kill it. You need me on this?"

"You mean like the flowers need the rain?" I said.

"Gringos are loco," he said, and hung up abruptly.

Since I couldn't argue with that, I got back to business. Fortunately for us, most of those eight members and a few other stragglers gathered nightly for a little business and poker, probably wagering the day's illicit gains. Tonight, we decided to pay them a little visit and make a little wager of our own.

We rode out to the warehouse district that was in relative proximity to Smythe's little neighborhood in the driving rain and kept ourselves busy by dodging rats and potholes as the darkening night clamped down upon Tacoma's forgotten detritus. The potholes were also making it extremely difficult for us to finish our Diet Cokes and soft bean burritos with extra cheese that we had just picked up at Taco Time. The path of justice is often times strewn with adversity . . . and cold mexi-fries. We were riding in a brand-new black Ford F-350 that looked like it could have scaled Everest. Deity said he had "borrowed" it and I left it at that. He was riding shotgun next to Gio and I was in the back with Koda.

Koda's and my family went back a couple hundred years. His great, great, great, grandfather had been an Apache chief and mine had been a Territory Marshall appointed by the president and somehow our families had run together to various degrees ever since. He had spent ten years with the Night Stalkers, which was a Special Operations Aviation Regiment called SOAR, whose motto was "Death Waits in the Dark." In fact, Koda's real name, Miakoda, meant "power of the moon" in the Apache language. Now, he ran security at the Issaquah Indian Reservation Casinos, and since he was a ghost in the dark, whenever I had some night work, his presence was always requested and appreciated. I would have liked to have used him for daywork as well, but he was a little too big and too ethnically conspicuous for jobs done during the illuminating light of day.

I looked out of the window into the bleakness and despair that surrounded us like fog. "When you said it was dark, smelly, and ugly, I thought you were exaggerating, D. Now I know you were sugarcoating it. This place is a dump."

Deity turned in his seat and said, "But the perfect place for a bunch of pierced and tattooed skinheads to operate out of, without much notice. Most of the buildings and businesses out here are abandoned or condemned, so there's very little traffic. Wait til you see 'em, Bawse. They ugly even by Koda's standards."

Koda tried to smack Deity on the back of the head but Deity was too quick and Koda was partially restricted by his seatbelt. "I'd scalp you but you're already bald," Koda said.

"That's why I shave my head, I'm Indian-proof," said Deity, as he and Gio started laughing again.

I shook my head and said, "I'm on a job with Hewey, Dewey, and Louie."

For the next fifteen minutes, insults flew back and forth from front seat to backseat without respite. I tried to stay above it all, but in addition to being three of the toughest and deadliest guys I knew, they were also three of the funniest adolescents I knew.

A couple of miles from our intended destination, we killed the headlights and let Koda slip into the night. He'd make short work of anyone that was standing watch or loitering outside the warehouse that served as their base of operations.

The rest of us parked behind a neighboring warehouse still a couple miles out so that the diesel noise emitted from the F-350 wouldn't announce our arrival prematurely. We were all dressed in various versions of black-on-black, complete with full face covers, Kevlar-fitted fatigues, and black military issued boots. It would have been nice to have been able to use slickers on a rainy night like tonight, but they were a little clumsy and noisy for stealth work, and they reflected any light that might shine our way. Cotton and wool were still the choice of champions the world over.

Deity and Gio reached into their shoulder holsters and took the safeties off their big forty-fours, and slipped their sawed off shotguns into their backstraps for easier access. I was still partial to nines so I had one in each thigh holster that seemed to work best for me. We all carried extra magazines in elastic pockets too, just in case more than the planned eight showed up.

"What's that?" I asked Deity, as he put a small packet into his pocket.

"A rabbit's foot for luck, a Scooby-Doo band-aid in case I gets shot with a bazooka, and a sample of Gio's cologne to sniff in case I gets caught and needs to commit suicide."

Gio gave him a dirty look and said, "You better keep smiling or I won't be able to see you in the dark and accidently shoot you."

"With your aim, the safest place on the planet is right in front of you," Deity replied.

"All right, you two clowns, cut the comedy," I said. "It's showtime."

We showcased our best serpentine moves, reminiscent of Peter Falk in *The In-Laws*—one of my all-time favorite movies—toward their warehouse. We dodged behind whatever cover there was, in short, squatted spurts, making sure we weren't silhouetted against lighter backgrounds or the night sky, checking every twenty yards or so for movement from the warehouse perimeter. We were also hoping that we'd given Koda enough time to complete his portion of the mission. After about thirty minutes of what was probably excessive caution, we rendezvoused with

Koda on the west side of the warehouse which sheltered us from the majority of the wind and slanting rain.

Koda approached us out of the dark behind some old, rusted petrol cans; fifty-five-gallon drums strewn to eternity from past abandonment. He had a VSS sniper rifle hung chest high in his left hand, and a spec-op modified Glock with a silencer in his right hand hanging down by his thigh to keep the rain out.

"One target was watching the front from an outbuilding roof, but he was careless and kept lighting cigarettes either out of boredom or to keep warm," Koda said, just a little out of breath. "With the rain he had to keep relighting them so he was kind enough to offer me a great target about every three minutes. About ten minutes ago another target came to relieve him so I took him out as well, upclose and personal."

Koda looked around as lightning flashed and I could see the rain rolling off his face. He must have removed the hood when he was making the kills. "Looks like there are about nine of them left inside, one guy right inside watching what sounded like cartoons, and about eight others inside playing poker in an inner office, listening to some loud, heavy metal garbage that sounds like it's in German, and all getting drunker than ten Tanzanians."

Gio looked at Koda and said, "I thought the term was 'Drunker that ten Indians.'"

Koda smiled and said, "I cannot betray my people."

"All right," I said. "Let's get this over with, my feet are getting cold and I saw a burger joint selling bacon cheeseburgers and curly fries off the freeway on the way in. Koda, stay outside and outa-sight until we're in and organized. I'll take the lead and open discussions with the cartoon buffoon up front. Gio, you're in and on my right and have initial exclusive on anybody coming through the inner office door. Deity, you're in and on my left and have the perimeters."

Koda nodded and started to fade to black, disappearing into the night without a sound. "Happy hunting, Kimosabes," was all we heard for a moment and then the soft whistling of the theme song from the *Lone Ranger*. I strained my eyes to look deeper into the darkness after him but there wasn't any movement. I'd have to ask him how he did that someday.

We all removed our soaking wet masks and opened the graffiti-adorned wooden and sheet metal door. The light and heat were blinding as we entered, and the deafening music didn't help much either. There was a clumsily made two-by-four wooden desk about twenty feet in front of us manned by a rather large and lethargic skinhead. Triangulated forty-foot ceilings shouldered metal beams from which an array of pulleys and chains still hung in various stages of rust and disrepair. All types of large, mangled machinery littered each side of the dented steel-gray walls for about the first forty feet upon entry, meeting up with what looked like a quonset-hut office set in the middle of the expansive manufacturing area.

Behind the quonset hut and off to the side you could see newer crates sitting under old camouflage netting that had been partially opened, offering glimpses of what looked like stolen Harley Davidson motorcycle assemblies, though I always hesitated to cast aspersions. No wonder the Hitler youth were celebrating; it looked like a pretty heavy score for the home team.

Boy Blunder, behind his plywood desk, didn't look up from his cartoons at first, just yelling at us to "close the damn door."

"Hi," I said casually. "Are your mommy and daddy home?"

Our heavily tatted and pierced host looked over slowly at first and then more quickly the second time as he noticed we weren't members of the Heil Hitler Club. "Hey, I ain't no kid," he said with obvious irritation and in automatic defense.

"Actually," I patronized. "I was speaking more to your mental rather than physical development, but why sever semantic pretext upon first introduction."

"Huh?" was all he could deliver.

"Excellent response," I said. "Well said, well phrased."

"Uh?" he said with squinted eyes peaking out from beneath his Cro-Magnon brow, just now noticing the guns hanging down by our sides.

"Wow!" I continued. "Though my colleagues and I are intellectually aroused and cognitively captivated by your obvious elevated acumen, and would love to stand here and exchange one-syllable retorts with you, we need to speak with your boss. I was actually going to say we need to speak with your superiors but I don't have time to talk to all of the people and most of the one-celled organisms on the planet."

"I ain't the boss," he stammered while rising from the chair.

"Yes, a pity that a man of your caliber had been overlooked along the corporate ladder, but we'll put in a good word for you at your next quarterly review." I looked over at Deity, "Where was I?"

Deity never took his eyes off our host. "You was being well-built and eloquent, and he was being fat and stupid."

I nodded with remembrance. "Right. Okay then F&S, why don't you escort us into the inner sanctum so we can meet the rest of the gang. And remember F&S, fat will kill you slow, but stupid gets you dead in a hurry, so don't yell out or try for the gun on the back of your chair."

As we moved cautiously forward, Gio put his big forty-four in the back of F&S's neck and we entered the quonset. At first, no-one noticed our arrival since the alcohol seemed to have numbed their senses even if the music and smell of marijuana had not. All seven of them were in deep concentration, as a heated game of heads down Texas Hold'em was in raucous play. Large swastika'd flags and white supremacy posters littered the dilapidated and dented walls. A cheaply framed picture of Hitler, slightly askew, graced the wall above a table sporting an assortment of empty beer cans and opened bottles of Wild Turkey.

The hell boys all seemed equally tatted, scarred, and pierced. I knew this because they were all in various stages of dress and decoration, whatever clothes they were in were all military issue, done in various shades of camo green, brown, and black. It wasn't until Deity blew the boom box to smithereens with his sawed off shotgun that we finally got their attention. It got eerily quiet for a split second until one of them tried to go for his gun, which Deity took care of pretty abruptly. The bad news for F&S was that he also chose that moment to pursue hero status by trying to spin and grab Gio. Gio taught him a lesson; unfortunately the kind you die from, not the kind you learn from.

"All right, gentlemen, and I use the term extremely loosely, keep your hands on the table. Now, I know that this is not 'The Rocket Scientist Club,' so we'll keep it down to just one rule, . . . Do as we say or die."

I could see the music, drug, and alcoholic fog start to lift and they started to look at each other, and at the few guns on the table and those hanging from their chairs.

"Now, I'm already in a bad mood," I said, "a sad mood really. I just saw two of your psychedelic soldiers die of lung cancer outside, one die of lead poisoning inside, and my close personal friend and fellow cartoon watcher, F&S, just pass away from terminal stupidity. So I'd like your full cooperation." I looked around and asked, "All right then, who is the leader of this esteemed gathering?"

Because they lacked a frontal lobe, most of them automatically looked at the shirtless psychopath directly facing me. He looked back at all of them shaking his head.

"I'm Mace, and you're in a hell of a lot trouble," he said as menacingly as he could muster.

I smiled my most sympathetic smile at my new friend, Mace. "Actually Mace, with a quick visual inventory of your little rumpus room rowdies here, I don't doubt that I'm in hell, but if I have trouble, it will come in the form of something much more formidable than this motley crew of misfits."

Mace and his band of bad boys all glared at us. You could tell that all of them would have loved to have grabbed iron and taken their chances, but whatever brain cells that were left seemed to be prevailing.

"Who are you?" Mace snarled.

"We're Larry, Curly, and Mo than you can handle, Mace," I said. "So let's get back to business. Since four of your counterparts are already hip-hopping with Hitler in hell, I have a few questions while some of you are still among the living . . ."

"Boss!" Gio called out. "Koda said there were nine targets in here. There're two on the floor and six at the table."

One of the wunderkind's eyes darted immediately to his right and rear toward one of those green portable restrooms you see at construction sites. But before I could comment on that, the door kicked open and one of Hitler's finest came out screaming like a banshee and firing wildly. Shots rang out wide of us and a little high, but before he could get off the next series of shots, the thwap-thwap sound of a silencer ended his tirade as he fell heavily to the floor, two trickles of blood running down the back of his shaved and signatured head.

Koda stepped inside the back door with both guns hip high. "Good evening, palefaces," he said. "Pardon the interruption."

I looked at Koda and gave him a nod. "I always wondered why they called them 'silencers'."

"Now ya know, Kil. It's to quiet the crazy and the corrupt," Koda said with his ever-present smile.

With all eyes upon the surprise arrival and lethality of Koda, another of Mace's all-star team decided to Carpe Diem and Gio once again cut the rally short.

"Damn, Mace," I said. "It's not looking good for the home team. The survival rate around here is looking a little slim, quite unlike your fat and festively adorned friend here at the table." At that, the largest gollywonker started to stand but Mace put a hand on his shoulder and doughboy sat back down.

Mace looked back at Koda, and then slowly at each of us. He was probably a lot of things, but scared wasn't one of them. "What do you want?" he said.

"Macey, my boy, you're obviously a man of few words and I too am a friend of brevity, so I'll keep it short. Which one of you pushed an elderly Jewish woman down a few months ago during a 'mug and molest' that led to her untimely death?"

For being poker players none of these guys other than Mace seemed capable of a poker face. Three of the six remaining village idiots looked at the guilty pierced prince and he just glared at me. "Whadya gonna do? Shoot me cus I killed some Kyke granny?"

"Yes!" I said and shot him through the forehead as the others jumped up from the table and scrambled to get out of the way. All of them but dumbo, who was too big, too slow, too lazy, too stupid, or too brave to move.

"And then there were four," I said. "Which one of you Nancys is next?"

"Nazis," Gio said.

"What?" I said.

"They're called Nazis, not Nancys."

I looked at them and then back at Gio. "But they have earrings and piercings, and shaved bodies, and have adorned themselves in colorful murals. Are you sure they're not Nancys?"

I must have hit a nerve because two of the other boys on borrowed time put their hands on their guns and one said, "I don't hafta take that from no injun, no wop, and no n . . . ," and then, thanks to Deity, there were two shots followed by silence.

I looked at Deity and asked, "Was he gonna say what I think he was gonna say?"

Deity put his gun back down by his side. "I was in fear of a forthcoming racial slur and felt it better to relieve them of their overt bigotry."

"Well done, you've just made the NAACP Christmas Card list," I said. "By the way, how do you know he wasn't going to say 'Negro'?"

"I definitely heard the intonations of a short 'i' rather than a long 'e,' so I just naturally assumed the former," Deity said in his best professorial proffering.

I nodded and looked at the three remaining rejects. Mace and a young kid who looked a little slow mentally, and the fatman who remained seated and had yet to take his eyes off me.

"You think you pretty tough?" said the previously mute behemoth.

I looked at the solid mass of trash. "Excuse me?"

"I said you think you tough? I seen what you can do with a gun. I bet you a sissy with your hands."

"I don't have to be tough, el blimpo. I just have to be tougher than you. Which qualifies me and most skinny third graders."

He started to stand and said, "You wanna find out?"

"Actually, I already know tricera tubs, but if you'd like to find out, I'd be happy to educate you."

He must have been sitting on a pail or a five-gallon bucket and not on an actual full-size chair because when he stood, he stood all the way up to six foot eight inches tall and well over three-hundred and fifty pounds. And he was nowhere near as fat as he looked sitting down all scrunched up. I heard Gio say "Holy Moly" and Deity do an impressive whistle through his teeth. I looked over at Koda and he was smiling as always. "My money's on Mr. Potato Head, Kil, no offense."

"None taken," I said as I continued to gaze at his sheer size. "I think my money may be on him as well."

I looked over at Gio. "My eyes are a little blurry from the smoke. Is that four guys standing really close together or one gigantic near-human slug."

Gio was still looking at him in awe and shaking his head. "I do believe that to be a singular entity of enormous mass, Boss."

I looked over at Deity and asked, "What do you think?"

Deity, as always, had never taken his eyes off Mace, other than his quick initial glance at and evaluation of the human hippo. "If 'n I you, Bawse, right 'bout now I'd be rememberin' about a previous engagement I be late for."

Before I could respond either way to that lifesaving suggestion, we were interrupted.

"I am a bruiser," he said, and for the first time a faint German accent seemed to poke through.

"No need to apologize," I said, "a lot of guys drink too much."

"Not a boozer, I said bruiser."

"Don't be so hard on yourself, you're no loser either."

"Not loser . . . bruiser," he said, now a little meaner, a little louder, and a lot uglier.

I looked at him questioningly. "Why do you think you bruise so easily?"

He smiled and I was able to see all seven of his teeth in various stages of angle and iridescence. "I don't bruise, I bruise other people."

"Are they typically tied down or unconscious at the time?"

The Michelin Man must have gotten tired of our friendly verbal discourse since he reached up and grabbed his black "The Devil Made Me Do It" T-shirt at the neck and ripped it off his body like it was wet tissue.

Not to be outdone, I shoved my nine back into its thigh holster, removed my Kevlar vest, and grabbed the top of my sweater with both hands. But before I could do any damage, Gio kept me from making a costly mistake. "Isn't that cashmere, Boss?"

I looked over at Gio appreciatively. "Good point," I said as I pulled it off over my head instead. "And hopefully he's a bruiser and not a bleeder as advertised."

He flexed his massive arms out in front of him. "I have killed nineteen people with no gun to help me." He was starting to sound more like Arnold Schwarzenegger as he warmed to his role, and as his emotions and adrenaline started to percolate. "And you will be my twentieth."

"Do you think they died of your bad breath first or your body odor?" I asked.

"I killed them with my bare hands," he said, cracking the knuckles on both mitts loudly.

"That's impressive," said Koda from across the room, enjoying the forthcoming melee way too much.

I looked over at Koda. "You've killed guys with your hands before, what's so impressive about that?"

"No," Koda said shaking his head, "the fact that he can count to twenty."

The Goodyear Blimp finally screamed in frustration. "Enough talk coward, let us do this."

I looked at Gio. "Coward? I do believe I've been insulted."

"Well, now ya gotta fight 'em, Boss. You've been maligned by a rather large doofus."

I walked over to a side table near the door we entered earlier and took off both thigh holsters. "Mace, my boy, you giving odds?"

"You're actually going to fight him?" he asked in astonishment. "He's going to tear your arms off and beat you to death with them, and I'm going to love every minute of it."

"No commentary, Mace," I said as I looked over at the money still piled on the poker table, "just odds. I have a Benjamin in my pocket, how about a hundred to one?"

"You're on sucka," Mace said, true madness now in his eyes. And then he looked at his one-ton wobbler, and said, "Kill him, Von!"

He started to walk toward me slowly, so I started to circle.

"We gonna arm wrestle, Avon?" I asked.

"Nein, we are not going to arm wrestle," he said.

"Rock, Paper, Scissors?" I asked.

"Nein, no Rock, Paper, Scissors."

"Patty Cake?"

"Nein, no damn Patty Cake neither," he hissed.

I stopped. "Either."

He stopped too. "Huh?"

"You seem to be intellectually as well as grammatically challenged, my ruthless and toothless friend. Typically a singular verb is called for, but that singularity is by no means invariable. Try to remember that *neither* emphasizes the separateness of items. It doesn't add them together, at least not grammatically. Am I right, D?"

"In neither/nor constructions, the verb should always agree with the noun nearest it, Bawse," Deity said in his best professorial diction once more.

"I stand vindicated, Avon," I said, proud not only of myself but of my wingman's grammatical gifts as well.

But before I could bump knuckles with Deity, I was about to butt heads with a buffalo. I had a couple more one-liners and insults I wanted to try out on old Avon, but he lunged and threw a sweeping right hand before I could wax comedic, probably hoping to knock me down and then kick the comedian out of me with his size fifteen steel-toed military boots. I ducked the big right and as his momentum carried him past me, I hit him as hard as I could twice in the ear and temple, which seemed to faze him only slightly. If I was going to hit him in the head with my fists, I was going to go for the soft spots; I didn't want to break a hand on a rock hard, albeit hollow, head. As he advanced a second time, he tried a right feint and threw the left, but it got him the same result to the face, this time with my forearm and elbow.

"Have you actually ever hit anybody, Avon?" I asked. "If you get any slower, I can snack between punches."

Avon just ignored me and shook his massive skull to get rid of the bells that were surely ringing in his head and came more cautiously this time, hands still held high, and just a little crouched, stepping relatively light and quickly for a man of his mass. He tried a few jabs and grabs but they were too slow. Fortunately my right crosses over the top of his massive arms and an occasional uppercut weren't, and I opened up deep cuts on a cheekbone, above one eye, and under his chin within minutes. My footwork was important here too since getting in close enough to hit him, and getting out quickly enough to evade a significant punch or hold was crucial to my long-term health plan.

In between punches by me and advances by the large barge, I stole quick glances at the boys, but for the most part they had maintained their focus and vigilance; Deity on Mace, Gio on the interior, and Koda along the exterior perimeter. I'm sure they stole occasional glances to see if I was in need of help or if chubby checker was in need of a bullet, but we'd been in this situation enough times to not be distracted by me fighting a rhino.

For a few minutes, I thought maybe that I was winning, but as bloodied and winded as Avon was, he wasn't slowing down. There seemed to be a distinct separation between his mind and body, which meant he was probably too stupid and too mean to realize losing was an option. Since I was sure Avon's fights typically only lasted a few minutes at best before he pummeled his opponents to perdition, I was hoping he would have tired before now.

We continued to circle, with Avon getting in an occasional hard, dull blow which racked my whole body. I was throwing various head and body shots that even now didn't seem to do anything other than slow him down and bloody him more. Sweat intermixed with blood as we exchanged punches for the next ten minutes and danced around each other in pugilistic pink.

With Avon finally starting to look a little winded and arm weary, I took two quick shuffle steps in to throw some world-class body blows and ended up slipping on the aforementioned puddle of pink. The good news was that I caught myself before I went down; the bad news was that Avon caught me as well. I did manage to knee him in the face as hard as I could before he could get his big arms around me, but two seconds later my feet were off the ground and he was squeezing the life out of me.

I tried to reach down with both arms to pry his grip off me but got several hard headbutts to the face for my efforts and saw blackness interspersed with fireworks all around as explosions went off in my head. He squeezed tighter still and I could feel ribs start to tear away from the muscle sheath.

I had no more sense of time or spectators, just a fight for survival that didn't seem to be going my way. I tried slapping both of his ears simultaneously with my cupped hands to try and break his eardrums but he seemed more than willing to endure pain and deafness if it meant victory. As he kept trying to headbutt me into submission and unconsciousness, I managed to get my hands in front of me and jabbed both my thumbs into his beady little eyes that resided beneath his caveman cranium. Fortunately for me, he drew the line at blindness and he threw me to the floor with a scream and grabbed involuntarily at both of his eyes, still trying to kick out and connect with his boots where he thought I might still be. Only the first one connected, and only on my forearm as I tried to block it, but I could tell he had either broken or fractured it by the sound it made and the pain I instantly felt all the way up my left arm.

I was hunched over, trying to get my breath back, as it came in great gulping rasps. Since he was still hunched over with his hands on his face, I closed in quickly and kicked him as hard as I could in the head a couple of times, and as he turned his back on me to shield his face, I kicked him in the side of the knees repeatedly, which eventually brought him to his knees. As I stepped back to catch my breath, he rose slowly and hobbled over to me once more.

Probably deaf, half blind, and crippled, but definitely game, he started to circle again. I held my torn ribs with my fractured left arm and tried to get in as much air as my bruised lungs would allow, hoping that I was going to be able to end this soon. With as winded as ol' Avon was, his mouth was hanging open like an attic trapdoor, and bloody drool was running down his chin. I dropped my arms a little in feigned exhaustion and he took the bait and rushed me once more. As he got close enough, I lifted my left knee to make him hesitate a little and raise his head, and then dropped it quickly and did a right snap kick with all the remaining strength I could muster, that caught him squarely under the chin.

The sound of his lower jaw hitting his upper made a crack so loud that I thought a gun had gone off. Avon's weight and momentum had knocked me back to the wall and him into an old pile of discarded rebar shards embedded in concrete. I must have kicked up a few when he knocked me past them because as I scrambled to stand up I could see that two pieces had impaled him through the right side of his rib cage and in all likelihood had pierced a lung and possibly whatever heart he ever had. Had the kick not knocked him out, he probably could have managed a more graceful landing, but three-hundred and fifty pounds coming down unabated on jagged rebar didn't give him much of a chance.

There were about ten seconds of pristine silence after that as we all took in what had just happened. I looked up and Deity was nodding his head in approval but still with his complete focus on Mace, who was looking at the ex-Avon in obvious disbelief, and then up at the ceiling in obvious defeat. "I never woulda believed it," he said. "I never woulda believed anybody coulda taken Von in a fair fight."

Now that the show was mostly over, Koda gave me the thumbs-up and stepped out the back of the Quonset hut to do an outside perimeter check. Gio checked to make sure I was okay and then went out the front door to check on the rest of the warehouse.

I leaned up against the side of the building, still trying to catch my breath and spit up a little blood. I could tell my nose was broken for the hundredth time and I felt the multiple, deep cuts from the series of irregular head butts. With my tongue, I could feel the cuts on the inside of my mouth and at least one loose tooth.

When I looked over at Mace, he was looking at me and then down at Avon. "Didn't think it could be done," he said, still shaking his head. He looked around the room then, at the bodies and probably at what he thought he had accomplished prior to our arrival. He looked back at me for a long time and seemed to come to some sort of self-realization. "You gotta kill us."

I looked at him, and when I had finally caught my breath, I said, "Sorry, Mace, but yeah, I gotta kill ya."

He looked at the one remaining soldier who had moved slowly behind him now, almost as protection. As their faces came side by side and profiled, it dawned on me that they looked vaguely similar and were probably related somehow.

"Brothers?" I heaved heavily through bloody and swollen lips.

Mace looked back at me and answered, "Cousins. He's a little slow, but I'm all he ever had."

The slow cousin looked back at him blankly and then down at the ground. He smiled as Mace rubbed his shaved head. I don't think he had ever uttered a word the entire time we were there.

"Hard," I said breathlessly, "hard to take care of family, even under the best of circumstances."

Mace turned and looked back at his cousin and smiled, then grabbed him gently by the back of the neck and kissed his forehead, which made the cousin smile big again as well. "Not too hard though."

Mace turned to take another slow, encompassing look around and then looked at his cousin and then back at me, and said, "I gotta favor to ask."

It was a slow drive home, the wind still howling, the rain still coming down sideways and in sporadic sheets. Deity was at the wheel with Gio riding shotgun. I was in the back, laying down—the shock and numbness starting to wear off, and the aches and pains starting to make their presence known.

"Koda finishing things up?" Gio asked quietly, almost respectfully, over the front seat.

I was staring at the ceiling of the crew cab, not really there, not really anywhere. "Yeh, he's gonna stay and clean the scene. I told him to make it look like it was an internal dispute. He's obviously had extensive experience along those lines. Plus, he had to stay and make sure Mace was good to his word. Said he'd maybe wander around for a while afterward and then get home on his own. I asked him to stop on the way and phone in an anonymous tip to Chief Tanner since he wouldn't recognize his voice."

"I never knew nobody who loved the dark and lousy weather as much as Koda," Deity said. "It's gotta be in the genes, man. He be a ghost out there."

Gio looked back again. "D said Mace asked for a favor. What was the favor?"

I started to answer but we hit a pothole and the pain that racked my whole body was instant and lingering. When I got my breath back, I said, "Rather than shooting them, he asked if I'd let them OD. Better to go happy, I guess."

They both were quiet for a minute before Deity broke the silence. "I know they a bunch of sleazebags, and I know it's probably crazy to say, but I think Mace loved that kid. Another time maybe, another place maybe, and maybe under other circumstances, Mace probably be a pretty straight up cat."

"I was thinking the same thing, D," I said as I fluffed my coat for a pillow, hopefully without further injury. "I was thinking the same exact thing."

The night grew quiet once again, and the rain on the roof and windows seemed to abate as we drew closer to Seattle. I could hear both Deity's and Gio's voices in the front seat, and Dean Martin and Doris Day doing a duet on the radio, but I think I was too tired to discern much of anything else.

Gio pulled down his visor and opened the mirror and positioned it so that he could see me. "You all right, Boss."

"No, not right now, guys," I said almost in a whisper. "Don't really think I ever have been . . . don't really think I ever will be."

I saw Gio and Deity exchange a glance and then there was nothing—just the sound of the tires on the road, the cacophony of the wind-swept rain, the melodic movements of the windshield wipers, and the deep sleep of catatonia that only accompanies exhaustion and delusion.

CHAPTER 12

The next morning came early. It was around noon, but it felt early after the previous night's exploits. Deity and Gio had carried me up to my apartment and called a buddy, who was a doctor, to patch me up without a hospital visit on record.

"What the heck happened to him?" Dr. Aaron Gaudin asked when he was led into my room.

"Pillow fight, Doc," Deity said with a straight face. " . . . he lost."

"Well, next time, take the anvil out of the pillowcase prior to striking," Aaron said shaking his head. "I'm going to give him something for the pain and something to help him sleep now that I've sewn and set everything that I can, but call me in the morning if there are problems during the night."

"You got it, Doc," Gio said. "We're gonna crash in the spare bedrooms tonight and take turns checking on him, so we'll let you know if the injuries sustained during the pillow fight continue to worsen."

Aaron looked at them, and then shook his head again in frustration. "If I remember correctly, the last time you guys called I had to plug up a couple bullet holes."

"Those weren't bullet holes, Doc," Deity said. "We'd left a bag of popcorn in the backseat, and when the car got too hot, the popcorn bag started to pop on its own. We was popcorn shrapnel victims."

"That's the best story you can come up with?" Aaron said, rolling his eyes.

"That's our Orville Redenbacher story, Doc," Gio said, "and we're sticking to it."

Aaron zipped up his bag and grabbed his coat. "Just so you know, in my esteemed medical opinion, you guys are lousy liars."

"That's all right, Doc," Deity explained, "we ain't married, so we don't get no practice."

And that, I was told later, was how the night went, though they were able to talk Aaron into some thirty-five-year-old scotch and Cuban cigars before he left . . . the usual payment for medical services rendered.

In the morning, just getting showered and dressed was a process of pain suppression, especially with a fractured arm, and looking in the mirror didn't lift my already dulled spirits much either. The deadly duo suggested I remain lo-pro for a while as well, at least until some of the more severe swelling and bruising went away. The late, great Avon was right, he was definitely a bruiser.

But based upon the scarcity of time, I couldn't really put off tonight's meeting with Kathryn's friend Casper. So at seven o'clock, we once again found ourselves together and at the door of the unknown. This time though, we were inside a climate-controlled apartment building, we were dressed for success, and the chances of getting shot seemed rather remote for a change.

"Casper?" Deity asked, as we got off the elevator and walked to apartment number nine-nineteen.

"Ya got me," I said. "But I hope he's a friendly ghost."

When we got to our appointed destination, I rang the bell, which took the melodic form of *The Entertainer*. As the door opened, I think our host was as taken aback by my looks as I was by his. He was an albino—replete with white hair, pale skin, and pink eyes. But remembering the mirror this morning, he definitely had more cause for alarm. And at least we knew why he was referred to as Casper.

After both of us recovered from our initial shock, he opened the door wider and led us into his darkened den.

"I'd heard you were ugly!" he said, extending his arm to shake my hand and laughing at his own joke.

"I like him already," Gio said from behind me.

"You should see me without makeup," I joked back.

"Or not," he said, one-upping me again.

But to my slight dismay and great discomfort, I had forgotten my current state of being, and as I laughed, I felt my swollen lips split open, and I was once again deemed dracularian, as I dined on my own blood for the twentieth time that day.

Once the introductions were completed, he escorted us further into his apartment, with the most obvious aspects being the lack of light, the sparse furnishings, and plethora of computer and IT equipment. It was a relatively large three-bedroom apartment, with one bedroom reserved for what looked like his place of rest and repose, another adorned with a series of monitors, and the other racked and arrayed with computers and servers.

"Dr. Strangelove, I presume," I said.

Casper followed my gaze and said, "Of a sort. Part IT nerd, part mad scientist, and part child of the night. Since I am obviously albino and not so obviously allergic to the sun, my days are spent sleeping or at my computer banks, and my nights are spent roaming the streets and trying to assist those that anoint the night as well."

We were interrupted by a noise from what I assumed to be the kitchen, and much to my surprise and delight, Kathryn appeared looking even more beautiful than the previous evening. When she saw me, she was nearly as surprised, but much less delighted.

"Oh, good Lord!" she practically screamed and ran over to me. "What in the world happened to your face?"

"A shaving accident," I said, with as much compunction as I could muster.

"Oh, pooh!" she said. "You've been badly hurt." She studied me some more. "Your poor, sweet, handsome face. Are you okay?" She then proceeded to give me a hug around the ribcage that almost brought me to my knees.

She looked at Deity and Gio. "Shouldn't we call a doctor?"

"He's already seen a doctor," Gio offered.

"And?" she said, apparently frustrated with Gio's lack of forthcomence.

"Doc say there ain't no cure for ugly," Deity said. "He think it be terminal."

Kathryn laughed her great laugh and then looked back at me. Her eyes started to moisten as she touched my face tenderly with both hands, like the blind with Braille; first my swollen eyes, then nose, then lingering on my lips. I looked down at her and she met my gaze. "It's amazing to see you again," I said.

She wiped the tears away with the back of her hands. "You always know just what a girl wants to hear." And then she wiped under her lower eyelashes with her finger, as women tend to do, to make sure no imperceptible trace of mascara was running. "I must look horrible," she said, walking over to the mirror in the entry.

"Attrocious!" Deity said.

"Grotesque!" Gio said.

"Hideous!" Casper finished.

Kathryn turned from the mirror immediately with her hands on her perfect hips. "How wonderful, in my time of great doubt, despair, and obvious disrepair, to have such a sweet support system here to strengthen and fortify my fragile feminine ego."

"Beautiful!" Deity said.

"Gorgeous!" Gio said.

"Stunning!" Casper finished.

Kathryn turned her piercing gaze to me. "And you, Mr. Kilbourne? What have you to say for yourself?"

"Prettiest girl in the room," I said with a painful wink.

"Well," she said, shaking her head, "it's a start."

She walked over to Deity and Gio and held out her hand. "I'm Kathryn Rae, universally regarded and currently acknowledged as the prettiest girl in the room."

"In all rooms, Ms. Rae," Deity said with a slight bow at the hips as he shook her hand.

"In all universes, Ms. Rae," Gio said while kissing her hand.

"You may both stay!" she said with obvious glee. Then, she looked back at me. "They're very charming!"

"Yes, their mothers sent them to the finest charm and finishing schools in the country. We're all very proud of them."

Casper took this opportunity to clear his throat, and as we all turned, he said, "Now that we're all members of the Kathryn Rae Fan Club, shall we forgo future accolades and commence to the task at hand, the exact nature of which I am still in ignorance."

We all walked across the dark carpeting and sat on the dark couches, and looked around at the dark furniture and furnishings, encapsulated by the dark walls and ceiling.

"My apologies for the dramatic and depressed color scheme, guys, but my afflictions make me very light sensitive. Televisions and computer screens are only tolerable with extremely dark sunglasses, and I can only be outside if I have on special dark contacts or wraparound shades, and then only for a few hours before they start to burn."

Deity looked over at Gio. "See, I told you black folk are easier to look at than white folk."

I tried to ignore the daycare duo and get back to basics. I explained our current situation to Casper, or Cas, as he liked to be referred to. I was appreciative of the fact that he let me go through the entire chronology without interruption. When I was finished, he sat back, and I assumed assimilated the information that had been presented.

"Okay," he said. "I am up-to-date on a historical level. What have you done in regards to locating her to-date, so that I might know how best to further aid and abet."

"Gio and Deity have talked with all the local authorities and assistance programs on both sides of the law. I've had some personal acquaintances go a little deeper than that." I looked over and gestured at Kathryn, "Our mutual friend, Jenner, has had some folks at Vertical Alternatives run the name and aliases through their public and private databases as well, and they go dark about a year ago. The information gleaned so far has her heavy into drugs and prostitution up until then, and then off the map."

Kathryn chimed in at that point. "Cas, maybe you can tell these gentlemen a little about why I thought you might be able to help, over and above their already exhaustive efforts. And while you're doing that, I'll pretend I'm domestic and get us each a nice glass of wine."

We couldn't argue with Kathryn's domestic pursuits, so we settled in to listen. Casper sat back in his chair, unconsciously tucked his long, white, page-boy hair behind his ear, and took a deep breath.

"Well, since I have been saddled with my afflictions since birth, I have always been somewhat of a night owl as you might expect—sleeping or lounging around during the day and working or heading out at night. Since I have always had a passion and natural inclination toward technology, multiple companies employ me to manage and oversee their nocturnal networks. It's easy and it's excellent pay with only the occasional e-commerce emergency."

Kathryn reemerged with a couple of bottles of Napa Valley's finest and five glasses and handed me the wine opener. "Would you care to do the honors, my charismatic Quasimodo?"

"I knew you only loved me for my looks," I said, while pretending that opening the wine was easy and painless in my current state.

She patted me softly on the head. "Unfortunately, for you my little troglodyte, it appears that you'll now have to live your life without love or looks."

Since I wasn't making any headway with Kathryn, I turned my attention back to Cas, and he continued.

"By heading out at night, and by that I mean the witching hours, typically two to six in the morning, I became more and more familiar with the Seattle's nightlife, and they with me. I became somewhat of a trusted oddity in a sea of other oddities. And as I have become more and more of a trusted confidant over the years and more accepted within the inner circles, I am exposed to more than I care to talk about. There is a subversive subculture that most day dwellers are unaware of, a nighttime network of people, places, and possibilities that would boggle your mind; hookers, drug dealers, robbers, thieves, partiers, city workers, nightshifters, the homeless, and an equal amount of miscreants that are there to partake of or participate in the sins the cover and cancer of night can provide."

As I watched Cas, I could almost see his pink eyes look inward as he mentally recalled every after-dark atrocity that he had either been told of or exposed to. Kathryn had mentioned that Cas was acting as an intermediary to the nightlife in respect to making them aware of the free services and programs available and helping to staff and operate many of the volunteer agencies—health, education, housing, fund raising, etc. Cas was a frontline guy, and probably trusted as one of their own. Just another 'midnight misfit', as Jenner referred to them, who had made his work life his life's work.

" . . . so I guess what I'm trying to say is that I may be able to track her whereabouts," and then he paused, "or remains. There are definitely a number of folks who would talk to me that would trust and talk to no one else. As I mentioned before, there are places where hookers and drug addicts go as they continue down the spiral staircase. Places unknown to most and unimaginable to all."

"Like chicken ranches and body farms," Gio said. "Yesterday's high-priced harlot turns to or gets turned on to drugs, and he or she become's today's half-hour hooker, and eventually tomorrow's body by the minute."

Cas gave him a knowing nod. "Exactly. If they can remain just a drug addict or just a prostitute, their lives typically will stay within the worst-case clinical definitions of use and abuse, but it is the combination of the two that leads to eventual scenarios definitively less kind than death. In its kindest classification, it is torment, terror, and torture, but I've heard of places that facilitate a laundry list of atrocities and perversions that only the sickest and most deviant minds can conjure up."

"So where does that leave us?" I asked, not sure where he was going with his monologue. I appreciated the background information, but most of those in attendance already knew ninety-nine percent of what he had just iterated. My guess was that it was his way of leading into his conclusion, whatever that may be.

Cas grabbed his wineglass and stood, smiling weakly to Kathryn as he walked over to the blackout curtains. He parted them only minutely to check if it was dark enough to open them, and after some equivocation, went ahead and drew the curtains. Though it looked pitch black to me, whatever light he sensed made him visibly recoil. And he turned immediately away from the window and back to the four of us.

"Okay, here are my four educated options. The first option is the dream that she somehow relocated, in or out of the profession, and that she is now a loving wife and mother somewhere in suburbia. That she had the mentality, money, or means to move on her own is pretty slim. But reality dictates that since she hasn't been seen or heard of in a year, the next best option, oddly enough, is that she is dead, a Jane Doe death certificate at any number of morgues never to be heard from again. The third option is potentially more dire than death, and that would be that she was sold off to a body farm anywhere in the world. Death at that level is indiscriminate and inevitable anyway, so option three is just a brief reprieve from option two."

Cas moved away from the window, checked his watch, and then sat back down. "So in my expert opinion, if you want to call it that, is that she has either died or distanced herself. With your connections and resources, and those of the city, county, state, and non-profit, surely she would have turned up somewhere. She could very easily have died or been murdered anywhere within a hundred-mile radius and been dumped in the forest, the desert, a body of water, or an abandoned building. The scenarios are endless in the dark depths of the human condition. And she may have just as readily hopped on a bus or boat and be a corner cutie anywhere in the world."

We were all quiet then, each alone with our own thoughts and conclusions. Cas looked at his watch again and excused himself to check his array of computers and servers. I looked at Kathryn, and she took my hand and squeezed it, her amazing eyes moist with emotion.

"Is it Cas's story or my face that brings tears to your eyes?" I said gently.

"Both," she said sweetly. "Both are hard to look at or think about in the light of day."

I'm sure I was about to respond with a brilliant comeback, but I was interrupted by Gio.

"I hate to always be the math genius here," Gio said in a semi-whisper, "but Cas mentioned four options, and I'm pretty sure he only gave us three. Could be a simple mistake on his part, or maybe there's another option he's reluctant to talk about."

We could hear Cas in the other room keyboarding, checking monitors, replacing disks, and hot swapping hard drives. Inside his sanctuary, a rainbow array of iridescent lights bounced off the walls, floor, and ceiling, as the monitors and computers traded bits and bytes and ran the web-weary world.

"Where were we?" Cas asked as he reentered the room.

"We were wondering about option four," Gio said.

That stopped Cas in his tracks. "Did I say there was a fourth option?" he asked with a smile and a little hesitation.

"As a matter of fact, you did," Gio added. "But what we're trying to figure out is if you want to talk about it and if we want to hear about it."

Cas continued to stand there a minute looking at all of us and taking in our expectant stares. He placed his hands behind his head and interlaced his fingers and looked up at the ceiling and then out the window. After another long look at us, he puffed out his cheeks and exhaled heavily.

"I don't even know where to begin, guys," he said, now once again at his post in front of the window. I casually looked down at the carpet beneath his feet and noticed the wear and tear, but only in that spot. I couldn't even imagine the hours it would take standing in that one spot, in front of the window, to compromise the carpet in such an emaciated manner. His life must have truly been the vigil of the voyeur, bereft of the physical faculties that would permit a normal life in the light of day.

"In fact," he started again, "I don't even know for sure if it exists or why I really brought it up. It's rumor and innuendo and speculation and conjecture and legend, and a thousand other synonyms that in the aggregate still don't really amount to much more than myth. Over the last couple of decades, I've heard it whispered about and alluded to, but never confirmed or substantiated by anyone with a sane or sober moment. Anyone I've ever pressed hard on the subject got either instant amnesia or a look of terror in their eyes that basically rendered them mute."

"Sewer City. Tunnel Town. Devil's Dungeon," Deity said, almost in a whisper to himself.

Cas looked over at Deity with wide eyes. "You've heard of it."

By the expression on his face, I don't think Deity even knew he said it out loud. "Yeh, I heard of it, but I heard of it like I heard of Atlantis, and King Solomon's mine, and women who don't want a commitment. Nobody thinks any of them really exist."

I couldn't really argue with that since I'd never come across any of them either, but keeping quiet with Kathryn within face-slapping distance didn't sound like too bad of an idea.

I looked back at Cas, who was grinning widely at Deity's statement. "So do you think this place really exists, and if so, why do you think Chrissy might be there, and if she is, why do you think she'd still be alive?"

"Whoa, one question at a time," Cas said, as Kathryn poured us more wine and put a little hummus on a cracker for me. "But okay, here's my hypothesis. I think it may exist based upon the fact that everyone seems to be afraid to talk about even the possibility that it does exist. I think your client's daughter may be there because she, so far, appears to be nowhere else and in a downward professional spiral with drug addictions. And if she is really there, I think she may still be alive because she's, according to you, abnormally attractive and also because they may be marketing her as a senator's daughter or future president's progeny or Little Rich Girl, or maybe a hundred other titles they could utilize to entice or appease prospective buyers. I imagine generic Jane Doe's are used, abused, and disposed of rather quickly if this place actually exists. But a girl with a certain look, talent, or pedigree might be kept alive for a while . . . fortunately or unfortunately, depending on how you look at it."

"So where do we go from here?" Kathryn asked.

"We?" I said looking at her with a surprised look on my face.

She smiled her sweet, sorrowful smile at me, almost like she was looking at a poor, lost dog. "Jenner said I am to take care of you because you are on a path of self-destruction; and based upon your face, I think he might be right."

I looked at Deity and Gio for help, but I could tell they were already happily on her side and loving the grief she seemed predisposed to heap upon me. Fortunately enough for me, Cas interrupted the assault on my autonomy and offered reprieve.

"I'll tell you what. Today is Thursday, why don't you give me the weekend to try and do a little detective work and see what I can verify either way. I'll touch base with you on Monday, and we can update. I'm taking for granted that your twin towers here will be running down their own leads as well, and maybe we can find enough consensus or commonalities to either semi-confidently confirm or deny the existence of this place. Deal?"

I looked at everyone for their acquiescence, and we all seemed in agreement. "Okay," I said. "Let's all plan on meeting here on Monday night, and we can exchange notes."

After a few minutes of small talk, Gio and Deity went with Cas into the techno-world and got a tour of Cas's midnight madness in the two adjoining rooms.

"Well, my disfigured dreamboat," Kathryn teased, "are you going to tell me what happened to your face?"

"Is there something wrong with my face?" I responded in mock terror. "What will happen to my modeling career?"

"I believe radio may be your best medium now," she said patting my leg.

We looked at each other then for a moment, and I'm sure it was more fun for me that it was for her, but whatever it was, it was the most fun I'd had all day.

"So, Ms. Rae," I said, with as much charm and as little pain as I could muster, "would you like to come to the City this weekend and dine with me? And feel free to invite Jenner if you'd like."

She looked sorrowful. "Actually, I am flying to New York this weekend to meet Victoria and do Broadway. But I am touched and honored by the offer."

"Is Victoria the striking blonde in the photos back at your place?"

"Yes, she is my close friend, and we are infinitely and intimately connected. Her husband is of wealthy European aristocracy, so we don't get to see each other often. Just when she can say she's getting away with friends for an American shopping jaunt."

"Are you in love with her, if you don't mind me asking?"

She smiled sweetly. "I think you and I are beyond secrets at this point. I love her dearly and deeply, but I'm not sure 'in love' is the correct term. I think 'in love' means commitment, and monogamy, and normalcy, and family, and future, and planning, and permanence. And I don't think we'll ever have any of those to share with each other. And I think we are both okay with the ambiguity and nebulousness that that engenders."

She got up and walked to the window. "Besides, I don't have time for much else anyway. I have my art and my causes and my home," and then she looked at me, earnestly, almost expectantly, "and now, I have you."

"Your corsair and confidant," I said as I walked over, and stood behind her looking out the window. She leaned back against me, she with her arms folded, me with my arms hanging at my sides. After a while, I put my arms on her shoulders and kissed the back of her head.

"My good, my bad, and my ugly!" she said, and started to laugh again. So I took a quick step back, and she almost lost her balance and fell. But being the fully ingrained gentleman that I am, I caught her, painfully, before she could drop completely to the floor.

"Unhand me, you beast," she said in feigned fury.

So I said, "Yes, beauty," and let her drop unceremoniously to the floor.

The sound of her fall brought the techno-three out of the other room in a hurry, but the sound of her laughter caught them equally by surprise. They looked at her still on the floor in hysterics, and then at me. I just looked at her, shaking my head, and then back at them with my hands out and shrugging my shoulders, "It was the wine, I think. She's drunk. Poor girl can't handle her alcohol."

I walked over and carefully picked her up off the ground. She was breathing heavily and tearing greatly from the laughter. "You big jerk," she said between fits, "I can't believe you dropped me on the floor."

I was dabbing her eyes with a napkin that I picked up off the end table. "Just following orders, ma'am," I said. "Just following orders."

"Well, the next time I ask you to do something, it will be definitively more pleasant than a bruised bottom."

"It looks swollen," Gio said from behind her, and we all started laughing again.

"Oh, shut up!" she said with a smile and trotted off mid-tirade to the nearest bathroom to fix her face. I envied her the ability to fix her face with mere water and makeup; mine would take an indeterminate amount of time and a team of plastic surgeons.

As I started to crumple up the now tear-dampened napkin to throw it away, I noticed the Holiday Inn emblem. I looked up at Cas, "Holiday Inn napkins?"

Deity looked at him in amusement. "Say it ain't so, Cas!"

Cas just smiled coyly and shrugged his shoulders. "What can I say guys, I'm on a budget. But I swear that's all I took."

"I believe you, Cas," I said. "That's why I'll just leave this Holiday Inn napkin in the Hilton Hotels ashtray, next to the Marriott pen, and never mention it again."

"Oops!" he said sheepishly and with a guilty grin.

Later, when Kathryn finally came out of the bathroom looking sweeter than a platter full of rice crispy treats, we bid a fond farewell to Cas, and the four of us rode down the elevator together.

"May I have a ride home?" Kathryn asked as we walked outside to the calamity and cacophony of the city streets. "Jenner dropped me off after taking me to dinner to gossip about you and said you'd be a dear and drive me home."

"Well, I don't want to lose my reputation as a 'dear', so I guess I'm obligated."

"G and I may as well do a little rummaging around, while we're down here, Bawse, and see what we can dig up on the down low," Deity said. "We'll be back at the City in a couple of hours and help Diane and the boys lock up, so you's can go home after dropping off little missy and get some beauty sleep."

That said, they both turned and gave Kathryn a warm hug good-bye.

"It was great meeting you both," she said. "Thanks for letting me into the boys club for a night."

"Class and beauty negate the need for an invitation, Ms. Rae," Gio said in his best Italian accent. "And it was a pleasure for us as well."

"And tell Cas we appreciated his help and hospitality," Deity said. "Casper definitely be a friendly ghost."

Kathryn smiled brightly. "He's a sweet and decent friend, and an honest and dedicated humanist. Though I did notice the towels in his bathroom all had The Four Seasons logo embroidered on them."

Gio, Deity, and I all looked at each other and burst into laughter.

Kathryn just looked at us in obvious confusion. "What did I say?"

CHAPTER 13

A slight veil of mist began to envelope the city as I tucked Kathryn safely into my Mercedes CSR500 and turned on Tchaikovsky for a symphonic serenade.

"Why a Mercedes?" she asked, "why not a Lexus or BMW?"

"Because I can afford a Mercedes," I said.

"Only the best?" she said.

"Only the best!" I said. "In luxury sedans, Mercedes is unparalleled. In SUVs, sans kids, I'm a Range Rover guy."

"Whatever happened to Baseball, Hot Dogs, Apple Pie, and Chevrolet?"

"An antiquated theory, 'tis the dawn of a new generation. Now it's Football, Hamburgers, Cherry Pie, and Ford."

"Oh, I see!" she said as she tilted her seat back slightly and closed her eyes either in appreciation or exhaustion. I grabbed the royal blue Polo cashmere blanket off the backseat and spread it over her. She never opened her eyes or offered to assist, she just smiled and whispered a thanks. Since she had her eyes closed, I surreptitiously maneuvered the rearview mirror, so that I could steal a glance at her as I drove. She was unquestionably one of the most stunning women I had ever seen, but it wasn't overt beauty, nor was it ostentatious in its grandeur. None of the theatrics or flamboyance of Jess's beauty; it was an exceptional aggregation of looks, brains, compassion, and humor.

"Are you looking at me in the rearview mirror?" she said without opening her eyes.

"No, I'm trying to avoid ambient illuminated glare from the overhead streetlights and headlights, so as not to incur or encounter star burst or strobe blindness while operating passenger-laden high-performance machinery, therefore adjusting all rear-facing reflective devices to a thirty-degree optimal performance angularity."

"Oh, that was my second guess!" she said with a giggle and reached out and held my hand. "Where are we going?"

"I assumed we were driving you home," I said.

"Oh."

"Oh?"

"Oh!"

"Would you like to go get a glass of wine somewhere?" I asked.

"Yes, please."

"Do you care where we go?"

"Yes, I do." She said.

"Care to share the destination with me?"

"Well, it's still early, and Jenner said your penthouse is spectacular and must be seen to be believed," she said, still with her eyes closed.

"That's because he was the interior designer."

"I know, he mentioned that too!"

"Whatever happened to women playing hard to get?" I asked.

"An antiquated theory, 'tis the dawn of a new generation," she said. "Now women don't play hard to get, we play hard to forget."

"Oh, I see," I said.

Fifteen minutes later, we arrived at my building and handed over the keys to the valet. As we walked into the building and to the private elevator for the penthouse suites, I looked through the lounge and saw Roiko. He was talking to the cocktail waitresses across the bar as he was polishing glasses, and looked up as he heard the elevator ping its arrival. He smiled as he saw me and raised his dark Russian unibrow when he noticed Kathryn. I smiled and winked at him, and he just shook his big head and mane. I was sure the "Russian Inquisition" would continue the next time we talked.

My penthouse, atop the Rothschild Building, was angled much like the triangulated top of the Washington Monument. The three-thousand square feet on the main floor offered a grand great room and four corner guest suites, each with it's own private bath and corner-based dual views. In between each bedroom were four ancillary rooms; an exercise room, an office, a mini-theatre, and a library/den. In between each of those eight rooms was a small, secluded sitting area that looked out over each area's vista of choice via the large floor-to-ceiling windows.

The master bedroom sat on the upper floor open balcony, centralized within the free space that Jenner had so meticulously engineered. It looks, at first glance, that it is suspended in midair by eight large naval anchor chains in retracted repose, the individual links the size of dinner plates, but was actually supported by the half-circle kitchen and half-circle bar that sat directly beneath it in the center of the main floor. Two sets of staircases granted ingress and egress in traversed fashion. Jenner called it his "hi-tech retreat, meets alpine chalet, meets bachelor bravado, meets intellectual adolescent, meets nautical noir" creation. Basically, lots of polished woods, darkened blues, and lightened upholsteries.

I felt about my penthouse much the same as I'm sure Kathryn felt about her home. It was refuge and sanctuary, and an elevated escape from the diatribe and detritus that seemed to encapsulate and categorize my current existence.

As the elevator doors opened, Kathryn emerged with a look of wonderment. "Wow!"

I looked at her. "By golly, I believe that is exactly the response that Jenner was looking for. And it is exactly the same thing I said when I first saw the finished product."

"Oh, Shad, I love it!" she said excitedly. "May I wander, may I meander, may I muse?"

"Mi casa es su casa, Senorita," I said. "I'll check messages while you peruse the premises."

And with that she slipped off her shoes and spent the next twenty minutes going through every room, touching every fabric and piece of artwork, and it sounded like she was also looking in every drawer, cupboard, and closet upstairs.

"If you'd like," I yelled up to her, "I could empty the vacuum bag and dump the trash cans on the floor just in case you missed anything. I'm glad the maid was here this morning; you left no stone unturned."

"You big liar," she said, bouncing buoyantly down the stairs from my bedroom. "You don't have a maid; Jenner says you rarely let anyone up here and you do all your own cleaning and washing."

I gave her by most self-effacing grin. "Well, you know the saying, if you want it done right . . ."

"I know," she said, and she dropped luxuriously down on one of the couches. "I don't let anyone invade my inner sanctum either. And it was part of the reason I asked to see your bachelor pad, to see if a person of your extreme privacy would allow me the merit of a visit."

"Feeling honored?" I asked.

Kathryn looked at me comtemplatively for a few seconds before answering. "Touched, actually."

I smiled at her and grabbed a seat on the couch across from her. "Well, I tend to make rare exceptions for the exceptionally rare."

The brilliance and staccato of lightning interrupted our conversation, and the ensuing roll of thunder made Kathryn close her eyes and visibly shudder.

"Are you cold?" I asked. "Can I get you a blanket?"

"You're sweet, no. Thunder tends to frighten me. Typically, Daddy was always gone, so I had to weather the storms by myself, and thinking of him off flying somewhere in those storms always scared me as well. I was always afraid, prophetically enough, that someday he would not return."

"Well, you're safe here, little lady," I said in my best impersonation of John Wayne. Unfortunately, the gesture tore open my cracked lips, and I felt the warmth in my mouth yet again.

"You're bleeding," she said, "I'll be right back."

"Where are you going?" I inquired to her backside as she navigated the furniture and mounted the stairs once more.

"To get your first-aid kit," she said, "you're a mess."

"How do you know I have a first aid kit and where it is?" I yelled.

"I saw it earlier as I was rummaging through all your things, you dolt."

"Oh, silly me, I forgot about the 'help yourself' policy to my life."

"Take solace, dearheart," she called from up above, "all men are silly."

I was wondering what was taking so long when she finally descended from on high.

"Ta da!" she said, stopping to pose on the balcony's edge with hips to one side and both arms high in the air. She had changed out of her faded, form-fitting jeans and silken sapphire blouse, and donned my Notre Dame sweats which were about ten sizes too big for her. She had put her thick and lustrous hair back in a ponytail and grabbed a pair of my wool socks as well.

"Sexy," I said, "very elegant, very glam."

"'Snuggly couture' is the proper vogue terminology, you boorish cretin. It was all the rage in Cannes this year."

"Actually," I said in my snobbiest voice, "I was in Cannes this year for the film festival with friends and none of the starlets wore sweats, baggy socks, or ponytails on the red carpet."

"Harlots in Babylon," she said. "What could the fabulously rich, gloriously attractive, and internationally famous possibly know about current fashion trends?"

"Good point, Ace. My mistake." And couldn't help but laugh once more at her continuing antics.

"Okay," she said, as she straddled my lap and opened the first-aid kit. "No more laughing. Doctor's orders."

She proceeded to carefully dab my mouth with medicated lip balm and expertly touch up the cuts and scrapes with a Q-Tip and anti-bacterial cream. With the scissors, she trimmed the stitches, and with a pair of tweezers, gently tucked some of the skin back into proper alignment. With her face only inches from mine, it was fun to see her concentrating so hard on the task at hand.

"You smell wonderful, Doc," I said, as she blew gently on the scrapes when she saw me wince at her mending.

"Shush, vermin, you're violating the doctor/patient relationship," she said as she continued to clean and repair my damaged face. "And your ugly mug is in dire need of my experience and expertise, and deepest sympathies."

I let that slide. "By the way, Herr Doktor, how is it that you seem so adept at this calling?"

"I volunteer occasionally at the Free Clinic on the weekends with the employees of some of the art galleries I own. So I see a lot of this type of thing, along with the occasional gunshot or stab wound."

She grabbed my chin and moved my head side to side and up and down, and seemed to be pleased with her work; but probably not with her patient.

"There, all done, Scarface." she said.

"Am I beautiful?"

"Hmmm," she said leaning back in evaluation mode. "You're less ugly."

"Well," I said, "it's a start. So what's on our agenda? What would you like to do, Ms. Rae?"

"Can I spend the night?" she asked, biting her lower lip in anticipation of my response.

"Yes," I said without hesitation. That was rule number one in my book of wisdom: that whenever a beautiful woman asks to spend the night . . . always answer in the affirmative. You can always figure out the motives later.

"Even on my terms?"

"Even on my couch," I said.

"You're sweet and chivalrous, but I trust you," she said, her eyes wide with excitement. "So how 'bout we open a bottle of wine, pop some popcorn, lay on this gigantic and comfy couch, watch an old movie, I can fall asleep on your chest halfway through, and you can make me a fabulous breakfast in the morning."

"Well," I said looking contemplative, "you're very bossy and obnoxious, but you're also bright, beautiful, built, and bemusing, so I guess you can stay!"

"Yay!" she said. "Okay, what are my cabernet choices?"

"They are numerous, but of what is readily available, I would suggest the Krug, the Cakebread, the Clos Du Val, or the Hourglass."

"Okay, Hourglass," she said with much enthusiasm. "What about popcorn?"

"Orville Redenbacher or Cinema's Best."

"Okay, Orville. What about the movie?"

"They too are numerous, what is your heart's desire?"

"Do you have Casablanca or Dr. Zhivago?"

"Both."

"Really? I'm impressed. But let's go with Bogart, because of the stormy weather outside, because I'm gorgeous, and because you're in love with me and can't have me, and because you're a bar owner and a sucker for lost causes."

"I'm not in love with you," I said defiantly.

She grabbed my face with both her hands. "Yes, you are, you big dope. You just don't know it yet."

"Oh!"

"What music can I listen to while you change?"

"If you can figure out the universal remote, I believe the first five cds are the Rat Pack, Andrea Boccelli, the London Philharmonic Orchestra, the Carpenters, and the always fabulous John Denver."

"Okay, let's go with the Philharmonic," she said. "You go change."

I started to get up, and she continued to sit on my lap.

"Well?" I asked.

"Well, what?" she said with a slight smile, feigning ignorance.

"Are you going to get off me?"

"What'sa matter, big fella, too weak to move me?"

Not one to be denigrated without a fight, I stood up with her still on my lap, but now hanging on for dear life with both arms around my neck and her legs wrapped around my waist. "Kiss me you fool," she said with much laughter and teasing.

Instead, I peeled her off me and threw her gently back on the couch. "Not on the first date, you Mata Hari."

As I turned and started to walk away to go change, I could hear her start to laugh. "You big lummox, I can't believe you just cast me aside like chattel."

"If you gain any more weight, you'll be cast aside like cattle," I said, and made a run for the upstairs before she could find anything to throw.

As I was changing into my BYU sweats, Kathryn called up to me and said, "Do you want me to make you a quick drink?"

"Sure, what are you having?"

"I thought I'd slip out of these wet clothes and into a dry martini," she joked. "What about you?"

"I'll take a tall Barbancourt and Diet Coke, thanks."

"Hey, you own about fifty bars," she said. "What is the official ruling on the proper number of olives in a martini?"

"Two," I yelled down.

"Say's who?" she asked loudly in return.

"Says Frank Sinatra, the martini master."

"Oh," she said in a preoccupied voice.

I came down the stairs and walked around the corner, and she handed me the olive jar to open. I took the jar from her and popped it open. "Are you admitting to my superior physical strength?"

"No," she said, taking the opened jar from me and plopping a green olive into her mouth. "I'm reminding you of my superior mental strength by forcing you into servitude."

She looked more closely at my sweats and then at hers. "BYU and Notre Dame sweats in the same drawer? Aren't you afraid of inter-drawer hostilities?"

"No, the socks and boxers act as peacekeepers," I defended. "Besides, both are Christian universities, so we celebrate the similarities. I got the Notre Dame gear from a couple buddies who graduated from there, and the BYU stuff from one of my bouncers at the City. Most of the big islanders in my employ are Mormon, which means they're impeccably honest, hard working, don't fool around, and don't drink or steal, and are predisposed to service and charity. A dishonest employee can cost me a fortune, and the waitresses love having guys around they can trust. Plus, because they're Mormon, most have served two year missions abroad and most of them are bilingual, which is always a bonus in the international melting pot that Seattle boasts."

Kathryn grabbed the drinks and I gathered the rest of goodies, and we traversed the expanse back to the main couches.

"Why two olives?" she asked.

"What?" I said, a little preoccupied with proper furniture, food and beverage placement.

"Why did Old Blue Eyes say there should always be two olives in a martini?"

I smiled at her. "One for him, and one for the next beautiful woman that walked into the room."

"Always the romantic," she said. "Why can't all men be so lovely?"

I looked at her in disgust. "Probably because all men are scared to death of being referred to as lovely."

"Good point, Poindexter," she said. Then she looked around, "Hey, there's no TVs down here. What are we going to do?"

"If you'll hand me the universal remote, I'll show you a little Jenner magic."

Kathryn handed me the remote, and I pushed a few buttons in each of the specific zonings, and TVs started to pop up out of the large end-tables like meerkats throughout the great room. I pushed another button and the music shut off and the lights dimmed.

"Very high tech," she said. "Jenner loves gadgets. What else can that thing do?"

"If you try to make a pass at me during the movie, there's an ejection seat button that I can push to grant you the gift of flight. I call it the anti-hussie button."

She rolled her eyes, "I'll try to refrain from any overt physical gestures. And speaking of physicality, give me some background on Gio and Deity. How long have you guys been together?"

I tried to think back chronologically. "I guess Deity and I have been together almost five years. He was initially special ops in the military, then turned global mercenary with a group of his comrades, and then came back to the states and started his own private security firm. While he was doing security for various clients at my clubs, we kept running into each other and became friends. He eventually got tired of the wide array of hours and egos and took me up on an offer to come be my head of security, and we've been together ever since."

"What about Gio?" she asked with genuine interest and concern. "Jenner said you guys weren't always the best of friends."

I laughed at first, thinking back on Gio's initial dislike and distrust of me. But in order to tell Kathryn the whole story I had to make sure we were equally as informationally exclusive with each other. I looked at her frankly. "To what extent can I trust you?"

She looked back at me equally as frank. "You can trust me to the extent you need to Shad, and I think you know that. But know that I understand the seriousness of what I think you are sometimes forced to do, and I take no umbrage at you needing to hear it from my lips as confirmation."

"Thanks," I said. "I am comfortable sharing my life with you as you know, but this touches on the lives of others, and I needed your word."

"You have it, Semi-Handsome," she said, caressing my cheek with the back of her hand and fingers. "Now, open the wine and commence with the story."

I opened the Hourglass Cabernet as she ran over to the bar and popped the popcorn. "Do you have a large bowl or do all confirmed bachelors eat their popcorn right out of the bag?"

"I think there's a big tupperware thingy in the bottom cupboard, smart aleck."

"Hey, there's a whole cupboard in here full of Pop-Tarts."

"That's my health food cupboard. Don't mess with the breakfast of royalty."

"Yes, Your Majesty," she said.

After we had settled in on the same couch facing each other, I gave Kathryn the background on Gio. "Gio is the urban assailant version of Deity—high school, college, FBI, police detective, and currently one of the reigning three stooges."

She laughed. "Why FBI and then detective? Did he not like it?"

"Actually, he was married at the time to his college sweetheart. He was going through the academy, then national postings, and she was going through med school and then her internship and they encountered a little relational rift. So he quit the bureau and joined Seattle's finest to help ease their angst, and she cut back her hours and her ambition at the hospital to do the same."

"It's tough when two ambitious and driven individuals are matrimonialized," she said. "It doesn't leave much room for romance and relational reinvestment."

"And there were other issues as well," I added. "They had both initially wanted kids, and now she didn't. She was going to have a small private practice and a modest income, and now, she wanted to be the world's foremost pediatric cardiologist, and it brought with it substantial notoriety and compensation. They swore they'd always reserve weekends for each other, only to find out that criminals and cardiologists are disrespectful of design and work within their own pathologies."

"So Gio was being trivialized relationally, financially, professionally, and socially, rendered childless, and therefore minimalized and emasculated."

"Exactly. And as their hours and separations got longer, their tolerances and tempers got shorter, and their relationship digressed and eventually disintegrated."

"That's so sad," she said. "Especially, when they were both securing the success that they had both always wanted for themselves and each other. But how did you two come into contact and contention?" And then she straightened her legs and put them in my lap. "And how come you're not rubbing my feet and filling my glass?"

I laughed at the non sequitur and hurriedly went about my domestic duties. After the wine had been poured and the foot rubbing had commenced, I continued the quasi compendium. "Gio was the rising star within the force—a no-nonsense detective of great intellect, energy, ambition, arrogance, and attitude; and because of his FBI ties . . . unlimited resources; he could outwork, outsmart, outfight, outmaneuver, and out-discipline all his contemporaries within the department. He was a man possessed, a man on a mission to 'out relevant' his wife." And I thought about it for a minute. "But he was also a boy scout, a by-the-book bastion of letter-of-the-law ludicrousy. He was the reigning king of 'Quid pro quo.' And since I am more interpretive and selective in my definition of justice, we'd continue to run into each other at both ends of those initiatives and energies. He was the very visible long arm of the law; I was the almost invisible strong arm of the just."

"But wait, aren't they basically the same?"

"Yes, and no," I equivocated. "If a guy molested a child, Gio wanted the law to prevail, I wanted justice to prevail. I was all about outcome, Gio was all about procedure."

"How did he know it was you behind the scenes?"

"Rumor, reputation, research, relationships. The Seattle chief of police and I have become amicable antagonists. Most of what I do that he knows of he privately lauds and publicly loathes. But we both pretty much agree on the same 'bad guys off the streets' premise. So in regards to my existence in their realm of responsibility, Gio had always pushed for a 'terminate' stance, whereas the chief had always sided with a 'tolerance' stance."

Kathryn sat there in full repose, wide-eyed and attentive, her wineglass resting on her lower lip as she listened with full focus. "So how in the world did two adversaries become two associates?"

"As fate would have it, and to make a long, complicated story short, Gio's wife ended up having an affair with another prominent surgeon who she thought shared her same adorations, hours, and ambitions; only to find out that he was pursuing the same activities and abuses with other ladies of equal status. When she confronted him about it and iterated her decision to end it, he beat her up and pushed her down a flight of stairs, resulting in the breaking of her back and being reduced to a wheelchair."

"Oh my God, how tragic," she said with her hand now over her mouth. "I'm so sorry for them both."

"It ripped Gio apart. He almost felt like he was the one that pushed her down the stairs, since he felt like he was the one that pushed her into the arms of another man in the first place. She clearly felt embarrassed and humiliated and all the other requisite shades of human emotion, and didn't want to prosecute. Both she and Gio were guilt ridden and both felt at fault, but the only difference being that Gio wanted to prosecute to the full extent of the law, and she blamed herself and didn't want to drag Gio into a public scandal or ruin her hard-earned reputation. Even when Gio did some investigative background on the guy and found out he was a habitual user and abuser, Angela's psyche was still too fragile to press charges."

"What about the medical community and the press?" she asked. "Wasn't she pretty prominent in those circles?"

"With Gio's obvious connection to the police and Angela's connections at the hospital, they were able to get away with calling it a random act of violence conducted during an attempted mugging or rape. So rather than the humiliation and condemnation of an affair, she was allotted the sympathy and compassion of an arbitrary attack. There was a lot of skepticism and conjecture within the press and both professional communities, but if she was sticking to her story, there wasn't much anyone could do. And visibly in her condition, and with the sympathies of the city and medical community, no one tried too hard."

I poured us some more wine and grabbed a couple handfuls of Orville's best. "So anyway, one night, overwrought with guilt, anger, and alcohol, Gio tailed the doctor to a club, and as he got out of the car, he beat him unconscious, dragged him under a parked car, punctured the gas tank with a screwdriver, and torched the guy. After that, he drove around for a while and then showed up on my doorstep in somewhat of a mental stupor. After a couple hours of coffee and conversation, we figured out he didn't want to go to jail for life and that I could use a man of his special qualification and experience. So Deity and I immediately took Gio on a camping trip for about five days up on the northern border, supposedly with no access to paper, internet, or phones, and fortified our alibi. Koda came up every other day with supplies and updates. It also gave Gio time to heal a little mentally, and time for any dermatological traces and physical abrasions to disappear. By the time we got back into town, most of it had blown over based upon no real known connection between the two anyway. When the eventual and inevitable leak came out about all the interrelationships, it was two months later, the police force was unified behind him, Shane Lowe was representing him, and Deity and I were offering a rock-solid alibi. Two weeks later, Gio was in my employ, and he, Deity, and I have been a trio ever since. Almost four years now that I think about it."

I looked across at Kathryn again and saw the sorrow and compassion on her face. She got up and crawled over and rested her head on my chest, and curled up into a ball. After a few minutes of silence, she finally spoke up. "What a horrible, dreadful story. And what a waste. It pains me to my core to think of what promise they all had, what all of them had to go through, and what they still probably must go through on a daily basis."

I rubbed her back a little. "Well, if there's a silver lining, it's that the bad guy dies, Gio and Angela have salvaged a friendship, and I have gained a trusted friend and partner."

"So they're friends still?" she asked sitting back up.

"Yeh, good friends. There's still a lot of love and pain involved, but they continue to work through the webbing."

"Does Gio have any regrets in relation to killing the nemesis?"

"At first, I don't think he really did because of the revenge and rage that compelled the act in the first place. And he knew that the doc had no wife or kids and no living family, but when he had some time to contemplate the full ramifications of his actions, he realized that a gifted pediatric surgeon was gone and that that might cost some children their lives or at least the quality of their lives, which is why we spend a lot of time, money, and energy on research now, to make sure that if someone goes away, the reverberations aren't crippling or catastrophic to those intertwined with the target."

"Yuck!" she said as if she had a bad taste in her mouth.

"I know, it gets yucky a lot, but hopefully justice prevails in the majority of cases."

She looked up at me. "I'm sure it does, and I'm sure Edmund Burke applauds your efforts."

"As in '*all that is necessary for the triumph of evil is that good men do nothing*?'"

"Yes, my good man, that is it exactly," she beamed. "Now, should we watch Casablanca and seek the relative safety, security, and solemnity of celluloid?"

"Absolutely. Hollywood awaits, as does Casablanca." I pushed a few buttons and the magic of technology once again transported us through the looking glass.

"Will you rub my back during the whole movie?" she asked.

"Yes."

"Will you pop more popcorn and pour more wine when needed?"

"Yes."

"Will you pause the movie for bathroom breaks and not roll your eyes?"

"Yes."

"Shad?" she asked softly, once again lying down on my chest, the opening credits starting to roll in the reflection in her eyes.

"Yes?"

She raised her glass and said, "This could be the beginning of a beautiful friendship!"

We clinked glasses. "Here's lookin' at you, kid."

CHAPTER 14

Night dissolved into morning as I prepared my world-famous omelets for Kathryn, and this was the good stuff . . . morel mushrooms, smoked Canadian bacon, beluga caviar, and old country sour cream. Fortunately, Roiks was able to run down to Ramone's Eggery to get it and get back before Kathryn was out of the shower. Unfortunately, she busted me when she remembered that the only thing in my refrigerator the night before was Diet Coke, Dom Perignon, and some Pop-Tarts, my three staples.

But it was as nice a morning as I could remember, and I almost hated to see Roiks come get Kathryn to take her back to her place and then run her out to Sea-Tac International to spend the weekend with Victoria. But business and the weekend were at hand, and it was best not to get used to having someone so incredibly encompassing around too much.

Upon my mid-afternoon arrival back at the City, I was met by the resident beauty who once again spoiled me with a quick kiss on the cheek and smack on the bottom.

"Good morning, Di," I said as I conquered the steps and accepted her affections.

"Ouch," she said, examining my face. "It's actually the afternoon, and it looks like you took a beating, you poor thing."

"Quite the opposite, actually," I said. "I was able to block all his punches with my face, so he was never able to land a clean blow to my ego."

"Are you insinuating a victory?"

"I am," I said proudly.

"Well, for future reference, it doesn't look like it was worth it."

I was busy looking through the reservations and the litany of messages that littered the hostess stand. "You should have seen me two days ago. I am George Clooney-esque compared to then."

"Too bad it's not closer to Halloween," she said playfully. "You could have saved a mint on a cadaver costume."

"Hell's not a place, it's a gender!" I said to her to counter the verbal onslaught.

Diane grabbed the messages from my hand and stuffed them in my pocket. "But I'm a brilliant businesswoman, Grumpy, and you absolutely adore me. So go up to your office and return these calls, and I'll have the kitchen make you some lunch. Gio and Deity said they'd be here in about an hour."

"Were they much help last night in my absence?" I asked.

"Professionally, they were perfect as always, but relationally, they let me down."

I had been heading up the stairs, but turned around. "Oh, really, what happened?"

"Well, I needed some manly advice from them about a guy that I am so in love with I can't see straight, unbeknownst to him, so I made the mistake of asking them both what they looked for in a woman."

"Uh oh," I said. "I think you were asking the wrong two guys. What'd they say?"

"Well, when I asked Gio what he looked for in a woman, he said 'an exit strategy'. And when I asked Deity what he looked for in a woman he said 'high heels and low expectations'!"

I laughed all the way to my office, and once seated, pulled out the messages and laid them out according to importance. But the first call I made was to Jess, since it was almost seven in Stockholm and her concert would be starting in just a few hours.

Robby, her manager, answered her cell phone. "Hello, Shad, guess who's running around in mass panic?"

I smiled at the thought of Jess in clinical distress, trying on ten outfits, while her hair and makeup gals tried to keep up. "Slip her a micky, Rob, or at least a cleverly disguised valium."

"I'd love to, but I think it states in her contract somewhere that you're not allowed to drug the world's fastest rising star. Are you going to meet us in Paris next month?"

"I'll be there, Robby. I'll see you then."

For the next hurried and harried fifteen minutes, Jess and I talked as best we could while her assistants painted, prodded, poofed, and poked her to perfection. After she had shooshed them away, we finally got a couple of minutes to ourselves.

"I love you and miss you desperately," she said. "Are you sure you can't come over before Paris? Like maybe Oslo or London?"

"I wish I could Jess, but you know what your life on the road is like. It would drive us both nuts. Besides, in Paris, you'll have a week off, and we can just travel and relax."

"I hate it when you're pragmatic," she said with a laugh. I heard someone say something to her in the background and then her tone changed, and I knew that she'd have to get off the phone soon. "I miss you so much, my heart hurts, and there's this void in my soul that wreaks havoc with my world when we're not together."

"You'll be happy to know I suffer the same afflictions in relation to you, but we are but a few short weeks out, and then we can explore the theory of exclusivity with each other."

Jess was quiet then, and I could sense the tears behind her eyes and hear the words that would have to be left unspoken.

"I have to go," she said, her voice broken with emotion.

"I know," I said. "It is how we end every conversation, and I think somehow defines our relationship."

"I love you, Shadoe Kilbourne," she said, "please don't let me lose you."

"You can't lose me, Jess. I am infinitely yours."

"Promise?"

"Promise!"

I heard her start to cry and laugh at the same time. "I think I need to redo my makeup."

I laughed too. "No finer face ever graced the stage. You are in less need of makeup than anyone in the world."

"Does that mean all I need is you?"

"No, that means all you need is you."

"Thank you, Freud."

"You are most welcome, ma'am."

Again, the voice in the background. "Kisses in the wind," she said.

"And in sweet return," I replied, and then a soft click, and the finality of transatlantic static.

I went through the rest of my messages, weeding out the good, the bad, and the boring. Eddie Murphy was in town and was going to stop in for dinner solo, so wanted to know if I and the dinner would be free. I started to smile already, a dinner with Ed and you'd be laughing so hard you wouldn't need to do sit-ups for a week, and an evening with Ed adds at least a month to your life.

A few messages from the nefarious that I had contacted in relation to the senator's daughter, but all said, they had come up blank based upon the photos, descriptions, and events. Hopefully, Cas was having better luck. My list of to-dos were interrupted by Deity and Gio coming up the stairs, once again in great debate.

"Boss, who's better looking, Shania Twain or Faith Hill?"

"How come you guys never ask me about dissident influence in the Middle East or fusion extraction after thermonuclear events?"

They both looked at each other. "What?"

"Never mind," I said. "What's the question again?"

Gio took his position down on the couch while Deity went over to the bar fridge and grabbed each of us a Gatorade. "Bawse, educate my Italian stallion friend here on the finer aspects of horse flesh. Would you rather date my girl Shania Twain or Gio's girl Faith Hill?"

I thought about their world-altering question for a minute. "If I'm thinking night time, I'm going with Shania. If I'm thinking day time, I'm going with Faith, but if I'm thinking lifetime, I'm going with Sarah Evans."

They both just looked at each other with smiles on their faces. "Gentlemen," Gio said, "it looks like we have the makings of a triple date."

"Okay, but who has the better voice?" Deity continued.

We thought about it for a second and then we all said at the same time, "Martina McBride!"

I gathered my messages together and swept them into my "I'll do it later drawer" and joined the boys in the pit. "How come you rarely see any brothers or sisters in country music?" I said, accepting the ice cold Gatorade from Deity.

"Cuz there ain't no horses in the ghetto," Deity said. "'Ceptin' at the butchers."

Gio looked at Deity and tried to keep a straight face. "Can't you just steal one?"

Deity looked back at Gio as if he was actually giving it great thought. "Yeh, but there ain't no grass and hauling hay sounds like too much work for the bruthas."

"Good point," Gio said. "Maybe someday."

I looked at Deity and shook my head sadly.

"What?" he said.

"I hate to be the bearer of bad news, my brutha, but there won't be a 'someday'. Current empirical data dictates the extinction of the African Race and future radical eradication of all dark-skinned lineages."

Deity squinted his eyes and glared at me suspiciously. "What empirical data?"

"You ever watched the Jetsons cartoon?" I asked.

"Yeh," Deity said.

"What's it about?"

"The future," Deity said.

"You ever see any bruthas on the show?"

Deity thought about if for a minute. "No."

"I rest my case," I said smugly.

"Can't argue with irrefutable proof like that D," Gio said. "You best be paying your last respects soon."

"I gonna miss you honkies," Deity said while pretending to wipe tears from his eyes. "Hopefully, in heaven, they'll be other white folk like you who can't dance, dress, or dunk."

The next half hour went much along the same lines as the previous, one insult exchanged after another.

"By the way," I said, "to what do I owe the honor of you boys down here early on a Friday?"

"We be havin' us some bartender problems down at Aquanauts," Deity said. "It be rumored that Little Ricky be spendin' some time with some of the military misses, and me and G figured you'd want to have a word with our young friend. He's on his way over as we speak."

Aquanauts is one of my large clubs that catered to the hospitable cohabitation of parents and teens. It is split down the middle with floor-to-ceiling acrylic partitions, so that the youngsters have a lowered, fun, safe, alcohol-free dance venue on one side and the parents have a raised bar and lounge setting on the other. Parents can go out and cocktail by themselves or with friends and still keep an eye on their kids, and vice-versa, through the acrylic partitions.

The teens' side has open-couched and booth seating areas along the perimeters, all kinds of food and mocktail options, and a large open-pit dance area complete with all the latest techno-pop light and sound systems. It is also fully equipped with all the latest fun gadgets—confetti drops, balloon drops, sud machines, dry ice mist machines, rain-misters, etc.

The parents' side is a typical bar/lounge setup, but is raised fifty feet above the teens' side, and partially tiered as well, so that they can sit or go to the viewing area and watch their kids if the need or want arise. The "scenic overlook" area even has mounted spotting scopes and video zoom cameras with video screens and toggle switches, so that parents can keep an eagle eye on their offspring, or at least check in on hopeful appropriate behavior occasionally. The parents and their kids are also fitted with co-electronic monitors that beep, vibrate and light up when one is in need of the other. This allows parents to occasionally make verbal or physical contact with their kids in a roped-off neutral area, which we affectionately call the DMZ (Dennis Miller Zone) for exchanges of hugs, kisses, money, or reprimands.

Because of the military wives' vast network, word of mouth and media have made Aquanauts a particularly favorite destination for them. They can go out with their kids, both have a great time, and both sides are held responsible for each other's behavior. So the military husbands/ wives know their spouse and kids are in a fun, safe environment and that their families are getting great military 'food and drink' discounts as well.

Security is also very tight there, so that there would be no problems on either side. If the military is going to ensure the freedom of my family, I was sure as heck going to ensure the safety of theirs. And part of that is making sure the military wives were free of inappropriate overtures from marauding morons. All of my staff is aware of my feelings toward the men and women of the military, so to hear that one of my own is causing consternation in the ranks was highly unacceptable.

Rick is the son of an acquaintance of mine who had asked me to hire his son to bartend as a personal favor. He is about twenty-two, good looking in a soft kind of weasily way that some women liked, and lifted enough weights to think himself more than what he actually is. The bouncers refer to him as Slick Rick, much to Rick's enjoyment, because he is young and dumb enough to think it a compliment. What they really mean is that he is a slippery character that none of them particularly like or trust, which is why he isn't working in one of my elite clubs. But he has less than six months until he graduates from UW, so his presence is tolerated and his inevitable departure greatly anticipated.

When Rick was beeped into my office, he walked up wide eyed as he looked around. "Whoa, this is amazing, Mr. Kilbourne. I'd heard your office up here was tight, but this is radical, man."

"I'll let Jenner know you concur with his thematic extravagances," I said. "Sit down, Rick."

"Sure, Mr. Kilbourne," Rick said as he walked over to the couches and noticed Deity and Gio for the first time. "Hey guys, what's hap'nin'?"

"S'up Rick?" Deity said without affect or emotion. Gio abstained from any comment but nodded his head in acknowledgment.

Rick had on a LeBron James jersey over a white T-shirt and faded jeans, with designer loafers and no socks. "Rick," I said, as I came down from my throne to sit across from him on the couches. "I'll make this short and sweet, and get right to the point."

Gio and Deity came down and sat on the couches as well, one on each side of Rick. "First of all, I promise not to tell LeBron you're wearing his jersey and tainting his hard-earned reputation. Secondly, rumor, real or imagined, has it that you've been going above and beyond the call of duty with some of the military wives at Aquanauts, and it stops right here, right now, permanently."

Rick started to say something, and I raised my hand and cut him off. "Whether you are or not isn't important, Rick. Military wives are a federally protected national treasure, and since you don't work for the Treasury, you're held to a strictly hands-off policy. Got it?"

"But Mr. Kilbourne," Rick tried to explain, "those women were sorta coming on to me, I'm just . . ."

I held up my hand again and he stopped in mid-sentence. I looked over at Deity. "Can you please clarify to young Rick here his options?"

Deity looked at Rick coldly. "Nobody much gives a damn, little Ricky, who comin' on to who. If you so much as look at another military missy with anything other than bartending on your mind, Mr. Kilbourne here will fire you, Mr. Giovanni here will beat you to a pulp, and I, Dr. Death, will kill you. You understand what I'm telling you, kid?"

Rick looked at Deity like he was going to wet himself. A glance at me and a look at Gio took away any doubt he had about the serious nature of his indiscretion and the repercussions thereof.

"I . . . , I . . . , I didn't know, you guys," he stammered. "I was just having fun, you know, guy stuff." He looked around to all of us, all youthful bravado and cockiness now carved out of his voice and demeanor. "I mean it, I didn't know, I swear. Honest guys."

Gio looked at him hard in the eye. "Rick, we like you, when you're not being an egotistical little punk. And we know you didn't know it, which is why we're here talking to you now rather than in the alley watching you count the broken bones poking out of your skin. The important part is that you cease and desist. And you don't have to just worry about us. Have you ever seen what military personnel do, upon their return stateside, to lecherous little losers who violate code with their wives or girlfriends?" Gio shook his head slowly from side to side. "It ain't pretty, Rick. In fact, in most cases it ain't even human."

As Rick was still transfixed in terror on Gio, Diety reached over from the other side and tapped him on the shoulder to get his attention, and Rick just about jumped out of his skin: . . . and did jump off the couch.

"Oh my God, don't hurt me!" he yelled to Deity as he staggered back and almost tripped on the coffee table. "I won't do it again, I promise you guys. Just don't hurt me!"

We all started to laugh at his fright. "Nobody's going to hurt you, Rick," I said. "Just stay away from military wives for the rest of your life, and you'll live to see grandchildren."

"Are you kiddin' me?" Rick said rapidly with eyes as big as saucers and still breathing heavily from his near death experience. "I'm not going within a hundred miles of another one. I swear, I swear, I swear. Honest guys, don't hurt me, I'll never fool around with anybody ever again. Oh, man, please don't hurt me!"

I started laughing again. "Well, Ricky, I appreciate your bravery and unwavering strength in the midst of crisis." I looked over at the boys and asked them to give us a minute or two alone.

When they had left, Rick finally breathed a sigh of relief and almost fell back on the couch in exhaustion. I could tell we'd put him through the wringer, and he'd gotten the ever-so-subtle message.

I stared at him, and every few seconds, he'd look up, see me staring at him, and look back down at the carpeting again. Finally . . . "I'm so sorry, Mr. Kilbourne, I really am," he said almost in tears. "I never even thought about it. I'm just a kid. I didn't know I was hurting anybody."

"Knowing is key, Rick. Thinking helps too, and I probably should have let you in on what I consider the obvious when I hired you, but let me give you some advice that will help you live a little longer. Don't try so hard to be somebody. It just proves you're nobody. With the guys around here, hard work, humility, and character are everything, that's how you earn respect. You don't buy it, you don't dress it up, you don't sleep with it, and you don't lie about it. Be earnest and honest, and these guys will take you under their wing and treat you right. There are no better guys than the hundred or so guys I have working for me in security in the clubs. But if you're a pretender, you'll be the butt of their jokes and the recipient of their disrespect forever. Understood?"

"Yes, sir," he said in a quiet voice, still with his head down in reprimand.

"And as far as this military thing goes, how many friends do you have that would either kill or die for you? I'm thinking none, and those are your friends, Rick. The men and women of the United States military are sworn to protect the lives of its citizens. People you don't even know, people you've never met and are never likely to, are willing to kill and die for you, Ricky. What do you think you owe them?"

"My respect and my freedom, Mr. Kilbourne?" he stammered.

"Everything, Rick. You owe them everything. And what do they ask of you in return for this risk, Rick?"

"I don't know, sir." he said, fighting back tears.

"Not much, Rick. They ask for a little thanks, a little love, and a little respect. And they ask that maybe since they are out there on a global basis eating dust, drinking mud, breathing smoke, and risking death, all the while looking out for the welfare and safety of you and your family, that maybe you'd like to do the same in return for them. Got it?"

"Yes, sir, Mr. Kilbourne, sir."

I stared at him hard for a few more seconds, so he would know the absolute importance of this conversation. "Okay, enough said. As far as I'm concerned, this is a dead issue, and you're a better and brighter young man for the experience. I'll let everyone know that you've had some issues that have affected your past behavior, but that you're back on track and deserving of their respect and reconsideration. Fair enough?"

"Everyone will still think I'm a jerk."

"No, they won't," I promised. "They'll think you are how you present yourself to them from now on. Most everyone in my employ has learned tough lessons and has been in need of second and third chances. It's part of the learning and maturation process. It's a new day, Rick. Be excited about it. By the time you get to work tonight, everyone will treat you how you've always wanted to be treated. Just continue to earn it on a daily basis. Deal?"

He finally looked up with a smile on his face. "Deal!" And then he thought for a minute. "What about Gio and Deity?"

"You've got the beginnings of being a good man, Rick, just like your dad, so man up with them on your way out. Go find them downstairs, pull them aside, hold your head high, look them in the eye, apologize, and give them your word that it won't happen again."

"And then?" he asked.

"And then shake their hand, live by your word, and know that those two will be there for you whenever you need them from now on. You'll earn the right to their friendship and respect." I stood up. "In fact, the three of us will come by tonight to see you as a show of love and support, how's that?"

"You mean it?" he said excitedly as he stood up as well.

"We'll be there. And if you really want to impress us, keep a couple of Coronas in the ice for me, Michelob Light for Gio, and St. Paulis for Deity."

"Yes, sir!" he said with obvious enthusiasm as he was walking down the stairs to leave.

"And Rick," I said, "don't forget . . ."

"I know," he said, "don't forget that it's a second chance for me and not to screw it up."

"Well, that too," I said with a smile. "But what I was going to say was not to forget to keep the pretzel bowl full for when we get there."

He laughed. "I won't, I promise." And then he made it down to the slidey door before turning around. "Mr. Kilbourne?"

I looked down at him. "Yes, Rick?"

"Thanks for everything—for the job, and for the talk, and for Dad, and everything."

"That's what friends are for, Rick," I said as I headed back to my desk. "That, my young friend, is what friends are for."

The rest of that night was a restaurateur's dream—lots of people, lots of profit, and a lack of problems. Eddie Murphy was a big hit with all in attendance, as he always was, and we got a chance to sneak away later on for dinner and cocktails with the boys. He was just in town for a day for a benefit and was catching the red eye to Europe for a little family vacation, so we didn't get much time, but the time we had was time well spent. Ed, bigger than life and pound for pound the funniest man on the planet!

Since Gio, Deity, and I were already on the cocktail caravan, we headed over to my other clubs for an alcohol audit, and all the world seemed to be as it should. We popped in on Rick and showed him a little extra love, so all would know he was back in good graces.

By the time we got back to the City, it was the wee hour and we were way drunk, so we decided to hole up in my office for a "cocktail coup de gras," or "drunken détente," as Diane usually referred to it the next day.

"What time ith it?" Gio asked as he practiced his mixology skills at the twirly bar, starting to slur his words a little.

"Taco Time!" Deity yelled from behind the closed bathroom door and then started to laugh with inebriation.

"Do they deliver?" Gio asked.

"Fellas, it's three in the morning," I said. "And besides, only Karl 'The Mailman' Malone truly delivers."

"Good point," Deity said coming out of the bathroom. He threw a wadded up paper towel at Gio and ended up hitting him in the side of the head, which started Gio laughing too. "Do you think the Mailman will go pick us up some Taco Time?"

"I don't know,' I said. "I'll call him and find out."

I hit the speed dial on my desk, and after six rings, a large, deep, sleepy voice was finally heard on the other end of the line and the country.

"Karl 'the Mailman' Malone!" I yelled into the phone.

"Yo bros," he sleepily drawled, "what's going on down at the City?"

"Liquids!" we all yelled in unison.

"Aptly named, you drunken buffoons."

"You got that right," I said.

"What time is it?" Karl asked groggily.

"Taco Time," I said. "We already established that."

I could hear Kay, Karl's wife, start to laugh in the background. "You morons," Karl said, "it's 5:00 a.m."

"Hey," I said, "we're hungry and we were wondering if you would go get us some Taco Time?"

"I'm in Tennessee, man. The tots would be cold and the tacos would be soggy by the time I got there. Besides, I can hear the deadly duo giggling in the background, which means they'll be passed out in about fifteen minutes. How many cocktails have you boys downed?"

"How many cocktails have we drowned?" I yelled down to my two partners in crime.

"Eleventy-thirty!" Deity said, and both of them fell back over the couch in hysterical laughter.

"You have any adults working for you?" Karl chided.

"Naw, they're boring," I said as I opened my drawer and pulled out a Cuban cigar, "and they make you do your homework and eat vegetables and stuff."

"Good point," Karl said with a yawn. "I hadn't thought of that."

"You and Kay wanna come out in a couple of weeks? Play a little golf, take a little cruise, do a little shopping?"

"Yeh, sounds good. I'll get grandma to watch the kids. You gonna send the Lear?"

"Sure," I said. "Maybe we'll come down with it and pick you up."

"If you do, you should spend a few days down here at the ranch first, and we can ride the horses, chop some wood, and do a little fence mendin'," Karl said. "Let Frick and Frack there with you put in an honest day's work for a change."

"What about Barkley and MJ?" I asked. "Are they up for a little weekender?"

"I'll give them a call," Karl whispered into the phone. Obviously Kay had fallen back to sleep. "But if they're going to come I'm flying solo."

"A guys' weekend?" I asked, while trying to light my cigar evenly and failing miserably.

"Dats what I'm talking 'bout," he said, still in a secretive whisper.

"I hear ya, my brutha," I said and practiced a smoke ring at the same time. "Make it happen."

"Count on it, Homeboy," he said.

"Okay, I'd better go. I haven't heard anything but snoring out of the gruesome twosome since they fell back over the couch."

"Love to Jess," he said.

"Love to Kay," I said in return. "Hey, wait a minute, what about getting us some Taco Time?"

"Adios, tostitos!" he said, and then the line went dead once again.

And so for the first time in his life, the Mailman didn't deliver!

CHAPTER 15

It took us an hour and a half in the gym and another half hour playing chess in the steamroom on Saturday morning to finally feel human again, which made me glad I was going to stop drinking tomorrow. We had also promised Pablo that we'd take him with us, so we had the added benefit of laughter as he huffed and puffed his way through all the Nautilus machines and free weights, all the while checking himself out in the mirror looking for increased muscularity. But he picked up the lifting techniques and chess game quickly, so we made him an official member of the club where he could workout with us or his dad, and not suffer through "Guest" status. Deity and Gio also charmed the membership gal into granting Pablo's two little sisters "Pool Only" memberships, so that Pablo's mom could bring the whole family on occasion.

Our arrival back at the City proved to be just as adventuresome. As we parked Gio's Hummer in his reserved spot, in the parking garage, Deity spotted two sedans idling softly with multiple occupants on our way in.

"Looks like we got comp'ny fellas," Deity said. "Lock an' load. Danger abounds."

Gio and I followed suit and jacked a bullet into the chamber and got out and behind the adjacent cars. The two dark blue sedans with the heavily tinted windows pulled in behind us, and what looked like three wise guys got out of each car. By the look of their sports coats, all of them looked to be wearing shoulder holsters, but none of them had actual firepower in their hands, so we came out from behind the cars with guns at our sides, each about ten feet from the other, me in the middle. From experience and training, I knew that Deity and Gio would each take the two end targets and leave the middle two for me, and that if it went down all of us would drop and move to our left. I also knew that if it came to a shootout, there'd be six more speed bumps in the parking garage. We wouldn't have to dispose of their bodies, we'd just paint'em yellow and go about our business.

As is typical with most parking garages, the lighting was poor; what was atypical with this parking garage was the Seattle weather, which meant it was always dark and overcast, making it even worse. A second look at my two central targets brought with it some recognition. I smiled at who I now knew to be the leader.

"Mario!" I said.

He grinned. "Hello, Sheriff Taylor. Glad to see you still have Barney Fife and Goober Pyle in your employ."

Gio and Deity didn't respond or look at Mario, nor did Mario expect them to. He knew that both of them would be focused on the empty space between each of their two targets and wouldn't allow peripheral distraction. Mario was the striker within John Rawls's army of miscreants. Johnny Rolls, as he was often referred to because of how he looked and what he ate; operated most of the drug distribution that went down along the I-5 corridor. He was also one of the fattest and most arrogant guys I ever met on his side of the law, and ruled more by brute force than by brains. He preferred to kill rather than compete; but then again, drugs weren't a rocket science business, so fear mongering probably looked pretty good on a resume.

"You still with Johnny Danish?"

A couple of Mario's guys started to laugh and stopped immediately, when Mario looked slowly in their direction. "I don't think Mr. Rawls would appreciate your sense of humor, Kilbourne."

"Tell him to take it on the chins."

Again, some laughter from his group, but he just let it go this time and shook his head. "You're gonna be a very funny dead guy someday, Kilbourne. Someday, it's gonna get you killed, but good."

"But not today, Mario," I said.

Mario thought about that for a second and did a quick glance down at the guns at our sides. "No, not today," he said. "Today, we're just talkin' like a couple a regular Joes."

All of Mario's regular Joes, of irregular size, were in tan slacks with ill-fitting navy blazers over what looked to be polo shirts, Mario was the exception. Fashion and grooming were big with Mario, and he was always decked out in the best that money could buy. I admired Mario greatly for this.

"I have a global enterprise to run, Mario," I said. "What do you want to talk about?"

"You global now?" Mario asked.

"I just opened a taco cart in Tijuana," I said.

"Congratulations," Mario said with a slight smirk. "I heard it's tough to get good Mexican food south of the border."

"Thanks, should be a big hit, we're all giddy with excitement," I said blankly, "as you can probably tell."

Mario did a half smile and glanced at the blank faces of Deity and Gio as well. "It has come to Mr. Rawls's attention that you are looking for a certain girl. He asked me to inform you that she went . . . ," and he paused for a second and did his signature half-smile, "went global too, over a year ago, and therefore to leave it alone."

I stared at Mario for a few seconds. "That's it?"

"That's it. We got a deal?"

"You got a phone number?"

"What?" Mario asked.

"If you got a phone number, or an address, or a body, or a grave, or death certificate, we got a deal. If not, I gotta keep looking until I find her."

Mario looked at me and shook his well-coiffed head. "Don't be stupid, Kilbourne. Some scragged-out hooker ain't worth the price."

"I have a few problems with Johnny's generous offer, Mario. Why would he volunteer the information unless she was into something or tied to something? Telling me the truth requires a friendly call or visit from you with proof. Trying to scare me away with a lie brought out you and two tons of terror. Now, I know that the round mound you work for is long on lard and short on cerebellum, but if according to you she's alive, bring her by the City. If she's dead, bring me proof. Do one or the other, and do it quick, or stay out of our way."

Mario had nothing to say to that, and wouldn't have offered anything he wasn't told to offer anyway. So we just stood there and stared at each other while he thought about it. For a parking garage, it was dead quiet in the mid-afternoon malaise; you could hear seagulls somewhere out of sight, begging for french fries at McDonald's. Seagulls aren't very bright, but even sheep know that McDonald's holds the world title on french fries.

Another ten seconds ticked slowly off the clock, when all of a sudden the hatch release on the trunk of one of the cars was triggered, and the noise and movement made everyone jump. Deity and I brought our guns to bear immediately, before the sociopathic six could even think about clearing leather, but by then Gio had already put five bullets into the trunk, all evenly spaced.

"Nobody move!" I shouted. "Everybody just relax."

All of us were looking around, tensions were high, when all of a sudden one of the hired help spoke up. "My bad, Mr. Moretti," the nervous and embarrassed driver said. "I hit the trunk release button on my key fob by accident."

Mario looked at him, and then at the trunk, and then back at him.

"Better get Maaco," I said.

Mario grinned at me, and then looked over at Gio. "Nice shooting," he said. "You're quick."

Gio, once again, didn't respond, his eyes still firmly fixed on his two targets of responsibility.

"You!" I said to one of Gio's targets furthest to the left. "Open the trunk slowly so Gio can look inside."

He looked over at Mario. When Mario nodded the okay, he opened the trunk slowly, and Gio peered inside and smiled. "It looks like I killed a case of Pabst Blue Ribbon."

I looked at Mario in disgust, "Pabst?"

Mario just shrugged, "Heineken taste, Blue Ribbon budget."

We stood there for a few more seconds before Mario told his boys to get back in the cars. Mario continued to stay where he was. "Mr. Rawls ain't gonna like your response, Kilbourne."

"I know," I said regrettably, "but think of all the sleep I'll lose over disappointing a human hippo."

Mario just half-smiled once again and shook his head as he headed back to his car. A few seconds after they pulled away, their brake lights came on, and all of us pulled our guns again in response. Mario got out of the car and took another look at the five bullet holes in the trunk, "You owe me five beers, Kilbourne!" And got back in the car and drove off.

"Well," I said optimistically, "who's up for some McDonald's fries?"

CHAPTER 16

When I got back up to my office, I called my beer distributor and had him send over five cases of Heineken to Johnny Rawls's warehouse down by the docks, in care of Mario Moretti. I had a message from Kathryn saying she'd be flying back into town Sunday night and asking if I could pick her up at the airport, and, saying she'd make me dinner in return. I also had an urgent message from Malcomb Arbreau, the senator's campaign manager, asking me to call him right away. So I immediately grabbed four Advil out of my drawer: two for the headache I had, two for the headache I was about to have.

"Well? What have you got?" Malcomb asked quickly, as soon as I navigated the senatorial switchboard.

"Mostly, a hangover, Malcomb. Thanks for asking."

"Mr. Kilbourne," Arbreau said impatiently, "though I am appreciative of your sizable frame, intellect, and wit, I am also paying you a sizable sum of money to gather intelligence on our project and would like an immediate and exhaustive accounting of your efforts to date."

"I'm looking into it," I said, matter-of-factly. "And I'm making progress."

There was a palpable pause on the other end of the line. "That's it? That is the extent of two weeks of research and reconnaissance? Surely, you have more to proffer than that?"

"If I had more, I'd offer more, Malcomb. I have considerable resources that are checking with their resources who are looking into still more resources. I imagine I'll have something concrete for you in two weeks or so as promised. Reporting progress, or lack thereof, to you was not in the contract, nor was any guaranteed success or grand effort on my part. I've promised to look into it and I am . . . end of story."

Arbreau was clearly exasperated at this point. "Well, that sounds like pretty easy money to me, Mr. Kilbourne. Maybe we should just shut down this operation, take back our money, and save you the effort."

"Don't throw false fits, Arbreau. You and I both know you've already paid me the money and that it is contractually nonrefundable. You and I also know nothing of each other's lives, and if we did, I believe we'd find the situations we sometimes deal with equally as vexing, and the people we sometimes deal with equally as revolting."

"I deal with politicians, not prostitutes, Mr. Kilbourne."

"You just proved my point, Arbreau," I said. "And no need to apologize for servicing the lesser of the two. Though I am impressed that you can even tell them apart since their job descriptions and clientele are identical."

This seemed to further infuriate my fuzzy little friend, so I did us both a favor and hung up on him.

I went through the rest of my messages and to-dos that Diane had left on my desk. The only one looking like much fun was to proof the invitation for the celebrity croquet tournament that I sponsored each summer. I had met Michael J. Fox four years ago at my New Year's gala and was so impressed with him and his cause, as well as his wife and kids, that we'd put together this benefit to raise money for Parkinson's research. It is officially known as the "Back to The Future Benefit" since its sole/soul purpose is to raise money so the proper institutions have the funding to get back to the business of finding future cures. But unofficially, it is locally and affectionately referred to as the "Stick It in the Wicket and Whack Off at One in Your Whites" celebrity croquet tournament. Everyone is expected to wear their dress whites, but two years ago, we let everyone wear whatever headgear they'd had an inclination to sport as long as it has some white on it. As a result it's now turned into Seattle's version of London's Royal Ascot, each hat a masterpiece in the making, and each one more outlandish than the next. Friday night is the grand ball and auction, Saturday is the tournament, and Sunday is the corporate brunch.

Michael is always the tournament grand marshall, but John Travolta and his wife, Kelly, have volunteered to host every year, and John has even donated his time, piloting, and plane to pick up celebrities all over the country for this grandest of all games. Tickets are sold at a hefty price to the public for the Friday night festivities; corporate CEOs, who have donated mightily, are paired with celebrities for the Saturday tournament; and the Sunday brunch is set aside for the celebrities, sponsors, volunteers, and their families. Stadium seating tickets are also sold to the general public for the tournament, and all proceeds of the entire three days go to the Michael J. Fox network of charities.

I met some good friends for dinner in the Falling Waters Restaurant at seven, and most of the boys showed up around ten for cocktails and tall tales. Shortly after midnight, Gio and Deity joined us after their appointed rounds, and the night took on the glow of good friends and great laughter until shortly after two when the majority of the group headed over to H2O. H2O was another water-themed private bar and dance club I owned that was open on the weekends until six in the morning. I had modeled it after some of the hottest LA, NY, and Miami clubs that were now so popular with the "dance til dawn" crowd. The place didn't really pick up until around two-thirty in the morning, when the regular bars were shutting down and shoving out the clientele.

Once again, I'd been begged to accompany my fellow rowdy and raucous revelers, but the prior night's escapades with Gio and Deity were still taking their toll on my ever-aging body. Plus, there was always work to be done on the computer, and if I was to spend Sunday evening with Kathryn, then I'd better get a start on it. But after a couple of hours, my back hurt from sitting in my ergonomic engineered chair for too long, and my neck and eyes hurt from working on the computer. I think my brain hurt, too, but that could have been from the crossword puzzle this morning. And come to think of it, I was trying to chew gum at the same time, so maybe I pulled a gray matter muscle in the process.

I had just finished totaling the bank deposits and putting them in the biometric wall safe when the buzzer from the Atlantis bar brought me out of my accounting stupor. I checked the monitor and saw Trey Deuce standing at the door down below, moving lightly in rhythm to the headphones on his iPod that he never seemed to be without.

I punched the intercom and said, "If you're the Avon Lady, I think there're steroids in the lipstick."

I could hear TD start to laugh and then look up into the camera high above his head. "Nah, man, all of us Avon Ladies is hired outa East Germany," he said in a high-pitched feminine voice. "If you can't make the gymnastics team they hire you at Avon."

"In that case, gorgeous, I'll buy whatever you're selling." And I buzzed him in.

TD walked up the few stairs from the bar into my office; and since it was late and I had the lights muted, at first all I could see was a huge white smile and eyes against an alabaster face. I'd hired TD four years ago as a favor to Shane Lowe, who had represented TD pro bono in a rape case that Shane thought smelled a little of setup and racism. Shane had gotten TD off, but figured a full-time job in a fun but disciplined environment would be the only way to keep TD from further mischief, or worse.

TD was about twenty-eight or nine, he wasn't sure which. He had dropped out of school when he was around twelve and joined the gang circuit before using his brother's driver's license and social security card to walk on at a junior college outside of Los Angeles. He was big and quick, but had hands of stone and couldn't post the grades to stay. So TD has been one of my best and most popular bouncers ever since, and has done a pretty good job of staying out of trouble; just a simple, black kid in a man's body trying to make something out of his life.

"S'up, Bawse?" TD said, as he plopped down on the couch in his light blue, silk sweats with the three navy stripes going down the side, the multiple gold chains jangling around his muscular neck and pecs as he landed and crossed his legs in one smooth movement.

"Actually," I said, "I was contemplating not having another drink and was hoping someone would stop in and talk me out of it."

TD smiled the big smile. "I yo man, Bawse. Want me to pour?"

I was already headed to the twirly bar. "No, sit tight, and let the oppressor pour the drinks. I've got two-hundred years of slavery-induced guilt to make up for!"

"Well, as along as all ya'll are feelin' guilty, how 'bout bringin' a po' boy over some pretzels too, I is hungry as heck."

"Want me to make you something in the kitchen?"

"Nah, kitchen food would turn to fat this late. I be better off sticking with the stix."

I brought the pretzel stix over to the sunken couch area in front of my desk and set them down in front of TD. He took a handful and popped them in his mouth as he looked around the room and took the crown and coke that I had made for him.

"Y'all are livin' large, Bawse. Sweet face."

"Face?" I asked, always one step behind on the latest black vernacular.

TD shook his head. "C'mon, Bawse, y'all been hangin' wid da brutha's long 'nuff to pick up da rhythm. 'Face', man! How folks see you, how you is looked at by others. Y'all are clickin'!"

"Well," I said modestly, "I actually took a semester of 'clickin' in college, so I can't take all the credit."

TD started to laugh again as he rubbed his hands over the Corinthian leather couch in appreciation. I slid into the chair across from him and sipped my tall Barbancourt and Diet Coke from the heavy, leaded Waterford tumblers the mayor of Seattle had gotten me for Christmas. *La Dolce Vita!*

"So what's up, Trey? You on your way home or on your way out?"

TD looked down at his Air Jordans for a full ten seconds, and when he looked back up, the ever-present mirth had left his face. He seemed tight all of a sudden, and so did his voice when he finally spoke.

"You ever think 'bout dying, Bawse?"

I looked at TD and kind of half smiled. "Yeah, all the time."

"What you think 'bout that?"

I couldn't quite figure out where TD was going with this, but I was sure he'd get around to it eventually. "I think it's inevitable, and I think in a way it will be a relief."

TD nodded to himself and was quiet for awhile as he took a sip from his drink.

"You ever think about suicide?"

I smiled again, and gave the same answer. "Yeah, all the time."

TD seemed to appreciate a positive response. "Me too. What you think 'bout that?"

"Well, first of all, let me just say that I don't think mine is a shared perspective. But that being said, in specific situations, I think it's a viable and valuable option."

TD got a quizzical look on his face, and since I could tell he'd been drinking, I elaborated a little bit. "I think life is too hard sometimes. I think life is too confusing sometimes. I think life is too painful sometimes. I think life is too tiresome sometimes. I think people screw up too badly sometimes. I think suicide would be a nice out sometimes."

TD nodded his head in what I took for agreement. "So you don't think it's chicken sh . . . Oops! Sorry, Bawse. You don't think that person be a coward?"

"Heck, no. I don't think there's anything easy or cowardly about suicide. In specific cases, I think it can be a little selfish, and it's extremely self-serving by design and definition, but I've never thought of it as simplistic or uncourageous." I took a sip from my drink and silently congratulated myself on another perfect pour. It made me sad I was going to quit drinking tomorrow. "Probably, more so the opposite."

TD started to laugh. "Y'all are killin' me, Bawse. I was with you up to 'heck, no!' and then I didn't know what the heck y'all were talkin' 'bout."

I laughed with him for awhile on other topics and then we both got quiet. "What's on your mind, TD?" I asked softly and almost hesitantly.

TD got tight again; I could see the pain in his eyes and demeanor. I also noticed for the first time that he had a nine mm in a shoulder holster under his sweat jacket, even though he had no shirt on underneath it. It was always tough to tell on TD because his pecs were so big. When he looked up, the trail of tears were already evident. "I got me a call from some friends back home last night. They said my mama done died last week. Funeral was two days ago. Said they couldn't track me down. Said she been feeling poorly for some time now. Said she askin' for me, said she callin' out my name 'fore she died. Said she just wanted to see her baby boy one more time. Said she just wanted to hold her baby in her arms once more 'fore she passed."

TD started sobbing heavily and dropped his drink on the carpet. I put down my drink and walked over and sat beside him. When I put my arm around him, he leaned over into my lap and cried all out. I hugged him as hard as I could and naturally started to rock him a little, as he continued to cry without respite. I'm not sure what the rule books say about two full-grown men hugging and crying together, but being a surrogate mother wasn't an area I was familiar with, so I just went with it and kept saying, "I'm sorry, TD. I'm so damn sorry," over and over again.

And it was gut-wrenching. This kid had been through so much and was just starting to get his life back together. He'd met a nice gal named TaNisha that he was thinking of marrying, and they were going to start a little bar and restaurant together using both their mothers' family recipes. I was going to finance it as a silent partner until they could afford to buy me out.

"Where's TaNisha?" I asked after most of the hard sobbing had abated.

He sat up then, with his elbows on his knees and his head still in his hands, tears running down his forearms. "She with her sisters down in Louisiana. They digging up their mama's recipes for the restaurant. Don't have no phones where dey at, ain't sure when she'll be back."

I got up and made TD another drink and set it down in front of him. "Are you gonna go home?" I asked. "Whatever you need in regards to money or transportation you know I'll take care of it."

TD took a sip of his drink, still with his head down. "Thanks, Bawse, but Mama was my home, she ain't there no more. I got me some aunts an' cousins down Atlanta way, but I ain't seen them in a little whiles neither."

"You want to crash here or come flop at the penthouse?" I asked. "I can make us something to eat, and we can figure out a plan. I can call some of the boys too if you want. We can all hang out with you and drink ourselves into a coma."

TD finally looked up, and even had a smile on his face. "You'd do dat for me, huh, Bawse?"

I smiled back at him. "'Course, I would, TD, you're family, man. And I know you'd be there for me too. So no worries, just let me know what you want or need, and I'll fix it."

He looked up again, but this time the smile was gone, and his voice was almost a whisper. "Bawse, I done something I don't think y'all can fix."

I felt the jolt in my solar plexus, and the darkening cloak of dread and despair. I sat back down across from him and took a deep breath.

"Okay, TD, what'd you do?"

CHAPTER 17

The staff Sunday brunch came early that Sunday. I was tired and surly, and not much in the mood to entertain or uplift the troops. The clouds hung dark and foreboding over the partially domed sky tiles, and the rain seemed to batter down with furied intensity and purpose.

To make matters worse, I was just about to bite into a carefully prepared lobster-stuffed sirloin, made especially for me by a guest chef, when the Seattle chief of police ascended the stairs with two other of Seattle's finest. All of a sudden my appetite was gone and the jolt to my solar plexus had returned.

"Just in time for brunch, Chief. How do you like your eggs?"

My entire staff stopped what they were doing and turned to look at our three guests. All of a sudden I knew how quiet the City could really get.

"This is business, not breakfast. We need to talk," he said. He gestured to the police officers in tow. "You two wait here."

I told the two officers to help themselves to the buffet, took one last look at my lobster-stuffed sirloin, and led the chief up to my office.

"Working on a Sunday, Chief? I'm impressed. You want me to have someone fix you a plate while we talk?"

"I'm not hungry, Kilbourne," he said with as stern a look as he could project. "This is a serious police matter."

"Chief, you lie like a larcenist. You're just like me, you've never not been hungry in your entire life. I have a premonition that neither one of us is going to enjoy your visit, so you may as well enjoy my hospitality."

He perpetuated the stare for about another five seconds and then finally gave in. "All right, nothin' wrong with good food accompanying bad news, I guess," he said reluctantly.

I buzzed Diane's headset on the speakerphone and asked if she'd please have someone fix the chief a plate. "I'll do it myself. Does handsome want the usual?" she asked teasingly.

I looked over at the chief. "Chief Handsome, you want the usual?"

He finally broke into a smile. "Yeah, that'd be great. Tell Gorgeous I said thanks."

I spoke back into the phone, "Handsome said to tell Dog Face he said thanks."

"Nice try, big fella," she said with much good humor. "You're on speakerphone, I heard him say gorgeous."

Damn!

"Oh, but this is serious police business," I pretended to whisper to Diane, "so don't arrange the two eggs and bacon into a smiley face. We need to keep some semblance of decorum up here."

"You're only half as funny as you think," the chief said after I had disconnected with Diane.

"That's okay," I said, "that still makes me hilarious."

The chief just shook his head and took off his raincoat as I walked back down to the couches. He folded it twice along the creases and then placed it carefully over one of the stools next to the bar and library shelves. He was only about five-foot eleven, but he was hard and thick in both manner and build. When you crossed him, he looked about eleven foot five, and didn't mind getting physical with either his mensches or his menaces if the situation required it. He looked a little like Sergeant Carter in the *Gomer Pyle* sitcom, replete with crew cut and temper. He was old army and about as regimented and regulated as it gets. But he was also old school and knew that it's not as much about the law as it is about the interpretation and intent of the law.

The chief and I had always had a pretty good relationship, or at least a decent amount of respect for each other. He knew that sometimes I did things or had things done that were vigilantic by deed and definition, but he also knew I usually came up on the right side of wrong. And we both knew that if I ever pushed the envelope past the point of perdition, he would be forced to come down on me like a ton of bricks. He was too honest and apolitical to probably ever make lieutenant, but sitting behind a desk all day would probably be the genesis of his demise anyway.

"How's Marie?" I asked with some genuine concern, knowing that she had some pretty severe health issues.

"She's in a lot of pain most of the time, which means she's angry, and she's spiteful, and she's unhappy. She could take more medication to ease the pain, but then she'd lose the ability to function, and she knows it's just a matter of time until she starts to lose some more mobility." He sat down and crossed his legs, wiping the raindrops off his shoes with a handkerchief from his suit pocket. When he was done, he folded it neatly in on itself and put it back. "And she takes it out on me, but you can't really hold it against her with everything she has to deal with."

"So how's the marriage?" I asked, hoping I hadn't crossed any boundaries.

He looked at me for a second, probably figuring out how honest he wanted to be. "It sucks!"

"But you stick," I said.

"But I stick," he said, almost to himself. Validating a decision I'm sure he made long ago. "My old man abandoned my mom and my two brothers and me when I was ten, and it gutted all of us because up until that point we worshipped the ground he walked on; he was super-dad. But the one gift he gave us, which is actually a gift to our wives and kids, is that we'll never do that to our families. What's the old saying? 'Real men don't leave' or something like that. So anyway, that's his lasting legacy, that the sons will never repeat the sins of the father."

"Tough price to pay," I said. "You still love her?" Once again probably prying too much, and by the look on his face, I could tell I was getting close. But he thought about it for a minute, like maybe he hadn't thought about it before, and stared off into space.

"I love her for who she was and what we once had. It's not romantic love or friend love, it's more like respect love or memory love. I'm not good with words like you, but remember that old Redford/Streisand movie about a hundred years ago?"

"You mean *The Way We Were*?"

"Yeah, I think that's the best way to describe how I love my old man and my wife, because of the way we were, because of what we once had." He looked back at me. "That make any sense?"

I smiled. "It makes perfect sense, Chief." But before I could elaborate, Gorgeous arrived with Handsome's breakfast on a silver serving tray, inclusive of coffee and orange juice. He stood when she entered, and when she put the tray down, he gave her a hug. She responded with a kiss on the cheek and departed with a twinkle of her fingers and a swish of her hips.

We both watched her go. Long auburn hair, off-white wool slacks, a light blue cashmere sweater, matching off-white sandals and pearls, and the always understated makeup over her semi-freckled tan skin.

I looked back at the chief, and after Diane was completely out of sight, he looked back at me and smiled. "But if I wasn't deliriously happy in my marriage . . . !"

"If only," I said in commiseration.

We spoke casually for another few minutes about first crushes and *Sliding Door* scenarios while he finished his breakfast, and then it was time for whatever had prompted the visit. He didn't mince words. "We found one of your bouncers," he said apologetically.

It was as if I knew the second I had seen the chief walk into the restaurant, but I was hoping I was wrong, resurrectively wrong, restoratively wrong, regeneratively wrong. Like maybe if I lived in denial, TD could live in perpetuity.

I took a deep breath and tried to exhale the hurt. "Damn it!" I stood up and walked over to the aquarium and looked down through the glass at all the employees enjoying their brunch and their friendship, minus one.

The chief looked at me. "Don't you want to know who?"

I shook my head sadly. "Nope, I can guess who."

"You want to know where?"

"Nope, I can guess where."

"You want to know how?"

"Nope, I can guess how."

"You want to know when?"

"Nope, I can guess when."

"What about the why?"

"I know the why, too."

The chief sounded irritated already. "All right then, Sherlock, you want to tell me who, what, when, where, and why?"

I turned around and looked at the chief still sitting on the couch, only mildly interested in what was left of his breakfast. "My guess is it was TD because he was asking me about suicide last night. My guess is he shot himself in the heart because that's where it hurt. My guess is he did it down by the docks because he loved to watch the big cargo ships come in and unload. My guess is he did it early this morning because his world spun out of control last night. My last guesses are because his mom died last week without him and he beat a pimp to death last night, and because he was never quite right, and because life can be damn hard sometimes for a good kid with a bad start." I hadn't noticed it, but as I ended my impromptu speech, I realized I'd been shouting.

"You knew he was gonna kill himself?" he asked, some of the irritation now out of his voice, replaced possibly by a little understanding.

"I didn't know for sure, but it was looking that way."

"And you didn't try to stop him?"

"Didn't seem to be any reason to," I said. "He said he'd been seen with some of the hookers, and there were plenty of witnesses to the beating to death of the pimp, and he was scared to death of going to prison."

The chief nodded as if he was running it all through his head. "Did he say what started the altercation with the pimp?"

"Yeh, he said he was talking to a few of the corner coquettes that he knew and must have either spent too much time, or not enough money, or the pimp was jealous, but regardless, the pimp took a swing at him, and he said something in his head just exploded and he went beserk. He said he didn't even know what he was doing until some of the girls and passersby started pulling him off the guy."

The chief got up from the couch, picked up a link sausage, and joined me at the aquarium. "Sorry about the kid," he said after a while.

I nodded a silent thanks. "He was a work in progress, but he definitely put the *fun* back in dys*fun*ctional," I said. "He was a good kid with a good heart, but without a clear concept of right and wrong. Just that 'do what you got to do to survive' mentality. He may have been a good man someday."

"He still might," the chief said casually.

I looked over at him as he put his hands in his pockets and stared down at Diane, who was laughing with the two officers at her table, always the perfect hostess.

"He still might?" I asked.

The chief didn't answer for a while as he continued to watch Diane interact with his men. "You never know." And then he looked at me and smiled. "A couple of long walks and talks with God could straighten anybody out."

I laughed at the thought of God and TD walking together among the clouds; TD probably asking a ton of questions, and God smiling inwardly at his newest "eager-to-please" apprentice.

We continued to stare into oblivion, with the occasional large denizen of the deep swimming buoyantly by. The chief tapped on the glass to see if he could get the leopard eel's attention. "That looks like a mean old ugly devil," he said.

I looked at the chief, who was looking at the eel, who was looking back at the chief. "A thousand dollars says the eel is thinking the same exact thing," I said.

The chief snorted and laughed. "Could be," he said. "Could be." He watched Diane get up from the table and smiled like a proud father as both his men rose as well in polite conformity.

"Want to hear a story?" he asked, after Diane had disappeared from view.

"Sure," I said.

He continued to watch the gathering below. "Couple a weeks ago, an old man walks into our station downtown. His wife was killed sometime back by a possible harassment, but nobody would testify because of the threat of retaliation by the alleged neo-nazis who did the original accidental offing. Since he wasn't there, he wasn't sure exactly how it went down, but a few weeks passed and a couple of the storekeepers who had witnessed it coughed up that it had been the skinheads knocking her down while trying to grab her purse. She fell and hit her head on the cement sidewalk outside their store, and probably because of complications due to advanced age and ill health, died within a few minutes due to compromised trauma."

I, too, continued to watch the gathering below, knowing fully now where this was headed. He continued as if he was telling it to the eel, no real emotion or effect, just a monotone restatement of fact. "Upon his urging and our never-ending pledge 'To Serve and To Protect,' we sent some uniforms and a couple of detectives back to reinterview the same folks with the same results. They were either still too scared or too smart to risk reprisal, so we came away with zip once again. My guess is he turned to another source."

The chief turned and looked at me. I looked at him and smiled politely and impartially and returned to my voyeuristic pursuits. He plodded on, "So much to my amazement, last week I get an anonymous call, at home on my unlisted phone number, mind you, saying shots were heard out by the abandoned warehouses in the old steel district south of Tacoma, somewhere between here and hell. We sent a couple squad cars out to investigate, and lo and behold, the aforementioned skinheads seem to have suffered some internal strife and eleven of them ended up shooting each other to death or were off'd by a competing faction. Except one individual, who was either a very large man or a semi-small sasquatch, who seemed to have taken a beating by someone who was either very skilled, very tough, or both. Another individual, who we believe was the sect leader, must have gotten overcome with dismay and accidently OD'd on some of his own product." The chief was quiet for a moment as we stared off into space, both alone momentarily with our own thoughts. After about two minutes, he looked over at me casually. "What do you think?"

I looked at him compassionately. "Tragic."

He turned back to the aquarium. "Ain't it though?" He put his hands behind his back and rocked back and forth on his heels. "You think maybe I oughta investigate further or do you think maybe I oughta let dead Nazis lay?"

I pursed my lips and nodded my head as if in deep thought. "Looks pretty cut and dried to me, Chief. Those skinheads are a passionate lot. Hair-trigger tempers. Dare I say incendiary by nature."

The chief folded his arms in front of him and rested his chin in his large and calloused hand. "Incendiary by nature?"

I smiled. "I kind of liked that myself, but you started it with 'aforementioned'."

The chief smiled back. "I was just showing off and trying to keep up." He walked over to the barstools and grabbed his coat. "And luckily for us, there was also a very large shipment of stolen Harleys in the warehouse, which we were able to confiscate and return to some very happy suppliers. There was also a large cache of drugs and weapons, in addition to the dearly departed eleven who have pulled their last caper. I'll probably get some kinda commendation from the governor and my picture in all the papers."

I walked over and slapped him lightly on the shoulder. "You do good work, Chief. Don't ever let anybody tell you any different."

He looked at me hard for half a second. "You wouldn't happen to have an alibi for that night, would you?"

I thought about it for a second. "I believe we were having a knitting bee right here in this very office, Chief. Nothing like a good crochet contest to really get those competitive juices flowing. In fact, I knitted you some body armor." I looked under a coaster. "Now, where did I put that?"

"I didn't tell you which night," he said.

I smiled innocently. "Doesn't really matter, Chief. You can pretty much find us here any night crocheting holsters and making needlepoint bullets . . . knit one, pearl two."

Again, the hard stare. "Absence of evidence is not necessarily the evidence of absence," he said, now studying my face. "And you seemed to have run into a door in the night."

"Actually," I said, "it was a head-butting contest I entered over the weekend."

He took another look. "You lost."

"Thank you, Chief. I realize that."

"Always happy to offer a professional opinion," he said on his way down the stairs. "Words of wisdom and fists of fury, one low price!"

"Chief?" I said before he walked out the door. "I told Diane I'd take her to dinner next month with Jess and me. But since Jess is becoming somewhat of a celebrity, I know she'd feel better if there was some type of security there. The pay is good, the food is good, and the company is slightly better than average."

"You, Jess, Diane, and me for dinner?" he asked.

"And possibly a cocktail cruise along the Sound afterward," I said innocently. "Strictly business."

He smiled a mischievous grin. "To Serve and To Protect!"

CHAPTER 18

I picked up Kathryn at the Sea-Tac Airport at seven fifteen, for which I was repaid with numerous hugs and a kiss on the cheek. She looked dazzling coming off the plane in a short, tight-fitting wool dress with matching tights and heels.

"You look like you just came off a fashion runway, not a plane runway," I said as I took her carry-on bag.

She grabbed my free arm with both of hers and rested her head on my shoulder as we walked to baggage claim. "You're sweet!" And then looked up at me. "Your face looks better."

"Is there a worse?"

"Good point," she said with a ready laugh and held on to me tighter.

"How's Victoria?" I asked.

"Just like you . . . flawless, fabulous, and funny. And she said to tell you hello by the way, and that she looks forward to meeting you someday."

"Please extend to her my greeting and salutations as well."

"I already did. What do you want me to fix you for dinner?"

"We can go out if you'd like. I don't want to force domesticity on you upon recent arrival."

"No, I just want to get into our comfy PJs, cook young steaks, drink old wine, and make new memories . . . and have you all to myself."

We stopped at the baggage claim carousel. "That sounds great," I said, "but I spot a flaw in your well-conceived plan. I have no PJs with me."

"You You do now," she said, visibly pleased with herself. "I bought you some pajamas and a matching robe in New York."

"You think of everything," I said.

"I think of you," she said with some sentiment. "The word 'everything' would therefore be deemed redundant."

We sat at the carousel and waited for her baggage to arrive. People continued to eye her covertly as she told me about her weekend. Not only was she beautiful and brilliantly engineered, but she laughed without reservation and was equally as dynamically demonstrative in her story telling, with arms and overtures everywhere. There was about her an animation, innocence, and enjoyment that people were immediately drawn to. As I thought about it, it was probably the part of her that her father had left alone and intact: the little girl quality that often emerged, and refused to age and accept serious adulthood.

Halfway through one of her stories, she stopped abruptly. "Did you bring the Range Rover or the Mercedes?"

"The Range Rover," I said. "Why?"

"Because I don't think we'd be able to fit all the luggage into the Mercedes."

I looked at her with mild confusion. "But I clearly remember being impressed when Roiks told me that you had only two suitcases when he dropped you off."

"Silly boy," she said, as she rolled her eyes. "Both suitcases were full of other suitcases to fill with newly purchased fashion necessities."

And almost as if on queue, six ebony ostrich skin suitcases of varying sizes lumbered ungracefully down the luggage ramp and onto the carousel. I found a cart and a team of sherpas, and we exited without further incident.

Once home and only appreciably unpacked, and donning our newly purchased PJs, we migrated to her large kitchen that vista'd imperially over the great room. Her animation and inherent excitement continued as she spoke in rapid fire, all the while securing pots, pans, and utensils from every drawer and cupboard. As always, I couldn't help but laugh, even during her most serious of conversations. Occasionally, she'd pause, get her bearings in quick staccato'd glances, and then continue unabated and unconcerned with the extraneous world around her.

I was being treated to her top-secret, world-famous, award-winning, Zagat-endorsed aged Kobe beef and morel mushroom stroganoff. It looked like the secret ingredients were butter, sour cream, red wine, and a hint of garlic; not only because I saw her put those in the oversized sauce pans, but mainly because those were the secret ingredients to every good meal.

As I was opening the second bottle of Jordan Cabernet, my cell phone rang and Jess sounded like she had just awoke. "Hi, Prince Charming," she said in a sleep-inflected foray.

"Hey, Sleeping Beauty," I said. "You're up early."

"Unfortunately!" she said with an obvious pout. "But I have to do some ballad recordings for the new European album, and Robby insists my voice has a richer quality and lower timbre to it early in the morning. I'm not even allowed to shower or drink anything until afterward. I asked him if it was okay if I swallowed or breathed in the meantime, and he had to think about it for a minute."

"You poor little rich girl," I said in mock compassion. "But if it's any consolation, you are following in the footsteps of the greats. Bing

Crosby, Dean Martin, Frank Sinatra, etc, all did the same thing for their albums and movie musicals. They swore by the early morning medium. Your success is therefore guaranteed."

I heard a luxurious yawn with a surmised stretch at the other end of the transatlantic line. "You're sweet. I miss you so much I could scream. Where are you?"

"At Kathryn Rae's home, she's helping with a project I'm working on."

"Kathryn Rae, the artist?" she asked.

"Yeah, do you know of her work?"

"Who doesn't?" she said as if I'd been raised on another planet. "Her work is all fraught with emotion and innuendo and experience and erotica. She's incredibly gifted. I adore her work." And then there was a pause. "Hey, wait a minute, isn't she supposed to be gorgeous in the classical sense?"

Kathryn was standing across the breakfast bar from me stirring our dinner and eavesdropping on our conversation. She sipped her wine happily and smiled widely at Jess's overheard compliments.

"Actually, she's gorgeous in every sense," I said as we clinked glasses. "Supernal in repose."

"Yikes! Is she well built too?" Jess asked a little hesitantly.

I winked at Kathryn and looked her over analytically from ponytail to painted toe. "Incredibly compelling construction actually. She seems unnaturally immune to both gravitational force and caloric intake."

"Tell her I hate her guts!" Jess said.

"Jess hates your guts," I relayed.

"Tell her I'm a lesbian," Kathryn said.

"Kathryn's a lesbian," I relayed once more.

"Tell her I love her guts," Jess said.

I laughed as I relayed the message. "Jess now loves your guts."

"She'd be crazy not to," Kathryn laughed as she motioned for the phone. And for the next fifteen minutes, the two femme fatales chatted rapidly and laughed uproariously as I'm sure they exchanged a fact and fiction fair at my expense. Thick as thieves. When they were done, Kathryn handed me back my cell phone.

"She's adorable," she said while tasting her extreme cuisine with a wooden spoon.

"Yes, she is," I said in complete agreement.

"Do you think you'll ever get married?" she asked while turning away toward the refrigerator, as though an answer either way was sufficient.

"No."

"No to Jess, or no to ever," she shouted with her head now deep inside the refrigerator, pretending to be looking for something.

"Both, and it has nothing to do with either for I am a huge fan of Jess, a huge fan of marriage, and a huge fan of forever. But I don't necessarily think I'm worthy or likely to live long or love well."

When she finally exited the refrigerator and turned around, she was in possession of only a large smile. "I was hoping you'd say that," she said with obvious glee.

"That I'm not likely to live long?"

She rolled her eyes. "No, silly, about not getting married." She came around the island and sat on my lap as I sat on the barstool. "I don't think I'll ever get married either, so maybe we can grow old and adorable together. What do you think of that?"

"Hmmm," I said. "Let me think about that for a minute. Drinking wine, eating popcorn, and watching old movies with a beautiful but slightly obnoxious feline for eternity . . . well . . . if you throw in Pop-Tarts, sushi, Diet Coke, and the occasional slow dance, you got yourself a deal."

"Deal," she said. And we shook on it. "I'll have my attorneys draw up the contract in the morning just in case you get cold feet and try to get out of our ironclad handshake."

"Fair enough," I said. "Now get off me, your sauces are starting to scorch."

She must have thought I was joking at first because she continued to gaze deeply into my eyes until her nose got the best of her. With one quick sniff and a kiss on the cheek, I was alone once again on my barstool, and she was back to the epicurean, if not herculean, task at hand. I watched her with mild fascination as she was everywhere at once, and then she would catch up and become contemplatively inert, staring at me or the darkening skies, with her glass of wine resting against her voluminous lower lip.

We spoke of things both grand and bland, just enjoying each other's proximity and friendship. We ended up dining trailer-park style on the couch with our plates on our knees as we enjoyed the ubiquity and infinity of the raging rainfall. Kathryn hadn't bothered to turn on additional lighting as the skies had darkened in grayed anger, the only light being that of dusk's ambient offering and the staccato'd brilliance of flames at play. Laughter was in great supply in between bites and sips, and the entire night took on the surreal tonality of abundance and satiation. The sweet paean of catharsis permeated the room; an unexpected Zion of the night, as the week's ebb and flow of emotion and energy seemed to finally dissipate and dissolve into Kathryn's contagious laughter and innate grace.

"Slow dancing, eh?" she said as we quietly placed our fine china on the massive wood-and-glass coffee table.

"The romantic rogue," I said in an "ahh shucks" shrug. "What can I say?"

She smiled at me. "A man of merit, in search of means, must be tried and tested on those things for which he boasts and waxes bold."

"Are you saying I'm all talk and no action?"

"No, Curtis St. John, your idol is saying that," she said as she uncoiled seductively from the couch and walked the few feet over to me with an outstretched hand. "I'm saying you're all show and no go, big fella."

"Then let us 'trip the light fantastic'!" I stood, bowed elegantly, and then took her hand and led her to the hardwoods in front of the bay windows.

"'Trip the light fantastic', is that Faust?" she asked as we navigated the furniture maze.

"Milton, I believe, from the poem L'Allegro, directed to the goddess Mirth. Strangely apropos, wouldn't you say?"

"Mmmhmm," she said as she pressed her head against my chest.

"I'll take that as an emphatic yes," I said. I wrapped my arms around her tiny waist and she placed both arms around my neck, her face still buried in my chest.

"Your waist is miniscule," I said. "It's perfect."

She looked up at me dreamily. "And what would you say about a large waist?"

"I'd say it's a large waste."

"Ugh, that's what I thought you'd say."

Lightning crackled and thunder rolled as we both looked out the windows and then back at each other.

"Enough with the small talk," I said. "Prepare to minuet!"

And dance we did, into the wee hours of the morning. Quickly at first, slowly after a while, and later . . . not at all.

CHAPTER 19

Morning crept silently through Kathryn's diaphanous drapes, the too bright stiletto'd prisms of sun exposing the floating dust motes dancing on the air; each buoyant by origin; weightless, and without urgency. I loved the transient tranquility of mornings, especially those governed by quiet and calm. I looked down and Kathryn was still lying lightly on my chest, her breathing soft, slow, and even; her breath sweet with the nuance of fine wine. Her hair and pajama top slightly askew.

I kissed her cheek and then eased her off me as gracefully as I could and positioned her deeper onto the couch. I found a blanket in her immaculate and spacious bedroom closet and draped it softly over her feet, torso, and shoulders. There were no Pop-Tarts that I could find in the dark walnut cupboards, and no Diet Coke in the large Sub-Zero, so I figured I'd make it another Sausage and Egg McMuffin morning on my way to the office.

Back at the City, fresh from the shower and smooth from the shave, I put my office chair in full ergonomic recline and did a mental update of life's most pressing issues. Most of the detritus involved in our continuing call to justice was still laden with the daily dealings of the deadly, but none were too far parsed along the spectrum to cause us much duress. I still wasn't sure about Gio and Deity doing Phinny themselves, but a guy like that sometimes deserves the personal touch. And there was no real reason why the long arm of justice couldn't reach all the way to SoCal.

The senator's daughter, though, had me a little puzzled and perplexed. All paths to progress seemed to have hit dead ends, dead hookers, or dead memories. But there was about it an aura of secrecy and concealment that gave credence to the existence of some type of salaciousness beneath the city streets. The world was well aware of the Seattle underground that came to be when a cabinet maker accidently ignited a glue pot in 1889 that burned thirty-three city blocks of what is now historic Pioneer Square, and because of that, stone and brick replaced wood. But more importantly, rather than rebuild the embers, they decided to regrade the streets one or two stories higher to reduce the tideland flooding that had historically plagued the city as well. So now, twelve to thirty feet below the city streets exist the remnants of an underground city, complete with a maze of underground tunnels, alleys, and passageways.

I knew that opium dens, speakeasies, gambling halls, and other assorted atrocities used to thrive in that environment, so it wasn't too far-fetched to think that some of that could still go on behind the walls of the typical tours. But where beneath the city, to what extent, and was it organized? These, I thought, were the burning questions that inquiring minds wanted to know. And the fact that we'd recently been warned away by my friend and foe Mario Morreti granted even greater speculation to the whole debacle. I was about to give my sometime nemesis a call, when Diane buzzed to let me know he was already downstairs.

"Send him up," I said. "And make sure you count the silverware before he leaves."

When Mario came up the stairs, I expected to see GQ photographers snapping photos behind him. He was always decked out in the latest fashions, inclusive of a Dobbs Milan walking hat and cane, and a Burberry camel-hair trench coat, which I'm sure covered a litany of Armani underneath.

Mario had his arms spread in innocence. "Stealing silverware?" he said. "Now, that hurts."

"Someday, when I'm really rich, I'm going to be able to afford a pair of your socks," I said as he continued to saunter up the stairs. "You're ruining the 'Crime Doesn't Pay' campaign that Governor Mitchell is currently engaged in."

Mario passed up the couch and chose one of the firmer easy chairs that wouldn't compromise him as much if a quick response was required. He unbuttoned his overcoat and jacket prior to sitting and moved his holstered gun more comfortably over to his hip. "That's okay," he said. "Mitchell is on the payroll, the socks come free with membership."

"Good to know the incentives," I said.

Mario looked at me with a cold grin on his face. "The other incentive is we let you live."

"Also good to know." I threw him down a small bag of Jordan almonds that I had stolen from First Class, and he automatically caught it in his left hand, his right hand moving quickly and unconsciously to his gun.

He realized it was a test and started to laugh. "You spend way too much time trying to amuse yourself, Kilbourne."

"Just seeing how careful you were, Mario," I said. "Wanted to make sure you weren't getting soft and losing your edge."

Mario, again out of habit, tore open the small bag of nuts with his left hand and teeth rather than tying up his right hand. "You'll know I lost my touch the day you read my obituary."

"You gotta be good to do what you do," I said as I tried to open a bag of nuts with both hands.

Again, the cold grin from Mario. "You don't gotta be good to do what I do, you gotta be good to do what I do and live."

"Excellent point," I said. "To what do I owe the pleasure of your company, Mr. Moretti?"

Mario looked around the room appreciably and then looked back at me. "Nice digs," he said. "You wouldn't happen to have any recording devices among your long list of electronics would you?"

I smiled back with a warm grin to counteract his cold grin. "I would, but they're not active right now, and you're gonna have to take my word on that."

"Your word's good enough. I got no issues with that."

"Our word is about all you and I have to deal with each other, Mario," I said. "'Tis the currency of the criminal world. Honor among thieves."

"You talk funny," he said.

"Interesting comment coming from an uneducated Italian wise guy," I said.

"But smart," he said, pointing to his temple. "Smart in all the stuff that keeps me alive and the other guy dead."

I would have thought I had hurt Mario's feelings, if I had thought Mario actually had any feelings to hurt. "I was questioning your elocution, not your evolution."

Mario got a quizzical look on his face. "There you go again, talkin' your funny talk. Anyway, I ain't here to chat at ya. Mr. Rawls was hoping that you and I could come to some kind of agreement on this chicky you're chasing all over town."

I leaned back in my chair and threw a couple almonds in my mouth. "That's sweet of Johnny to want to appease me, what does he suggest?"

Mario was shaking his head. "He suggests you drop it or he'll suggest I bounce a bullet around in your brain, though I told him the chance of actually hitting something that small was pretty slim."

I laughed at Mario's sudden light side. "Mario, I didn't know you had a sense of humor. Careful though, it'll ruin your tough-as-nails reputation."

Mario shrugged. "All work and no play, ya know?"

"Plus, shooting me in the brain would be like me trying to shoot you in the heart. But here's the deal, I already took money from a guy to find his daughter and I spent it all on Pop-Tarts, so I'm kinda obligated. It would be a lot easier if he just coughed her up, and he and I went back to being the great pals that we are today."

He made some kind of chuckling noise in his throat and shook his head. "Mr. Rawls don't own her, this other guy must if she's still around. Mr. Rawls is doing this other gentleman a favor."

I thought about that for a minute. "Rawls wouldn't do his mother a favor. This other gentleman must have big bucks, big connections, or both."

Mario just shrugged, reached into his coat pocket and pulled out some lip balm with his left hand. "None a yer business, probably none a mine neither, but either way, you stop or you drop, s'up to you."

At that point, we just continued to look at each other while Mario applied his balm. Not to be outdone, I reached into the top drawer of my desk and grabbed some Blistex cherry lip balm. I did notice however that as I opened my drawer Mario's hand automatically got nearer to his gun. So I pushed in my drawer a little and his hand went back toward his lap. So I pulled it out again and his hand went back toward his gun. So I pushed it in again and his hand went back toward his lap. So I pulled . . .

"Knock it off, Kilbourne. You're driving me crazy," he said as he got up. "I should just shoot you right now and get it over with."

I put my lip balm back, pushed my drawer in for the final time, and walked down to the couches where Mario was standing. "Doesn't make sense, Mario. You kill me; Gio, Deity, or Koda kill you. Johnny tries to kill them, Chief Tanner busts your boss, and on and on."

Mario looked up at me from under his brow with his big Italian eyes. "Tanner is in on this?"

"He knows I'm looking into it, and he knows you and your boys braced us in the parking lot the other day," I lied. Typically, I liked to reserve my lies for women, poker, and the IRS, but I thought it would be okay to utilize one here as well.

Mario buried his hands in his trench coat and walked down the few remaining stairs. When he got to the bottom, he turned around and stared at me for a few seconds. "I ain't authorized to make any decisions on this, but I'll talk to Mr. Rawls and get back to you."

He stood there for another few seconds looking around my office, then over to the aquarium wall, then finally back to me. "What kind of Pop-Tarts?"

I smiled at him. "Frosted Blueberry."

He smiled too and nodded his head. "It's just one more thing we got in common Kilbourne. Be a shame to kill you."

"If you can."

He looked at me hard. "I can."

I shrugged. "Maybe someday we'll find out."

He grabbed his cane and put on his hat. "I'll look forward to it."

I quoted the legendary Loius L'Amour. "And I'll look back on it."

CHAPTER 20

Gio and Deity joined me downstairs at the bar later on that afternoon to share theories. Our original plan was to get together to share facts, but since we didn't have any, we went with the next best thing. I was enjoying a rum and Diet Coke to wash down the rest of my smoked almonds. Gio was doing his usual vodka and Red Bull. Deity was drinking his usual afternoon cordial, a tall Seven and Seven, which he said is commonly known as a "Thirteen" in the ghetto, the public school system being what it was.

"Nobody knows or claims to know nuthin'," Deity said with no small amount of frustration. "Only a few folk I talked to even said they'd heard of it, but it goes by a bunch of different names—Sewer City, Tunnel Town, Devil's Dungeon, . . ."

Gio broke in. "Same deal with my connections in every city, Kil. Most of my guys haven't heard of it, or if they have, they take it as urban legend and dismiss it as myth." When he finished, he looked over at Deity. "But . . ."

"But what?" I said as both of them grinned at each other.

Deity was the first to speak up. "We was accosted."

I smiled at the thought of someone trying to accost Gio and Deity. "How'd it turn out for the accosters?"

"Depends on their medical and dental plans, I s'pose," said Deity. "We roughed'em up pretty good, but while all the fun be goin' on, a little brutha of anutha cula steps outta the car with a piece and tells us to skee-daddle."

I looked at them with raised eyebrows. "A brother of another color? Black, Hispanic, Russian, Italian . . . ?"

"Asian guy, Kil," Gio said. "We were downtown on First Avenue hanging with the hired help about three in the morning, showing the leisure ladies and passersby Chrissy's photo and asking questions when the four horsemen showed up. Big white guys, looked like powerlifters who probably did hard labor during the day, all casually dressed, with an aggregate IQ and tooth count of around ten."

"The boys were tough, Bawse," Deity continued, "but they was definitely local and definitely not professional. Hired muscle to scare old ladies and small children. But when we started to get the better of them, this gentleman of Asian persuasion, Chinese, I think, hops out of the car, dressed in some expensive threads, and waves a pearl-handled NP-20 at us, and the boy blunders pick themselves up and wobble away."

"So what did he say?" I asked, always up for a good story.

"He just sneers at us and says 'Leave it alone, no more warnings', and then gets back in the car and drives away. G and I notice that he's got some magnetic dealer plates on the big caddy, so we figure it's stolen or temporarily commandeered. So we hustle on down the street to see if we can find our newfound friends and get some answers, but by the time we catch up to them, they already pulling away."

"Did you make the plates?" I asked, though I presumed I already knew the answer.

Gio nodded. "I made a few calls Sunday morning, and it looks like the old, beat-up suburban was registered to a Grayson Construction down in Kent by the docks. Owner is a guy named Micky Gray who has an arrest record that would make Mario proud. Mainly small time stuff, but enough to let us know that he stays dirty and busy."

"Curiouser and curiouser," I said, as I took another sip and commandeered some of Gio's pretzels. "First, we get warned off by the Mario brothers, then some rent-a-thugs try to dissuade you from further followup, and then a personal appearance today by Mario to warn me off at risk of death. Methinks the local lawbreakers doth protest too much."

Gio pulled the pretzels back toward him. "I say we mosey on down to Kent and pay a visit to the too live construction crew."

I was trying to remember the last time I'd moseyed. I was sure I'd done it more recently than Deity, particularly since I was pretty sure that brothers don't mosey, especially in public.

We finished off our drinks and the rest of the pretzels and crossed the great divide that was Lake Washington on the 520 and then headed south on the 405 past Bellevue and Renton down to Kent. It took us a while to find the palatial estate of Grayson Construction, but if you hit enough potholes and followed the foul smell, you were bound to find it sooner or later. Fortunately, we were in Gio's Hummer again, and we survived both perils.

Grayson Construction was true to its name, it looked like a thousand other construction companies anywhere in the world. Multiple outbuildings and storage sheds, front loaders, back hoes, pavers, graders, packers, dump trucks, water trucks, etc, were all over the place in various stages of use and abuse. There was also the usual activity on the main grounds as hard-hatted individuals walked back and forth to their appointed rounds and responsibilities. At two o'clock in the afternoon, it all looked as it should. We asked a grizzled old man, who was writing down truck numbers as they ingressed and egressed, where we could find Micky Gray. He said something about a "shack in the back" through a toothless mouth and a heavily tobacco-stained gray beard.

Deity looked over at Gio and started to laugh. "How long your pappy been working here, G?" To which Gio tried to backhand him and drive at the same time.

The "shack in the back" turned out to be about three or four mobile homes L'd and T'd together like a poor man's dominoes to form the glamorous global headquarters. Most of them were dirty, dented, and in a general state of decay and disrepair. With our combined genius, we figured where the office was. It was the door that actually said 'Office' on it. As we started to enter, Gio grabbed us by the backs of our shirts and pointed over to the side of the dilapidated building. "Those junkers look familiar, D?"

We both looked over and an old suburban like the one they had seen the prior evening was sitting off to the side next to a newer LTD and various other nondescript cars, trucks, and motorcycles. Upon entry, we were met with the overpowering stench of cigarettes and sweat. I wasn't sure which was worse. Fortunately, there was a nice old lady at the reception desk who was more than happy to assist us.

"Whadya want?" she bellowed above the noise of the general goings-on outside and the rickety old electric fan on her filthy desk that produced no perceptible current. Her shapeless gray dress covered her shapeless gray frame, but at least it was adorned with gray ash that even now was about to fall from her cigarette.

"Greetings, benevolent beauty," I said. "May I get you an ashtray?"

"What?" she cackled, not even bothering to look up.

"I said I admire your ability to smoke without an ashtray. Not many folks actually like to wear the remnants of their cigarettes home in sweet remembrance. But it's nice to have a little keepsake from your day, before you go home and hit the whiskey, isn't it?"

"Are you smart-aleckin' me, boy?"

I looked shocked. "No, ma'am, I was just thinking that you remind me of my sweet grandmother, about three years after her demise."

"Dem eyes?" she shouted as the cigarette bobbed up and down with each word. "What about my eyes? My eyes may be old, but I can see you three are full of tomfoolery and are gettin' persnickety." She squinted her old eyes and glared at us intently, or tried to focus, either one. "I asked ya what ya'll wanted, or gitouta here."

"Actually," I said, "we're here to see Micky. We met him at the Mary Kay Cosmetics conference, and he's won a free herbal facial and rose petal pedicure."

She must have finally found me funny because she started to hack and wheeze and slap her ancient thighs. "You young'ns must be off your rockers," she said in between fits of laughter and coughs. "Nobody here but me that would take to all that fussin', and I can't 'ford it."

Behind me, I could hear Deity talking to Gio. "If'n your mammy laughs herself into a stroke, you doing the mouth-to-mouth."

After a few lengthy minutes, she finally got hold of herself and dabbed her moist eyes with an old tatted handkerchief. "Ain't no one here in need of a makeover, but yours truly," she said. "Hoooweee, I haven't laughed that hard since the Red Skelton show. You young'ns remember Red Skelton?"

"I'm sorry," I said. "What color skeleton?"

This too sent her into fits of laughter, so I decided to turn down the charm a notch and get back to the task at hand. I moved an old invoice that was partially covering her plastic name plate.

"Marge, though I've enjoyed our exchange of words and secondhand smoke immensely, would Micky happen to be in today?"

She took a few more seconds to gain composure, all the while shaking her head. "He's here, but he don't see nobody unless they have an appointment. And since he don't take appointments, I'm afraid you fellas are outa luck, outa time, and outa that there door." She pointed to the wobbly old aluminum door on the bent hinges, through which we had just entered a few merry moments before.

I looked at her with great confusion on my face. "Well, that is peculiar. Normally, when we OSHA inspectors arrive, we are seen right away."

You'd have thought the late great Red Skelton himself was standing right in front of her. Her eyes got big, her cigarette dropped out of her mouth, and she stood up so fast the invoices on her lap flew hither and yon.

"OSHA?" she exclaimed. "Well, why didn't you fellas tell me you were from OSHA. Yes, you can see Mr. Gray right away." She fluttered in five places at once, not quite sure how to regain our respect or her integrity. "Can I get you some coffee or a donut or something?" And then she was off in a flustered tear, apparently scared to death that she had just alienated the occupational safety and health administration inspectors.

"Just have a seat gentlemen, and I'll be right back."

We looked around, but couldn't see any chairs, donuts, or coffee, so we remained steadfast and standing. Within just a few minutes, she came back wiping the ashes and cobwebs from her dress. "Down the hall, gentlemen, last door on the left."

We did as we were told and managed not to get lost or pull out our GPS. Micky Gray was all that we'd dreamed he'd be; short, fat, bald, ugly, old, and ornery. He was sitting behind a battered metal desk that looked like six inches of the legs had been sawed off unprofessionally to accommodate his vertical challenges. His office was like the rest of the structures, faux wooden paneling, cheap carpet, and punchboard ceilings that were either cracked, water stained, or both. It was a large room with beat-up lazy boys and well-worn couches interspersed throughout what must have been originally designed as the living room. Micky himself was dashing in a blue denim shirt unbuttoned to his navel with a stained wife beater on underneath. Tattered khaki pants and tan engineering boots completed the rest of his ensemble, other than the multitude of gold chains that hung down his neck, only to get lost in the plush jungle that was his chest hair.

He spied us suspiciously as we entered. "You fellas better check with your supervisor; we took care of Charlie last week."

"We're not with OSHA, Micky. We just said that to get in here. We're actually starting a shag carpeting business, and we're here to harvest your chest and back hair."

By the time I had finished that first sentence, a door opened on either side of Micky and four leg-breakers came in through each. At closer look, a few of their faces were still tattooed with some of Deity's and Gio's best pugilistic work. And as usual, both my boys turned to face the opposition, while I focused on my fuzzy little friend.

Micky's muddled Irish face got a lot redder and his small reptilian eyes got even smaller. "Before I have you taken outside and beaten into wood pulp, I'll give you one more chance to state your business. And it better be damn good, or I sweartagod you'll be leaving in a cement suit."

I'm sure Micky would have loved to have had his boys jump us right there, but he noticeably wasn't sure yet exactly who we were and why we felt confident enough to give him some grief.

"We just got a few questions for you, Micky, but don't worry about it, I'll speak slow and keep it to only a few syllables. A few of your cavemen tried to roust my companions here a few nights ago, and we'd like to know why."

Micky continued to stare at me, and without looking away, called to one of his overly fed but undereducated employees. "Jax, you know these guys?"

Jax was evidently one of the guys who had bit off more than he could eschew the other night. A few Band-Aids and bruises still graced his face. "These are the guys that you asked us to have back off the hooker downtown, Mr. Gray. At least the spook and the wop, I don't know this other guy."

"Spook?" Deity said.

"Wop?" Gio said at almost the same time.

"As long as we're all denigrating racial backgrounds," I said, "you guys can just refer to me as the honky, so I feel like I fit in."

"Enough," Micky said, more than a little irritated, "who are you guys?"

"Just think of us as a triumvirate."

"A what?" he said.

"A trilateral commission," I said.

"Huh?"

"A triangulated partnership."

"Eh?"

I sighed. "There're three of us!"

"Oh," he said. "Why the hell didn't you just say so?"

"I thought I did," I said.

The room was quiet for a few seconds until Deity spoke up. "I say we shoot 'em, he'd be too stupid to notice."

"Dammit," Micky said, slapping his hand down on the table. "I'm busy, what the hell do you guys want?"

"Actually," I said, "we're professional bounty hunters and we get paid for catching guys that are fat, dumb, or ugly, and we get a special bonus when we find someone who's all three." I looked at Micky and grinned. "We could retire on you."

"That's it," Micky said. "Jax, get these bozos out of my face and off my property. And I don't care how you do it, but I sweartagod you better not do it gentle."

Jax and his boys started to take a step forward, and the three of us casually pulled our semis out from underneath our baggy button-ups.

"Micky. Micky. Micky," I said, shaking my head sadly. "Where's the love?"

I walked over and sat on the beat-up old file cabinet next to Micky's desk. As I got closer, Micky got a little nervous and stood up.

"Stand up, Micky," I said. "I want to make sure you're not carrying."

"I am standing up, you jack . . ."

I put a bullet past his ear. "Micky, please, let us hold a civil tongue. We merely came by to inquire as to why the harassment, and who put you up to it. No need for foul language." I squinted my eyes in exaggeration and looked more closely at Micky. "Are you sure you're standing up?"

"Yes, damn . . ." And he stopped when he saw me raise my gun.

I bent down and looked underneath his desk. "Are you standing in a hole?"

"No, you piece of . . ." And he stopped himself again. He looked at the three of us with our guns pulled on his party of eight, and figured maybe it was time to deal before he lost any more face in front of his men. "Listen, I didn't get any loyalty pay on this deal, so here it is. Sweartagod, some Chinaman walks in last week and says he needs a little muscle to scare a couple guys off one of his hookers. Now, I know the prostitution in this town is run by the n . . . ," he caught himself once more and looked peripherally at Deity. " . . . by the darkies, so it don't make no sense that no Chinaman would be giving out orders. You know what I mean? So I tell him 'sure, I got guys that can handle that', and he throws ten K down on my desk and says to have four guys downtown on the corner of first and main at midnight on Saturday, and he'd point you out if you guys showed up again."

Micky looked around and licked his lips in a nervous twitch. "That's it, I sweartagod, just a little harmless arm twisting to stay away from the dame. Sweartagod."

I looked at my little man Micky some more, but he seemed to be telling the truth. And there was realistically no reason for him not to if he hadn't received business from this guy before and probably wouldn't again.

"All right, Micky," I said, as I stood up and put my gun back in its back holster. "We're working with Chief Tanner and the Seattle PD on this, so don't show up downtown again and hope to fare any better. Next time, it'll be a little jail time for your eight maids a milking, got it?"

Micky just nodded. What I'd just said was a lie, but the last thing I needed was one of Micky's guys trying to prove how tough he was to the others or get a gun and friends and give Gio and Deity another try.

"And one more thing, Micky," I said, "it looks like Marge could use an ashtray and a raise. I'd appreciate it and take it as a personal favor if you supplied her with both."

He just stared at me incredulously and shook his head. "Why'n the hell should I do that?"

"Because I asked you nicely, Micky. Because I said I'd appreciate it, Micky. Because I'd owe you a favor, Micky. Because you're a man of immense warmth and wealth, Micky. And because, Micky, if I check back in and find out you haven't, I will pound you down from five-foot four to four-foot five, and you won't be tall enough for any of the rides at Disneyland anymore. And if you get any shorter, first graders will be pummeling you for milk money."

He just stood there.

"Micky?" I said.

"Yeah, yeah, I'll take care of it," he said reluctantly.

I smiled. "Sweartagod?"

Again, the evil eye, and then finally, "Yeah, my word."

I turned my gaze to Gio and Deity. "Shall we depart the premises, gentlemen?"

Geo and Deity both nodded and walked backward to the door after me, making sure as to not take their eyes off the adversary. Gio came next as Deity stood there for a second with his big, broad, Magic Johnson smile. "Memorize the face, boys. It's the face of death if'n y'all ever come near us again. And if'n any of you village idiots so much as stick your nose out of this door as we be leaving, I will personally provide you with a third nostril."

With that said, he saluted with his gun, put it back in his shoulder holster, and we navigated our way back out to where it all began. Marge was still standing guard, still curious as to our intent and the earlier gunshot. I pulled my money clip out of my pocket and peeled off three one-hundred dollar bills and held them out to her.

"What's that for?" she asked a little leerily.

I smiled my award winning 'I love the elderly' smile, the one officially endorsed by the AARP. "It's for a day at the spa," I said, as I placed them gently in her hand. "No beautiful woman should go without one."

After a few seconds of realization, her eyes started to moisten, either from my gesture or my aftershave, I wasn't sure which, and she looked at the money and tried to speak, but no words came. So I just patted her hand and turned to leave. Gio and Deity looked out the smoke-scarred windows and then walked cautiously outside. As I started out the door behind them, I looked back at Marge and said in my best vocal imitation and facial expression of Red's famous nightly closing, "Good-night and God bless."

Her watery eyes got big. "You do remember Red Skelton!"

I smiled at her warmly. "That I do, Marge. That I do. I was a big fan of Red Skelton as a youth, and I'm an even bigger fan of the lovely ladies that still hold him in their hearts."

CHAPTER 21

We stopped by the club for a quick workout on the weights and heavy bags, and then dropped by Taco Time to carbo load on the way back to the City, Mexi-Fries once again being the super nutritional source for elite athletes the world over.

Monday night was Lady's Night at the City, both down at the Island Bar and upstairs at the Falling Waters Restaurant; and since we had nothing productive to do until we met with Cas and Kat at eight o'clock, we decided to sit in the bar and see whether Gio or Deity could pick up the most attractive female.

It was the typical target-rich environment that the City was known for, and we enjoyed the spectacle of beautiful women trying to outdo each other for attention, either by dress or demeanor. Both Gio and Deity had mastered the art of passive pursuit, so they'd occasionally look around, make eye contact, hold the look for a few seconds to imply interest, and then casually turn back to their drinks. They also always strategically placed themselves on the path to the ladies restroom as well, therefore giving the ladies multiple opportunities for contact should they so desire. Plus, according to Gio, all women used the facilities at least sixty times a night, typically in herds, so we were bound to see all potential candidates eventually. I wasn't aware that women traveled in packs to the powder room, but Gio and Deity swore by it.

After a while, they'd both find a false excuse to saunter off separately on reconnaissance missions and return to trade notes. Gio thought he had a good read on a table of young flight attendants over by the window, but came back with disappointing results.

"How'd it go?" I asked. "Any prospects?"

He looked at me as if in pain. "There were four of them. So the odds were good, but unfortunately, the goods were odd."

"Ouch, that's too bad," I said. "Love at first sight is often cured by a second or sober look. May I suggest thirteen more cocktails and another look later on?"

Gio laughed. "Finally, a plan that has never failed us. People never bite the hand that feeds them drinks."

"Where's D?" I asked, looking around.

Gio pointed to the back access to the kitchen and service bars. "He was talking to two beauty queens earlier in the corner, so he may be the winner tonight."

Deity came back to the table as a striking young lady of African heritage walked by with a large chest and a purple afro; so in her honor, we clinked our glasses in a toast to good plastic surgeons and bad hairdressers.

I looked over at Deity who was busy trying to put a dead fly in Gio's drink while he wasn't looking. "The latest scouting report from Gio says that you're the odds-on favorite tonight after being spotted with two rather attractive females."

Gio turned around before Deity could complete his mission, and he returned to the conversation in resignation.

"No such luck. The dark-haired gal was good from far, but far from good, and the other one turned out to be a lesbian."

Gio looked at Deity in disbelief and then over at the striking and well-structured blonde at the bar. "She's a lesbian? How do you know?"

Deity looked at Gio with a straight face. "I asked her out and she said no."

We all laughed at that, and once again toasted to the 'key lesbian indicator' . . . a 'no' to a date with Deity.

This time Gio looked at Deity with a straight face but kept out of striking distance. "If that's the criteria, that's the twenty-third lesbian you've asked out this week."

Unfortunately, for Gio, Deity's reach was a little longer than he had anticipated, and he got slapped, quickly but softly, on the side of the head.

I ordered another round while Gio went to take another look at the flight attendants. I looked at Deity. "Ever walked into a room and felt like the best-looking guy there?"

Deity smiled. "Every time I walk into a room, Bawse. What 'bout you? You ever feel like the best-looking guy in the room?"

"Yeah," I said.

"On those extremely rare occasions," Deity joked, "is there ever anyone else in the room?"

"No," I said dejectedly, "but it's no less rewarding." I was about to elaborate when Gio rejoined us. The next two hours were much the same, with a plethora of pejorative banter and numerous nubile young women eager to make Deity's and Gio's acquaintance. I tried to stay away from the fray by hopping behind the bar to help out and happily watched my boys do their social networking. It was always a sight to behold and well worth the price of admission.

At eight o'clock, we were back comfortably at Cas's apartment and ready to update each other on our dealings with the dubious. Cas was in his typical all-black ensemble and in monochromatic fair play, Kathryn was in a stunning off-white business pantsuit that accentuated the obvious. I'd forgotten that I'd seen her just that morning until she skewered me with guilt for sneaking out unannounced. I retorted that she lacked proper high-level hospitality since my search for Diet Coke and Pop-Tarts had gone unrequited.

"How do you look like you do with a meal plan of Diet Coke and Pop-Tarts?" Cas asked.

"I augment it with Taco Time and rice crispy treats," I said.

"Oh, good plan," he said.

I looked over at Kathryn, and she was just shaking her head in motherly fashion, but luckily decided not to reprove me in public. Gio and Deity finally came out of the kitchen; each had a bottle of wine in one hand and a drumstick in the other.

Deity smiled brightly at his find. "Kentucky Fried Chicken," he said. Gio joined in with equal enthusiasm. "Original Recipe!"

"Feel free to help yourselves, fellas," Cas said in mock hospitality. "There's a container of spicy Thai beef in the refrigerator too if you're still hungry."

Deity looked over at Cas. "Not no more." And he and Gio broke into guilty laughter.

Cas looked at me blankly, and I just shrugged. "You know what the current labor market is like Cas. Good help is hard to find."

"If not impossible," he said, while looking at my two ravenous assassins and shaking his head.

"Okay, I'll pour the wine," Kathryn said, "if someone will please tell me if that underground city exists or not. I've been waiting patiently all weekend and patience is not my middle name."

I looked at Gio and Deity and they began to tell Cas and Kathryn various versions of the same story that they'd told me. That though they strongly suspected it existed in some fiendish form, they were not able to substantiate it to a point of proof positive or even proof probable.

"The funny thing is," Gio said, "is that people have never heard of it, or they have and think it's a myth, or they get a look of fear in their eyes and vehemently deny its existence."

I took it from there. "And it's the latter that we think provides the greatest evidence of some actual truth to the tall tale other than numerous warnings to stay away. And again, these aren't the city's best and brightest that we're talking to, so it's all conjecture and supposition on our parts, but I think it's enough to pursue further and adds a certain amount of trace validity to our suspicions." I looked over at Cas. "If Cas has experienced the same scenario and concurs with our rather bleak findings, I think we should interrogate more severely those who seem to know something and those who seem to deny its existence too strongly."

Cas got up and walked over to his well-worn spot in front of the window without comment and looked down on his pet project, downtown Seattle. He stood there for a few minutes without saying anything, while we just looked at each other and decided to await a response. Finally, Kat's curiosity got the best of her.

"Cas, are you okay?"

Cas didn't bother to look over, but continued to stare into the darkening night and see the things that probably only he could see. After a while, he smiled a humorless smile. "I found a guy."

We all looked at each other in surprise and waited for further information. He maintained his vigil at the window, and when he spoke, he spoke as if he was speaking to others unknown, in ominous tones. It was as if we were merely eavesdropping on an account he was giving to his street corner constituency.

"I know a woman, her name is Grace Simmons, who works with those beyond help, those that are irretrievable and without hope, destined for death and destruction. Most of those she works with are extremely mentally and physically damaged, and so addicted to so many things that they are usually delusional, either by nature or narcotic. Some inert, some feral, all in various stages of decay, their bodies ravaged beyond repair. All Grace can typically really do is give them some dignity in death. She runs a clinic in Gig Harbor, out of some abandoned apartments she's remodeled beautifully, funded by those agencies and foundations that have nowhere else to send the human refuse."

He turned and looked our direction, but probably didn't see us. "She's amazing," he said, almost to himself. "She runs that clinic on a shoestring or more like a wing and prayer."

This time he did see us. "So I talk to her, and she says she's heard the stories of Tunnel Town at different times and actually had a ward there who spoke, though basically incoherently, about Tunnel Town and that he used to be what he called a Tunnel Runner for them—someone who would mule cargo, human or otherwise, in and out of there. He told her all kinds of wild stories that she declined to go into, but did say it was along the lines of deviance and drugs. Grace said she doesn't necessarily believe him, but since she's experienced so many other things in the last eleven years that she never would have believed, she doesn't doubt anything exists anymore."

I looked at Kathryn, and she shivered visibly and wrapped her arms around herself as though she was suddenly cold. She looked over at us. "Could someplace like that really exist under the public radar?"

Before I could reply, Deity spoke up. "Heck, yeh. There's rat holes like that all over the world. Not all of them underground, but most of 'em remote and generally unknown 'cept 'n by those that frequent those kind of places. It's big money."

We all thought about that for a minute as Cas turned back to his window to the world.

"If it does in fact exist," I said, "and no one seems to really know much about it, it is either run really well, really deadly, or both."

"Too bad, he's not still around," Gio said. "He could have been the missing link."

Cas surprised us again with a smug look on his face. "He's still around and Grace was pretty sure she could track him down if we gave her a couple days. She said he comes by occasionally when he gets low on food and medications, or when he's just strung out again, and she said the next time he came in she'd talk him into hanging around for a while and giving us a call."

I smiled at him. "Cas, you are the man. Great work. Hopefully, this will lead us somewhere. Especially since every other turn has been a dead end."

Cas came back and sat down with us. "Grace is an incredible woman," he said with no lack of affection, "and intensely protective of those she has the honor to care for, so we'll have to tread lightly and play by her rules. But I have a feeling from what she said that this guy is legit."

We sat there for the next hour and played out scenarios of what we envisioned Tunnel Town to be, on what scale, with what offerings, and with what management. Fortunately, as the night unwound, we found lighter topics to discuss, and it turned into a nice evening of good friends, great wine, and bad pizza.

Kathryn had driven to Cas's apartment on her own since she had been at a friend's private showing, but asked if I could take her home and leave her car here. I had a better idea, and asked Gio and Deity to follow us and drop her car off at her place, on their way back downtown.

When we were both safely tucked in the Range Rover, Kathryn immediately leaned over and hugged my arm and put her head on my shoulder as I drove.

"What a ghastly world we live in sometimes!" she said with evident distaste. "It makes me happy that I don't have children that would someday have to deal with the world's pervasive social sicknesses."

"Me too," I said. "It's funny, most of my friends with kids question whether I love kids or not, and tell me that if I really loved kids that I'd have some of my own someday. My response to them is always the same . . . if you love kids, you have them. If you *really* love kids, you don't. I love my potential children too much to bring them into this global cesspool the way it is."

She looked up at me with her sweet smile. "I never thought of it that way, but subconsciously, I've probably always been an advocate of exactly what you propose."

"I remember a line in *Parenthood*," I said, "that has always stuck with me where Keanu Reeves makes a statement along the lines of 'you have to undergo background checks, credit checks, criminal checks, and fill out a hundred forms to get a business license to sell hotdogs on the street corner, but they'll let any loser have a kid'. It makes me angry that there's no justification needed or minimum requirements mandated to be a parent."

"You big softy," she said amidst soft laughter. And then she leaned all the way over to the other side of her seat and leaned her back against the door as much as the seat belts would allow. "You remember the first time we met, and you jokingly referred to yourself as the great dichotomy?"

"Yes," I said hesitantly.

"In many ways, maybe most ways, I think that is exactly what you are. When Jenner first told me a little bit about you in confidence and how vengeful and vigilantic you sometimes were, I thought, to do what you do, you must feel nothing. But now, I know you do what you do because you feel everything."

I looked at her a little self-deprecatingly. "Number one, let's not talk about me. Number two, let me put it as simply as I can . . . I hope that everyone gets what they deserve. I hope the wonderful live a wonderful life, and I hope the horrible die a horrible death. And I personally feel that it is my privilege, my honor, and my responsibility to expedite and augment either scenario."

She came back to her original position, which I preferred, and kissed me on the cheek. "All you need now is a suit of armor and a round table."

"And a damsel in distress," I said in my best Groucho Marx mimickry.

"Well, Mr. Marx, I am in a bit of distress if you really must know. I want to go to your place and snuggle on the couches and watch a movie, but I also have an insatiable craving for sushi." She looked at me with enlarged eyes and fluttered her long natural lashes. "What's a distressed dame to do?"

"Well, Lady of This Evening, allow me to demonstrate my super powers."

I pressed the button on the steering wheel that activated the audio phone system and clearly stated the name I wanted it to call. Charles, a good friend and fellow restaurateur, who just happened to own the best sushi restaurant in Seattle, answered the phone on the third ring.

"Need bail money?"

I laughed at his usual greeting. "No, not this time, Chuckles. I am actually with a rare beauty with unrequited sushi aspirations, and I told her I could wield my magic wand and make it happen. What are my chances?"

"Chances are always good for you, Kil. You know that. We're typically booked a couple weeks out, but if you two want to swing by, I'll gladly give you the best table in the house."

"Actually, my good friend, I was hoping you could deliver. And before you answer, remember you're on speaker phone."

There was a slight pause on the other end of the line. "You know I don't deliver."

"I was merely under the assumption that you didn't deliver to regular people."

"Oh, them!" he said, and again, the momentary pause of thought.

"I'll owe you a favor," I said.

"You can do me a favor right now and close a half dozen of your restaurants. The competition is getting a little tight in these tough economic times."

"I've already done you a huge favor by not opening up a sushi restaurant of my own."

"Splendid point," he said, and paused for a moment. "Did you say a rare beauty?"

"Remember the brunette in the periwinkle bikini at the Four Seasons in Maui, who you said you'd kill and die for, right before you tripped and fell in the pool?"

"Yeh, she was stunning," he said thoughtfully, and a little painfully.

I winked at Kathryn, "a comparative pig to the celestial beauty that radiates within the Range Rover as we speak."

"Then I'll deliver it myself," he said, all of a sudden decidedly more excited. "And I'll do you one better. I'll corral one of the guys I use for caterings and bring him with me if you break open some of that Bordeaux you have stashed away."

"Deal," I said.

"Sucker!" he said. "See you in an hour."

I punched the 'disconnect' button and looked over smugly at Kathryn. "Ask, and ye shall receive, my lady."

She smiled in complicity. "I'll never doubt you again, Sir Laughs-A-Lot."

We held hands the rest of the way to my penthouse and had the extreme pleasure of not speaking and just enjoying each other's proximity, until we were almost home.

"By the way," she pondered, "why did he call you a sucker?"

"Because the Bordeaux of which he speaks is a Lafitte, and is of rare vintage. Chuck's been begging me to crack a seal on one for years."

"And you finally acquiesced to make me happy?"

"I finally acquiesced to make both of you happy. You are two of my most favorite people, both of whom also appreciate fine wine, and I can't think of a better time to taste the grapes of Bordeaux than with each of you."

"Told ya you're a softy," she said teasingly. "Is the Lafitte of which we are about to imbibe dusty, web ridden, and epochs old?"

"Actually, even the finest Bordeaux's aren't typically palatable after fifty years, and no wine of any stature can typically endure a second century. Wines older than that are quite literally collectables, not consumables."

"Well, either way, I'm honored, Kind Sir," she said with much affection.

"I drink, and drink with, only the best the planet can proffer," I said in my best Ivy League snobbery. "And speaking of snobs, let's call Jen and invite him over."

"What if he already has plans?"

"Tell him we'll be sipping Lafitte, and he'll be at the penthouse before you can hang up the phone."

And not to be outdone, Jen showed up with an array of Sicilian breads, English crackers, Parisian cheeses, and Grande stories. Charles's sushi chef was also of top quality, and we therefore dined graciously, drank royally, and talked joyfully late into the night.

CHAPTER 22

The next three days passed without incident as we continued our search for the prodigal daughter and awaited a call from Grace. Friday morning though, dawned with a call from Mario.

"Mr. Rawls wants to see you."

"Squirt guns at fifty paces?" I asked. "Slingshots from rooftops?"

"Knock it off, Kilbourne," he said.

"Raindrops on roses and whiskers on kittens?"

"Quit screwing around, Kilbourne. You coming by or not?"

"Yeh, Grumpy, I was just letting you know that those are a few of my favorite things. I'll be there, give me an hour."

"You drive me nuts!" he said and hung up hard.

I looked at my to-do list on the desk and scratched off "drive Mario nuts." And since I had just irritated him as well, it made for a pretty successful and full day for me already. I had half a mind to call it a week and hang out at Barnes & Noble, but the other half of my mind, the half that occasionally worked, insisted I go see Johnny Rawls. I let Gio and Deity know where I was headed, just in case, and hopped in the car. They wanted to come along, just in case, but if Mario was going to whack me he wouldn't be giving me a heads up beforehand. They did offer to take over my penthouse, cars, and girlfriends if I was killed though, so I appreciated their sacrifice and magnanimity.

As I drove down to Burien, I surmised that from the amount and diversity of unwanted attention we seemed to be getting lately, it looked like we had actually stumbled onto something of significance. A lot of people fail to see the value of good stumbling, but it remains a key crime-stopping tool for those of us who lack any real investigative training. Now, bumbling on the other hand is never a good thing, but stumbling, like patience is a virtue.

I pulled up to the maze of warehouses that was part of Rawls's evil empire: cargo containers and truckloads sitting idly by or getting aggressively loaded and unloaded; men, materials, and machinery everywhere. A large part of what Rawls controlled was arguably legit, and his aggressive industriousness a great cover for the underground criminal activity of which he was both progenitor and propagator. I was relatively sure that he was a multi-millionaire several times over even without the illegal dealings, but some guys are pointed in a questionable direction early on and tend not to deviate from their chosen path of prosperity.

As I pulled up to the warehouse that I knew to contain Johnny's main office, I saw Mario and a few of his goons leaning against a large crate outside of the main doors, some of his guys smoking cigarettes, some squatting down and rolling dice against the warehouse wall. It looked like all of them had different denominations of bills between each finger and they passed around the winnings or losings as the dice chose their fate.

I parked and walked up to Mario, and we shook hands. His goons stopped and walked over as well.

"You guys playing jacks?" I asked innocently.

Evidently, that hurt a few of their feelings. "You got a smart mouth, pal," one of God's larger creations said. "Maybe I should shut it for you, permanent like."

I looked at him and couldn't help but laugh. "Anytime you feel lucky, dumbo, draw a gun or throw a punch; it's a happy hospital holiday for you either way."

"This guy thinks he's tough," Dumbo said to Jumbo.

"It's not a question of thought," I said, "it's a point of fact."

Mario had had enough already. "All right, knock it off, fellas. He's here at Mr. Rawls's request. And I hate to admit it, but he'd put each of you on the ground or in it within seconds."

I tried to look humble and turned to follow Mario inside under the oppressive glare of his henchmen. I could see them staring at me in the reflection of the glass doors, so right before we went in, I spun around and dropped to a knee with my forefinger out as a pretend gun. Mayhem ensued. Two of his guys dove for cover, one fell over backward, one dropped his gun trying to get it out too fast, and the others were caught awkwardly reaching for their guns with little or no success.

Mario grabbed me by the back of my suit jacket and pulled me up and inside.

"You idiot, Kilbourne," he said heatedly, "what if one of those guys would have shot you?"

I looked at him blankly. "From what I assumed and just witnessed, I don't think there was much danger of that."

"Kilbourne!" he said, walking away and shaking his head.

"What?" I said innocently.

We went through two inner edifice doors and around a barrage of ocean containers stacked to infinity. Finally, Mario was speaking to me again.

"Thanks for coming," he said reluctantly. "I know you didn't have to."

"Just think of me as the traveling intellectual," I said.

"I was thinking more along the lines of the wandering imbecile."

I stopped and looked at Mario. "See, there you go again, Mario. Every time I start to think you have no personality, you crack a joke."

He shrugged and continued to walk between and around crates and boxes of every size and shape. "I was funny when I was a kid," he said. "I used to try to crack up my grandpa all the time, who was dying of cancer. That old man raised me. He was my whole life, ya know?"

"So you're not funny anymore?" I asked, trying to keep up.

"No," he said rather sharply.

"Why not?" I said.

This time he stopped and looked at me, and this time, there was no humor in his voice or eyes. "Because he died anyway." And then he turned back around and mounted the steps up to Rawls's office. Maybe Mario had a heart after all. First the Tin Man, then the Grinch, and now Mario. Maybe it was catching.

We scaled the fourteen or fifteen steel-meshed steps up to a double-doored entry that stated in raised black lettering on frosted glass "Global Import & Export," and underneath that in larger raised gold gilt lettering "Jonathan Rawls—President."

While Mario was punching in the code to gain entry, I tried to make polite conversation. "Why a double door? Has Johnny gained even more weight?"

"Kilbourne!"

"What?" I said innocently.

Mario just turned and looked at me blankly. "Kilbourne, I realize you're rarely serious and find yourself immensely amusing, regardless of the rest of the world's opinion to the contrary, but don't mess around with Mr. Rawls, he ain't in the mood today, trust me. Got it?"

"Good plan. We'll just pretend Johnny is thin and a thinker."

"Kilbourne!"

"What?" I said innocently.

The outer office had a series of metal and faux leather chairs and couches, stamped linoleum tiles, and ornate metal walls. Industrial chic! In those chairs and along both sides were four guys of varying sizes and shapes, but all were in standard slacks and jackets . . . to promote their solidarity and hide their weaponry, no doubt. A plethora of plastic plants adorned each table and barren corner.

"Are the plants plastic so Johnny won't eat them?"

"Kilbourne!"

"What?" I said innocently.

The fearsome foursome stood up heavily as I followed Mario into the room, and he waved them back down with a "sit" hand gesture. I made a "rise" gesture with my hand and they stood back up, not knowing who I was or why I was there, and because they were, by nature and conditioning, heavy on following orders and light on independent thought.

Mario looked at them standing at attention and then at me.

"Kilbourne!"

"What?" I said innocently.

Another door, another keypad and identical interior design; this time, though, there were just two hitters, both of whom must have had some seniority, because each stayed languid in his seat and just nodded lethargically under heavy eyelids at Mario as we moved through and into Rawls's inner sanctum. There was also a desk that was currently uninhabited, but based upon some of the pictures on the desk, the missing occupant looked promising.

When we got to the door, I looked at Mario. "Hey, what's the name of that big, fat, ugly worm in Star Wars that's the galactic crimelord?"

"Kilbourne!"

"What?" I said innocently.

Mario gave the door five quick taps, waited five seconds, and then led us into Rawls's office. Johnny waved us in and Mario immediately went and sat down on the black leather couch to the right and picked up a *Sports Illustrated*. Johnny was on the phone, negotiating some kind of contract and motioned for me to sit in one of the two matching black leather chairs in front of his desk.

On the couch against the wall to the left was the obvious denizen of the desk from the other room. She was blonde, built, and may I say brazen in her choice of wardrobe, or at least, what there was of it. She had on a black one-piece stretch mini that hugged every curve the gods had given her and a few she had augmented on her own.

She was sitting sidesaddle on the couch with her very tan legs crossed demurely. Black high heels and a gold ankle chain completed the look. She had a pen in one hand and a pad in the other and she bobbed her right foot up and down as she looked me up and down with a seductive smirk on her face. Johnny saw her giving me the once-over, so he snapped his fingers and waved her out of the room. She looked at me and made a pouty face that Johnny couldn't see, so I gave her a reassuring wink to let her know that her dress and its inhabitants were still all that she had hoped they'd be and hadn't gone unnoticed . . . or unappreciated.

When the stunning stenographer had left the room, Johnny stood up, still on the phone, and walked over to the windows behind his desk that allowed him to look down upon but a small piece of his empire. It also gave me a chance to see Johnny in all his girth and glory silhouetted against the painfully bright and artificially lit window. It seems Johnny had missed a few Pilates classes, but no meals.

I glanced over at Mario, who was looking at me over his magazine with a look of warning on his face.

"Jabba," I said to him. "Jabba the Hutt."

Mario's eyes got bigger than dish plates.

"What's that?" Johnny said, putting down the phone and sitting heavily back down.

"Java," I said. "I was asking Mario where in this hut I could get a cup of coffee?" I looked over at Mario and he gave me the "you're playing with fire" stare of incredulity.

"Oh, yeh, come to think of it, I could use one too," Johnny said, and punched an intercom button. "Daphne, could you hustle us up three cups of joe?"

"And some donuts," I said.

Johnny looked over at me. "Maybe we'll get along better than I thought, Kilbourne," and forwarded the additional request on to the blonde bombshell in the anteroom.

Johnny got up and walked over to the wall directly behind me. On it was an eight-foot high, twenty-foot long, floor-to-ceiling map of the world. At various points on that map were little, push-pins of various colors. I had a feeling Johnny was going to tell me how great he was. It was time to pack my bags: I was going on an ego trip.

"You see all these pins, Kilbourne?"

"No," I said.

He looked back at me and noticed I was still facing the other way, busy filing my nails. "Well, dammit, Kilbourne, turn around when I'm talkin' at ya."

"Kilbourne!" Mario said for the seventh time in the last five minutes.

"What?" I said innocently.

I turned around and faced Johnny and tried to look as interested as the prospect of a big man with small pins could infuse.

Johnny, on the other hand, didn't seem to be too put out. He was apparently still too titillated by his own success and couldn't wait to share it with his newly-found, captive audience. Fortunately, before he could once again defend his dissertation on global domination, the much anticipated and long awaited Daphne knocked five times and then entered in a breeze of excellent perfume.

She handed us all our coffee, replete with company logo'd napkins, and placed a large purple box of donuts on the coffee table in front of Mario.

"Will there be anything else, Mr. Rawls?" she asked.

"No thanks, Daph," he said, eyeing the donuts instead of the dolly. "That'll be all."

She turned and walked past me with a wink, to which I took as a good omen. Hopefully, she had something on her mind and not something in her eye.

I watched Johnny as he looked from the donuts, back to his map, and then back to the donuts once again. I could tell his stomach was fighting with his ego, and since they were both large and equally in charge, I decided to put him out of his misery.

"Mind if we grab a donut before we reengage?" I asked. "I'm starvin'."

"All right, but let's make it quick," Johnny said halfheartedly. And then grabbed two jelly filled and a powdered, and walked back to his aircraft carrier-sized desk and put his feet up.

Everything had to be big with Johnny. He was big, his stretch limo was big, his reputation was big, his personality was big, his ego was big, his bank account was big, his office was big, his enterprise was big, and I'd heard his temper was big. I don't think he even minded being fat because it just made him that much bigger.

I walked over and grabbed a chocolate éclair and sat down on the couch next to Mario. He seemed mildly displeased with this, but didn't say anything since he had full access to the donuts. I made a mental note later on to ask him if he was homophobic.

"Ahh, Jabba," I said out loud as I took my first sip.

Mario started to choke mid-sip on his coffee as soon as I said it.

"Java," Johnny corrected me, with a mouthfull of donut from his executive perch.

"What?" I said innocently.

"It's pronounced Java, not Jabba. You got it right earlier."

"Oh," I said with a straight face. "Thanks, Johnny."

"Don't mention it," Johnny said, "easy mistake," and went back to his donut deluge.

When Mario was done choking and glaring, I decided to ask about what I suspected to be Johnny's most valuable asset. "What's the status report on your receptionist?" I asked. "Is she free to wed whom she pleases?"

"The little ice princess?" Johnny said, as he and Mario both laughed. "She's an MBA broad at the university and built to kill, but she's cold as ice. The only reason she's here is as a favor to a guy I know. It's his daughter and he don't want no funny business. So I gotta pay her a ton to do a whole lotta nuthin'. But she's great to look at, so I do the guy a favor, and someday he does me a solid back. S'how it works, ya know."

It wasn't a question, so I didn't bother with a response. I looked at Mario in surprise. "She hasn't thrown herself at your feet yet?" I asked.

He grinned with a mouthful of donut. "I know, can you believe it? All this, here for the taking, and I can't even get the time of day outta her. She's either gay, engaged, or extremely guarded against handsome Italian men who dress nice and talk good."

"I just hope she doesn't jump me in the hall on the way out," I said.

Johnny couldn't wait to shut me down. "Ain't a snowball's chance in hell, you making any time with her, Kilbourne. Lotta guys been in here with more moxie than you, and they ain't got nowheres."

I was about to form an impressive rebuttal, but as I removed the napkin from underneath the coffee cup to wipe my hands and face, I noticed a telephone number, a smiley face, and the words "Top Secret" within the circled indentation that the cup made on the napkin. I slipped it into my pocket for further review . . . after I memorized the number of course.

"Oh, well," I said, "nothing wrong with the occasional cold shower."

"It improves the circulation," Johnny said with a mouthful of jelly donut, always willing to exercise his immense intellectual prowess. "I take one every day after my steam. Good for the heart."

Always nice to hear a man talk about healthy heart maintenance as he washes down his third donut with a coffee, full of cream and sugar. The only thing I found more dichotomous was when I watched CNN's coverage of another "Right to Life" lunatic who had just killed another "pro-choice" advocate. The world ain't crazy, it's just gone insane.

Finally, Johnny rose from his donut-induced delirium, rubbed his palms together aggressively to magically eradicate any trace of residue, and marched confidently back to his map of monarchia.

"Kilbourne, this is my empire, and these pins are all the places I got a physical presence." Johnny stopped and stepped back at that point to bask in the absolute majesty of it all. Mario elbowed me in the side, so I immediately complimented him on his vast and varied accomplishments.

"The green ones mean I own it," he continued. "The yellow ones mean I have ownership in it, and the red ones mean I'm in the process of obtaining it. Shipping, trucking, manufacturing, warehousing, all of it, Kilbourne. I got it wired from cradle to grave. Within a couple of years, I'll get into industrial loans and commercial insurance and have to deal only with me." He started to laugh, not a normal laugh, but the satanic and somewhat insanic laugh of a Simon LeGreed.

"How much of that is legit?" I asked, tensing my obliques in advance of another elbow from Mario.

Johnny spread his large, soft arms wide, and smiled an innocent smile. "It's all legit. It just depends on which side of the swinging cell door you're on."

Though the "pin" demo and following narrative were somewhat impressive, and I do thoroughly enjoy a good smoke and mirrors magic show, I knew the truth to be somewhat different. Johnny's vast enterprises were notorious money pits, where money was hidden and not made. He ruled with too much supposition and not enough substance. The washed money made it look and feel lucrative, but none of his legitimate businesses could probably stand on its own two legs without infusions of illicit funds and illegal aliens.

Since he didn't have any living blood relatives and didn't trust anyone, and probably couldn't, he tried to run things himself and was way out of his league. What he needed was the business equivalent of a Mario, but last time I checked, the universities weren't offering any Mobster MBAs. Previous conversations with Chief Tanner pointed in the same direction; that in order to hide finances, his books had to be pretty loose, and loose books provided plenty of variance. As sad as it was to hear, and in contrast to what I'd always heard, the chief said there was in fact no honor among thieves. Henceforth, their penchant for felonious pursuit I suppose.

Johnny walked back to his desk of gargantuan proportions and seemed well pleased with his criminal dominion. "So, Kilbourne, as you can plainly see, I have dealings in many countries. In order to do that I gotta work with them that can guarantee my continuing success and survival in those countries, and in return, they like to do a little business here in the states, and I guarantee their continuing success and survival. You understand what I'm sayin'?"

"Quid pro quo!" I offered.

"Yeah, that, what you just said. And the reason you're here today is because you're treading dangerously close to one of my foreign associates' areas of interest, and he has asked me to insist you back off the girl or he will deal with you himself . . . permanent like."

I looked at Johnny for a few seconds. "I got a few questions. One, why tell me? Two, why not just have you do it? Three, why not just give me back the girl dead or alive? And four, what's he into that makes one girl an issue of significance?"

Johnny probably couldn't remember four questions in a row, so he nodded to Mario, and he took over the conversation.

"We're telling you so that maybe you'll be smart enough to drop it and alive enough to enjoy it. Mr. Rawls don't want to do it because he don't want no unnecessary heat from the local fuzz and your two wombats. We don't know who the girl is or what Mr. Chang is doing with her, so we don't know why she's worth the effort, or why he don't just give her back. It's probably a prostitution slant and hookers ain't our bag, and the General rules that track with terror as you know. And he clearly can't be any help because if he finds out somebody else is trickin' skin on his turf, it'll get bloody."

"So you're out of it," I said.

"After our conversation here today, we're Switzerland," Mario said. "We're just the messenger here, but don't take Mr. Chang and his associates lightly. Those little Laotians or Vietnamese kids or whatever they use would just as soon shoot somebody as not, they got nuthin' to lose. For them going to prison is a permanent family reunion with free bed and breakfast thrown in . . . if they get caught."

"Do they ever get caught?" I asked.

"Naw, or at least not unless they get busted red handed," Mario said. "There's too many of them and they all look alike. None of them are listed in any official database and they ain't got no permanent residences. Once they do a job, they fade back into the shadows. Slippery little devils, but deadly as hell."

Johnny came around his desk, leaned up against it, and crossed his arms. "If I was you, I'd drop it. Hookers typically ain't worth dying for."

"What about Julia Roberts in *Pretty Woman?*" I asked.

Johnny actually smiled. "Well, most hookers ain't worth dying for."

CHAPTER 23

I bid Johnny and Mario adieu, gave Daphne a knowing wink and a smile on the way out, and vacated the premises under the scornful eye of the dice-throwing dandies.

When I arrived back at the brain trust around four o'clock, my faithful companions were sitting on opposite couches tossing the tennis ball back and forth and discussing life's most pressing issues once more.

"Okay, for one hundred dollars . . . off the floor, onto the coffee table, onto the end table, off the marble pillar and into the vase, nuthin' but net."

"Who needs to work," Deity said, "when fools be givin' money away. You're on, my idiotic Italian friend."

I walked up to my desk and looked down at the deadly duo. "What's going on?"

Gio smiled. "I bet Deity a hundred smackers that I could take this tennis ball, bounce it off the floor, onto the coffee table, onto the end table, off the marble pillar and into the vase, nothing but net. It's merely the physics of angle and velocity, Boss. Piece a cake."

Deity looked up at me. "It's still a white boy and round ball, which means it ain't gonna happen, Bawse."

"He's got ya there, G," I said. "We're sadly compromised by our ethnicity. But what we lack in athleticism, we make up for in intellectualism."

"That's what I been sayin' all these years, Bawse," Deity said while nodding his head at Gio. "That's why ya'll make good coaches, cuz ya'll are smart enough to let the brutha's play the game."

Before Gio could coordinate a comeback, I interrupted.

"Wait," I said. "This is big. We'd better share this with the rest of the team." I called down to Diane and asked her to assemble everyone in my office immediately for an event of gargantuan proportion. When the bouncers, waitresses, cooks, cocktail waitresses, and bartenders arrived, I had them encircle the couches, adding an auditorium-like feel to the event. You could cut the tension and suspense with a knife, maybe even a Ginsu.

Diane finally arrived and came up to my desk for a kiss and a better vantage point. "What's going on?" she asked in a whisper. "Are you going to make some big announcement?"

"No, but this is big, really big," I said excitedly.

"Negation of world hunger big, or genesis of world peace big?" she asked.

"Both of those pale by comparison," I whispered. "Gio is going to try to bounce the tennis ball off the floor, then have it bounce off the coffee table, then bounce off the end table, then bounce off the marble pillar and then into the vase, nuthin' but net."

She looked at me blankly. "You called all of us up here for that?"

"I thought you were a sports fan," I whispered back. "It's never been attempted before in the modern era of target tennis ball bouncing. This could be a historical moment and thanks to me, you can tell your grandchildren that you were here to see it."

Nothing, still the same blank stare from Diane. "Sheesh, Women!" I said.

"Ugh, Men!" she retorted.

Gio was up, stretching and talking to the gathering hoards, and Deity was rubbing his shoulders and trapezius muscles, so I took a minute to call my good friend Dan Cunningham, who was a Pulitzer Prize-winning columnist for the *Seattle Times*. He answered the call on the first ring, just like a seasoned veteran.

"Cunningham here!"

"Danny C, this is Kilbourne. I have some breaking news for you," I said.

"Just a second," he said, "let me grab a pad and pen."

Within seconds he was back on the phone. "Thanks, Kil, what do you have?"

"Do you have a senior writer and an experienced photographer there? You'll need 'em?"

"Yeh," he said, starting to feel the excitement. "Marty and Kris are right here, what's going on?"

"Remember Gio, one of my codirectors of security at the City?"

"Yeh, yeh," he said anxiously, "what about him?"

"Well, he's here in my office as we speak, and he's getting ready to bounce a tennis ball off the floor, onto the coffee table, onto the end table, off the marble pillar, and into a vase."

Silence. I could almost hear the crickets chirping in the background.

"What?" he said, evidently dumbstruck with excitement and the majesty of it all.

"Let me recite it to you slower so you can get it all down on paper . . . I said, Gio is getting ready to bounce a tennis ball off the floor, onto the coffee table, onto the end table, off the marble pillar, and into a vase."

More silence.

"That's why you called me?" he asked.

"I call you whenever I have a hot scoop with global ramifications."

"A hot scoop of what?" he asked, evidently not a sports fan either.

"Hey, who called you last week with earth-shattering news?" I asked.

"No offense, Einstein, but finally setting the time on your VCR correctly is not necessarily considered earth shattering within Pulitzer circles."

"That's the problem with you, Danny. You're a pessimist and out of touch with today's readership."

"The problem with me, Kilbourne, is that I have morons for friends."

"How unfortunate for you. Have I met any of them?" I asked, but decided not to wait for an answer. "Anyway, feel free to forward my call to the global sports desk, at least they'll recognize the technical and athletic merit involved in an undertaking of this magnitude."

"Remind me again of your educational background?" he said.

"A PhD in Pop-Tart toasting," I said.

"That's what I figured. And from what esteemed university was this rigorously pursued acumen obtained?"

"Martin and Lewis," I said proudly.

There was another slight pause. "Would that be Dean Martin and Jerry Lewis?"

"You've heard of it?" I asked eagerly.

Click!

I looked at Diane who was now sitting on my desk facing me. "There goes his shot at a second Pulitzer," I said.

Diane rolled her eyes once again. "I'm stunned he's not running right over with a media team to document every second of this glorious event."

I patted her knee. "Thanks, Diane, your sincere and heartfelt support is always appreciated."

She just shook her head. "Do you realize how embarrassing it is for me to have my Bryn Mawr co-MBA friends know I work for a mental midget?"

"I believe the politically correct term is mental small person."

She smiled sweetly. "See what I mean." And with that, she kissed me on the forehead and left the room. I guess women will never understand sports at the elite level.

I looked down at the gathering and stood up. "Ladies and gentlemen, let the games begin. And to add more drama to our quest for athletic immortality, if Gio makes it, with his 'nuthin but net' shot, everyone will get a five-hundred-dollar bonus immediately after this amazing spectacle."

Yahoos and Hoorays echoed off every wall, and just as I had envisioned, this was truly turning into a seismic event with their newfound vestment.

Gio took his position on the couch with great fanfare and backslapping from the growing crowd. Once again the room grew quiet; nary a breath dared escape the lips of the onlookers so great was Gio's focus and concentration! He looked at the floor, then the coffee table, then the end table, then the pillar, and finally the vase with the five-inch fluted opening. He squeezed the tennis ball to gauge its bounciness, wet his index finger, and stuck it in the air to factor in whatever wind disturbance the AC may be causing.

Gio looked at Deity who nodded the go-ahead, then he looked at me, and I gave him the thumbs-up. With one smooth, graceful movement, Gio threw the tennis ball down relatively hard on the floor, and it bounced up majestically about ten feet in the air and then landed squarely on the coffee table, bounced up about six feet, seemed to stop and pose in midair much like Michael Jordan with the Nike swoosh clearly visible, hit a little wide on the end table but the uneven marbled glass straightened its trajectory, bounced up two feet, careened off the pillar, hit once on the wide mouth of the vase, then bounced again on the other side, its momentum almost forcing it to fall off the other side, and finally circled the rim . . . once . . . twice . . . and then . . . in. Tiger-esque!

A giant roar and an explosion of applause overcame the office as we realized we had just witnessed one of the greatest athletic performances in the history of the world. The employees stormed Gio with more backslaps, high fives, and attaboys. Rarely in life do you get to witness such graceful athleticism, such poetry in motion, or such technical artistry. Truly a moment of epic proportion!

But all of a sudden, a pall came over the crowd as Tree-Top stood up on one of the barstools and waved his hands. Not that he needed to stand on a stool since he was six feet nine inches tall, but maybe he was going for effect.

"Wait a minute! Wait a minute!" he yelled, trying for quiet and vying for everyone's attention. After everyone quieted down, he looked up at me, or down at me in his case. "Boss, you said we got five hundred dollars only if it went in and didn't touch the rim. Do we still gets our monies?"

It suddenly grew quiet, dead quiet, morgue quiet, middle of the Sahara quiet, a rap concert without tattoos, piercings, or felons kind of quiet. Extremely quiet! And all eyes were upon me in great expectation and anticipation. I thought about it for a few moments and came up with a solution.

"Clearly, a deal is a deal. And my promise was that it had to go in without touching the rim, but what constitutes a rim?" I looked down and rubbed my chin in deep thought as I'm sure Solomon might have done in his day. "That, ladies and gentlemen, is the five-hundred-dollar question."

I looked back up at the crowd. "What we need here is a ruling by a man of impeccable honesty, a man of utmost character, a man of such unimpugnable ethics and steely moral fiber that his ruling for or against can stand the test of time and a federal appeals court. A man who, when his name is mentioned, strong men kneel to, weak men run from, and women swoon over. A ladies man, man's man, man-about town. Ladies and gentlemen, I am obviously speaking of the great . . . Pablo Ramirez."

The crowd parted, much like Moses' parting of the Red Sea, and there Pablo was in the back, sitting on Dyno's broad shoulders, wide-eyed and surprised.

I called down, "Pablo, join me on the dais, if you would, please."

Dyno set Pablo down gently and he serpentined his way apprehensively through the crowd, climbed the few stairs and stood beside me behind my desk, looking a little scared but eager to lend a hand in this most critical of matters.

"Mr. Ramirez," I said loudly so that all could hear. "You have heard the question from Tree-Top, and you have heard my response. What we need from you is a thumps-up or a thumbs-down on whether or not five hundred dollars should be issued, based upon the question of . . . 'is a rim an outside edge, or is a rim the upper part of the inside of a rather beautiful and rare, ridiculously expensive, azure and ivory, fourteenth century Ming Dynasty vase'?"

I looked at him and gave him a quick wink and said, "A thumbs-up for dough, a thumbs-down for no."

All eyes were upon Pablo as he held out his arm, thumb to the side. You could have heard a grenade pin drop. With his left hand he rubbed his chin as I'm sure he had just seen me do two minutes before.

Finally, after what I am sure was a deep, exhaustive pondering of issues pertaining to quantum physics and the relativity theory, a ruling was made . . . thumbs-up!

Another roar from the crowd, equal to or greater than the original. Pablo surprised all of us by running around my desk and jumping into the crowd mosh-pit style. But he was caught by strong hands and loving arms, and was soon carried down the steps and out onto the deck of Atlantis by his fellow employees for a celebratory toast of sparkling cider.

I went to my biometric wall-safe and pulled out a large stack of one hundred dollar bills, each of which made me wish that they still circulated the McKinley five hundred dollar bills. I know that they used to print one thousand, five thousand, and ten thousand dollar bills too, but I think Nixon nixed that back in the late sixties to combat money laundering. I even tried to get a one-hundred-thousand dollar bill once from my bank for a charitable donation to a National Rifle Association fund-raising event, especially since the back of those bills are hunter orange, but was told that those were only used for intra-government transactions and were illegal to own by the public. Though it would have been nice to have pulled one of those out on a first date—the definitive guarantee of a good-night kiss!

After dispensing five one-hundred dollar bills to each of the employees and asking Diane to add equal bonuses to the checks of the employees who weren't in attendance, I felt pretty good, especially to see the look on Pablo's face when I counted out his money. But what really made him happy was me giving him a stack of ten thousand dollars and asking him to help me count out the winnings. I did ask Diane to give Pablo's father, Rama, a call and ask him to please pick Pablo up tonight, so that Pablo wouldn't accidentally buy five hundred dollars worth of bubble gum on the way home.

I had done a similar bonus for the employees at our last company Christmas Party. I'd had bingo cards passed out and we'd given out prizes to those with bingos at various times during the evening, but on the last bingo round of the night, I told them that I'd throw in an extra thousand dollars to the winner. What they didn't know was that it was rigged, and as Diane called out "I-1," everybody excitedly yelled "Bingo" at the same time and then looked at each other in disbelief. Thinking it was a mistake, they all looked over at me dejectedly until I raised my champagne glass and said, "Merry Christmas everyone, thanks for a great year and jobs well done!" The only problem now was trying to be even more creative next time.

Back to just being a threesome and all relaxing on the couch, I said, "You know what the best part about being me is?"

"The shame, the ridicule, the pity?" Gio asked.

I looked at him in disbelief. "Pity? Who'd pity me?"

"Mr. T. He pity all the fools," Deity said.

"Excellent point," I said, now in resignation.

"By the way," Gio said, "how'd it go with Super Mario today?"

I gave them the synopsis and told them that Mario and Johnny agreed to put Mr. Chang off for a couple of days by saying they hadn't contacted us yet.

"What'd that cost you?" Deity asked.

I looked at him and winced, "Ten cases of Michelob, fifty pounds of Maine lobster, fifty pounds of Alaskan King Crab, and a box of Cuban cigars."

"Ouch," Gio said. "Tis a high price you pay for bribery."

"I know, but remember the old adage . . . 'keep your friends close and your enemies closer'. Plus, it can't hurt to be on Johnny's good side . . . 'better the enemy you know,' you know?"

"Ya'll are making my head hurt," Deity said as he walked up and over to the twirly bar. "Maybe a couple of cocktails help ease the pain."

"I'll take some of that action, too, Mr. Jones," Gio said, "though I feel no pain."

Deity looked at Gio and smiled, "You know what they say my brutha . . . no brain, no pain."

When he turned to fix the drinks, Gio threw the infamous tennis ball at him but Deity had expected it and turned around just in time to catch it.

"Never turn your back on an Italian," Deity said and laughed as he threw the tennis ball back to Gio.

When Gio caught it, I noticed some writing on it and looked over at my bookcase that covered the entire wall to my left where Deity was fixing drinks, and noticed an empty space.

"Hey, is that my autographed tennis ball?" I asked.

Both of them turned and looked at me like two kids caught with their hands in the cookie jar.

"Oops, sorry, Boss," Gio said. "We couldn't find our other one so we borrowed yours."

I shook my head at them is disappointment. "That's my Tiger Wood's autographed tennis ball. Careful with that thing."

"Hey, speaking of that," Gio said as he walked up to put it back on my bookcase in its special holder, "Deity and I noticed you have a tennis ball autographed by Woods and a golf ball autographed by Federer. How come?"

"Because they're both smart alecks," I said. "When we were sitting together at the same table for the Diamond Jubilee on New Year's Eve, I asked Diane to get them a tennis ball and golf ball to autograph. And you know Tiger and Roger—just to mess with me and still fulfill my request, they both signed the other's. Now I just gotta figure out a way to get them both back."

But before I could figure out my revenge the phone rang.

"Greetings from the Gray Ghost," said Cas.

I put him on speaker. "Cas, I'm here with Deity and Gio. How goes the search?" I asked.

"So far so good. What are the 'Three Muscatels' up to?"

"Speaking of muscatels," I said, "we're just sitting here sipping alcoholic beverages and waiting for our thoughts to coalesce."

"I thought alcohol made your thoughts coagulate," he said.

"I think alcohol brings clarity," I said.

"I thought religion brought clarity," he said.

"I think religion brings salvation," I said.

"I thought alcohol brought salvation," he said.

"Ah, the circle of life," I said. "From whence it began so shall it end."

"From the Genesis to the Apocalypse," Cas said, "it's a wild ride."

"Amen, my brutha. What do you have for us?"

There was small pause and then a smug reply. "I got the call."

All of us sat up in our chairs in unison. "Seriously?" we asked.

"Yeh," he said. "All kidding aside, a gal that works with Grace just called and said that the gentleman that Grace had spoken to me about earlier in the week had just been admitted and would likely be able to receive visitors sometime late tomorrow."

"Wow, that's excellent news, Cas," I said. "Great work." Deity and Gio clinked glasses and bumped fists.

"Thanks. I'll give Grace a call in the morning and get the scoop, and then we can see what time we can head over there tomorrow. Hopefully, the guy will be coherent enough and brave enough to tell us what he knows."

"You always know just what to say."

She laughed her infectious laugh. "And who to say it to."

I thought of Yogi Berra and said, "It's déjà vu all over again."

"Yes," she said serenely. "Isn't it wonderful?"

There was a long pause, but it was calming and reassuring to just know that she was in town and on the other end of the line.

"I realize I'm on speaker phone," she said. "But I assume you're alone."

"Yes, just the fish, Ron Bicardi, and I," I answered.

"A motley crew . . ." she said.

"If ever there was," I said, finishing her sentence.

Again a pause—and then a voice—different from before, more emotional, less sure, and maybe a little afraid.

"Shad?" she asked almost in a whisper.

"Yes?"

And then, barely audible, with much effort, accompanied by what I assumed were tears . . . "I think I'm falling in love with you."

I was about to take another drink and stopped halfway. I thought about those words, what they meant, what they required, the lives that would be impacted, and that telling her that I wasn't in love with her was definitely the best thing for everyone and everything involved.

But, "And I with you," was all I heard me say in the gathering darkness.

CHAPTER 25

I once again ascended Kathryn's meandering boarded and roped walkway, and couldn't help but think of *Swiss Family Robinson* again. I was sure that somewhere in Kathryn's past it had something to do with memories of happier times with her father; a tree house maybe, or an adventure, or maybe just a book or movie they had shared.

As I got up to the doorstep, I noticed the glass door was slightly ajar, the bright light escaping in rectangulated prisms into the night. I pushed it open with a little hesitation and was relieved to hear Andrea Bocelli in the background and Kathryn singing in concert from a back room. I decided a long time ago to never care too much for one person ever again, much like a burn victim who stares into a fireplace, fascinated by its lingering brilliance but fearful of its devastating potential. It was also the reason I owned no plants, nor pets; her death was still too recent a memory and I didn't want to experience loss ever again, for any reason, on any level.

"Hey!" I called out and then heard a familiar squeal from her bedroom. Two seconds later, she came running out and jumped athletically into my arms, wrapped her legs around my waist, and gave me a giant hug and a quick peck on the lips.

I looked at her affectionately as she leaned back with her hands clasped behind my neck and her legs still wrapped around my waist.

"You seem a little ambiguous as to whether or not you're happy to see me," I said.

"That's because I'm playing hard to get, silly," she said.

"I thought you 'Thoroughly Modern Millies' played hard to forget?"

She unwrapped her hands and legs from around me and walked with exaggerated seductiveness back to the kitchen.

"The night is young and so am I, so we'll explore the hard to forget part later," she said over her shoulder.

"Well, since the wine and I are both old, I'll play sommelier."

She looked at me skeptically as she placed two Tiffany crystal wine glasses on the black granite counter. "Since when is being in your thirties considered old?"

"Since my life expectancy is probably forty, being in my thirties is probably the twilight of my life."

"And to what do you owe your perceived early demise?" she said, now a little concerned.

"I believe it would stem from too much lead in my diet."

She had to think about it for a minute but then got the connection and laughed. "But I thought you were faster than a speeding bullet?"

"I am," I said. "But occasionally the bad guys don't warn you prior to pulling the trigger."

"How inconsiderate," she said in mocked anger.

"I know," I said. "Think how I must feel?"

I opened a bottle of Cakebread Cabernet and poured a little into her glass for her to taste test.

She took a small, experienced sip. "Yummy. Pour on McDuff," she demanded.

"So," I said, "I either need to concede to dying young or start eating better."

She was once again foraging in the walk-in pantry and came out with multiple cheeses and crackers. "And what have you decided?"

"To start eating broccoli," I replied.

She started to laugh. "My experience with broccoli dictates that it could serve as either death or diet."

"Good point," I said. "Maybe broccoli is where they got the line 'what doesn't kill you makes you stronger.'"

"Death fought off by broccoli or death brought on by broccoli?" she pondered out loud.

"Is it 'Give me broccoli *or* give me death' or is it 'Give me broccoli *and* give me death'?" I posed as well.

We stared at each other for a minute wondering how we'd gotten off on such a sour-smelling and tainted-tasting tangent.

"On the topic of wonderful smells," she said finally, "will you please make us a fire, while I clean, cut, and coordinate the crab, clam, and lobster cuisine?"

My stomach and I smiled brightly at the menu, as I once again attempted man's quest for fire; fortunately, for us modern-day Cro-Magnons there were matches on the stone hearth and paper in the basket. "You know just what to prepare."

"And who to prepare it for," she uttered, equally as brightly from the kitchen.

I built the Dante of fires and returned to my barstool at the counter, so that I could watch her as she prepared our seafood feast.

"Are we movie watching tonight?"

"Yes," she said excitedly. "*The Thomas Crowne Affair.*"

I nodded my approval. "Any particular reason or just a mad crush on Pierce Brosnan . . . or Rene Russo as the case may be?"

She gave me a dirty look. "Actually, smart aleck, it's because the hero and heroine end up together at the end, regardless of the risk, ruin, or ramification."

I lifted my glass in a toast. "Love conquers all."

"Correction," she said as she clinked my glass, "*true* love conquers all."

I laughed. "Once again I cede to your wisdom and experience."

She winked and continued in her culinary craft by licking her fingers and snitching pieces of lobster. "Better for a man to do what he is told than to be told what he is."

"That sounds familiar."

She walked over to the end table and held up a large tome I knew to be the writings of Curtis St. John. "Voila!" she said triumphantly. "Since you quote him so often, I picked it up at Barnes & Noble. He's wonderful, by the way."

"He is the king of wit, wisdom, and womance, to coin his alliterative phrase," I said. "And he thinks 'womance' should be spelled that way too since it contains both the words 'man' and 'woman.'"

She smiled. "And who are we to argue with he who waxes poetic perfection?"

"I'll toast to that," I said. "And I will also toast to the fact that Cas got the call from Grace today, and we're meeting with the mystery man tomorrow night at Genesys. Would you care to come with?"

"Well, Mr. Kilbourne, that is toast-worthy," she said with obvious excitement and her typical facial animation. "And I would love to go with. What are you expecting?"

I shook my head. "I don't know. There's a lot of 'depends' woven into this deal. It depends on if he's there tomorrow, it depends on if he'll talk to us, it depends on if it really exists, it depends on if he'll show us how to get down there, and it depends on if it does exist . . . is she there or was she there, and then pull on that string and see where it leads us. If everything goes according to plan, I'll take Deity, Gio, Koda, Cas, and Rama with me to Tunnel Town and we'll see what happens."

"Why five and why them?" she asked astutely.

"It's actually very few for an operation where you have no idea what you're up against. And each of these guys, with the exception of Cas, are all experienced fighters and shooters. Plus, between those five guys they are pretty fluent in about six different languages, which may help. I have to take Cas, because I am assuming he'll want to go, that the informant will want him there, and because he might possibly know some of the individuals involved once we get down there."

"My God," she said, coming over to hug me and have me hold her. "I wasn't scared until just now, but I never thought of this as a bunch of armed men going in against another group of armed men." She looked up at me with moist eyes. "I'm afraid for you, Shad. I just found you. I don't even want to think about losing you."

We walked arm in arm into the great room and sat down next to each other on the couch with our wine and oceanic hors d'oeuvres. We tried to steer the conversation away from the weekend's potential consequences and ended up getting lost in each other's laughter and companionship, rising only occasionally to feed the fire or replenish our wine glasses. I rose once again to put in our movie and seek the relative safety of cinematic seclusion, but before I could push "Play" she asked if we could talk first about our earlier exchange over the phone.

"All right, young lady, what would you like to do about us?" I asked, relatively ignorant of what her expectations would be.

She had her arm through mine and her head on my shoulder as we stared into the night's fire and occasionally the night sky—the lights of a few homes and a myriad of boats reflecting spectrally off the lake, dancing buoyantly with each passing wake and undulation.

"Well," she said. "I know we are both in long-term committed, though not necessarily monogamous relationships. I know that we both would not care to hurt those unnecessarily for whom we care so deeply. I know that I have unresolved issues that I still need to sort through on multiple levels. I know that I adore you and you've reciprocated in kind. I know that this has been a wonderful friendship so far, and I don't want to disturb or destroy what we already have . . . so, if you wouldn't mind and are in full agreement, I would like to leave it pretty much as it is, except with the knowledge that we feel the same way about each other and with the hope that maybe someday with you will turn into everyday with me."

With that said, she turned to look at me with her dazzling smile. "What do you think?" she asked.

"Well," I said, "let me state that I too adore you, and have from the second I met you. I think that I have genuinely met my soul mate and potentially my sole mate. I think pleasantly, long, and often about a scenario that someday materializes with our lives permanently intertwined. I think that to be the recipient of your love and affection is one of the greatest honors that have ever been bestowed upon me. I think I potentially have the future emotional bandwidth and the physical discipline to do both eternity and monogamy with you and probably only you, but because of who I am and what I sometimes do, I don't think I am capable of marriage, cohabitation, or kids. But I do know that the thought of you not in my life pains me greatly, and it is not something I will willingly let go of unless you so desire."

I wasn't sure how she'd take the no marriage, no living together, and no kids declaration, but I didn't want there to be any misunderstandings or false promises. And I knew that for her to make the emotional investment of change in life and change in lifestyle, she needed as much clarity as I could possibly provide.

She was quiet for quite a while after I had finished, so I just held her close and let her sort things out in her head. I knew that we had crossed the Rubicon relationally and emotionally, but that the physical abyss might be the largest impasse for her to potentially navigate someday.

"If we end up together someday, will you promise to spend the night, any night, I ask?" she asked.

"Yes," I said.

"Will you promise to love me forever and never leave me?"

"Yes."

"Will you promise to tell me how beautiful I am even when I'm old and gray?"

"Yes."

"Will you promise to ravish me in the bedroom even when you're old and gray?"

I looked down at her face of infinite possibilities. "Yes," I said slowly, "probably not often . . . and probably not well . . . but yes."

She kissed me tenderly on the mouth for just the second time since we met, and for just a moment, and then said in a barely audible whisper. "I now pronounce you friends for life."

CHAPTER 26

I knew it was love when in the morning I awoke and there were Pop-Tarts in the pantry and Diet Cokes in the fridge. I knew it was true love when there was a Rice Krispies treat with a ribboned bow around it on the counter. She was still asleep on the couch and I was once again sneaking out so as to not wake her mid-dream. I tip-toed over to the couches, stealthily pulled the covers over her, and risked a kiss on the cheek. As I went to grab my keys in quiet exodus, there was a note on the entry table with a small envelope.

> *Dear Loving Friend,*
>
> *I am assuming you will depart quietly in the wee hours of the morn so as to not disturb my slumber. I will miss the welcoming warmth of your presence upon dawn's awakening. As you already know, you have the key to my heart, and that being said, I would be honored if you would please accept the key to my home as well, for it will be merely a house until you return. I will see you tonight (don't be late!).*
>
> *With you always,*
> *Kathryn*

I took the key out of the envelope and placed it on my keychain, I would have left her the key to my penthouse but it is merely a code punched into the private elevator's security system. So I wrote her a quick note back and slipped surreptitiously out of the door, locking up after myself with my newly awarded key.

Around noon, I met up with Gio, Deity, and Koda and we headed down to Southeast Seattle to an area called Rainier Valley and a nightclub called Pandora's Box, which was owned by the General and also served as his base of operations.

We were in Deity's black Cadillac DTS, or 'The Fine Ride,' as he referred to it. Koda was in the front with Deity, and Gio and I were in the back, watching Seinfeld on the TV monitors hooked up inside the back of the headrests.

Deity looked over at Koda, "If 'n you and Gio weren't here, I could pretend I was driving Ms. Daisy with Kil in the back."

"I'm sure it will be a thrill for the General to see you chauffeuring us around," I said. "Make sure you get the doors for us, too. That'll drive him nuts."

"Yessa, Bawse!" Deity said in his best black-de facto imitation.

When we arrived at Pandora's it was around one o'clock and there were already cars in the parking lot, the Saturday crowd hitting the cocktails early to get the party started. Pandora's used to be a large, old bowling alley that the General had remodeled into a disco-tech-esque nightclub replete with lighted floor, strobe lights, mirrored balls, and plenty of neon. He had actually applied for and been granted matching redevelopment funds from the city since he had called it a community center in the application. The city council had tried to repeal the award after its true purpose was discovered, but the NAACP had jammed the race card down their throats so hard that they had to uphold the original award and amount.

Four huge, black bodybuilders were hanging around out front playing mumblety-peg in the dirt with switchblades. As soon as we pulled up and emptied the car, two of them walked inside while the other two stood at the front of the main double-doored entrance. They kept the switchblades out, but down at their sides, and both of them produced nines out of their baggy military pants.

My security guys at the clubs were all big and well built, but these guys were poster children for steroid use and abuse. They had muscles on muscles, with the skin pulled taut to the point of stretch marks. As we walked up, the two roid boys paid Deity a little deference and bumped fists.

"S'up, D?" they said in unison.

"S'happ'nen fella's," Deity said in return as they did the now common half hug.

"Ya'll know the routine fellas. Hands high," said the larger of the two as they started to pat us down, guns and knives still in their hands.

The less gargantuan of the two started to pat down Deity, but large-and-in-charge stopped him. "Just ask him if he's carryin', Coop. Don't be dis'n the brutha."

"No 'fense, D, I be forgettin' maself." Coop said to Deity. "Ya'll packin'?"

"Yeah, we all carrying a piece," Deity said, "but the General will be okay with that. We ain't warring. We're just here for a cold beverage and a warm hug."

Large started to laugh a big deep laugh, "Beverages be inside, D, but the huggable honies don't start work until around nine."

"Maybe I go in and give Gat-Gun a big hug," Deity said as we started to walk in.

Smiles left both of the roid boys' faces. "Man, don't even be jokin' 'bout dat 'round Gat-Gun man, GG will slit yo throat. You know he ain't got no sens'a humor and he be homophobic as hell."

Deity looked at them both with his big white and wide smile. "You're right, my bumpy bruthas. Maybe I jus' give him a little kiss on the cheek!"

As we entered the dark and cavernous building, I expected to feel the cool relief of air-conditioning, but it was hot, humid, and sticky, much like a night in New Orleans, minus the beads and bedlam. The black ceilings were about twenty feet high, the walls and flooring done in the same black, reflective tiles. To complete the ebony theme, the furnishings were composed of black, faux leather chairs and reflective black-topped tables. There were three different dance floors and five bars, with numerous small dance platforms and cages so that the daring could swing a solo once enough liquid courage had been consumed.

"This place must pop with a decent light show," Deity said, already dancing to the music that only he heard. Life was one continuous rhythm to Deity; even the way he walked seemed smooth and sinewy as silk.

We were met about halfway through the entryway by Gat-Gun and the other two muscle-bound militiamen who were posted outside just a few minutes prior. They were probably considered the height of fashion since they had forgone the tank tops and opted for white, short-sleeved Under Armor tops and blackened camo pants instead.

Gat-Gun looked at each of us without a word, finally nodding silently and slowly when he saw Deity.

"I don't know him," Gat-Gun said in his high voice, pointing to Koda. It was always funny to hear Gat-Gun speak for the first time because he had that Mike Tyson little girl lilt to his voice, except that Gat-Gun was dumber, meaner, and madder than Iron Mike. He had a hair-trigger temper and would just as soon shoot you as look at you. He was not to be messed with too casually or too often.

"Friend of mine," I said with a straight face and a serious tone. Shad Kilbourne . . . all business! "The General said I could bring one friend of each ethnic background. I got a Chinaman, an Irishman, and an Ottoman still in the car."

This was way too much information for Gat-Gun's mustard-seed intellect. He looked hard at me for a few seconds and then switched back to Koda.

"Aw'right," Gat-Gun said tapping his big forty-five against his thigh. "As long as the General okayed it." And then he turned his "nobody home" gaze back to me. "But those other three guys stay in the car."

I almost started to laugh, but thought better of it after I heard a "Careful, Boss" whisper behind me from Gio. We all knew that Gat-Gun was more than a little off mentally and didn't need much provocation to start shooting us just for the sake of saying he did it.

"First time off the reservation, Tonto?" one of the two muscleheads asked as they both laughed and bumped fists.

The other went with the flow. "Let us know if you be get 'n thirsty, Tonto. I sure we's got some fire-water here somewheres." More laughter and more fist bumps from the dianabol duo and a high-pitched giggle from Gat-Gun. I looked over at Koda and he just smiled . . . which didn't bode well for them.

We followed Gat-Gun through the maze of tables, chairs, lighting units, and audio pillars, with the rest of his black militia following closely behind. Before we got to the main hallway, there were three doors along the far wall, one marked "Men," one marked "Women," and one marked "Whitey." I stopped out of curiosity and opened the one marked "Whitey." It had clearly once been a broom closet. It was probably two feet by two feet with an old, rusted bucket nailed to the floor, a roll of toilet paper made out of sandpaper, a sink with no faucet, and an old dim light bulb that came on when you opened the door. The only ode to decor was an old copy of a photograph blown up to poster size that showed a huge old sprawling oak tree with six Klu Klux Klan members hung to death on its formidable branches, still in their white sheets, surrounded by a squadron of black men in Union-blue uniforms. Cheery!

I looked at Deity, "I hadn't realized that the General had a sense of humor."

"I don't tink dat he do," Deity said in his best Michael Clarke Duncan impression.

Gat-Gun turned around to tell us to quit wasting time when he noticed our foursome was suddenly a threesome. "Where's the Mex?" he said to the two subordinates behind us. They just looked at each other and then looked around hurriedly, hoping he was still in sight.

I smiled inwardly, so as to not get shot, at the thought of Koda seeing if he could "go ghost," as he called it, right in front of their eyes. Nobody does a disappearing act better than Koda.

"You idiots," Gat-Gun yelled. "Go find'im. How you lose somebody who's right in front a ya?"

"Apache Indian," I said.

Gat-Gun looked at me like I was speaking French, except that he'd think I was speaking German if I was speaking French. "What?" he asked.

"He's not Mexican," I said. "He's Apache Indian, and I know you wouldn't want to hurt anyone's feelings by hating them for no reason."

"I hate everybody," he said pointing his gun at me, "you 'specially."

I had a special knack for making friends wherever I went; it was a gift.

Another hallway branched off toward the interior of the building, and at the end was a single door of some obvious size and expense, which was in direct contrast to the rest of the bleak and barren hall.

Gat-Gun knocked on the door with the barrel of his gun and it was opened by the first tall, thin, lightly hued black man of immaculate and fashionable dress that I'd seen since I arrived.

"Attorney or accountant?" I asked him as I walked in.

He looked at me behind rimless glasses with a faint smile. "Both, actually," he said with his hand out to shake. "I'm Roland Tate, MBA, CPA, and JD, but mainly legal counsel and business advisor."

I shook his rather delicate looking and feeling hand. "Shad Kilbourne, GED," I said, "working on my PhD in longevity."

He laughed gently. "Good luck with that."

The rest of our entourage filed into the redoubt to what could only be categorized as early-seventies *Shaft*. Lots of what was neo-modern at the time that now went for retro-ugly: blue velvet couches, orange-and-brown wall-to-wall shag carpeting, leopard- and zebra-patterned lounge chairs, lava lamps, beads, glass coffee tables, stained glass lights, Formica counters at the bar . . . shaga-delic baby!

The General was sitting behind his desk with his feet up in authentic *Shaft* attire as well—his leather zip ankle boots showing a little hairless leg where his stove-pipe plaid slacks couldn't quite stretch—his tight lime green Neru jacket showing off his prominent pecs and thick neck.

"S'up, D? When you coming to work for me and quit serving white bread over here?" he said, gesturing a thumb at me.

"That be a very kind offer, General, but I'm not sure you can afford what Kil be paying me," Deity said. "'Sides, I be a loyalist; wouldn't be the honorable thing. And you don't be need 'n me; Kil does."

I put my hand behind my back, palm up, and Deity slid me some skin. I loved my boys.

"Your loss, D," the General said.

"And yours, General," Deity said in return as he and Gio moved to either side of the doorway.

"You prob'ly right," the General said, nodding his head in thought. "So shut the damn door already, Kilbourne. You born in a barn?"

"No," I said humbly, "in a manger, under a star."

Mr. Tate was the only one who got it and laughed; the General and Gat-Gun looked a little perplexed.

Gio shut the door for me and all that was left was our threesome and the four horsemen that were the General, Gat-Gun, Mr. Tate, and another gentleman of African American descent I had just noticed who neither moved nor acknowledged us in any visible fashion. He was inert in a chair in the far corner, with an expensive suit and designer sunglasses as his only calling card. He seemed to be looking at everything, or nothing maybe, or maybe he was asleep, or maybe dead and embalmed to look like high-priced backup. And since no one bothered to do the intros, I made a note of where his hands were and let it go at that.

"Honky-Tonk," the General called me from his desk after popping a few gummy bears in his mouth. "To what do I owe the displeasure of your annoying and worthless existence?"

"I just wanted to see what unlimited power and inexhaustible wealth could provide in the way of office décor," I said. "Does Super-fly know you stole his stuff?"

The General attempted a smile, without much warmth or humor, "Just because I let you keep your gun doesn't mean you won't need it. Gat would consider it a personal favor if I let him put a cap in yo' ugly mug."

"Gat would consider it a personal favor if you let him burn ants with a magnifying glass out in the parking lot," I said, "as long as he gets to kill something."

"Enough," the General said with a dismissive hand gesture. "You asked for this meetin' and cus I feel sorry for white folk I 'cepted. What you want, Honky-Tonk?"

Gio and Deity leaned against the back wall, probably excited to lean up against authentic shag carpeting on a wall, since none of us were alive yet when it was en vogue back in the early seventies. I walked over and sat in the faux leopard skin chair; as I did so the room's attention was directed to the door behind me. Koda walked through and leaned up against the door between Deity and Gio.

"Who are you?" the General asked, all of a sudden unsure of the situation.

"He's with me, General," I said. "He was out practicing his YMCA moves on the dance floor."

"And he ain't Mexican," Gat-Gun said proudly, happy to potentially know something his boss didn't. "He's a patched Indian."

The General looked at Gat-Gun as if he had told him the sun was hot. But he did relax a little bit that it wasn't some kind of power play on our part.

I looked over at the mystery date in the corner and he was putting a gun away that I hadn't seen him draw. I needed to be a little more careful, or someday I'd be a little less alive.

The General studied Koda some more. "Do you know who you look like?"

"The Indian on *Predator* and *48 Hours*?" Koda asked.

The General snapped his fingers and grinned. "Yeah, that's it, Man: the injun on *Predator* and *48 Hours*."

"Except I'm bigger, tougher, and better looking," Koda said.

"You look a lot like him, though," the General said.

Koda smiled. "He's my cousin."

"No foolin'?" the General said while popping a few more gummy bears in the process. "What's he like?"

"Like me," Koda said with a straight face, "just smaller, weaker, and not as good looking."

The General didn't get it at first, but then shook his head and pointed at Koda as the fog cleared. The conversation was cut short, though, when the General realized Koda had entered unescorted.

"Wait a minute, how'd you get in here? Where're Rock and Daman?"

Gat-Gun spoke up. "I sent them to go look for the injun," he said nodding toward Koda. "They must still be lookin'."

I smiled and looked back at Koda. "Did they find you?" I asked.

He smiled as well and answered, "I found them."

"And?" the General said, clearly starting to get a little annoyed at this point.

Koda looked at him without expression. "And they are resting peacefully in the shed out back."

"What?" the General said, coming out of his seat, "Gat, go check on Rock and Daman." And then he looked back at me and Koda. "And they better not be dead, or you four are going to join them."

"They're not dead," Koda said. "They had quick mouths and slow reflexes. And they confused size and strength with toughness and technique, so I taught them the difference." He smiled again. "The education was free, by the way. There'll be no charge."

"Dammit, Kilbourne," the General said, slamming down a pencil on his desk. "You're gonna meddle once too damn often."

"Actually," I said, "I've always wanted to be a gold meddle winner. This could be my shot."

Mr. Tate interrupted calmly at this point. "Gentlemen, if you could please state your business, it would allow us to get on with ours."

The General looked at Tate and then back at the silent partner, and a nod from him seemed to calm whatever agitation the General happened to be feeling at the time. "What is it, Honky-Tonk? Make it fast."

"I'm with Weight Watchers," I said in an official voice. "I'm here to confiscate your Gummy Bears."

"Quit screwing around, White Meat," he said, pulling his tasty treat closer. "And don't touch the bears. It's my last bag of a brand you can't get anymore. So start talkin' or start walkin'."

I took a folded picture of Chrissy out of my jacket pocket and showed it to the General. He looked at it. "So?"

"One of yours?" I said.

He looked at it again, and then looked at Mr. Tate and the henchman behind him. Both of them arose and walked over for perusal. Both took a long look, which I appreciated, and then shook their heads in the negative.

"Not one of ours," the General said, spinning the picture back across his desk toward me. "Never seen 'er before. You can check with Gat and the boys on the way out, but she ain't ever shimmied for us. I may not know all their names, but I know the faces that pay the bills, and she ain't one. Why you want t' know?"

I handed the picture over my shoulder to Deity so he could go check it out with Gat-Gun and a few of his cronies. "She's important and she's missing; just thought she may have spiraled down in your direction."

I thought about it for a minute and then went ahead and asked. "You know anything about a place beneath the city that might be running a little skin-game of its own?"

"Tunnel Town, man?" he said with much laughter. "Man, that rumor's been 'round long as I been. There ain't nuthin' to it or I'da put it outa biz'ness a long time ago and put the management even deeper in the groun'. Hell, if anything it's probly a brutha sellin' his girlfriend and sister for pennies in the pits." He spread his arms to encapsulate all that around him. "Too small for me to bother with. I runnin' an empire here, not worryin' about no nickel and dime nookie 'neath the streets."

He started to laugh again, grabbing some gummy bears out of the bag on his desk and popping a couple in his mouth. "Tunnel Town! That cracks me up, man. Ain't no tunnels that ain't on the tour and there ain't no undergroun' town that's trickin' without my knowin'. From the boardroom to the bathroom, my brutha, the action be mine. Least ways in this here state, White Bread."

The phone rang and the General picked it up, listened for a minute and then held up his index finger to mean he would be a minute. I thought about all we'd learned and some of what we'd surmised. Either Tunnel Town didn't exist, which was possible and probable, or it existed in such a vacuum that great lengths were taken to keep it so quiet for so long. Which meant the security was great, the secrecy was great, or someone ruled with such absolute control and utter terror that people were too afraid, too discredited, or too dead to bring down the house. And if that was the case, it wasn't just about prostitution; it was probably something so far beyond the bizarre that I didn't even want to think about it.

Fortunately for me, I wasn't going to get a chance to think about it, because the General's phone call came to a close and for the first time that day, a large smile adorned his face.

"Looks like Gat-Gun ain't gonna get the pleasure of killin' you, Milk Bone," the General said. "Just got word that somebody already put fifty large on your honky head this morning." He started to laugh with genuine humor and enjoyment. "You musta really jacked someone 'round this time, Tonk, cuz I'm lookin' at a dead man for that kinda bread. Bes' you be watching yo baggy behind."

"First of all," I said, "I prefer the term 'buns of steel,' and secondly you probably heard them wrong and someone is willing to pay fifty grand to feel me, not kill me."

The General actually continued his laughter. "You wish, and anyway, I jes passin' on the info as a favor to D. But fifty K in this here town can buy a brutha some serious comfort, so I'd be keeping your boys close if 'n I you, least ways 'til you find out who be financin' your finale."

There didn't seem to be much else to say, so I stood up, walked over to his desk, and held out my hand to the General. "Thanks for the heads up on the potential hit."

The General stood as well and matched my grip in a momentary test of strength; we both gave each other a knowing grin and then released. I looked past the General and shot the dark knight with my thumb and index finger. Everyone turned to look at him as he just nodded once behind the sunglasses and stayed true to form . . . mute and resolute.

We all piled back into Deity's Caddy and started to turn out of the parking lot when all of a sudden we heard shouting behind us as Gat-Gun and his cronies came running out the front doors of the club in angry pursuit.

I told Deity to hit the gas and we skidded out of the parking lot and headed for the relative safety of the freeway.

"Kilbourne, you son of a . . . ," was all we heard as the rest of it was lost in the roar of the massive engine and the squealing of tires on the rain-slickened pavement.

Gio, Deity, and Koda looked at me wide-eyed. "What the heck do you think that was that all about?" Gio asked. "I thought we parted on pretty good terms?"

I shrugged my shoulders innocently, reached into my jacket pocket and pulled out the General's coveted Gummy Bears. "I have no idea," I said, and passed out the spoils of victory amongst much laughter.

CHAPTER 27

We called Cas from the car phone and he informed us that we were on for eight o'clock tonight at "the place of Grace" as he affectionately referred to it. He wanted some time with Grace before we got there so we told him we'd meet him there. Gio and Deity could head over there early to make sure everything was copacetic and I'd pick up Kathryn and we'd rendezvous with the others around 7:45 p.m. There was probably no reason to have Koda or Rama there at this point since we could hold a briefing later, to update them on what we'd established, if anything.

Deity interrupted my thoughts, which bummed me out because getting my brain to engage for an extended period of time was such a rare occasion anymore.

"If'n Mr. Chang put up the fifty G's for yo hide," Deity said, "maybe Gio, Koda, and I be hanging out in yo hip pocket until we gets some closure on this deal."

Both of them were looking back at me. I looked at Koda, who was nodding his head. "Probably not a bad idea, Paleface," he said with forged accent and genuine concern.

"Though I appreciate the concern, fellas," I said, "I'll kindly defer your offer for now. Number one, we're not sure it's Mr. Chang yet who put the hit out on me; and number two, I think this thing is either going to blow up or blow away within the next couple of days, anyway. But I'll try to stay inside and lo-pro until we get a grip on this deal."

It was already around four o'clock in the afternoon, so the boys dropped me off at the City and went to check on the other clubs. I knew Diane would be dropping by the other restaurants as well to check in with the managers and make sure we were all set for another solid Saturday night, which meant that the restaurant would be relatively quiet except for the prep crew, and I could make some calls in undisturbed tranquility.

I checked the reservation list at the Falling Waters restaurant and made a note to drop by at some of the VIP and celebrity tables later tonight. It looked like both the Reef and the Breakers restaurants were booked as well, so I started to get excited as I always did. The energy and aura that the packed bars and restaurants emitted was both cacophonic and contagious. Something about the physics of controlled chaos always fired up the staff and made for a pleasurable and profitable evening for all.

I hit the stairs once more and emerged on the third floor of Atlantis. The giant islanders, Tui and Tevi, were busy prepping the bar, but Tui dropped back in the pocket, planted his back foot and threw me a bag of pretzels quarterback style as I went by. I made a miracle catch because of my two-and-a-half-inch vertical leap, and gave the boys a head nod, and the barstool a Heisman, as I ran by.

Back at the safety of my own enclave, I poured myself a Barbancourt and Diet Coke and opened the bag of pretzels that I had just recently scored a touchdown with.

There were a couple dozen messages from Diane on who had called and who I needed to call back, but first I called Rama and asked if he could possibly join us the next day for a potential operation and told him a big Indian would be there to pick him up, and as a professional courtesy to please not shoot him.

After that I called Kathryn to see if she wanted Roiks to pick her up and bring her to the restaurant for dinner, to which she readily and romantically agreed.

I then placed a call to a little Cambodian importer/exporter gentleman I knew through various nefarious dealings, who went by the name of Imex. I wasn't sure what his real name was, but now that I thought about it 'im' and 'ex' were the first two letters of import and export, . . . clever little devil. I pulled the empty gummy bear bag out of my pocket and read him off the brand name and the other markings on the bag. Imex was about four-foot-two-inches tall and weighed about ninety pounds but most of it was muscle and all of it was mean; however, through his global underground networks he could locate anything in the world, legal or illegal, for a price, and he was a good guy to know.

"How soon you need?" he asked without any exchange of pleasantries.

"Don't get mushy on me, Imex," I said. "I know you miss me when I don't call, but try to be strong for the kids."

There was a brief pause. "How soon you need?" he asked again, but with less patience and more irritation. Imex was great at hiding his love for me, but I hated to see a guy in denial.

"You get?" I asked.

"I get," he said.

"How soon you get?" I said, trying to mimic his tone, pattern, and accent.

"I find out," he said, my attempt at humor wasted once again. "You call Monday."

"Imex?"

Another pause. "Yeah?"

"I met a guy shorter than you last week." I said in my friendly pro-Cambodian, fan-of-the-little-man, making-friends-wherever-I-go, and international-man-of-magnanimity voice.

Still another pause—probably wondering if he should just hang up or not! "Oh yeah, who he?"

"I'm not sure," I said, "he was late for kindergarten and took off on his tricycle before I could get his name."

'Click,' was all I heard until the dial tone kicked in.

Ah, another day, another fan.

I called Mario and asked him if he could track down the source of the contract on my head. He seemed irritated at first that I had asked him for a favor, but seemed to cheer up significantly when he realized people were trying to kill me.

"I'll see if I can get a name and an address," he said.

"I don't need an address, just a name will do," I said.

"I know," Mario said. "The address is for me, I need to find out where to send the thank you card." And then another click and a dial tone. I sensed a trend.

I had messages from about a dozen other people, of which two were the senator's partners in crime: Nicholas White and Malcomb Arbreau. They said the senator was in town this week and wanted to meet me for a complete debriefing. I'd have more for them on Monday, so I figured they could wait out the weekend. Another message was from Smythe, so I called and left him a message telling him that Diane was missing and asking if the two of them had run off together and eloped.

The bird in the cuckoo clock on the wall moo'ed five times to let me know it was five o'clock, so I turned on the array of monitors and cameras and surveyed the business at hand. The crowds were already lined up at the doors and my staff seemed to have everything ready and under control as always. I caught a glimpse of Diane as she walked by one of the cameras, so I punched her headset code and started to breathe heavily into the microphone.

I heard her start to laugh. "Is this Brad Pitt or George Clooney?"

"Neither," I said. "It's their better-looking friend."

"Tom Selleck?" she said.

"No, better looking than that," I said.

I could tell that she had just entered the kitchen by the rattle of pots, pans, and plates in the background. "I hate to break it to you, my heavy breathing heart-throb," she said, "but there is no 'better looking' than Tom Selleck."

"Good point," I said, "everything okay?"

There was a pause and then some hesitation in her voice when she continued. "The restaurants are fine, but I miss you, and so does Taylor."

I smiled. "I miss you guys too. Sorry, I've been so busy lately. Let's do the zoo and a picnic that we were talking about or go on a lunch cruise next week, just the three of us. How does that sound?"

She laughed. "Not as good as a sleepover with just thee and me, but Taylor will love it, and I would love to pretend we're a family for a day again."

I felt us getting on some rather egg-Shelley-ian ground here. "You and Taylor are the only family I have, Di. You know that."

"I know," she said with burgeoning emotion in her voice. "But little girls - and big girls too - dream marvelous and magical dreams where the handsome prince comes and carries them off to his penthouse castle and they all live happily ever after."

"I didn't know you felt that way, Di." I said as sweetly and carefully as I could. "Why didn't you say something?"

She started to laugh and cry at the same time. "Because they teach you in business school never to fall in love with your boss . . . and your best friend."

She must have gone into her office because the background noise came to an abrupt halt after the sound of a door closing, and the flood of tears finally gave way.

"I'm sorry, Shad, I just thought that maybe if anything ever happened to you and Jess, that maybe you and I would finally be more than just great friends and pajama partners. But then when I heard you were seeing that Kathryn Rae woman, too, I guess I just lost hope. And the fact that you didn't even know I'm in love with you makes me think that you needed to know, especially if Taylor and I are to ever have a chance at being your real and only family."

I hated these conversations, which was ironic because I seemed to have them all the time. "You know me, Di, probably better than anyone else in the world, and you know who and what I am. Why in the world would you be in love with me?"

She started to laugh through the tears again. "Because I probably know you better than anyone else in the world, and I know who and what you are."

I started to laugh too, which helped us both out of our tenuous circumstance. "You're sweet. I love you, you know that. I just didn't know being 'in' love with you was an option or an opportunity. You have a great life, an incredible daughter, your pick of great guys to date, I pay you handsomely, and you have a boss-slash-friend that adores you in every way."

"I know," she said between sniffles. "And I'm sorry to bring it up now, at work, over the headphones, during the rush, but I'd rather you knew and turned me down, than not ever know what could have been."

"Me, too," I said. "And I am incredibly honored to have your love, your affection, and the opportunity to love you in return. We'll talk about it next week, but instead of going to the zoo, why don't I take you, or you and Taylor, to Hawaii for three or four days in a couple of weeks and we can discuss it over too much sun, too many margaritas, too many lobster tails, and too much time in the kiddie pool?"

"You mean it?" she said excitedly.

"Yes, of course, I mean it," I said. "I'm sure we could both use a little time and distance from this place. And why don't we bring your mom too? She's wonderful and we'd have a built-in babysitter for midnight strolls along the beach."

I expected a "yippee" or maybe a "hooray," but all I heard was more sobbing. "What's wrong now?" I said.

She started to cry even louder. "That's why I love you so much, you big, fat idiot, because you're always so wonderful."

"I'm not fat," I said, foregoing the indefensible "idiot" battle.

She laughed. "And because you're funny, too." And then she seemed to get her breath, her emotions, and I'm assuming her makeup, back in check.

"Better now?" I said.

"Yes, sir," she said with newly found composure, "much better now."

"Okay, then," I said. "Get back to work so we can afford an ocean-view suite at the Four Seasons in Maui."

"Aye, Aye, Captain," she said, back to her old confident and competent self. And then after only a moment's thought and pause, she said, "I love you."

"I love you too, Sailor," I said. "Don't forget."

"I won't," she said softly and sweetly, "you're already all my memories."

CHAPTER 28

I picked up Kathryn at seven o'clock on the dot for our drive south to Gig Harbor and the Genesys Clinic, and as a reward for me being on time, she came running down the delta'd landscaping in an athletic rush. When she jumped in the car, her forest green eyes were big, bright, and alive with energy and excitement. She was also drenched from the cantankerous rain that grew heavier with darkness and louder in accompaniment with the itinerant thunder and lightning. Her cobalt blue rain gear took the brunt of the abuse, but those areas exposed due to fashion's whim were soaked. She put her hand on my face and pulled me close for a quick kiss and a hug, all the while unbuttoning her coat as the rivulets of rain drained to the Range Rover floor.

"I'm so excited to see you," she said as she checked her look in the visor mirror. "I know I shouldn't be, based upon the essence and importance of this errand, but seeing you and embarking on this great adventure together is thrilling to me."

Lightning lit up the sky in electrical pulses, and the ensuing thunder rattled the car and some of Kathryn's nerves. The rain continued to pour, poke, and pummel from every direction, and the wind gusts pushed us from median to shoulder as we entered the I-5 Freeway South.

"I am actually a little excited myself, if you want to call it that. It will be interesting to hear the tall tales from the tunnel and finally put it to bed or put it into production, depending on what we hear tonight, and if he's willing to provide directions or guidance."

We drove in silence for a few minutes and I sensed her staring at me.

"What?" I said.

She squinted her eyes, as if in deep analysis of my psyche. "You seem abnormally distant."

"I am distant," I said, wary of the power of a woman's intuition. "We're nearly six inches apart."

"Oh," she said happily, "that must be it." And she leaned over onto my side and rested her head momentarily on my shoulder. After a few minutes, she sat back up but placed her hand on mine on the shifter.

"I think we need an old, rusty pickup," she said out of the blue.

I started to laugh at the unexpected non sequitur. "And why is that pray tell?"

"Because they have those big, old bench seats, and that way I could sit right next to you and bother you while you drove," she said, "and when I'm sleepy, I could fall asleep on your lap listening to the oldies on the radio."

"And snuggle with blankets if the old heater didn't work," I said in mock excitement, "and drink hot chocolate out of a thermos as we drove to destinations unknown. And you'd pack sandwiches, cold fried chicken, and potato salad for our trip, and we'd take the road less traveled."

"Exactly, Senor Sarcastic," she said with a frown but then illuminated immediately at the return to her story, her hands everywhere as she elaborated. "And you could carry me to and from the truck when I'm too old and weak to walk, and you could take me on long drives when I get senile. And as we drove, you'd tell me how much you love me, and you'd tell me stories of our lives together and the magnificent adventures we'd had, the exotic places we'd traveled, and the wonders we'd witnessed."

I was laughing all out at this point. "Wait, let me guess. And as we reached the sunset of our lives, we'd lie down together in bed and pass peacefully over heaven's horizon in our sleep, only to be met by family, friends, and favorite pets at the pearly gates."

"Yes!" she said with continued excitement and looking at me matter-of-factly. "That's it exactly. That's how all great loves and golden romances turn out, you big dope."

I think we laughed, joked, and teased all the way to Gig Harbor, which was actually a nice respite as we weren't allowed to contemplate what was about to take place and what it might set into motion on this most stormy and spectral of nights.

We pulled up onto the long wooden-fenced driveway, amongst the lush foliage and water-laden indigenous hemlocks that drooped mightily under the weight of an unrelenting master. We saw Gio's black Hummer sitting empty near the entry, and Kathryn recognized Cas's Subaru a few empty spaces down.

I looked at the structure that was the Genesys Center and decided that it was perfect in its placement and profile. It had the look of welcome and warmth, along with comfort and calm. It was noticeably an old motel remodeled in requisite to its current career, with a main cinder block office as the hub of multiple-roomed spokes. Cas had mentioned that there were twenty rooms along each of the four spokes, which made eighty rooms. Some of the rooms were singles for some of the more serious afflictions, but most of the longer-term guests were put in two-room sets for greater camaraderie, cooperation, and co-observation.

It had none of the sterile, antiseptic look and feel that most modern-day clinics espoused, and there was about it a refuge and retreat aspect that I'm sure earned it its name.

I turned off the car, Kathryn and I counted down from three, and then we threw open the doors and bolted for the initial overhang and roundabout where the more seriously challenged patients must have been dropped off. A very striking woman who looked to be in her early seventies was standing behind the florally decorated check-in counter with another young lady who was busy on the phone and the computer at the same time.

"How may I help you lovely people?" the matriarch asked sweetly.

"Actually, we just came in to get our loveliness confirmed," I said, "and I wanted to prove to my friend here that beauty knows no age limits. Thank you for providing both."

She looked at me suspiciously for a minute and then broke into a wide smile. "Young man, you and I are going to get along just fine."

Her name tag said "Maggie," so I introduced her to Kathryn and told her that we were looking for Grace, Cas, and two very large adolescents.

"Dr. Simmons is with Mr. LaCroix," Maggie said, "and I think the two adolescents you speak of said they were off to reconnaissance the donut situation in the break room."

Our attention was turned to Cas as he walked toward us through one of the arterial halls with a handsome woman who looked to be in her early forties, but already prematurely gray. She was naturally attractive, without the adornment of jewelry, makeup, or styling. They exchanged a look of masked affection before they saw us, and upon so doing, Grace immediately embraced a more professional and clinical demeanor.

Cas did the honors. "Shad and Kathryn, this is Dr. Simmons. Dr. Simmons, these are my good friends, Kathryn Rae and Shad Kilbourne."

Grace shook Kathryn's hand in genuine warmth. "I am a great fan of your work, Ms. Rae."

Kathryn accepted the compliment graciously, as always. "And I of yours, Dr. Simmons."

I shook her hand as well. "It is a distinct honor and pleasure to make your acquaintance, Dr. Simmons," I said. "Cas speaks highly of you and your work, and the lives you so selflessly touch. There are not many who can truly live up to their name."

She looked at me carefully at first, then clinically, then affectionately. "I've heard of you too, Mr. Kilbourne," she said finally with a hint of a smile around the corners of her mouth. "I am an indirect and appreciative recipient of some of your fund-raising and bestowments, but to be honest, I was expecting something different."

"Like an adult?" Kathryn teased.

Grace broke into a smile for the first time, a smile tainted with the vestiges of sorrow and exhaustion, but a smile nonetheless. "In essence, I guess the answer is yes," she said looking once again at Kathryn warmly. "I expected a man of his generosity and philanthropic pursuit to be older and of more experienced and antiquated stock."

"Well, if it makes you feel any better, Dr. Simmons," I said. "I am void of the ages of wisdom, but not the wisdom of the ages."

Now she looked truly bemused. "You speak well for a man of your musculature, Mr. Kilbourne. I expected more ego and vanity than ergo and validity."

"You are kind, Dr. Simmons," I said with a slight bow. "Though I'm afraid I am more Pathos than Logos."

"Quite appropriate under the circumstances, Mr. Kilbourne," she said. "Besides, it is your Ethos that I find most compelling."

"Thank you, Dr. Simmons," I said, suddenly proud of myself. "And I would be honored if you called me Shad, as well as friend."

"And I am Grace," she said, "and I would like and expect all of you to use it. There are no titles here other than respect and no positions here other than caregiver."

"I hate to be rude, Grace," I said, pointing to Maggie, "but you interrupted me mid-flirt with this charming creature before I could sweep her off her feet."

She looked at Maggie. "Dr. Simmons?"

Maggie looked at her guiltily. "Yes, Dr. Simmons?"

"Must I remind you, Mother," Grace said, "that it is counterproductive to our cause if all the visitors fall in love with you. If you could ratchet back your radiant beauty for a minute, I could make some real progress around here."

Maggie turned to look at me with a mischievous smile and then exhaled heavily in jest. "Just like a daughter . . . she asks for the impossible."

I walked over and kissed the back of Maggie's hand. "Young lady, you and I are going to get along just fine."

She blushed and brought the back of her hand up to her cheek. "Oh, I bet you say that to all the septuagenarians."

"Just the genetically gifted septuagenarians," I said. And then, unfortunately, it was time for the business at hand.

Grace gave her mother an exasperated look and then turned to walk down the hall, and we automatically followed as expected. "We serve all here. None are ever turned away unless they pose an overt and immediate threat to the staff or other patients. There is no cost other than donations of time, energies, money, or means. On one day, we may have five patients and on others over fifty. Some are in need of nothing more than coffee and companionship, while others are literally knocking on death's door," she spoke over her shoulder as she continued down the hall, nodding and smiling to the occasional fellow staff members and hugging the occasional grateful patient.

"Dignity, compassion, and respect are the hallmarks of what we do here. The medical and clinical aspects are just dressing to the human body in the nurturing of the human spirit."

We came to the end of the hall, and she stopped and stood in front of a door marked "Observation Room East." "Archie, the patient you've requested to speak with, is in his sixties. Because of the life he has led, and more appropriately and prophetically the life that has led him, he will look to you to be in his eighties. Historically, he is an addict and an alcoholic, and mildly psychotic and schizophrenic as well. He is heavily sedated right now and has been for about forty hours. I have given him a lucidity drug along with a vasodilator a short time ago. That should keep him relatively coherent for about an hour, depending on the number, seriousness, and experience of the questioning."

She looked at all of us. "I have asked Mr. Giovanni and Mr. Jones to sit in the mirrored observational booth. Cas, Kathryn, Shad, and I will speak to him in the main recovery room along with one of our volunteer registered nurses, to whom he is very attached and finds comfort and trust in. She will also be monitoring his vitals and will, therefore, let us know when it is unwell or unwise to continue."

Thor, the god of thunder, once again voiced his presence, and the reenergized rain battered the building voraciously and voluminously. Grace stopped and looked at the ceiling as the wind whistled its presence and potential. Kathryn, standing at my side, stood a little closer.

Grace looked at her watch and then continued. "My suggestion is that you make the questions quick, easy, and specific, and that there is only one questioner. As Cas has already told you, I have heard many of these stories before and have no professional opinion as to their truth or validity. He may lie or he may tell the truth—his truth may be our lie—he may say nothing at all or ramble on without respite. There will be real fear bordering on terror, as we've experienced it before."

She looked sweetly at Kathryn. "I would also suggest to Kathryn that if she suffers from too tender a heart then she recuse herself from the proceedings. I will neither pretend nor predict that it will be pretty or pleasant. Based upon past conversations I've had with Archie, it will rack your soul and shake your faith." She stopped then to look at us all individually and to gauge consensus. "Shall we venture forth undaunted?" Grace asked a little ominously.

"We shall," I said. And with that, we entered the realm from which there would be no emotional or psychological return.

CHAPTER 29

When we entered the semi-lit room, there was the smell of flowers and incense, and maybe even hope. I looked at the mirrored panel along the south wall and waved at those I knew to be standing behind it. We were introduced to Sally, who was the RN volunteer. She was sitting next to Archie, holding his hand and reading him a Louis L'Amour. His eyes were closed but there was none of the even breathing of sleep: it was irregular, raspy, and regrettable. Sally was little, blonde, and probably in her early twenties. The fact that she was a little overweight and that her voice was soft and high made her seem like she was in her early teens. But her bedside manner, intelligent eyes, and efficient movements made her seem like she was in her early thirties. Sally asked us to please be kind and gentle and then touched his brow and whispered his name.

"Hi, handsome," she said softly, smiling as his eyes opened groggily.

"Hello, young Miss," he said, smiling back at her weakly but affectionately. "Is it coming time to be gettin' married yet?"

She giggled softly. "No, not yet, handsome. You promised you'd get better first, remember?"

"Ah, with women there always be a catch," he said and then closed his tired eyes again.

Sally nudged him gently, propped him up, and helped to turn his head as she pointed toward us. "Your guests are here, Archie, –the ones we told you about, the ones that will put that awful place out of business, the ones that will save the little girls like me."

I noticed and took note of the fact that Sally's comments were short, soft, and simple, and not by accident. I was sure that Archie's cerebral faculties and intellectual capabilities were highly diminished from his age and addictions, and from forty hours of drug-induced sedation.

Sally pressed the motorized bed controls and raised him so he was sitting at a better angle at which to converse and maintain consciousness. Sally retreated to her bevy of electrical monitoring equipment along the wall and Kathryn joined her. I guess Cas had met him with Grace right before we got there, and he sat down next to Archie and grabbed his hand. Grace did likewise on the opposite side.

Archie looked from one to the other and then back again to Grace.

"Hi ya, Doc," he said.

"Hello, Archie," she said sweetly.

Archie looked over to Cas and the recognition took a few seconds before Archie smiled. "The Ghost."

We all laughed along with Archie and then he noticed my presence.

"Who are you?" he asked, looking happy to have all the company and gaining strength.

"A friend," I said.

Archie looked to Grace and she nodded. "I could use more a them," he said.

"Me too, Archie," I replied. "And you'll have one in me. But I was wondering if you could help me. I lost a young friend of mine, some years ago, and we haven't been able to find her. Grace said that you may know of a place where we might look for her?"

Grace had made it a point to let Archie know the topic of our discussion prior to our entrance and arrival, but it still didn't soften the impact on Archie's psyche when the subject was subtly broached. He tried to hold it together as best his condition allowed, but his eyes welled up immediately and tears streamed down his old, creased cheeks. After a few seconds he started to cry softly, whimper really, like a small child who's had a bad dream.

"It's a horrible place," he said between sobs. "You stop them, you make them go away."

I waited a minute for Archie to calm down after a certain look from Grace and a peripheral raised hand from Sally. Archie was old, skeletal, and fragile looking, with sparse white hair on his head and a white grizzled beard. His skin was loose and wrinkled from what I could see, and his hands and feet seemed to fidget and flail without motor control.

After two minutes, I got the high sign from Sally and proceeded carefully. "I'll put that place out of business, Archie. I promise you, my friend. But I need to know what it is and where it is."

Archie trembled visibly and then looked at me directly with eyes so wide and so expressive of terror that it took me aback for a second. "It is concentrated evil, mister," he said. "People go'd in, but they never come'd back out, least ways not through my tunnel. Called 'em 'One Way Willies,' cus we knew the ones that ain't coming back out. The rich ones and the important ones cames and wents as they pleased cus they had lotsa money and wouldn't say nuthin' cus you wouldn't want no-ones to know what you was doing down there no how. But we knowed the ones that had the smella death on 'em, and once they did their awful business, you knowed they'd be put to work or put down the hole." He stopped for a second to cough and catch his breath, and Grace gave him some water to sip through a straw.

"What were they doing, Archie?" I said softly. "What goes on down there?"

He looked at Grace frantically, but she just smiled, patted his hand, and nodded sweetly to continue. "Anything you wants, mister. Any kinda sick, perverted, thing you wanted to do to anythings or anybodys. And any kinda drugs, too. S'all down there fer a price, if 'n you got money. I was a tunnel runner down there goin' on six years and them there Chinamen started to trust me some. Sometimes I'd bring them stuff, or if somebody died or didn't show up, I'd git one of the up close sections of the tunnel and I'd see and hear tell some a what went on in them there tents and behind them there blanket rooms." He shuddered violently. "It's awful, mister, just the most awful that ever there was . . . and them poor little boys and girls. I'll tell ya sumthin else, mister . . . the good Lord don't know 'bout it neither, cus there ain't no way he'd let things like that happen ta folks."

Archie was energized by his fear and audience, and you could tell that as he was talking that he was reliving the sights, sounds, and smells of what must have been a nightmarish existence. For the next thirty minutes, he relayed stories of one sadistic atrocity after another, some of it supposed, some of it witnessed, some of it hearsay from the other miscreants he worked with. I looked at Kathryn and she had her head down, sobbing softly in her hands at what we all now knew . . . that it did indeed exist, and it was significantly worse than we'd allowed ourselves to imagine. It was a body shop for the worst kind of fetishes, perversions, and depravities that anyone could possibly conjure up, and it was also probably the first floor of hell.

After a while, Archie seemed to slow in both speech and energy, and I knew our time was short. "Archie, the girl that is lost was pretty but nothing special. She was just another lost teenager at the time. Why would she be taken down there?"

Archie took a deep breath. "Lotsa reasons, mister. The fact she's a warm body woulda probably been reason 'nuff, lotsa needs for bodies. But if 'n she's a down there fer that she'd be dead by now anyhows." And then he paused and thought for a much longer time than I thought we had time for. "Fer them to keep 'er alive, she'd havta be special fer some reason, or can do special things, or used to be somebody special, or 'lated to somebody special, or lookin' like somebody special. Lotsa folks out there only willin' to pay fer sumpin' special." He leaned over toward Grace and took another sip out of the straw and dropped his head back heavily on the pillow. "The Chinamen like to market sumpin' special, they surely do."

I had almost missed it, and I think Kathryn and Cas were so dulled by the details or lost in their own thoughts that they almost missed it too. About the same time it dawned on me, there was a soft tap on the glass and I nodded to the mirrored wall that I'd picked up on it as well. Deity or Gio had been paying close attention and thankfully hadn't overdosed on donuts.

"Archie?" I said, trying to hide my sudden heightened interest.

He opened his tired eyes, and looked at me a little blankly.

"You just said something about being related to somebody special. This girl is the daughter of a powerful United States Senator who might run for president someday. If they knew that, would that be enough to keep her alive?"

He thought about it for a minute. "Well," he said, "I reckon that'd be more 'n enough reasons to keep her live if 'n theys could sell her like that. There's been lotsa kids down there that theys sold as sons and daughters of famous folk, or related to famous folk, or used to be famous folk, or looks like famous folk, so's maybe she coulda been one a them." I started to get excited, but then Archie continued. "Less 'n a course somebodys wanted to pay a heap more dollars to kills the daughter of a famous senator instead."

I kept forgetting about the kind of place and class of people we were talking about and would inevitably deal with. Of course, anything would go, and the notoriety that could keep her indefinitely alive could also get her definitively dead. We had about drained Archie's mental, emotional, and physical reserves, so now that we knew the "what" and the "why," we were in dire and expeditious need of the "where."

I looked at Archie, and it was obvious that he was about done in. Grace looked at me and held up her left hand to signal five more minutes.

"Archie," I said. "Would it be possible for you to tell us how to get there or maybe draw us a map?"

"I don't know no street names or alleys or stuff, mister," he said weakly, "but I's could show you one of them entrances if you don't tell 'em it was me that showed ya. Sunday nights is the slowest, and their ain't but a few of the tunnel gunnies 'round then."

I smiled at him, and at his bravery and willingness to help. "Thanks Archie, maybe you can show us the entrance tomorrow night and we'll take it from there. We'll shut that place down for you and for all the little girls you're going to help save. You'll be a hero, Archie."

Archie smiled big and seemed to extract some peace from my statement. "Did you hear that, Ms. Grace? Did you hear that, Ms. Sally?" he said, raising his head from the pillow and looking over at them both. "The man say I'm gonna be a hero, a real live hero. We're gonna save some of them little girls, Ms. Sally, and then I'm gonna get better, you just watch."

Archie's head settled back slowly onto the pillow, the last outburst draining all the remaining energy from his emaciated frame. With his eyes closed, he exhaled heavily and seemed to actually sink into the bed.

"And then we're gonna git married, Ms. Sally," he said on the verge of soporia, "then I'll take care a you, just like you take 'n care a me."

And then he slept the light snore of a deep and peaceful sleep, the only sound now in the room being the small, shrill beeps of the medical equipment. Gio and Deity walked into the room with smiles on their faces. "We on?" they asked.

I looked at Grace and gestured toward Archie. "Do you think he'll be up to it tomorrow?"

She put his hand back down at his side, and gave it an affectionate pat, and then checked his pulse with one hand, and felt his forehead with the other. She nodded to herself and then looked at Sally, who checked her monitors and nodded in the affirmative as well. "Let's give him twenty-four hours of sleep and IVs and then he should be well enough to load into a van for a short trip. That's about all I can promise you at this point. It will have to do."

I looked at all those looking at me. "If he can show us a legitimate point of entry, we can take it from there."

Grace looked at Cas with genuine concern, which I thought was very telling and very sweet, and then looked back at me. "What will you do?" she asked plainly.

I gave her my best Cheshire cat grin. "We'll go through the looking glass, Alice, and down the rabbit hole."

The rain had neither abated nor tired with the night as the Range Rover traversed its way through the incessant weather. Kathryn and I were both silent, holding hands and grateful for each other's company after the ordeal in the observation room. Occasionally, she'd begin shaking her head and start to say something, only to remain mute and squeeze my hand harder in frustration and fear. After about twenty minutes of mutual silence and with the London Philharmonic playing ornately in the background, she finally crafted the proper and perfect response once again.

"Yuck!"

"I concur completely," I said.

She searched further for the right words, but once again came up empty. "I want to be eloquent and exhaustive in my reiteration of what we just experienced, but dear God, based upon the enormity of the depravity, 'yuck' is the only encapsulation I can think of."

I looked at her and smiled encouragingly. "I think 'yuck' is a fine summation, Ms. Rae," I said. "All I could come up with was 'wow' so I kept it to myself. I feel exactly the same way leaving Genesys right now as I felt when I walked out of the movie theatre after *Pulp Fiction*. I'm at a loss for proper descriptors."

She rested her forearm on my shoulder and stroked my cheek gently with the back of her fingers. "I know you know I'm going to ask you this anyway, but would you mind if we spent the night at your house tonight? I want to be with you, and among your things, and immersed in your life tonight. I need to lose myself in you or I'll go bonkers by morning."

I took her hand off my shoulder and kissed it. "Is bonkers a technical term? I'm unfamiliar with artistic jargon."

"Just answer da question, pally boy," she said in the worst but most endearing Cagney impression I'd ever heard, "or you'll be sleepin' wid da fishes."

"Well," I said, "to answer a question you already know the answer to, yes, you may spend the night tonight. And I would love to lose myself in you, a bottle of wine, a comfy couch, and a funny movie tonight as well."

"Then would you mind if I stayed the weekend?" she asked. "I would love to be here when you come home tomorrow night after your little underground extravaganza. And notice I said 'when' you come home, not 'if' you come home. That's an order."

"Yes, ma'am," I said.

I looked over and she was looking straight ahead, but there were tears streaming down her face again. I patted her thigh. "Don't worry, I promise to return in one piece."

She wasn't weeping, but it was taking all the restraint she could muster. "I lost the most important man in my life once, and it would destroy me to lose him again."

I looked at her as she looked at me, and I pulled the tear-laden hair away from her face and placed it carefully behind her ear . . . and finally a smile surfaced from beneath the gloom. "What a magnificent obsession you are!" I said.

She placed her head on my shoulder, grabbed my arm, and closed her eyes. "Heaven must be a lot like this."

I kissed her on the top of her head. "Let's not find out for a while, okay?"

CHAPTER 30

If there was any truth to *Red Sky at Morning, Sailor Take Warning,* then there was about Seattle an ominous glow that portended disaster as we all met at the City around nine, the next morning. Cas, Gio, Deity, and I were dining on juices and donuts as Koda and Rama walked up the stairs to my office.

"Nine o'clock on a Sunday morning, Gringo?" Rama said to me incredulously as he entered. "I don't think I want to work for you no more."

I smiled serenely. "Free juice and donuts," I said.

"Free?" he said. "These free donuts could cost me my life from what Koda told me."

"Good point," I said. "But you're looking at it wrong: you're not fleeing death, you're chasing immortality."

He looked at me contemplatively for a few seconds. "Are there still Peanut M&M's in the drawer?"

"An inexhaustible supply," I said.

He smiled as he caught a bag of M&M's that Deity had pulled from the coffee table drawer and thrown to him. "Like I was saying earlier, el Jeffe, no other person I'd rather work for."

"Welcome aboard."

Koda grabbed some Gatorade, and true to his national heritage grabbed a bag of beef jerky from the cupboard instead of a donut. "So what happened at the Paleface Party?"

"Heap big fun," I said. "Grab a seat and we'll fill you in on what we're in for tonight."

Koda and Rama took the empty couch and settled back to get the grisly details. Cas looked at Deity, Deity looked at Gio, and Gio made a face at them both and got up to move around as he talked.

"We can go into greater detail later," Gio began, "and the rest of this esteemed gathering can augment and interrupt as needed, but in essence Tunnel Town does exist and it is ugly. From what we've gathered from Archie, he is a Tunnel Runner, which means he'd sherpa people and product from one section of one tunnel to the next. There are three other tunnels that he knows of and suspects there are others for private or emergency use. Each tunnel has about four or five sections, each navigated by different runners so that no one runner knows the entire route until he has established years of seniority and trust."

"What's the security look like?" Koda asked.

"Several different types, actually," Deity said, "the first being geologic. Archie said the tunnels have no lighting, so it's pitch black. The runners navigate by memory and Braille-like feel from markings cut into the cement and wooden walls. There are multiple switchbacks, roundabouts, and dead ends that complicate things for the untrained, and several deep chasms and steep drops for those who might wander in on accident or enter unauthorized on purpose. Each of the tunnel sections ends in blind turns as well, so that you can't accidentally stumble onto them without prior knowledge. But the real security is what Archie called Tunnel Gunners, affectionately known as Gunnies. They are of Asian descent—small, quick, and deadly. Archie said they stay out of sight for the most part so that you don't know where to expect them—the only way he ever knew they were around was because occasionally he'd smell cigarette smoke or see the glow of a cigarette set back in some of the holes they had carved out to perch in. He said they all squatted down on their haunches and smoked cigarettes and in the dark, they looked like gargoyles with glowing eyes."

Rama finished his M&M's and eyed the donuts. "Are they outfitted?"

"Roughly," Gio said, "mainly just nines and knives. Most of it's up close and personal. No need for expensive electronic gear: they know the sights, sounds, and subtleties of the area, and they don't need silencers or suppressors since noise is in their favor - it'll bring more gargoyles. The only good thing is that because it's a sea of cement down there there's no reliable communication other than written or verbal messages, which should work heavily in our favor. Another thing in our favor is that because there is no communication mode, everything is very regimented, with almost no random or subjective movement. Archie said shifts for security change out every four hours on the hour, and that's gonna be our block of time to get in, get the girl if she's alive and around, and make a rapid retreat."

Rama decided on the chocolate bar with the cream filling, my personal favorite; the man was obviously a genius. "What about us peons? What kind of gear we lookin' at?" Rama asked.

Koda anteed up. "I picked up standard issue black fatigues, black travel boots, and black hoodies for everyone. We'll also have Uzi semi-automatic subs with suppressors, silenced nines, knives, Kevlar vests, night vision goggles, and short range communication headsets with a range down there of probably only a couple hundred feet. You'll each also have some snap flares, and percussion and flash grenades. My man Cas here doesn't have a lot of arms or tactical training so he'll have a couple nines strapped to his thighs in case of an emergency and that's about it. He'll have the backpack full of extra nine mm ammunition, rappel ropes, hooks, first aid, and various other equipment."

Koda stopped and smiled, "All the conveniences of home, Kil."

I smiled back, "Just a walk in the park fellas."

"Now that we know the how, the when, and the where, how 'bout somebody telling Rama and I about the what," Koda said. "As in, 'what the heck are we getting into'?"

I decided to field this one. "From Archie's accounts, this place is run by an Asian mafia or a Chinese Tong . . . which one, we have no idea. It has supposedly been running down there in some version for decades. Historically, the first Chinese Tongs came up from Chinatown in San Francisco to Seattle in the late eighteen hundreds, selling opium, prostitution, protection, and illegal gambling. Archie said he hasn't really seen or heard of any gambling, and protection wouldn't be on the menu down there, which leaves us with drugs and prostitution."

I walked down to the lower level and sat among the boys, and helped myself to another donut or two.

"Archie said drugs are a big part of what they both mule in and mule out - we're not sure in what quantities or kinds but it sounds significant. But the main deal is the body farm down there. I won't go into the detail Archie did, but think of the most deviant acts that the most sadistic minds can come up with and you get a pretty solid and sordid picture. It's basically everything you can't get on the street corner. Supposedly, some of the activity is filmed and the tapes are sold on the black market all over the world. Most of the clients are supposedly wealthy Asians, Europeans, and Middle Easterners where it is heavily advertised in the deepest dens of iniquity, but anybody with enough money can pretty much purchase whatever fantasy in whatever form they want. Some of the stuff Archie told us about, that he's seen, heard, or surmised would make a mortician sick to his stomach—lots of death down there and plenty more where they came from topside. Sometimes the poorest clients without ties to anyone of significance on the outside are held in servitude, used as part of the practice, or killed outright for their money. Archie said he's heard that it's around five grand a day to do most anyone or anything you want, but that some of the more specialized requests can cost hundreds of thousands of dollars or even a cool million."

"The good news," Gio said, "is that one of those specializations is anyone that is semi-famous that fell through the cracks, or semi-related to someone famous, or looks like someone famous. If it was known that Chrissy is the daughter of a famous senator, who may someday be president of the United States, she might still be alive and relatively well taken care of by comparison."

Deity went and grabbed everyone another Gatorade and brought down more jerky as I continued. "Archie said that the tunnels all spill into a massive circular great room that is a hundred feet tall and probably several hundred yards in circumference. There are small blanketed rooms and tents for the basic stuff along the perimeters, and as you get closer to the middle of the room the tents get bigger and nicer. Early Asian army surplus, if you will. The headquarters, if you want to call it that, is in a raised middle section where supposedly the head honchos hang out. The ceiling is all concrete, pipes, and wiring conduit. Which is where they get all their power and plumbing from - they just tap into whatever's overhead. Those, I'm sure, are all major public utility sources, so what they would tap out of that would be comparatively small, and if they've been doing it for multiple decades, I'm sure it would continue to go on unnoticed by the large utility companies for multiple decades more. Most of the Asian security force lives in little hollowed-out caves or blanketed tents along the raised perimeter walls to keep an eye on what goes on, in, out, and around the main staging area."

Rama was still shaking his massive head. "How can a place like that exist and nobody know 'bout it?"

Cas, who up until this point was merely a spectator, finally spoke up. "I'll take this one, Shad. I know Archie went into it a little bit while we were there, but it was one of the questions Grace asked Archie multiple times when they spoke of it in the past. Number one, they only employed guys to run the tunnels like Archie who were addicts. The addicts wouldn't want to snitch on their source of free goodies, and if they did, people would just pass it off as the ranting and raving of a lunatic, and they could be easily killed by a night-dwelling gargoyle if needs be and nobody would care. But they had to have some non-Asians to sherpa the stuff topside and old addicts were the perfect dupes. Archie said the entire Asian workforce never went topside as far as he knew unless it was to kill a snitch. Two, the "One Way Willies," as Archie called them, were either kept as veritable slaves, used and abused as part of the offerings, or robbed and killed outright. You have to remember that most of their clientele was foreign by design. So those with limited means and resources, who had pulled together their life savings to act out their most disturbing fantasies, never left alive. And those of significant means and resources were not only great repeat clients, but they would be the last ones to squeal because of their own driving fetishes and fear of discovery. I think at one point Grace even said that Archie heard that some of the more wealthy and important guests were filmed for further financial blackmail and insurance against being ratted out."

"Aye, Chihuahua!" Rama said. "I, too, have heard of such things, but I never thought that it could be true. It will feel good to put such a place out of business, senors."

"What time you want to get this thing rolling tonight, Bawse?" Deity asked.

I looked at Cas. "Grace said she could have Archie ready by around seven," Cas said, "since supposedly Sunday nights are the slowest in Tunnel Town. There's a shift change at eight o'clock, and on Sunday nights the waste levels are low enough in some of the large, concrete drainage piping that you can walk on the sides and not actually have to wade through it. Should help keep the noise levels down too."

Deity looked at Cas in disgust. "Waste levels? Nobody told this brutha about no waste levels. Maybe I'll sit this one out, Bawse. I'll keep the engine warm in the van so ya'll have a cozy drive home. Make sure ya'll wipe yo feet before you get back in the van, though."

Finally, the seriousness was broken and levity ruled the rest of the morning. I went back up to my desk and looked down at the fearsome fivesome as they continued to joke with each other. There was a good chance that a few of us might not be coming back, at least not in the same condition we went in. Not knowing exactly where we were going and what we were getting into bothered me on multiple levels, but there was no logical or tactical alternative. Koda wanted to go in by himself and try to do some initial reconnaissance, but if he was discovered, with Mr. Chang already knowing our interest and intent, it would risk Chrissy's life if she was still alive.

I looked at my watch; it was almost 11:00 a.m. "All right, fellas, we'll meet at our storage warehouse at seven o'clock in the evening to get geared up. Grace will show up with Archie by 7:30 p.m., Deity will supply us with a van, and we'll plan on leaving the warehouse at eight, and entering the tunnel shortly thereafter, to let the gargoyles switch shifts." I looked at all of them individually. "Any questions?"

Deity spoke up. "Yeh, I gots a question: What kind of waste you think Archie be talkin' 'bout exactly?"

The rest of the guys started throwing napkins and paper cups at him and then they all piled on top of him. Deity was laughing too hard to resist and it took them fifteen minutes to finally get back in decorum. I didn't want to interrupt their play . . . who knew when we'd have reason for laughter again . . . and who'd be around to enjoy it!

CHAPTER 31

I called Shane Lowe, my attorney extraordinaire, that afternoon and let him know what we were up to. He was on the golf course and swore that his phone ringing had just cost him a thirty-foot putt and a thousand dollars.

"Why do you care about a thousand dollars?" I said.

"I don't, I actually just hate the judge I'm playing with," he said in a whisper. "What's up?"

I gave him a vague *Reader's Digest* version of what was about to go down and told him to handle my affairs if anything happened to us. I wasn't that concerned about myself, Gio, Deity, Koda, or Cas since we didn't really have families, but I wanted to make sure Rama's family and Diane were well-cared-for, should the operation not go down smoothly. Jess and Kathryn obviously had significant funds of their own, but I wanted to make sure the people I cared about most and my employees weren't hurt by my early and eternal absence.

Hours later we were in the warehouse, helping each other strap on our gear and going over some of the finer mechanics and machinations with Cas. I'm sure he was aware of the seriousness of what we were about to embark on, but you couldn't tell by the look on his face. Try as he would, he just couldn't wipe the grin off his face.

"I know I shouldn't be this excited," he said, "but I've never done anything like this before; it's amazing."

And I had to admit it, too; every time I got geared up, it brought a certain level of excitement and pride to me as well. Maybe it was hardwired in men, or maybe hardwired in warriors of any gender, but going to battle and matching skills with the enemy was actually a very cool thing. Dying, on the other hand, was a very uncool thing, and one should try to avoid it at all costs.

Cas was looking in the mirror, squinting only slightly as his special darkened contacts filtered out the damaging light, but admiring the hi-tech outfit and gear greatly. "This is every little boy's dream."

Koda looked at him as he tightened Cas's backpack. "Enjoy the moment, Ghost Man, cus in about an hour it will be every little boy's nightmare. I guarantee you that." He jacked a shell into the chamber of each of Cas's Glocks and shoved them into the laced thigh holsters, and then grabbed Cas's head with both his huge hands and looked him hard and straight in his artificially blackened eyes. "Whoever you are right now is not gonna be the same guy that crawls outa that hell hole later tonight, Ghost Man, if you crawl out of there at all. From this moment forward it ain't fun, and it ain't a game, and five other guys' lives and maybe a young girl's are betting on you doing your job and not getting us killed. You understand me, Ghost Man?"

Koda still had Cas's head in both his hands and had his nose about one inch from his. If it was possible for Cas to turn pale, this was the time, but he handled it well. He looked back at Koda and said, "Tell me what to do and I'll do it; I'll exceed expectations."

Koda stared at him hard for a full ten seconds and then broke into a wide grin and patted Cas's cheeks. "I know you will, Cas," he said. "I know you will. Let's go get you some scar tissue."

We piled in the van and sat on the aluminum benches that stretched out on both sides. Archie was riding shotgun in the front passenger seat, wide-eyed, energized, and excited as Grace drove out of the warehouse. It was another moonless night, and the weather flung its full fury at the van as we started the fifteen-minute trip to downtown. The well-known tourist attraction that was the "Underground City," was in Pioneer Park, but Archie said the entrance he thought would be the most deserted this night was closer to downtown, through an old deserted corporate basement and into the sewer lines that traced back toward the cavernous underground ruins.

As we drove, Koda went over the contents of the auxiliary pockets on our gear: mini-maglite in one pocket, clicker in the next, whistle, leatherman, lighter, compass, tourniquet string, mini cell phone, and on down the line as he elaborated on the use and misuse of each.

Cas was looking through his pockets. "How come all these pockets are held shut with elastic? Wouldn't Velcro keep them in place better and make them more secure?" He looked up and we were all smiling.

"Trust me, Ghost Man," Koda said. "This is soft and silent work. Tearing open a Velcro seal in a dead-quiet tunnel would sound like you just set off a dozen firecrackers. Stealth will be of key importance to this whole deal, especially the way sound carries down there. Ties and buttons, though quiet, are too task-intensive and time-consuming; Velcro, zippers, and snaps are too noisy and tend to stay open when opened. And down there, he who makes the first noise makes his last."

We pulled down an alley off First Street and handed out final instructions and possible rendezvous points and contingency plans. The alley actually led to a blind entrance to an old, condemned underground garage that was closed off by old wooden garage doors. Archie said that those doors pushed open only slightly and it would be a tight squeeze for us. Once we were in, we'd walk down some steps masked behind an old, rusted-out dumpster that led to a vertical drain only three feet in circumference. He said the steel bars would look formidable, but if you reached in and released a push hatch-lock on the backside, the bars were actually on hinges and would release individually to grant entry. Once you gained access to the initial entrance, a manhole cover would appear within twenty paces that dropped ten feet to the main tunnel. There was no obvious ladder, but if we reached in, there would be a nylon rope attached to a hook that we could pull up to produce an aluminum and rope makeshift stepladder.

Archie gave us the rest of the directions for the third time, as best he could remember, and we hopefully had them committed to memory. We each shook his hand, and Cas and Grace exchanged looks and kisses on the cheek.

"Tell your mother to wait for me," I said to Grace with a wink.

"I will," she said with a sad smile. "She's been picking out wedding dresses all day."

I handed her a piece of paper. "This number is for Chief Tanner. If you haven't heard from one of us by morning, call him and tell him everything you know."

She nodded her head and tried to speak, but her emotions got the best of her so she just smiled weakly.

"Wish us luck," I said.

"God bless and God's speed," she said in sad return, and then we were swallowed by the night.

Within minutes we had all made the ten-foot-drop to the main concrete tunnel, and had given up our last vestiges of light and hope, Koda taking the lead into the abyss. It smelled of mold, decay, and rotting vagaries, and the sounds of water were everywhere - flowing, dripping, falling, and rushing. It was also warm and humid, but I shivered involuntarily anyway, hopefully not as a harbinger of things to come. The darkness was all encompassing, it was physical, it was opaque, it was a resistant force and a tangible reality with which to be reckoned.

We turned on our night optics, and the concrete portal stretched out in greenish perpetuity before us. The tunnel was about eight feet in circumference and in various stages of disrepair, and fortunately for Deity and the rest of us whatever quasi-liquid resided on the bottom was only about six inches thick, with plenty of room on either side to maneuver unhindered and un-mucked. Three one-inch pipes ran along the top above our heads, and supposedly when the three merged to one, we'd backtrack thirty yards and see the next sectional entrance.

After about five minutes, the lack of noise was numbing in contrast to the sounds of the storm-ravaged surface we had just abandoned. We turned on our communication headsets, gave each other the thumbs-up, and initiated our endeavor. Koda took lead about a hundred feet in front of us, and the rest of us trailed behind in fifty foot intervals, Gio bringing up the rear. All we could hear was each other's breathing, and the omnipresence of water. I looked at my watch and it was eight forty-five, which gave us exactly three hours to get in and get back out. According to Archie, actual tunnel time should be around forty-five minutes each way. I was under the assumption that since we were moving cautiously going in and moving expeditiously coming out it would be more like sixty minutes in and thirty minutes out, depending on if we found Chrissy and in what condition, and who was on our tails.

"Hey, a cat," I heard Deity say into his headset. "Was's up, kitty?"

I also heard Koda laugh quietly into his headset soon after. "I'm not sure what you call them in the ghetto, but on the reservation we call those rats. I don't suggest you try to pet it."

Deity was about twenty yards directly in front of me and I swear I saw him jump about three feet in the air and onto the other side of the concrete conduit when he got Koda's delineation. "Damn," he said as he quickly moved past the cat-sized rat, "let's get in and get out of here; this place gives me the heebie-jeebies."

"Careful, that could be a cleverly disguised assassin," I whispered into the headset. "Deity, give it a kiss and see if it objects."

"If it objects to a kiss from D," Gio said from close to a hundred feet behind us, "that just means it's human and has good taste."

Whispered headset banter accompanied us for the next few minutes as we continued our slow descent underground. Each step we took was put down with caution, and each move we made was manufactured with care. With absolutely no cover, this was the last place I wanted us to be discovered, but Archie said the initial section was rarely traveled on Sundays and never guarded. Gio whispered a quick "Entrance" into his headset and we all turned about the same time Koda started back. Koda had probably seen the spot where the three pipes merged and since Gio was watching our back trail he'd seen the hidden entry first, mainly by accident.

We all fell back to Gio and waited until Koda got back and could do some quick reconnaissance inside the newly found portal. After a few minutes, he poked his head back in, "You're gonna love this!"

We entered through the small jagged opening, shards of broken concrete and exposed rebar tugging at our gear as we squeezed through. We immediately split up and moved both left and right of entry: armed, anxious, and anticipating anything. The confinement and claustrophobia of our concrete causeway gave way to the wide open spaces of antiquated urban ruin. A large clearing area spread out in front of us for the next hundred yards, the detritus and decay of rotting architecture everywhere. The rolling stone ceiling was only a couple of feet above our heads in most places, and most of what we saw was eroded concrete, brick, and piping - the majority of it covered in decades of cobwebs, dust, and despair. I was down on one knee behind an old cast iron bathtub, the rest of the team taking refuge behind various dilapidated walls or huge pieces of discarded machinery and giant rusted iron gears. The groundscape was littered with similar refuse all through the expanse, all of which would provide excellent strategic cover for armed gargoyles.

We were all quiet for a few minutes as we surveyed the terrain before us; our senses strained for the slightest sound or movement. Our green and black view through the night vision goggles added an aura and atmosphere of an alien-like martian expedition. I motioned for Koda to take the left exterior, and Deity the right, whispering to the others to stay stationary until the quad had been secured. After a few minutes, I sent Gio and Rama out in opposite search patterns to back them up as I scuttled back to the portal to make sure no one was following us.

Deity gave us the signal that his perimeter was secure, but as Koda was about to do the same he suddenly whispered "Contact" into his headset for all of us to maintain our positions. "Cigarette smoke," he whispered into the headset after a few seconds. I checked my weapons out of habit, making sure the safeties were off and the shells were chambered. I looked at Cas and he was the poster child for fright and flight. Fun and games had given way to life or death, and I'm sure he was wishing he was back at the relative safety of his apartment. He looked back at where we'd entered the arena, nervously adjusting his gear. As he looked back, he caught my gaze. "No worries, Cas, all is well." He gave me a weak smile in return and took a deep breath with eyes wide.

We could hear Koda's breathing get heavier as he was audibly nearing the origin of the cigarette smell; he had left the main area and entered into the next passageway. A few long minutes later his breath had normalized.

More whispering . . . "Two targets, adjacent entry, smoking, drinking what smells like hot tea or soup over small, smokeless fire.

Semi-automatics and pocket lights in both their waistbands, speaking Vietnamese, no detection," he said.

"You need Deity, or want to go it alone?" I whispered back.

"I'll take these two, but I'll need Deity to assume lead right away to make sure there are no strays or immediate forward positions."

"Deity," I said. "You read?"

"Got it, Bawse," Deity said. "I got Kod's back."

"I'd rather you had my front," Koda whispered jokingly in return, the sounds of him taking off some of his gear in the background.

"I seen yo' front," Deity said. "You lucky I got yo' back."

"I'm going dark," was all Koda said in return, and then his headset went dead.

I looked around our new environment and couldn't help but think of lost civilizations. Ruin and rusted dreams were everywhere. I looked down at my feet and could see my footprints distinctly in the decades accrual of dust; it looked like the astronauts' footprints on the moon. Five excruciating minutes later, we could hear the almost imperceptible ping of a headset coming back on. "All clear, targets down," Koda said.

"Forward sector clear," Deity said soon after. "Coming back."

The rest of us moved forward quickly, but still cautious of hidden assassins and red-eyed gargoyles. We reconvened with Deity and Koda at the juncture of the two sectors. They had carried off the two bodies and dumped them in an old, abandoned hand-operated cement mixer, kicking dust over the blood and wiping as many of the incongruent footprints away as possible.

"As expected?" I said to Koda and Deity.

"Just like ol' Archie told us," Koda said, "Vietnamese gunnies, carrying nines and small flashlights, wearing old army fatigues. Found a bottle of some kind of whiskey too. Looks like they were adding a little joy juice to their tea to help pass the night. They also had some small bowls of boiled meat and rice. These two had no communications and no other gear other than the nines and the flashlights—deadly, but basic."

"Good, I hate surprises," I said. "Okay, Archie said there are numerous turns and side tunnels from here on in, so Gio, why don't you start exit-marking with Cas, and Rama and I will take the perimeter. Deity and Koda can continue with the lead since it sounds like knowing a little Vietnamese will help at the forward positions."

"Okay," Gio said, "but if we smell pizza and hear Italian, I get to take lead."

"And if we smell tacos and hear Spanish," Rama said, "then I will join you, compadre."

Everyone looked at me and Cas and I just shrugged. "I guess Cas and I will take the lead if anyone smells Pop-Tarts and Rice Krispy treats," I said. "But let me know if you guys hear the King's English and my white and righteous friend here and I will translate for you."

"That's mighty white of you," Deity said in his best announcer's voice. "I skipped Honky 101 in college."

Gio reached into Cas's backpack and pulled out the spray cans that held the UV paint. It was invisible in normal light but if our UV headlamps were turned on, they showed up like a welcoming beacon, so that if we were coming out in a hurry we could spot the orange arrows about every twenty feet and wouldn't get lost or lose precious time arguing about the correct exodus.

Deity rubbed Cas's head. "How goes it, Ghost Man? You hangin' tough?"

"Tough enough," Cas said with a weak smile.

"You'll do well, my brutha," Deity reassured. "Just stay low, stay sharp, and stay alive."

We moved on at that point, cognizant of the fact that we'd been pretty lucky so far, and happy for the fact that the enemy's boredom often required cigarettes and alcohol for company. As we entered this new section, it seemed to grow colder and deeper; I took a marble out of my pocket and set it on the occasional solid surface in regular increments. Based upon what my trusty cat-eye and my pedometer told me we were going about ten feet deeper every hundred yards or so, on average.

We twisted and turned through differentiating terrain and architecture, sometimes missing the intended portals and having to backtrack after seeing what Archie called "wrong way rocks," which were a series of bricks and stones placed in premeditated randomness indicating misdirection to those in the know. Fortunately, we could see them - most had to stumble upon them if they didn't have access to a light source.

Etchings and carvings in the stone walls or wooden planks told those who knew their secrets where they were and how far they had to go in any one direction. Archie said it was how they navigated without light when needed, but that the coding was too elaborate and complicated for us to learn in a day and that it was an imperfect science to say the least.

Noises that I'm sure were normal for an underground labyrinth made us jumpy at each introduction. We tried to sooth ourselves with the knowledge that our silent but deadly hosts would not be making any noise at all, and that any ambient noise would help to cover our occasional misstep. We continued to navigate our way through the third and fourth sections, and as we were about to enter what looked like the fifth section we heard Deity again on the headset. "Voices," he whispered, "Vietnamese again and arguing something about one of them stealing cigarettes. Can't make out most of it! It's too fast for me. Koda, can you make it out?"

"Sorry, D, too distant for me - you're probably about fifty yards forward of my position. Hang tight, I'm on my way."

Gio, Rama, Cas, and I stayed back, strategically spread. After another few minutes of listening to the walls and ceilings groan under the weight of time and antiquity, Deity broke the silence once more. "This tunnel is reinforced with what looks and smells like old railroad ties, and because of that, there's not much cover . . . pretty much debris-free in this section, so be extra careful. The two targets are still arguing and I think now's a good time while they're distracted. If Koda doesn't mind, it's my turn to dance with the demons."

"What about me?" I asked.

"You too pretty and delicate," Deity joked as his breathing got a little louder and more intense. "And you don't understand Vietnamese any more 'n you understand women."

"Excellent point," I reluctantly whispered in response. "Hey, what happened to your ghetto accent?"

"Oops! I be forgettin' ma'self, Bawse," he said. "I's in commando mode."

"Well, don't let it happen again," Gio said. "I thought you'd been captured by an elocutionist."

We heard Deity and Koda laugh and then exchange a few tactical maneuvers . . . and then the ping of dead headsets. A few minutes later, we heard the repetitive spits of the suppressors and then the soft ping of the headsets coming back on line. "All clear," Deity said. "Targets down. Koda has lead."

And a few minutes later, an update from Koda: "Forward sector clear, soldier boys, and it looks like we have reached the promised land, looks like a light source about two hundred yards up."

We navigated a series of turns and saw Koda behind a bank of large aluminum cargo bins and miscellaneous storage equipment where the tunnel had widened greatly; this was probably a main staging area and the bins were used to sherpa supplies in and out of the tunnels. Deity was off disposing of the bodies and cleansing the scene, and joined us a few minutes later about thirty yards back of Koda's point position. We started to move forward after an "All clear" from Koda, but a quick and unexpected hand signal from him soon after, and we hit the dirt.

"We got company, send up D," Koda whispered after a few moments, and we all scrambled for any cover that we could find.

As we strained our noses, ears, and eyes, we could smell smoke and hear numerous Asian male voices and screams of objection in the form of females, audibly frantic for their release. Deity whispered into the headset. "Five more Asian army boys - looks like they be pullin' a couple of the tunnel hunnies aside for a little fireside fun." There was a brief pause as it sounded like Koda and D were crawling closer to the action as the voices grew louder. "All five have nines in hip holsters and machine guns on shoulder straps," Deity whispered. "They lookin' a little better outfitted than the tunnel gunnies we dropped earlier. Get up here if you want in on the action fellas, cus I surely do hates a rapist."

We moved forward in ten-second intervals and finally met up with Deity and Koda behind an old cargo container that smelled of rotting fish. I looked around the corner. They had turned on some sort of standing military-issued floodlights that shone unflatteringly on the two, small, terrified girls on the ground—most of their already tattered dresses torn from their bodies. Three of the men were smoking and occasionally turning to watch the passage from where they'd come, as the other two shared a bottle of an amber-colored liquid and started to unbuckle their belts.

"Let's make this quick, fellas, or it's gonna be too late," I said. "Cas, palm a weapon and backtrack about twenty yards and watch our back. Gio, Deity, Koda, Rama, and I will take the targets left to right on my count. Koda and Deity will move forward and take immediate lead after the first shots are fired. Go!"

Cas turned and ran, half crouched and clumsily to a dilapidated wooden handcart about thirty feet away from us. Koda took position along the perimeter at the other side of the container, trying to look past the flood lamp and the fivesome to the area beyond the light. The four of us crawled forward on our forearms and elbows with our Uzi's already in position. On my count, each of us took a specific left-to-right target and squeezed the trigger in a short semi-quiet burst, the familiar thwap-thwap-thwap of the military grade suppressors sounding incredibly loud a hundred feet below the busy streets above. All five targets dropped in unison before they knew what hit them, and by the time we were on our feet, Koda was already thirty yards out in front and moving quickly. We ran to the girls before they could start to scream, with Deity and Gio holding them gently, covering their mouths initially and whispering "shhhh" into the ears of the terrified young girls, letting them know that they were safe and we were friendly.

Rama killed the flood lamps, and we all retreated back behind the large cargo container with the young girls in tow.

Koda broke the silence over the headsets from his forward position. "All clear up here, no other targets and no noticeable disturbance. But wait until you get up here fellas - this is going to blow your mind."

Cas scrambled back and took over the duties with the girls as he held them both in his arms, both of them sobbing heavily and hanging onto him for dear life. I told him to extract whatever information he could out of them. I instructed Gio to go back a few hundred yards to see if anyone was coming up behind us and make sure he could see the exit markings with his UV headlamp turned on, and then to come back and assist Cas. I asked Rama to secure the immediate area while Deity and I moved up to where Koda was positioned. I looked at the five bodies as we went by and motioned to Rama, "Make sure they're dead and get rid of the bodies," I said.

"How do you want me to make sure they're dead? Take their pulse?" he said half jokingly and a little estranged to his new surroundings and duties.

"They're rapists," I said. "Do a little temple-tap with your Glock. One lead to the head should discourage any comeback plans they had."

As we neared Koda's position behind a crumbling concrete wall, a vista opened up before me that practically took my breath away. It was much like coming out of the darkened tunnels of large sports auditoriums and into the height, might, and light of the playing field. Except that this playing field looked more like a shanty town and was composed of hundreds of small tents and blanketed compartments, and it looked like the quality of accommodations got nicer, if you could call it that, as you neared the epicenter, just as Archie had related to us.

Dozens of huge, old lights dangled down from what must have been hundred-foot ceilings to barely light the vast area, and thousands of other pipes, wires, and electrical cords webbed their way to the ground as well—some of the thicker cords going to large electrical-bank boxes with dozens of cords streaming out from them as well.

Koda elbowed Deity and me to get our attention and pointed to the expansive ceiling. "They've tied into the city's electrical conduits," he said and then traced his finger over to the piping along the ceiling and walls. "And they've tied into the water systems as well. Unlimited free electricity and water, compliments of the city of Seattle, and the heat from the water pipes keeps this place hot and humid. This place is like Bourbon Street during Mardis Gras, complete with a hooker haven."

It was just as Archie had iterated for the most part—a little larger than two rounded football fields in length and width, with a slight raised perimeter, where it looked like most of the so-called security hung out in small recessed dugouts or military surplus tents—open cooking pots out front along with colorless, nondescript laundry hanging from rope or pipe clothing lines. I wondered how long would it take to dry something in this kind of dank biosphere, if ever!

We receded back into the safety of the shadows as a heavily tatted and pierced white guy staggered by with a girl under each arm—one of the girls just as inebriated as her client, the other more vapid and devoid of emotion, just pharmaceutically strung out on the drug du jour. We watched them as they entered a blanketed room and then continued our visual reconnaissance. A few minutes later, two sheik-ish Middle Eastern gentlemen walked from one tent to another with what looked like a young Vietnamese guide, shaking their woven kaffiyeh-adorned heads vehemently at they peeked in the open flap of each tent. Finally, after four failures, they peeked in the fifth, nodded in approval, and went inside.

Koda smiled at us. "I wonder who's in there!"

We heard the bleat of a goat.

Deity smiled back. "I wonder *what's* in there!"

Screams broke out from somewhere in the encampment, followed by laughter and then more screams. As we continued to listen, the screams, laughter, and sounds of both pain and pleasure were indiscriminate and ubiquitous. My first thought was that the sounds of agony were the victims, but when I remembered where we were, and who and what we were dealing with, I knew I could no longer be sure.

The heat and humidity were oppressive, as was the bright light after the darkness of our descent, but it felt good to remove the night vision goggles and lose our lime green existence for the moment. Two more security types walked by in casual conversation, smoking cigarettes, guns held lazily on their shoulders; probably the thousandth time they'd encircled the encampment, numbed by birth and boredom to this setting. Rama and Gio both joined us after a few minutes and we waited for about twenty more minutes, but there didn't seem to be any rhyme or reason to the patrols, so we retreated once more to the safety of the shadows to strategize with the rest of the team.

I checked my watch; it was 10:30 p.m. It had taken us almost two hours just to get to this point and we were still far from our main objective. "How are they?" I asked as we all squatted down and encircled the girls.

Cas was sitting on the ground, leaning up against a dilapidated storage bin with one of the girls curled up tightly in his lap, the other sitting next to her, rubbing her back, and stroking her hair. The one in his lap had her eyes wide open, tears streaming down her cheeks, but no sobs or facial expressions, just the watery remnants of unimaginable and unspeakable horrors.

"Scared, beaten, tired, hungry, and basically strung out," Cas said. He motioned to the girl who was stroking the other girl's hair and also seemed a little older, maybe eighteen, and the most coherent. "They said they are given "vitamin" pills each morning which must actually be laced with mild narcotics to keep the hired help in a constant state of comatose compliance. She said they search their mouths after administering the drugs to make sure they're swallowed, but that she's been throwing them up on purpose when she gets back to her bed to stay halfway alert just in case she saw a way out." He held the one in his arms tighter and patted her back. "Brave girls. They were making a run for it when the five guards grabbed them and pulled them into the tunnel to teach them a lesson."

Cas must have taken his black hoodie off to look a little more human and to not scare them any more than we and life already had. I could see the bright moisture in Cas's eyes. This was everything that he had spent his life fighting against, and it must have been hell for him, too, to know that things of this nature went on, and had gone on for decades here, and centuries in other countries.

Both girls were wearing tattered, nondescript dresses, in various stages of disarray. Their bodies filthy from being thrown on the dirt floor, water streaks marking their cheeks and neck where the tears had run unabated down their faces.

"I showed her the picture of Chrissy," he said, gesturing to the older and more alert girl, "but there're so many girls here and the picture's so old, she wasn't sure if she has seen her. She said the 'novelty properties' were closer to the center of the encampment and in 'cloth cabins,' tents, I think, instead of what she called 'blanket bedrooms' like most of the other product here."

I took off my black hoodie as well, and spoke to the girl sitting up. "My name is Shad, and we're going to get you out of here safely, I promise you that, but first we have to find out if the girl in the picture is here or ever was. Do you trust us? Will you help us?"

She looked up at me incoherently at first, as if she could barely see me and almost as if I was speaking another language. I could see where her nose had been broken before and some scars around her cheekbones and on one side of her mouth. It made my blood boil, but going ballistic and shooting up the place wouldn't get us anywhere.

She finally spoke after a few long seconds . . . softly, carefully, respectfully . . . probably from months or years of forced subservience. "I trust him, sir," she said pointing to Cas. "I've seen him up top before, on the streets. He helps people like us. But I don't know her, sir. Just like I told the pale man, there are hundreds of girls here and most die or are killed after a while."

I looked at her and could see the fear and pain in her eyes. She kept looking at Cas and then back toward the tunnel entrance, probably expecting men to come drag her back at any minute.

"What's your name, miss?" I asked softly.

She looked back at me nervously, as if any conveyance of information might get her in trouble. "It is Dru, sir. And this is Marcy," she said, pointing to the younger girl curled up in a ball in Cas's lap. "We've been down here for over six months, I think, sir."

I looked over at the vacant stare that was Marcy and was glad that Dru seemed to be keeping it together and was halfway coherent. "It is nice to meet you, Dru. I've heard life spans down here are short. How did you two survive for so long?"

Again, the premeditated and premedicated pause. "We're sisters, sir."

At first, I thought she was going to elaborate on their longevity here, but after a few seconds it dawned on me that she had just done that. It was the uniqueness of sisterhood, their status as a probable "novelty property" that had ensured their temporary survival.

"Well, Dru," I said softly, and with a slight smile to hopefully put her somewhat at ease, if that was possible after her recent incident and being surrounded by six hooded and heavily armed men. "The girl who we are looking for, who was in the photo the pale man just showed you, is named Chrissy, short for Chrystal. In fact, she has her full name tattooed on the underside of both her wrists, and . . ."

"Chrystal Meth," she said under her breath and almost to herself.

We all looked at each other blankly. "Well, kinda like that," I said. "Her first name is Chrystal and her last name is . . ."

"Marcum," she said for me, now with more energy and lucidity, and looking around at all of us. "She's the senator's daughter, a novelty property like us. Chrystal burned the 'Marcum' off her wrist a long time ago with a lighter, and had 'Meth' tattooed over the scar on her right wrist instead. She said that Meth was her new family. I do know her, sir. She's here!"

I felt the twin chills of excitement and anger go through my entire body. I looked up at the boys and they were all smiling and nodding to each other.

But before we could get too excited she continued. "But she's really sick, sir," Dru said. "She tried to OD again last week and I don't think she's gonna make it this time. And if they can't make any money off her, they'll shaft her, sir."

"Shaft her?" Deity asked.

His deep voice startled her a little bit and she cowered slightly as she looked back over her shoulder at him. "Yes, sir, there's a deep hole over by the far generators that they use as a well or drainage or something. I think it empties into the Sound somehow when the tide comes in. It's where they throw the bodies when they're done with them, sir."

"Dear God!" Cas said, "dear God, dear God, dear God!" We looked over as Cas held the younger girl tighter and rocked her back and forth as he started to sob, tears running rapidly down his cheeks, his face now buried in her hair. The young girl looked to be asleep now, or maybe more appropriately, unconscious after her ordeal. I looked at the rest of the team; it was heart-wrenching to see and listen to, but we still had work to do. It had been a long, strenuous, and emotional night for Cas, but we needed him to hold it together.

"Kemo Sabe, we need you to focus," Koda said softly but strongly, "we've still got a lot of work to do."

I looked over at the girl who was watching Cas and her sister. "Do you know where Chrystal is now, Dru?"

"Yes, sir, she's at the infirmary, over by the generators and the shaft, so's they don't have to cart'em very far if 'n they die, sir."

I thought about it for a minute. "Okay, unless anybody has a better idea, I'm gonna have Cas and Rama take these two out of here after Dru gives us some more detail and direction on Chrissy. Koda, Gio, Deity, and I will try to find her and follow you as quickly as possible, but at least you'll have a head start. The big question is how the heck do we get in there undetected?"

I started to continue, but Rama interrupted. "I would like to stay, senor. I have daughters . . ." And then his voiced trailed off with emotion for a minute and then looked at me hard, "I would like to finish this."

I smiled at him and knew how he must feel. "I know, Rama, and it is because of those beautiful daughters, and your loving wife, and a world-class son, that I need you to lead them out of here. It is also because Cas will need your manpower, and possibly your firepower to get these girls out of here safely. The four of us have worked together as a unit multiple times before, so we know the way each other thinks and reacts, it can make all the difference. You have a family, we only have each other."

I knew that Rama knew that I was right, but it was still hard for him to leave a battle unfought. He looked at me for a few seconds, probably thinking of a reason to stay, but came up empty. But, before we could continue, our entire world went instantly black. We all immediately hit the ground, pulled down our night vision goggles and had our weapons at the ready. I'm sure we all prayed to God that we hadn't been discovered yet.

"Hear anything?" Gio said into his mike a little too loud, all of us pumped up on fear and adrenaline. We listened hard, but all the now normal sounds were still there, an occasional scream or loud laughter, but no yelling, gunshots, or rush of men to be heard.

"It is all right, sir," Dru whispered from a few feet behind us in the complete darkness. "About every half hour or hour the power thingy overloads and the lights go out. It takes about sixty seconds for the generators to kick in and then they shut off automatically when the power returns after a few minutes. It happens all the time, sir. Nobody pays it no mind."

And just as described, about sixty seconds later, the loud rattling of multiple generators kicked in and the lights flickered once, twice, and then back on to full power—the radiant light from the main area casting a gray pall to where we were gathered in the shadows of the tunnel.

Koda turned around to look at us with a smile on his chiseled features. "You think'n what I'm think'n, fellas?"

I looked at Gio and Deity and they both nodded.

"What is it, sir?" Dru asked.

I reached out and squeezed her hand. "We just found our window!"

CHAPTER 32

Dru scrawled a rough map in the dirt by the low-glow of our penlights, and even gave us a guess of which bed in the infirmary she had last seen Chrissy occupy. There was a slight chance of great success and a great chance of slight success, or maybe none. But life was a gamble and rolling the dice was just part of the game. Since the last time Dru went by and saw her yesterday, Chrissy could have died, been moved, gone for a walk, be in whatever constituted a bathroom around here, or a dozen other possibilities that would more than likely get us killed rather than get us Chrissy.

Dru also gave us as close an approximation as she could as to what Chrissy now looked like. Her long blonde hair was now cropped short and dyed black to accommodate various wigs, and her once full, lush features had been thinned, scarred, and hardened by age and addiction.

I looked at my watch again and it was almost eleven, and twenty minutes had passed since the last power outage, so we were potentially short on time. We exchanged quick good-byes with Cas and Rama, and I took Cas aside as the boys gave Rama some quick instructions.

I checked both of Cas's guns and put them both back in his holsters. "Okay, Cas, you're locked, loaded, and lethal. Follow Rama's lead and he'll get you out of here. Hold Marcy's hand with your left and keep the gun in your right at all times. Same deal if you have to carry her, keep the gun in your hand at all times. It may make just enough difference to keep you alive."

He was looking over at the young girl he was going to escort out, hanging tightly in the shadows onto Dru. I grabbed his shoulders to get his attention, "Use the guns if you have to, Cas," I said, and then paused for a second, "or on yourselves if the situation demands it. You don't want to be caught alive down here, trust me."

With that, he looked up and once again realized the gravity of the predicament we were still in and what the possible conclusion might be. I think it also slapped him back to reality.

"We need you sharp, Cas," Deity said as he walked back up with the others. "She needs you sharp. Don't let her down."

Gio slapped Cas on the back and Koda turned on his UV headlamp for him. Rama went first, followed by Dru, who preceded Cas and Marcy.

They'd only gone a few steps before Rama stopped and turned around; he looked at each of us. "My family is your family now, amigos. See that you return to us."

And then they were gone.

We advanced to our previous position at the entrance to the main area, trying to get a feel for the normal sights, sounds, and sequences that could tip us off to any irregularities once the place went black again—the screams, yells, moans, and occasional manic laughter becoming commonplace as we awaited our extraction opportunity.

"Okay," I said. "When this place goes black, Koda and I will sprint for the infirmary to find Chrissy. You two hang back for three seconds and offer cover. If anything moves, take a millisecond to make sure it's not Chrissy, and shoot it. We can't afford to be discerning at this point with only maybe sixty seconds of darkness. Once we're in, Deity can take forward point, and Gio can take rear. Assume your positions for fifteen seconds and then get back to the tunnel, regardless of what else is going on or whom you have visual or audio contact with. If we're not back in fifteen seconds, we're probably not coming back."

They all looked at each other and mouthed the word "whom." "Bawse, be eloquent even in a time of crisis," Deity said.

"Good diction knows no bounds," I said.

Gio checked his weapons for the third time. "What if she's not in the infirmary? You wanna do a quick sector search?"

"There won't be time - we probably only have about fifty real seconds," I said. "If she's not in the infirmary, finding her at random would be impossible unless we run into her by providence. We'll get the heck out of here and let Seattle's Finest come back down here with a SWAT Unit and clean up whatever's left by the time they get here. At least we'll know that she was here and that she was probably alive."

Each of us held a silencer in both hands, our night optics and com-sets were on and functioning and we were about as ready as we could possibly be.

"My guess is that when the lights go down, the gargoyle gang will probably stop right where they're at until the lights go back on," Koda said. "So know that they won't be able to see us in the total darkness, especially if they're smoking and the red embers make them even blinder but better targets. They probably won't be able to hear us either if there's enough action and satisfaction going on in the blanket bedrooms. If you see a target, run right at it until you've confirmed a head shot. If one of those little tunnel gunnies gets off a loud round, the entire place will swarm us, and there are probably fifty to a hundred of them, so make every bullet count and make sure you save one for yourself just in case. You don't want some of these boys going medieval on you if you're caught alive. Torture is what they do best."

We all nodded in sober acknowledgement. "Okay, it should be any minute now," I said. "Set your watches for fifty seconds and remember . . . she's about five-foot-seven and, according to Dru, right around one hundred pounds with short black hair, multiple pierced ears, and has Chrystal tattooed on the underside of her left wrist and Meth on the . . ."

Blackness!

Fifty Seconds.

Koda and I came out from behind our barrier at a dead sprint. After maybe twenty yards, we turned a corner and practically ran over four gargoyles loitering behind one of the blanket bedrooms, both Koda and I firing at point-blank range into their chests to drop them and then headshots to confirm the kill. Forty yards and five seconds later, we dropped two more coming out of a large tent with an unconscious fat guy. We heard some shots behind us and were pleased to recognize the sound of suppressors from Gio and Deity and nothing more. Another five seconds, and two more were smoking cigarettes at the entrance to the infirmary and we shot them at a dead run, knocking the bodies back into the tent before they could even fall lifelessly to the ground.

Thirty-five Seconds.

I said, "We're in" into my headset and was met with an almost instantaneous "Rear secure" from Gio and seconds later three shots from a suppressor and then a "Forward secure" from Deity. My heart was pounding out of my chest and I could hear the adrenaline and exertion belabored breathing from the other three. Two would-be medical staff popped up from chairs behind patient gurneys as they heard us enter and Koda popped them with both guns before I could even bring my gun to bear. I envied him his lethal ambidexterity. I could faintly hear more silenced shots outside the tent, mixed with loud but indiscriminate screams and laughter, and hoped for the best.

Thirty Seconds.

The inside of the infirmary tent looked like an old *MASH* rerun with around fifteen beds along both sides and all kinds of bottles and tubes hanging from what looked like rickety, wire coat hangers. Koda went along the nearest wall, and as I looked over quickly, he wasn't even looking at faces, just grabbing sleeping or sedated Caucasian arms and checking the wrists for the identifying tattoos. I followed his lead and went bed to bed as we heard another round of shots from Deity's position; short near-silent spurts met with the clamor of silence. A scream echoed in the domed cavern, followed by another and then the laughter of inebriation or insanity.

Twenty-five Seconds.

I was almost at my last bed and starting to feel the emptiness of failure in the pit of my stomach when the "Contact" came over the headset. I looked over at Koda and he was quickly pulling tubes and tapes out and off her arms. Koda started to pick up her near-lifeless body, but I ran over and grabbed her instead.

"I'm stronger and faster," I said. "And besides, you're a better shot."

"And better built and looking," Koda said as we made a run for the tent exit.

Fifteen Seconds.

I would have liked to have thrown her over my shoulder, but with the shape she seemed to be in, I didn't dare. So I cradled her in front of me as gently as I could with a gun in each hand and a prayer in my heart. As we exited, Deity fell back into rear position and Gio took lead, with Koda two steps in front of me taking mid position. We were all at full sprint knowing that our time was about up, both literally and figuratively.

Ten Seconds.

Loud shots rang out and Gio went down hard, then struggled to get back up with an obvious leg wound at least. Koda fired rapidly in spray fashion as three gargoyles in full combat fatigues and old-school night vision goggles came out from behind one of the blanket bedrooms. These guys weren't the run-of-the-mill militants we'd run into prior to this; they were probably some type of elite unit for down here and we were lucky that Gio was far enough ahead of us that they assumed he was alone. Koda's automatic fire took them by surprise and dropped them almost immediately with some follow-up rounds from Deity, but they weren't using silencers and neither were the screamers coming from some of the nearby beds.

Five Seconds.

Shouting, confusion, and chaos were now all around us as Koda took lead and Deity grabbed Gio on his way by, looking like the losers in a three-legged race. More gunfire from Koda and Deity, as I too fired shots at random bodies with no assurance of accuracy, little green meanies seemingly coming out of the woodwork. I could see our tunnel now, fifty feet in front of us and off to the right, but it felt fifty miles away as I could see ten to fifteen fully outfitted gargoyles heading our way in a hurry. They were bound to get to the tunnel entrance prior to us, so we'd have to scatter and take our chances as singular units.

A new sound was added to the night as I heard the rattling of the generators kick noisily back to life, and I knew we had only a few seconds before we would be illuminated and probably eliminated shortly thereafter. But before I could give the "Scatter" order the staccato'd sounds of suppressed automatic fire rang from the tunnel as Rama stepped out and opened up on the green meanies as they passed him unnoticed. The majority went down right away as Rama continued to shoot without respite, only taking his finger off the trigger as we neared and Koda joined him in emptying their guns into the rest of the group.

"Hola, Gringo's!" Rama said as we ran past him into the tunnel, he and Koda now returning the majority of the gunfire behind the crumbling, concrete cordon. Gio fell again as soon as we entered the tunnel, out of exhaustion, blood loss, or both. Deity checked on Gio and then quickly walked over and gave Rama a big hug.

I looked over at Rama who was beaming brightly at both his timing and lethality. "I thought I told you to get Cas and the girls out of here safely," I said.

"I forgot that I had promised Pablo not to let you get killed before you signed his paycheck," he said behind his big Fu-Manchu covered smile. "And the senora, she has used a gun before, so they are hunkered down in section three." He looked down at my arms. "You found her?"

I had almost forgotten I was still carrying her with everything going on and her being near lifeless and weightless. She was in an old hee-haw country dress with yellow ribbons tied in her hair, iconically outfitted to satisfy a client's personal taste, no doubt. She must have only weighed about ninety pounds and wasn't only knocking on death's door, she was kicking it in. Her face was gaunt and pale, her eyes half open in a comatose stare. Her hair was falling out in clumps and her body was riddled with lesions and sores.

"She is alive, si?" Rama asked.

I smiled at my new best friend. "For now, but let's get the flock out of here."

"You got him?" I asked Deity as he bent down to pick up the 74 inches and 240 pounds that was Gio.

"He ain't heavy, he's my brutha," Deity said with a smile and hoisted him onto his shoulder.

"Take me home, Mr. Jones," Gio said and broke into semiconscious laughter, bordering on delirium. "And don't spare the horses."

Before Deity could reply, a series of bullets ricocheted off the stone walls above us and mineral fragments peppered our gear. Koda continued to return fire and Rama rejoined him, but it was only a matter of time before we ran out of ammo and they ran out of patience.

"Get everybody out of here, Kil," Koda yelled above the gunfire. "I'll hold them off for a while and then lose them in the tunnels."

I picked Chrissy back up and Deity shouldered his burden and followed. Rama decided to stay with Koda for a few minutes to help hold our position, plus, he knew that as slow as we would be traveling, he could catch up to us easily, being unencumbered. I gave Koda the thumbs-up right before we turned the first corner and he just smiled, pulled out a big cigar and jacked another magazine into the chamber. If ever Koda was in his element, it was now.

Rama caught up with us twenty minutes later, and five minutes after that we were able to find Cas and the girls as well. Cas had taken a bullet in his shoulder, and Dru had a bullet crease along her neck that she said stung more than hurt. There looked to be a lot of blood loss, but she was probably staying conscious on a high octane mixture of fear and adrenaline. Luckily, it was just a twenty-two caliber bullet and Cas had gotten the bleeding to stop. Both girls were now semicomatose at his feet.

"What happened?" I asked.

Cas was pretty shaky at this point—mentally, emotionally, and physically drained by the night's extracurricular activities. "I think it was a random patrol, just two of them walking around casually. They would have walked right by us but Marcy let out a little moan in her sleep, so Dru and I left her there so when they found her they would think that maybe they had just found a druggie or an escapee. When they found her we snuck back up on them and shot them both."

"Dru, too?" I asked incredulously.

"Yes," he said with a weary smile. "She wanted to. But after it was over, she said it didn't feel as good as she thought it would and threw up.

I went over to comfort her and forgot to check to see if both of them were dead and one of them got off a couple shots at us before we could kill him." He thought about it for a minute. "We were lucky, I think."

"Very," I said. "But I'm proud of you for taking care of the girls and for thinking of the decoy plan with Marcy. That was well done. We'll make a mercenary out of you yet."

Cas started to laugh and then got dizzy and had to sit down. "Speaking of that," he said weakly, "I'd like to turn in my two weeks notice. In fact, I should have done it two weeks ago."

I laughed and slapped him on his good shoulder as he sat. "Request denied."

After a brief rest and only one other minor altercation, which Deity and Rama dispatched relatively quickly and without major incident or injury, we were back on our feet. Cas was carrying Marcy, Rama was carrying Dru, and as I walked over to pick up Gio to switch loads with Deity, he stopped me.

Gio was unconscious now and Deity was checking his pulse. "I got him, Bawse," Deity said.

"Why don't you take Chrissy," I said, "you must be exhausted."

Deity looked up at me, and for the first time since I'd met him five years ago, I saw tears in his eyes. "I got him, Bawse," he said again with brittle emotion, and went back to tending Gio. I guess I never really knew for sure how strong the bond was between those two, but I knew it now and it made me proud that I could call men of that caliber my friends and family.

We hadn't heard gunfire for almost fifteen minutes, but we made a rapid retreat anyway, glad that the path was marked and that we had only a short distance yet to go. Within five minutes, we heard thunder and we all smiled at each other and started to laugh. We knew we had made it and that the exit and end were near. I looked back in the tunnel for any sign, sight, or sound of Koda, but there was nothing but blackness, eerily green as always through the night vision goggles. I thought he might try and catch up to us, but I also knew that he loved to play chess in the dark with the adversary.

We got back to the ladder and eased the girls up and out, struggling a little with Gio as we were all about done in. Roiks was waiting with the van when we emerged from the devil's playground. I placed Chrissy on the floor alongside Marcy and Dru. "Hang in there, little ladies," I said to them as we sped off to the Genesys Center. "Lord, don't let them die on us now."

Cas and Rama tended to and comforted the girls as best they could. Deity was sitting in the back on the floor, with Gio laying unconscious between his legs, the back of his head resting on Deity's chest. Deity's arms around him, holding him up and steady.

In most ways, it had gone much better than expected, but in some ways we would never be who we were just four short hours ago. It was true what Archie had said, those that went in never came out . . . at least not mentally or emotionally, and that would be true of all of us as well, a memory and a bond forever forged in darkness.

CHAPTER 33

Cas called Grace and let her know that we were safe and on our way, and that her expertise would be greatly needed . . . times three. Since both she and her mother probably had limited or no bullet wound experience, I called my buddy Aaron again to see if he could render his services as well.

"Who got shot?" he said when he answered the phone.

"Dr. Gaudin, is that any way to answer the phone when an old friend calls at midnight on a Sunday?" I asked.

"I have Caller ID, you dork," he said sleepily. "Bullet holes, broken bones, and abrasions are typically our only topics of conversation."

"Well, I really only called to say hello, but since you brought it up and you're already awake, we would like to make a donation to your private lead collection."

I could hear him jumping out of bed and scrambling to get dressed. "Anyone critical?" he asked.

"No, I don't think so," I said. "Gio took a bullet right below his left ribcage and in his thigh, another of our party took a twenty-two to his shoulder, and a young lady has a bullet crease along her neck. They've all lost a lot of blood and are currently unconscious, but other than that everybody's just a little beat up."

"Where are you?" he asked.

"On our way to the Genesys Center. Have you heard of it?"

"The dual Dr. Simmons's. Yeah, I've heard of them; I'm a fan."

"Good, I'll ask them to autograph your stethoscope. See you in a few minutes."

I hung up from the good doctor and called Kathryn at my place as promised. It rang only once and then it was answered, but there was no acknowledgement.

"Miss me?" I said to the expectant silence.

All I heard in return was Kathryn starting to cry and laugh simultaneously. I'm sure the last six hours waiting to hear from me had been hell for her, especially in relation to the painful poignancy of her paternal past. But after a precious few moments, she got it back together a little bit.

"I missed you so badly," she said between sobs. "My heart was breaking at not knowing if you were going to come home to me, and I wanted the phone to ring so desperately, but it scared me to think it might be someone else telling me you didn't make it, and I couldn't have handled that, Shad, and I kept telling myself that God wouldn't kill me twice, and that you were indestructible, and that you'd find a way to make it back to me, and that we'd be okay, and that I'd be whole again . . ."

And then she lost it completely and for the next few minutes continued her emotional release, a cleansing catharsis of tears. I could hear the sound of her body convulsing as she cried, and it made my eyes water to think of how excruciating it must have been for her to wait alone and unaware.

After a while, I heard the weeping give way to sniffles, and I knew that she was finally free of some of the demons she'd been carrying around for so long. Sometimes, the good guys win and get to go home again.

"Can we please get back to whether or not you missed me?" I said, and was rewarded with the renewal and rebirth that was her laughter.

"I love you, Mr. Kilbourne!"

"And I, you, Ms. Rae!"

I heard her take a deep breath. "Are you okay?"

"We're alive and optimistic," I said. "We found Chrissy and a few of her compatriots, and are on our way to Genesys. She's pretty emaciated but not dead, so there's hope."

"I can't believe you found her, Shad. How wonderful! I'll let you go, but I'm on my way."

"No," I said. "A lot of what you just imparted is intrinsic to me as well and I don't want you out this late alone, especially in this weather, especially after this ordeal. As soon as Roiks drops us off, I'll have him come get you. Promise me you'll stay until he arrives."

She laughed. "I promise, you big sap."

I laughed too, and it felt great. "Love," I said gently.

"Returned," she said softly.

I hung up—reluctantly. Like I had just shut off my only source of oxygen, but I knew that I had another phone call to make.

"What is it?" Ryles said groggily as he answered the phone.

"Ryles, it's Kilbourne," I said. "We found Chrissy and have her in our possession. How do I get a hold of Marcum?"

"Son of a . . . !"

"I know, we got lucky," I said. "But she's in critical condition. I'm on my way to a clinic right now to have some excellent people care for her, but I want the senator there."

"No, don't take her anywhere," he said adamantly. "My men and I will come to you. Where are you?"

"No deal, Ryles. It's the senator's daughter. She's a product of his parentage. He needs to come see his handiwork and accept that responsibility—no security, no intermediary, no management, no counsel, no politics, no PR, and no spin—just the senator and his daughter."

Ryles came unglued. "Dammit, Kilbourne. We had a deal. Bring her to me or suffer the consequences. Now!"

"Ryles," I said, evenly toned, trying not to disturb the van's precious cargo, "you have nothing to threaten me with. Either get Marcum down here, or I go public."

That seemed to bring Ryles back to some semblance of reality as the repercussions started to calculate in his mind. "I'll call Arbreau and White," he said. "I'll call you back."

"Do whatever you want, Ryles, but the deal remains the same."

The line went dead and I tried to figure out what to do. I couldn't give her to Ryles because I had no idea what he'd been instructed to do. And I didn't want the senator's usual passive involvement in this. This was his posterity and he needed to recognize his involvement and deal with it personally, not politically.

Within three minutes, and just as we were arriving at Genesys, my cell phone rang and it was Nicholas White, the senator's lead counsel.

"Democratic Headquarters," I said into the phone.

"Knock it off, Kilbourne," he said truculently. "Ryles said you found her. Is she okay?"

"She alive, but she's not okay," I said. "In fact, she's critical, so give me the governor's phone number so that he can come prove to her and to me that he's . . . how did you phrase it, White? . . . 'As good a father as he is a leader'?"

"Dammit, Kilbourne," he said in reiteration of Ryles's very same exclamation. "It's after midnight, the senator is exhausted, he's got national televised interviews all day tomorrow, and he can't be disturbed.

I know he'd love to be there, but let Ryles come get her and get her some decent help."

"She's getting world-class medical care. Are you going to give me the senator's number or not?"

"No," he said adamantly. "Turn her over to Ryles. That was our deal. I expect you to live up to your part of the bargain."

"White, I'd slap you ugly and stupid if life hadn't already beat me to it," I said coldly. "My deal was to find Chrissy, mission accomplished." And I hung up.

I looked behind me to Rama and Deity, both of them exhausted beyond comprehension from the night's activities. "Do you guys have enough energy to go grab me one presidential pain-in-the-rear?"

Deity looked over at Rama, who nodded in the affirmative. "How we gonna do that?" Deity asked.

"Break down his door and drag His Excellency's arrogant arse back to Genesys," I said.

"Oh, that's how," Deity said. "What about cops?"

"He won't call the cops," I said. "He's obviously been on the phone with his team by now and probably still will be when you get there. Cops bring press and publicity and he knows it."

As we pulled up, a number of nurses and gurneys met us at the doors, Grace and her mom anxiously among them. Grace gave Cas a rib-busting hug and her mom gave me a kiss on the cheek.

"Welcome home, warriors," she said warmly, "we'll take it from here."

Roiks jumped into the limo to go get Kathryn, and Rama and Diety jumped in Deity's Cadillac to go kidnap the senator after Grace reassured him that Gio was going to be fine.

"Don't let him die," Deity said to me as he headed to the car, obvious emotion in his voice, "he owes me a dollar."

"I'll let Grace know that if Gio lives, you'll split the money with her. Go on, he'll be fine." And then the big Caddy sprayed gravel as they peeled out of the parking lot, sending some of the orderlies scurrying for cover.

Within a half hour all was calm. They'd put the three girls in the same room so as not to split up the sisters and so that Chrissy might see some familiar faces if she regained consciousness. Grace was a flurry of movements and orders as she treated the girls with experienced but tender ministrations. Aaron was in removing the bullets from Gio's side and thigh, as well as Cas's shoulder, and had sedated them heavily in the process. Maggie was taking care of Dru's neck and my hand and arm, which had somehow gotten torn open sometime during our expeditious ascent from down under.

As I walked down the hall in search of donut and Diet Coke delirium in the break room, Kathryn came running down the hall and gave me a hug that took my breath away both literally and figuratively. She was dressed in one of my blue-striped polo shirts, tucked into turquoise jeans with gold rivets along the pockets. Over that, she had a gigantic down coat that went practically to her ankles. Her shiny, dark brown hair was in an erratic ponytail thingy, her mascara was running like the bulls in Pamplona from the tears and rain, and she still looked like a million bucks.

After a long and luxurious embrace, a torrent of tears on my shoulder, and a brief kiss, she stepped back to make sure I was all in one piece. "Your poor face," she said sadly.

I looked in the mirror that was affixed to the "Employees Only" door. "What? My face isn't hurt," I said.

"No silly," she said. "Not from tonight, I meant from birth."

"Oh," I said. "Well, I must be fine then, if you're already chipping away at my ego." I grabbed her again by the waist and she awarded me the longest kiss we'd had to date.

"Hey," I said, "you stole my shirt."

She smirked. "All's fair in love and war . . . you just stole my heart . . . and a kiss."

We both just stood there smiling at each other for a minute and then the smiles faded into words yet unsaid and a future yet unknown. But before either of us could comment on that, Deity and Rama pushed the senator through the door, much to his objection and dismay. He was dressed in a pair of baggy jeans, a pajama top, and slippers. And he was drenched and disheveled from the bipartisan rain.

When he saw me, he walked over briskly and started to pontificate. "I demand an explanation Kilbourne, what in the world is . . ." At that point, I gave him a hard, straight right to the chin that rocked him to his core and put him on his pompous glutei. It also knocked him out, which wasn't my intent, but something I probably wouldn't lose much sleep over.

After a few minutes and a Dixie cup of water in his face, the senator came around, physically, anyway.

He shook his head to get the cobwebs out, and the stars he was seeing in their proper alignment. "What in the hell was that for?" he asked as Rama helped him up.

"That was for and from your daughter, senator. And you're lucky I don't take you back to where I found your daughter and let the locals get to know you better."

The senator was busy brushing himself off with one hand and feeling the bump on his sore jaw with the other. I'm not sure he even heard me. "If my jaw is bruised, Kilbourne, I'm gonna . . ."

This time, something in *my* head exploded, and I grabbed him by his silk lapels and shoved him up against the wall as hard as I could, with my face two inches from his. "Listen, you diseased political appendage, this isn't about you. This is about a young girl who was abandoned by her functionally bereft father ten years ago, who has lived a life of hell from whence she has just recently returned in critical condition. Now get in there and beg for her forgiveness, or you'll be begging for mine."

I shoved him down the hall, not realizing that Rama and Deity had been trying to pull me off of him.

When he got to the end of the hall, he looked in the door that Grace was holding open. "I can't," he said sheepishly, standing with his arms down by his side, immobile in his inadequacies, "what would I do, what would I say, what *can* I say?"

I pointed to the door. "You're a politician and a public orator. This should be secondhand for you. Start with 'I love you' and end it with 'I'm sorry,' or vice versa, I don't really give a damn, but make sure she knows you mean it."

He walked to the door, his eyes pleading with Grace for leniency and compassion, and finding only anger and disgust. He looked in the semi-lit room and saw the three girls with various tubes, bags, and monitoring equipment, and turned to Grace bewildered.

"There're three of them," he said almost in a whisper.

"Yes, senator," she said. "Mr. Kilbourne rescued the other two along with Ms. Marcum."

"Chrissy," he said, and I was glad.

"Yes," Grace said, with the first hint of a smile of the night. "Chrissy."

He took a few tentative steps into the darkened room and looked at each of the girls for a moment and then back at Grace and me. I was only there because I still didn't trust him, his current state of mind, or his political ambitions.

"I don't . . . I mean . . . it's been so long and it's kind of dark in here," he said softly, apologetically, regretfully, I hoped. "Which one is she?"

Grace's first instinct, I think, was to slap him in a manner that would have probably put my previous punch to shame. But I grabbed her arm gently as she started to tense and she bit her lip in restraint.

"On the left, senator," she ended up saying tersely, with pursed lips. "She's been abused pretty badly, and recently attempted a drug-induced suicide. The cocktail of medications I've given her have brought her to a state of momentary semi-coherency, but in a few minutes they will also bring on a near comatose state for a couple of days as well, until we can get her better physically, emotionally, mentally, and spiritually."

He nodded slowly and shuffled hesitantly over to Chrissy's bed. The staff had changed her out of her ridiculous outfit and into a hospital gown, but I had specifically asked Grace not to have her team clean her up anymore than they had to until the senator could see the detritus of his desertion.

He just stood there and stared at her for a few minutes without saying anything, studying her face as if for the first time, and then the obvious trauma to her body. He looked over at us. "That's not my Chrissy," he said, tears starting to stream down his cheeks. "Dear God, don't let that be my baby girl."

Both of us just nodded and he turned back to her and started to pat her hands awkwardly, but gently, that were folded in her lap. He grabbed her left hand, hesitated for a few seconds, and then turned it over. Even from where I was standing, I could see the "Chrystal" tattooed on her wrist. He started to sob and his shoulders started to shake, and I almost said something to stop him from turning over the other wrist, but it was his legacy and he had to see it for what it was.

He grabbed the other wrist, expecting to see Marcum, and nearly lost it when he saw it burnt off and scarred, with a bold and scrawling "Meth" replacing his surname. "Oh Lord! Oh dear God, no. No, no, no, no, no, no, no . . ." And then he sank to his knees, still moaning repetitive "no's;" his whole body shaking with sadness and shame, racked with the ingloriousness of guilt.

His forehead was resting on her mattress as he continued to sob when all of a sudden, Chrissy slowly lifted her right hand from her lap and placed it softly on her father's head, her eyes still closed in catatonia, gently stroking his thick, white hair, weakly whispering, "Don't cry, Daddy, don't cry."

At first, he didn't even seem to notice, but as his sobbing subsided he must have felt her hand or heard her voice because his head came up slowly and he grabbed her hand in both of his.

"Baby? Baby girl?" he said gently, yet eagerly.

Chrissy's eyes fluttered for a second and then opened slightly.

"Baby, it's Daddy," he cried. "Baby, can you hear me? It's Daddy, and you're gonna be okay."

Her head turned slightly toward him, a blank and barren stare on her face for a long minute and then finally a cognitive click through the pharmaceutical fog. "Daddy?"

He looked over at us with an emotionally distorted smile, and quickly back to her. "Yes, baby. Yes, honey, it's Daddy. Daddy's here and it's gonna be okay. You're home now baby girl and we're gonna get you better. You just hang on for Daddy, little girl. You just hang on to life and my hand, you hear me? Can you hear me, Sissy?"

"Daddy?" she said, still trying to focus and fixate on the man at her side. "Daddy, is that you?"

"Oh God, yes baby, it's me. It's Daddy." Tears were cascading down his cheeks now in rivulets. He looked up to the ceiling, "Dear God, you let her go, don't you take my baby girl from me again. Please God, please let me keep her, don't take her away from me again."

A faint, almost imperceptible smile adorned her face as she looked at him in recognition, tears running down the sides of her face now as well.

"Don't cry, Daddy, it will be all right," she whispered. "You'll be fine." She shut her eyes then and her hand slowly went limp. "We'll be okay, Daddy . . . we'll make lemonade . . . and cookies . . . and . . ." And then she slept once more.

The senator looked up at Grace, startled and near panic, and got quickly to his feet. "What's going on? Is she okay? Is she all right?"

Grace walked over, her own face streaked in tears, and patted the senator on the shoulder. She looked at the blinking bank of technology on the side tables and grabbed Chrissy's hand and felt her pulse. "Yes, senator," she smiled. "Her pulse is weak but steady. She just needs rest now—time, treatment, and rest."

The senator looked over at me, still holding on to Chrissy's hand, tears still dotting his silk pajamas. "Thank you, Shad. Dammit, man, I've been a horse's hind end. Did you hear her? Chrissy was worried about me! How can I ever thank you?"

He switched his attention to Grace without waiting for an answer from me. "Doctor, whatever she needs, she gets. Whatever you need to get her better, I'll get for you. If you need more rooms, or more machinery, or more staff, or more money, whatever it takes I'll make it happen. You just tell me, Doctor, and it's yours, regardless of expense."

Grace put her hand on his shoulder again and he took the opportunity to hug her. "Thank you, Doctor," he said repeatedly. He looked back down at Chrissy as they separated. "When can I talk to her again, Doctor? When can I see her again? Can I stay here with her? I'll build a condo next door if I have to." He started to follow Grace over to the other two beds. "What about these girls? Are these friends of hers? I want to take care of all their expenses as well. What is your budget, Doctor? Do you have a board of directors or doctors or whatever you'd call it? What do you need in regards to funding?" He looked around the room quickly, yet evaluatively. "Let's saddle this horse and put 'er to work, Doctor, so we can help some more folks. Yessirree, Bob, we've got us some work to do. How many beds here, Doctor? How many rooms are . . ."

And then I left the room, the doctor to her work, and the politician to his newest cause. Kathryn, ever the eavesdropper, had been standing right outside the door, her face and my shirt adorned in tears. She looked happy, though, rays of hope and joy streaking across her face and throughout her compassionate being. "I think she's gonna be okay," she said hopefully. "Him, too."

I looked at her, grateful for her love, presence, and support—thankful for her kindness, humor, and wisdom. "Us, too," she said.

She grabbed my arm and got up on her tippy toes and kissed my cheek. "Yes, us too!" I said.

CHAPTER 34

A week later, all was back to normal, or in close approximation thereof. We had just finished having Sunday brunch with the crew on a beautiful Seattle spring day, and we were lounging around in my office, waiting until we could start planning dinner. Deity, Gio, and I were in our usual positions—I behind my desk and the deadly duo sprawled out on the couches. Gio was still wearing the elastic med-wraps around his waist, I was still wearing the bandages on my hand and arm, and Deity was still wearing the smile of indestructibility.

"Ya'll still wearing that wrap for sympathy," Deity asked Gio, "or to help reduce your love handles?"

"Love handles?" Gio said. "I'll have you know those are called well-defined lateral obliques, my friend."

"If 'lateral oblique' is Italian for 'sausage pizza,' then you probably right, my brutha," Deity said.

"All right, ladies," I said, passing my blue and white, Troy Aikman autographed, official Dallas Cowboy football to Deity, "enough banter. Where were we?"

"Ya'll was going to give us our daily Genesys update, Bawse," Deity said.

"Ah, yes. Well, I spoke with Grace this morning and Chrissy is doing quite well. She's up and around, taking nourishment, and seems committed to beating her haunts and habits by way of her father's sponsorship and strong support."

Gio moved to a more comfortable position and released some of the velcro'd tension in his bandages. "What about the presidential bid? Is he still gonna run?"

"I think so," I said. "Even though one of the orderlies at Genesys sold out to CNN and the cat is out of the bag, Arbreau was on it early and expertly enough to spin it into their favor saying that the senator had initiated a massive search for his daughter when he found out she was in Seattle and in jeopardy. So far nobody's tied it to the discovery of Tunnel Town."

Deity threw the football to Gio which made him visibly wince in pain. "That's what I love about politics," Gio said, "truth is always the first casualty."

"Okay," I said. "Now where are we with our continuing quest for karma?"

Gio threw the football back to Deity and winced in pain at that too, so I threw him the tennis ball instead. "Really only one thing left on the docket, Boss, since we been so busy with Chrissy. Maguire, the guy that killed his kids and beat up his wife because he lost the custody battle is history," Deity said. "Our Southeast body broker had some pull with one of the jail guards and he had his cellmate shoot him so full of junk in his sleep he was probably dead within fifteen minutes."

"What about D&L's?" I said.

"As far as dependents, he actually has some life insurance and some rental properties, so his wife will be taken care of," Gio responded. "He has a mother that's terminally ill in a nursing home, so that's not really a factor. As far as liabilities, the kill was pretty straightforward, the broker was one of our regulars, and the guard and cellmate can't talk without incriminating themselves. No one could ever trace it back to us definitively anyway, because of the triple-blind relay, but there obviously won't be much of a concerted effort on the part of Florida law enforcement to investigate a probable drug overdose by a guy who off'ed his own children."

"Good," I said as I took a deep breath. "I've got a couple other targets that are in need of our attention, but they can wait a month; I've had enough death for a while and those guys aren't going anywhere."

Deity and Gio maintained their gaze on me for a few seconds and then Deity finally spoke up. "What about Phinney?"

I thought about it for the hundredth time and came to the conclusion that I was too tired to think about it anymore. "You are both as bright and as deadly a duo as I know, so if you want to handle this one personally, I'm not going to stop you. Just be extremely quick, careful, and conclusive. No traces and no loose end. They'll probably assume it's a rival mob hit anyway, so keep the casualty count low."

Gio and Deity high fived, and Gio winced once again, much to Deity's enjoyment. My intercom buzzed and I picked up the phone and listened for a moment. "Send him up," I told Diane, "and no fraternizing with the enemy."

"I heard that," Chief Tanner yelled in the background. "And that'll cost you a cup of coffee and a Danish."

"All right, Diane," I said into the phone, "pay the man and make sure he tips you."

"Speaking of casualties," I said as I walked down to the couches, "we may all be one soon. Chief Tanner is on his way up."

Gio and Deity looked at each other. "Yikes," they said in unison.

A few minutes later, the chief walked up the stairs and then politely waited for Diane to proceed with her silver tray of coffee and pastries.

"Oh good," I said. "More food."

Diane brought the tray down and set it on the appropriately named coffee table. She gave me a wink and walked back up to the chief. "Tip, please!" For which she got a kiss on the cheek from the chief.

"Here's your change," she said, and smacked him on the bottom on her way out the door.

The chief turned to watch her go and then turned his attention back to us. "The usual suspects," he said.

"Wasn't us, Chief," Deity offered with an imperial smile.

He came down the few stairs to the couches and stood in front of us. "What wasn't you?"

Gio looked at him innocently. "Whatever it is that you think that we did, we didn't do, so don't think that we did, cuz we didn't."

"Thanks, men," he said. "I'll be sure to put that in my report when I want to go back and read something unintelligible."

"Always happy to help the local law enforcement," I said. "What can we do for you, Chief? Are you here for the coffee, the pastries, or just to tip the waitress?"

He grinned. "All three."

The chief sat and I poured all of us some coffee. Deity got up and grabbed the Baileys Irish Cream from the twirly bar. "Irish cream?" he asked the chief.

"I'm on duty," said the chief.

Deity held up the bottle in his other hand and asked, "Irish whiskey?"

"Yes, please," said the chief with a conspiratorial laugh.

Deity poured and the chief sat back with his large cobalt blue mug with the gold Liquid City logo in both hands and took a big sip. "Ahh, ya gotta love the Irish!"

"You talking about me or Notre Dame?" I said.

The chief looked over at me. "Actually, the whiskey. You Irish?"

"Black Irish," I said, "of Spanish descent."

"Is that why your skin is kinda dark?" he asked.

"And my heart is pure," I said. To which the chief almost choked on his coffee.

He set his coffee down on the coaster carefully, much like a guest who wanted to be invited back someday. "You're a lot of things, Kilbourne, but pure isn't one of 'em."

"True, I am but a humble barkeep," I said in my own defense.

"Well, no offense, but you ain't that humble and you're hardly worth keeping," said the chief.

I finally broke my resolve and laughed. "Well, thanks for coming by, Chief. Always nice to have you drop in to feed my ego."

"Actually," he said, looking around to the three of us, "I need your help. I have a mystery to solve, a conundrum if you will, and I know that your collective intellect can penetrate even the cleverest of capers."

"We're all aquiver with intrigue, Chief," I said. "Do tell."

"Well, I don't know if you geniuses read the front page of the paper or not, but a few days ago, I received another anonymous tip about an underground prostitution and drug ring of a most perverse and decadent nature. I, in my infinite wisdom, and trusting that this was my usual reliable source, quickly put together a joint task force made up of some of the DEA's, FBI's, ATF's, ICE's, and our own SWAT team's best men, and women, and followed a maze of tunnels, marked in fluorescent paint as promised, to a central destination of ill repute several hundred feet below our fair city."

"Wow," Deity said.

"Truly amazing," Gio said.

"Who'd a thunk it?" I said.

He made a "you're all a bunch of imbeciles" face and decided to continue without comment.

"Well, when we arrived, there was a small exchange of gunfire by a few holdouts, but most of the Vietnamese gunmen gave up without much prodding. We found almost one hundred troops and two hundred assorted men, women, boys, girls, and those in between, living in blanketed, toweled, or tented structures."

"Vietnamese, huh?" Deity said.

"South of China," Gio said.

"East of Thailand," I said.

The chief just shook his head. "We even found a few farm animals, on which we cared not to speculate."

"Pets are nice," Deity said.

"I always wanted a pony," Gio said.

"Chickens," I said. "Someday, I'd like to raise me some chickens."

"Knock it off, you morons," the chief said. "The gist of it is that it looked like a war had gone on down there prior to our arrival, and that someone had also knocked off the local management team."

"War is a terrible thing," Deity said.

"Management is a terrible thing," Gio said.

"Being called a moron is a terrible thing," I said.

The chief grabbed the bottle of Murphy's Irish Whiskey off the tray and poured more of it into his coffee. "This is going to be a long-drawn-out conversation," he said, a little under his breath. "I can tell that already"

"It's good to converse," Deity said.

"It's good to draw," Gio said.

"It's good to be long," I said.

We all thought about that for a philosophical minute and then we all nodded and clinked cups, even the chief.

"Anyway," the chief said, "would the three stooges care to speculate on any or all of what I've just disclosed . . . confidentially?"

"I don't know," I said. "Have you asked them?"

"I just did," the chief said.

"Oh," I said. "Well, in that case . . ." I got up from the couches and walked up to the aquarium and looked down on the City. I put my hands behind my back in my most professorial pose. "Though my esteemed colleagues and I would know nothing of such a secretive and insidious nature, I would be happy to offer an uneducated opinion."

"All your opinions are uneducated, Kilbourne," the chief said, "but go ahead."

I let that pass. "And mind you," I said, "that this is merely speculation and conjecture on my part, I read about something like this in a comic book once, so maybe there will be some similar parallels. In brief, it is my guess that a rescue and extraction mission of that magnitude would require a small, mobile, elite unit, say five or six guys, to move relatively unnoticed through the tunnels, but if noticed, be able to silence any objection or resistance with immediate and overwhelming lethal force. This small and elite group would also need to be genetically perfect, handsome, bright, articulate, well built, snappy dressers, replete with roguish charm . . ."

"Kilbourne!" the chief interrupted in frustration.

"Oh, sorry, I must have gotten carried away there," I said. "Anyway, it would also be my guess that they would need to proceed on a day and time when they would encounter the least amount of traffic in and around the tunnels. I'm going to venture a guess that it might be on a Sunday night, and that the window of opportunity would have to be short in order to circumvent any regimented or regulated changing of the guards or lookouts."

"So you think this may have been a rescue and extraction mission?" the chief asked.

I unclasped my hands from behind my back and rested my chin in one hand . . . very scholarly. "In the *Marvel* comic book that I read, that was the premise."

"I see," he said. "And why would the theoretical person be down there? Why would they still be alive? And why would that person be worthy of such a concerted and coordinated effort . . . do you surmise?"

"Wow, Chief, that's a toughie, I'm gonna have to really go out on a hypothetical limb here," I said. "If I were to venture another guess, I would say that maybe this theoretical person in peril was already in the business of ill repute and could, therefore, be absconded without fear of report or reprisal, and that maybe this person had a certain relational marketability to instigate such a ruse. I would also imagine that this relational marketability would make this person profitable if utilized properly, that this relational marketability would incentify them to keep this person alive and somewhat well, and that this relation that gave this person value initially would also give this person reason to be rescued by those to whom this person rightfully belongs."

"Ah," the chief said, which is what chiefs say, when they know that they're being bamboozled by three rather large and loquacious adolescents. "And how do you think this whole thing went down?"

"Well," I said, "you've already told us most of it. So I assume in this still strictly theoretical situation that they went in, marked their trail somehow for an expeditious exodus, shot who they had to in order to grab the person or persons of interest, made a run for it after a successful grab, had one of their team hold off the initial pursuit, and then circle back when the pursuit went after the main group to excise the management team because they deserved it, and to prove that he could."

The chief said nothing at first, just got up from the couch and walked up to where I was standing and we both looked at the aquanauts swim by.

"Well, that's quite a hypothesis, Mr. Kilbourne," he said.

"Well, that's because I have quite a fertile imagination, Chief Tanner," I said.

"And that must have been some comic book," he said as he looked over at me. "I'd like to take a look at that comic book sometime."

"Sorry," I said apologetically. "My dog ate it."

The chief smiled. "You don't have a dog."

I smiled back. "That's because he died of ink poisoning after eating my comic book."

"That's tragic," the chief said with a straight face as he looked out over the City once again, probably hoping to get another glance at Diane. "My deepest sympathies for your loss."

"Thank you," I said, my head bowed in sorrow. "I still get a little misty at the national CACB conferences."

He looked at me once again. "The CACB?" he questioned.

I wiped crocodile tears from my eye. "Canines Against Comic Books."

He snorted involuntarily. "Yes, well, I'm glad to see others in your painful paradigm have organized," he said.

"It brings us great comfort and closure, Chief," I said as I watched an eel devour a smaller neighbor. "And thank you for your heartfelt and sincere support."

"Like I always say, Kilbourne," the chief said as he looked at me, "To Serve and To Protect." The chief just stared at me for a minute, shook his head, and then walked back down to the couches and took a sip of his Irish-enforced coffee. He looked at Deity, Gio, and then up to me.

"What happened to your arm, Kilbourne?" he asked as he added more coffee from the sterling silver decanter.

"I sprained it helping an old lady cross the street."

"Oh," he said, "and what about you, Giannini? Why the bandages around the waist?"

"Those aren't bandages, it's an Abdominizer," Gio said as he looked reluctantly at Deity. "It helps reduce my love handles."

"Really?" The chief said. "The last time I saw you in the gym, you were ripped. I figured a guy like you would have well-defined lateral obliques, not love handles."

Deity smiled at Gio. "Nope, trust me, Chief," Deity said. "My boy here ain't got no self control, too many sausage pizzas."

"Uh, huh," the chief said, "and what about you, Jones? How do you navigate life unscathed?"

"My African heritage, Chief," Deity said with a wide smile. "I is genetically gifted."

"All right," the chief said, draining his coffee cup. "It's getting deep in here and my chest waders are in the trunk of my Chief-Mobile."

He looked at the three of us again and shook his head, then walked up the steps and stopped before heading out. "On another side-note, just in case you Boy Scouts don't read the *Political Section* either, it looks like our proud senator and local presidential hopeful has been reunited with his long, lost daughter after an extensive and arduous search by his security team. I guess she got caught up in the prostitution and drug culture a few years back and just recently and mysteriously reemerged. Anybody gotta theory on that coincidence?"

Gio and Deity looked up at me. "The Lord works in strange and mysterious ways, Chief," I said. "Never question a happy ending."

"I'm a police officer," he said. "I don't believe in happy endings."

I smiled a sympathetic smile. "Why don't Gio, Deity, and I take you out fishing on the boat next week, maybe spend a weekend on the San Juans, my treat?"

He laughed and walked down the stairs to the slidy door. "Maybe I do believe in happy endings after all," he said. "Dammit, fellas, maybe I do." And then he was gone.

I walked back down to the couches and sat heavily in my favorite chair, the one next to the Peanut M&M drawer.

"I'm beat," I said.

"I'm beat up," Gio said.

"I'm upbeat," Deity said, jumping up without effort and heading over to the twirly bar. "Tell ya what, I is gonna make you each a drink for medicinal purposes only and then ya'll be feeling better in no time."

"You guys go ahead," I said. "I'm meeting Kathryn for dinner. She's taking me to the Royal Ascot Races in London for my birthday and wants to show me all her brochures."

Deity went and fixed himself and Gio a drink as I headed back up to my desk. As I did so, they exchanged a glance that I caught out of the corner of my eye. "Diane said you and she were going to Hawaii in two weeks," said Deity.

"Yeah," I said, looking in my desk for my keys. "We have some relational issues we need to work through, and she could use the break, the distance, and the pampering."

"And the week after that, you head to Paris to meet Jess?" Gio asked.

I couldn't find my keys but I did find a Tootsie Roll, so rather than lamenting my lost keys, I counted my candy blessings. "Her concert series ends that weekend, so we're gonna take ten days to get reacquainted."

"And two weeks after that, ya'll are headed to London with Kathryn?"

I looked for more Tootsie Rolls but came up empty. "Should be fun. I've never been to the Royal Ascots, so I'm looking forward to it."

When I looked up from my treasure hunt, they were both staring at me.

"What?" I said.

"They be three mighty fine girls, Bawse." Deity said.

I looked at both of them a little suspiciously. "Yes, they are."

"Then how come you don't settle down with one?" Gio asked.

I reinitiated the search for my keys. "I don't know, just don't know if I want to go there again, I guess."

"Go where again, Bawse?" Deity asked as he exchanged looks with Gio once more.

I stopped what I was doing, realizing for the first time what they were getting at. The empty and agonizing feeling in the pit of my stomach started to expand into my chest and I tried to suppress it for the millionth time. How could I ever explain the utter desolation of absolute loss, of a void and an abyss that were beyond measure or mend?

I tried to make eye contact, but couldn't. "Sorry guys," I tried to say, "but I just . . . I mean, I can't . . . my whole world was . . ." I still couldn't go there, not yet, not without losing it, and I didn't want them to see me like that.

"I gotta go, guys," I said halfheartedly, trying to quell the quiver of emotion in my voice. "I'm gonna be late." Keys be damned, I'd just hail a cab or call Roiks.

"You can tell us anything, Boss," Gio said. "You know that, right?"

I nodded and tried to keep it together.

"We here for you no matter when, no matter why, no matter what," Deity said as his bottom lip started to tremble ever-so-slightly. "It's us against the world, Bawse. We be your family now."

I looked at these guys. These guys I had worked with, played with, and killed with; these guys that I would probably someday die with!

"I know, guys," I said. "I couldn't ask for more than that . . . I wouldn't want more than that."

I got up and walked to the steps above the door. I knew there was more to say, more that I owed them, but for the first time in my life the words wouldn't come.

"I'll see you guys in the morning," I said. "Thanks for always being here for me."

"Boss?" Gio said.

"Yeah?" I said as I turned around to face them.

"We been through a lot together. You, Deity, and I."

"Yeah, we have," I said.

"It would mean a lot to Gio and I to know her name," Deity said.

"Whose name?" I asked, feigning ignorance.

"*Her* name," said Deity.

I stood there and looked at them both for a long time. There was in me a piece that didn't want to say, the piece that wanted to keep it sacred and sanct, the piece that didn't want to expose the purity of the memory to the impurity of the world.

"Natalie," I said finally. "Her name was Natalie." And felt it deep in my gut.

"Is," said Gio.

I thought about it for a second and smiled. "Thanks."

"How long ago, Bawse?" Deity asked.

"Eight years," I said, purposely trying not to envision poignant vignettes from my past.

"Long time ago, Bawse," Deity said.

I shook my head to the contrary. "It was yesterday . . . It's today."

I turned and walked down the steps. "It's every second of every day."

The Beginning!